FAKE IT TO FOREVER

JONAS & CALLAHAN

SUMMER LOVIN' SERIES

RACHAEL OGLE

Fake It To Forever © 2023 by Rachael Ogle

ISBN: 979-8-9919576-3-2 (paperback)

FAKE IT TILL YOU FALL

SUMMER LOVIN' BOOK 1

For my forever wedding date who still shamelessly flirts with me after over eighteen years.

CHAPTER ONE

JONAS

"Come on, Jonas, you know you want to."

Any other time, the idea of Teagan's full mouth pulling into a pout would make my dick hard. Too bad I can't do anything about it tonight.

"Sorry, not tonight. I already have plans."

"And these *plans* supersede you getting laid? Wow, must be big plans." Her tone might come across as annoyed if I didn't know Teagan as well as I do. If she and I didn't do this song and dance every few weeks since college, I might worry I was gonna miss out on the opportunity of a guaranteed good lay. But it's Teagan, so I'm not.

"Yep, I'm going to see Nana, so I can't miss it. Maybe later?" I rake my fingers through my hair and check my watch.

"I might be busy, and besides, I'm only in town for tonight, so get it while you can, buddy."

I roll my eyes and chuckle. "Yeah, okay. Gotta go, Teag. I'm late." I disconnect the call and shove my phone in my pocket as I exit my car and jog up the sidewalk to knock on the door.

Nana answers a few minutes later and smiles when she

sees me. "Jonas, right on time." She kisses me on the cheek and I offer her my arm in assistance as we walk out to the car.

"Good to see you, Nana. How are things going? Got any hot dates these days? I bet you're keeping all the guys on their toes, aren't you?"

I open her door and ensure she gets into the vehicle before walking around to climb behind the wheel. My grandmother says, "No, but I will say this; you remember me telling you about Mary June and Harland sneaking around?"

I pull out into the street. "Yeah."

She shakes her head, eyes sparkling with the glee of juicy gossip. "Barb caught them together after bingo."

I widen my eyes in surprise. "No. What did she do?" I probably shouldn't get as much enjoyment as I do from Nana's stories, but honestly, it's some of the best entertainment I've got going on, so I look forward to hearing what goes down at the old folks' home when I take her out on our weekly dates.

"She tossed him out on his ass."

Smiling, I shake my head in amazement. "Wow, Nana. I tell ya, there's some major drama going on at the retirement community, huh?"

"Oh, yes; that's not the half of it. Apparently, there are so many cases of gonorrhea going around, they're making us attend a safe sex seminar."

I feel my eyes widen again. "You're joking."

She shakes her head. "Just makes me glad I'm not seeing anyone. I've survived eighty-one years without any STDs; I don't plan on getting any now."

I can't help but laugh. "Yeah, I guess that is something to be proud of."

Her expression grows serious. "I hope you can say the same, son."

"Nana, I'm not talking about this with you."

She dismisses my statement with a wave. "Oh, you young people think you invented sex. Just because we weren't as open about it in my day doesn't mean we didn't have plenty of it."

I huff a laugh. "That's quite the visual. Thanks."

"All I'm saying is, even at my age, it's perfectly natural. Why, right up till your grandfather died, we were still active at least a couple times a week."

I blush nearly to my toes hearing my grandmother talk about her sex life. "Nana, I don't want to hear about this."

"Then maybe you should settle down and get married and have some babies and I'll shut up." Her tone sounds as though she's trying to convince a small child that broccoli actually does taste good.

"I will. Someday. I've got plenty of time."

"Well, I don't," she states matter-of-factly. "I want to see you settled and happy before I die. Can't you grant an old woman one last wish?"

I roll my eyes. "Nana, you and I both know you're probably gonna outlive me. You're too stubborn to croak."

"Well, there's a lovely girl who works at the library. She's so nice. I think you two would hit it off."

Nice. Code word for ugly or boring.

"I'm good; I have plenty of dates."

She scoffs. "Plenty of hookups, you mean."

Surprised, I ask, "How do you even know what a hookup is?"

"Jonas, I wasn't born yesterday. I know a lot more than you think. All I'm saying is, all these girls you *date* are not gonna be any you can actually settle down with. And you're old enough to know what you should want in a partner; someone to spend your life with. Stop wasting your time on these stupid, silly bimbos"

"Nana, no one uses the term 'bimbo' anymore, I don't think."

"Well, whatever the current equivalent is, those are the girls you see. You need someone smart and kind, but who will still call you on your bullshit. Those are the relationships that last. Physical attraction is nice, don't get me wrong, but beauty fades. Find someone with a pretty soul, not just a pretty face."

After I drop my grandmother off following supper and pull in at home, it's still early enough to text Teagan to see if she wants to hookup. But when she doesn't text me back, I go ahead and change to head to the gym for a quick workout.

That's the good thing about summer break, I can stay up late and sleep late and pretty much do whatever I want. It's one of the main reasons I became a teacher; along with the fact I love kindergarteners. Their spunk, their creativity, their wonder. Probably doesn't hurt that I'm a big kid myself.

When I get to the gym, a woman I've hooked up with before is also there and I'm hoping she doesn't recognize me, because I don't remember her name and I don't want to make things awkward. I turn my baseball cap around the right way and pull it down low in the front and make sure my headphones are on.

Thankfully, she leaves and I dodge the bullet of having to speak to her. Maybe Nana's right. Maybe I should stop hooking up. Eh, who am I kidding? I have too much fun. Most of the time, anyway. What would it be like to wake up next to the same woman every morning again? What would even *wanting* that again be like? In general, I like the variety I currently have. No strings, no expectations, no heartbreak.

CHAPTER TWO

CALLAHAN

"Hey, Callie, would you care to shelve these returns?" Dorothy, my octogenarian colleague, asks me.

"Of course, Miss Dorothy." I push my glasses up my nose and hustle over to take the cart from her. "How are you feeling today?"

She gives me a wide grin. "Oh, you know me; still kicking."

"Well, you look very pretty today." Dorothy is white, with relatively unlined, creamy skin and is in her early eighties. She's dressed in a stylish pair of slim, navy slacks and a floral, tunic-length top and a pair of serviceable, white sandals and her short, white bob is accented with a spunky streak of hot pink at the bangs. "Are you still planning on doing the story time today, or do you need me to? I don't want you getting too tired on us."

She waves away my concern. "Callie, I may be old, but I'm still young enough to read a few books to some preschoolers. It's the highlight of my week; of course I'm gonna do it."

I smile, happy to accept her admonition. "Yes, ma'am. So,

how was your weekend?" I ask as I'm sorting through the returned books.

"It was wonderful. My grandson took me out to supper."

"Well, how nice. Where did you all go eat?"

"Over to the Cracker Barrel; he knows I love it. And since my Charlie died, he's been taking me out on Sunday evenings, since it's something we used to do."

"That's so sweet."

"He's a thoughtful boy." She eyes me. "You know, he's single and although I'm biased, he's awfully handsome."

I huff out a surprised laugh. "Miss Dorothy, are you trying to play matchmaker?"

"Well, why not? You're single, he's single. I'd love to have some great-grandbabies before I die. I'm not getting any younger, you know."

I pause cataloging the books to level her with an amused gaze. "Does he know you're trying to find someone to have his babies?"

She arches a penciled, gray brow. "No, but he's such a catch, I can't figure out why he's single."

"Maybe because his grandmother is the one who's trying to find his dates? Most men like to find their own. And has it ever occurred to you that he might be gay or something and that's why your efforts haven't worked thus far?"

"Oh, honey, trust me; he's not gay. He lived with me during high school. I saw all the girls he tried to sneak into his bedroom."

I can't help but smile. "*Tried* to sneak in?"

She taps her ear with her index finger. "I've still got perfect hearing and we lived in a creaky old house."

I try to think of an eloquent way to phrase my response besides *he probably likes easy hookups*. "Well, maybe the kinds of girls he likes aren't the kinds of girls you want him to date. Maybe he likes a... *specific* kind of girl."

She sighs. "Yeah, tramps."

"Miss Dorothy, you are something else, you know that?" I say and shake my head and laugh. I love this sassy old lady. She makes this low-paying, mind-numbing job at a small public library in Tallahassee worth it. At least, until I finish my Ph.D. and can get a job at a school or university. But working with Dorothy makes coming in day after day after spending nights and weekends studying and going to class and working on my dissertation worthwhile.

"So they tell me."

I roll the cart away and spend the next hour reshelving all the returned books.

When I get home and check my mail, while I'm expecting it, I'm still not prepared to see the wedding invitation. I wait until I get into the house to open it, even though I already know what it will say. My roommate and best friend, Elliot, is already cooking supper when I walk in the door. "Hey, El," I say, dropping my keys into the bowl by the door. "What's for supper?"

Standing at the stove, dressed casually in swim trunks and a tank top, his warm brown skin practically glowing from what I'm guessing was an entire day spent at our neighborhood pool, he stirs a large pot with a wooden spoon. His dreads, normally hanging down to his shoulders, are pulled back into a bunch and secured with a thick hair tie. He's right at six feet tall and spends a considerable amount of time in the gym. And with his honey-brown eyes and full lips, he's stinking gorgeous.

He turns and leans his hip against the counter. "Some pasta and a salad. How was work?"

"Fine, Miss Dorothy is trying to set me up with her grandson. I guess I should be flattered, but it just makes me feel pathetic."

Elliot quirks a dark brow. "Is he cute? Because if she's offering him up, I'd be happy to take a crack at him."

"Sorry, honey, not your type. I asked."

"Well, damn." He eyes the mail in my hand. "Anything good come in today?"

I hold up the fancy envelope. "Just this."

He glances at it and the calligraphy on the front. "Is that what I think it is?"

I tap the corner of the envelope against my palm and nod. "Yep."

"Are you gonna go?"

I give a halfhearted shrug. "Like I have a choice. If I don't, they'll assume—*he'll* assume—I'm still hung up on him."

Elliot frowns. "You are still hung up on him, honey."

"Yeah, well, it's not like I want him knowing that. I'm still gonna have to see him at family gatherings, whether I go to this wedding or not. I can't avoid Thanksgiving and Christmas for the rest of my life; he'll always be there. I already moved away so I wouldn't have to see them together. That probably broadcasted how tore up I was all on its own. I don't need to look anymore desperate than I already will."

"When is it?"

I sigh and stare at the envelope. *Rip off the bandaid, Callahan.* I tear it open, not even bothering to try to be neat about it. I pull the invitation and itinerary out and read over it. "Next month. Week of Fourth of July. Oh, look, it's a whole week of events leading up to the big day," I say in a false-chipper tone. "Gag me with a spoon."

"So are you gonna go for the whole week? Can't you only go for the wedding and call it a day?"

I shake my head, resigned to my fate. "No, my parents will expect me to be there for everything, and so will Maddie. I'm just thankful she didn't ask me to be a bridesmaid. I don't know that I could've done it. It's a good thing she's got a ton of sorority sisters, otherwise, I probably would be.

"It's not Maddie's fault we fell in love with the same guy and he picked her. She didn't know how I felt about him. And who can blame him; she's the epitome of class and elegance and charm. She got all the beauty genes in the family. And besides, Dom and I weren't *together* when they started dating, so I can't really even be mad at him. We were never official or anything. I was only a four-year hookup for him. He was upfront with me when we started hanging out. It's my own fault I let myself fall for him."

Elliot rolls his eyes and gestures wildly with the knife he's using to chop veggies for our salad. "Yeah, but Maddie knew y'all were a thing and she still went after him. She broke girl code. And for that, I'll always hate her."

"Nobody hates Maddie. You can't. She's too sweet. I wasn't honest with her, either, when she told me they'd connected over Christmas. I don't know if she actually knows how long we'd been seeing each other. She may only know about us hooking up in the beginning and for all I know, she may have believed it stopped years before she agreed to go out with him."

"He's still a douche for doing you the way he did."

I spread my arms, palms up. "It is what it is. You'll come with me, right? Be my plus one? It's not like I'm dating anyone these days. And you look super hot in a suit. My parents will pay for the plane tickets."

He considers for a moment and nods slowly. "I should be able to do it. Do you have any handsome cousins for me to try to sneak off with?"

I shake my head. "No, sorry. Maddie and I are the only cousins."

He scoffs. "Well, that's stupid. But sure; I'll go. Might be nice to spend the whole week at the lake. Maybe Dom has some hot groomsman I can check out."

"Maybe. And at least if you're there, my mother won't hound me about my life choices. Can you pretend you're *with* me when she's around? It won't be much, but if I bring an attractive man, she'll assume you're my boyfriend anyway, so it would save me a lot of stress."

He quirks a sculpted brow and the expression he wears is incredulous. "Pretend to be straight? For a whole week? Honey, I don't know if I have it in me."

"Please. Pretty please. I will love you forever and day." My tone is pleading and he sighs.

"Fine, but you owe me so big for this. I'm thinking dish duty for a month."

I throw my arms around him. "Thank you. Thank you. You are the best."

CHAPTER THREE

JONAS

As I'm cleaning up my apartment from last night's hangout with Kara—or was it Mara—my phone rings. I check the screen: Elliot Sanders. *Hmm. Weird, we've still got almost six weeks before school starts. What's he want?*

"Hello?"

"Hey, Jonas. What's up?"

"Not much, man. How're you?"

"Pretty good. Listen, you know the big favor you owe me for covering your bus duty all spring semester last year?"

Shit. I knew he'd eventually call it in. I was hoping he'd forgotten.

"Yeah, I guess. What do you need?"

"Well, I wanted to see if you were doing anything the week of Forth of July?"

"As in, next week? It's the thirtieth," I remind him.

"Yeah, are you busy next week? I'm kind of in a bind."

"I normally go to a party, but what's going on?"

"I have a free trip to a big lake house in Tennessee and I

wanted to see if you'd be interested in going. I have the plane ticket and everything."

"I mean, that sounds cool, but why would it be considered a favor? What's the catch?" I ask, unable to hide the suspicion in my tone.

"Well, see, my roommate has to go to her cousin's wedding and I was supposed to be her plus one and I can't make it."

There it is. "So you want me to go to a wedding in Tennessee with some woman I've never met for a week? Why can't you go?"

"I got invited to a big party in Miami with this delicious guy and I don't want to pass it up but I hate to disappoint Callahan. She's already dreading it since the groom is her sorta-ex. And she needs someone with her so her parents don't make a big deal about her not having a date or being in a relationship."

"Whoa. The groom is her ex? What kind of wedding is this? I don't want to be involved in any drama, man. Not how I want to spend my holiday at all."

He sighs. "The bride is her cousin; it's a long story. The reason I thought of you is because you're hot and you'll make Callahan look good. But all you have to do is show up, play pretend, hang out. She's cool. But she told her family she's bringing a date and she already feels like a failure compared to her cousin, so I hate to leave her hanging. I'm calling in my favor."

I blow out a breath and rake my fingers through my hair. "I don't know, Elliot, this is more than a simple favor. This is a whole week."

He's quiet for a minute. "Fine, how about this? I'll do your bus duty again for fall semester."

I consider. Getting out of another semester of bus duty would be pretty sweet. And spending the Fourth of July on a lake does sound appealing. "So, all I have to do is show up with your friend and play the hot boyfriend card; that's it?"

"Yeah. I mean, there's, like, a whole week of events leading up to the ceremony, but from what Callahan said, it'll be pretty low-key. Her family is snooty and loaded, thus the lake house, but Callahan's not like them. She's down to earth. You'll probably have to dance and pose for photos and stuff, but that should be easy for you. You're good with women. You'll need a suit for the wedding, but other than that, it's a casual thing."

"When does the flight leave?"

"Tomorrow morning."

I huff out a surprised laugh. "Shit, Elliot, I'm not gonna have any time to pack."

Elliot sighs in exasperation. "Jonas, you are a beautiful, straight, white man. You could wear a burlap sack all week and everyone would still say you're the hottest guy in the room. Trust me, you'll be fine. You always look great at work; you know how to dress."

"So, bus duty next semester and this wedding and we're even, right?"

"Yes. I promise."

I blow out a deep breath. "What does your friend look like? You said her name was Callahan?"

"She's pretty. Five-seven, strawberry-blonde hair, blue eyes. Maybe a little more on the nerdy side than you're used to, but she's adorable."

"How old is she? She's not, like, nineteen or anything, is she?"

"No, she's twenty-five. She's getting her Ph.D. Super smart and sweet, which is why I hate to ditch her, but I would have to pretend to be straight for the whole week and I don't know if I can do it. Plus, there's the delicious Miami guy. But if I can have a hot backup plan for her, she'll take the news better."

I frown in confusion. "Wait, so she doesn't know you're asking me?"

"No, but she'll be fine. She just doesn't want to go alone."

I think for a minute. A whole other semester getting to sleep in on my bus duty days and a week at the lake for free? What the hell? I sigh. "Fine. Okay. Whatever. Send me the details and the boarding pass. But after this, we're square."

"Jonas, you are a lifesaver. Seriously. I'll get it sent over to you."

I disconnect the call knowing I need to let Nana know I won't be able to take her to dinner this weekend. I dial her number and she answers on the second ring. "Hey, Nana."

"Jonas, sweetheart. How are you?"

"I'm good. Listen, I have to go out of town—kind of last minute—to do a favor for a friend from work, so I won't be able to take you to supper tomorrow night. I'm sorry, but I'll be back to take you next week."

"Oh, sure; don't worry about it. I'll see if one of the girls from the community wants to get together. I'll miss you, but I hope everything is okay with your friend."

"Yeah, he's fine. I'll tell you all about it when I get back. I have to pack and get ready to leave first thing in the morning or I'd give you the rundown now. I didn't want you to worry."

"Well, thank you for letting me know. Okay. Love you, Jonas. Have a safe trip, okay?"

"Will do, Nana. Love you, too." I disconnect the call and sigh knowing it probably won't be the last time this week I question what I've gotten myself into.

CHAPTER FOUR

CALLAHAN

When I wake up on the morning of my flight home, I'm overcome with the realization that I truly do not want to go to this wedding. I don't want to have to pretend Elliot is my boyfriend all week. I don't want to have to pretend to be happy for Maddie and Dominic. I don't want to have to sit through all the stupid events leading up to the wedding.

Honestly, though, I don't have a choice. Maddie is like a sister to me and I can't not be there for her on her big day, no matter how much watching the man I once loved—okay, maybe still love—pledge his life to the woman he loves. And the fact he's gonna be a part of my family for the rest of my life is the fucking icing on the cake.

It doesn't escape my mind that this wedding should be mine and Dominic's, not his and Maddie's. And the fact he was willing to commit to her and not me, makes me feel like life with Maddie always has. She was always the beautiful one, always the stylish one, always the elegant one, always the better choice.

Not me, that's for sure. I mean, I know I clean up nice. I

know how to look pretty but it's not my default. I'm nerdy, reserved, plain old Callahan. But on the bright side, at least there's an open bar all week, right?

As I gather up my last-minute belongings, I notice Elliot's not in the house. I check my phone and realize I don't have time to wait for him; I'm already later than I'd like to be. I guess he'll have to find his own way. *Maybe he had to run out this morning to get something?* But it's not like to not leave a note or at least shoot me a text.

I give myself one last look in the mirror before I head out the door. Yep, it's me. Cutoff shorts, tee shirt, ponytail, glasses, no makeup, flip flops. Travel ready, I guess.

I roll my suitcase out the front door and notice Elliot's car is gone. *Where is he?* And once I get behind the wheel of my car, I try to call him without success. I try to call him several more times on the fifteen-minute drive to the airport with no luck.

When I go through security and wait for my boarding to be called, I start to worry since I still haven't heard from Elliot. But once they call the plane, I get the impression I'm being stood up. Stood up by my fake boyfriend. *Well, isn't this peachy? Not even a fake boyfriend wants to be with me.* I want to cry, but I'm too mad, so instead, I roll my suitcase down the aisle of the plane and stick my bag in the overhead compartment. I drop into my seat and contemplate the odds of the plane crashing and how, in this moment, it might be preferable to me than showing up to this wedding with no date.

My phone rings and it's Elliot. I answer on the first ring, my tone angry. "Elliot, where the hell are you?"

"Okay, don't lose your shit, Callahan, but I'm not gonna be able to come to the wedding."

I lower my voice to a harsh whisper and turn toward the window. "What the fuck do you mean you can't come to the wedding? You are my plus one. You can't do this to me. You know how important it is for me to at least appear to have my shit together."

His tone is apologetic. "I know, I know. Something came up, but I promise, it's okay."

Panicked, I ask, "What do mean something came up? You've known about this for a month. I did dishes all this past month. How is it gonna be okay when I show up with no boyfriend when I specifically told my parents I was bringing a serious boyfriend with me? What am I supposed to do, pull a George Glass situation?"

"Oh, lord, you're bringing out *Brady Bunch* references? We need to get you some better TV shows to watch. No, I promise; it's okay. I've got someone coming in my place. He's a teacher I work with. He's super hot. He's good to play along. And believe me, he looks even better in a suit than I do. Jonas will be a much better fake boyfriend because at least he won't have to pretend to be straight."

"Elliot, I cannot believe you've done this to me." Hot, embarrassed, angry tears burn my eyes and I blink them away.

"I swear, it's gonna be fine. Jonas will do a good job. I'll make this up to you."

"I don't see how." I disconnect the call and turn to stick my phone back in my purse and I realize the seat next to me is now occupied. Occupied by one of the best-looking men I've ever seen in my life. And he probably overheard my entire, pathetic conversation. Perfect.

Fuck me.

I take my glasses off and pinch the bridge of my nose in frustration. *I'm gonna kill Elliot. Legit murder him. I'm gonna find a swamp and feed him to the alligators and they'll never even find pieces of his body.*

"You know, they say pigs are actually a better method for disposing of a body." My head snaps to my left and the impossibly handsome man is speaking. He has curly, dark brown hair that falls below his ears and dark brown eyes. His cheeks are dusted with freckles and the stubble on his jaw can only be intentional. And damn, it works for him.

Realizing I've said all this out loud and this gorgeous man has heard everything, color creeps into my cheeks and I'm about ten degrees warmer than I was five seconds ago. "I'm sorry?"

"You were muttering that you're gonna feed Elliot's body to the alligators. Pigs might be a better choice. Although, personally, he owes me bus duty for the fall semester, so if you could wait until after Christmas to murder him, you'd be doing me a real solid."

I nod. *Well, at least Elliot has good taste.* "Jonas?"

He smiles and his teeth are straight and white. "George Glass works, too. Been a while since I heard a *Brady Bunch* reference. I was impressed. Callahan?"

Fuck, he's good-looking. I'd never pull a guy this hot in real life. No one is gonna believe he's actually my boyfriend.

"That's me. I truly am gonna murder Elliot for bailing on me. I mean, it would've been nice not to have needed Elliot, but that's neither here nor there. It would honestly be great if I didn't have to go to this wedding in the first place. And probably par for the course for me, my fake boyfriend didn't even want to come with me and had to find someone else to come rescue my pathetic ass." *Shut up, Callahan. You're rambling.* I clamp my mouth shut and flush in embarrassment. After a beat, I say, "Sorry you got dragged into this. I'm sure you had a lot better things to do than get set up on the weirdest blind date ever."

Jonas's smile widens. "No worries. I owed Elliot a favor. If spending a week on a lake is paying him back, I'll take it. So, Callahan. Cool name. Callahan what?

"Thanks. Benson. Jonas..."

"Merritt. So, Elliot said the groom is your ex? And he's marrying your cousin?"

I blow out a breath. "Yeah, except Dominic—he's the groom—and I weren't ever official. We hooked up on and off for four years; I made the mistake of falling for him. But, instead, he fell for my cousin, so yeah, it's gonna be a great week for me."

His eyebrows lift in surprise. "Wow, four years. And your cousin is marrying him?"

"I don't know if she knows how long we were actually seeing each other. And it wasn't ever serious for Dom, I guess, so no big deal, right?"

"Still, if she knew you ever dated him, does that not violate some kind of cousin code or whatever?"

"I guess not because here we are." I splay my arms, gesturing to where we're currently located. On a plane. Heading to said wedding.

The pilot comes over the intercom and announces we'll soon be taking off and I inhale a deep breath as the plane begins to taxi and lean my head back and close my eyes.

"Nervous flyer?" Jonas asks.

I don't open my eyes, but I nod. "Yeah, it's not so much the flying part, but the takeoff and landing that always get to me." I wring my hands in my lap and try to relax.

Jonas asks, "You're getting your Ph.D.?"

"Yeah, at Florida State. I'll do my dissertation next fall. Hopefully. You know, if we survive the plane ride."

He chuckles. "What's your degree?"

"Library science." The plane leaves the ground and I open my eyes. "Thanks," I say.

"For what?" he asks.

"For distracting me."

"Not a problem." His eyes travel down my face and body

and I'm not used to someone looking at me so openly and my stomach knots up. I'm unsure how to read his gaze, even if he doesn't appear to be repulsed by what he sees. "So, librarian, huh? I can see that. You've got the glasses. Do you wear your hair in a bun and wear cute cardigans?" He grins and his tone is teasing and I feel myself blush.

Feeling as though he might not find me entirely unattractive, I relax. "Yes, actually, I'm a total cliché. But hopefully, I'll be able to get a job at a university or school once I finish. And you're a teacher, right?"

He nods. "Kindergarten."

I smile. "I bet all the single moms love you. And I bet they never miss parent-teacher conferences."

He chuckles. "Well, I've been hit on by some of the moms, and dads for that matter, but I make it a point not to date my students' parents. It muddies the waters too much. I like to keep my business and pleasure entirely separate."

I raise an eyebrow. "So are you saying once a student has left your class you've never gone out with a parent?"

"Rarely. I won't say never, but not in a long time."

I nod. "Okay, well, if I'm being honest, I'm not sure anyone in my family will believe I was able to pull you. Not sure they would've bought that Elliot was my boyfriend, either, after he started making passes at groomsmen, but I don't know if they'll believe you're actually into me."

CHAPTER FIVE

JONAS

"Not sure they would've bought that Elliot was my boyfriend, either, after he started making passes at groomsmen, but I don't know if they'll believe you're actually into me."

I tilt my head in confusion. "Why would you say that?"

Callahan lifts a brow and her expression blatantly says, *have you seen you?* "Because you're totally hot." Her cheeks turn bright pink and I can't help but chuckle.

"Well, thanks, I guess. But you think you're not?"

She shrugs and I realize she must not know how good-looking she is. She has her long strawberry-blonde hair pulled back in a ponytail and her glasses make her look adorable and magnify her dark blue eyes. She's got a fantastic figure. Great legs and a nice rack. Fuckable, for sure. She's quiet for a minute, her expression thoughtful. "I mean, I don't think I'm ugly or anything, but compared to Maddie—that's my cousin—I'm definitely the lesser of us."

"Why compare yourself to her?"

"Everyone always has. Growing up, we were pretty much raised as sisters, if not twins. Our birthdays are a week apart.

She's super tall and has all these gorgeous red curls and bright green eyes. She's like freaking Merida from the Disney movie *Brave*. And she's got this bubbly personality and everyone has always loved her."

I consider. "I mean, I know I've known you for all of about ten seconds, but you seem pretty cool."

"Yeah, except in my family, it's not about cool. It's about class and elegance. And that part, I've never seemed to master. I was always a little too backward, a little too clumsy. I always like to say Maddie got all the best genes, and I got what was leftover."

I study her for a minute. "Well, I'll take cool and clumsy over snooty and stuck up any day. And don't, for one second, sell yourself short. You're beautiful." She blushes and I can tell she's not used to receiving compliments. "If you believe you deserve something, others will, too. What's your goal for this week? What do you hope to accomplish or make people think or whatever?"

"Honestly?" she asks and I nod. "I guess to make them think I have my shit together, at least personally. Professionally, that's going okay. But I haven't dated anyone since Dominic and I don't want them to know I'm still hung up on him."

"And how long ago did y'all split?"

She looks down. "Eighteen months. He broke it off for good after he started seeing Maddie."

I feel my brows rise in disbelief. "So he was still hooking up with you while he chased your cousin? Wow, he sounds like a real winner."

She lifts one shoulder and drops it and her head tilts slightly. "I knew who he was when we got together; it was casual. At least for him, it was. Me, not so much after a while."

"So, do you want to make him jealous or regret that he let you go? Do you want to break up the wedding?"

She looks taken aback. "No. Nothing like that. I mean, the breaking up the wedding part, anyway. And I don't want to hurt Maddie at all. Because despite how much everyone loves her and dotes on her, she's a genuine and sweet person who truly loves Dom and I don't want to hurt her."

I smirk. "But you're not above a little jealousy, are you?"

She considers. "It might be nice for him to have a tiny bit of 'oh, man, did I screw up' or something like that. But I wouldn't want him back after he so easily picked her when I was there for four years and I wasn't enough for him." She clenches her jaw and looks down at her hands. "I don't want to be someone's second choice. I've had enough of that."

I nod. "I get that. So, what are we looking at when we get to Tennessee?"

"Well, we'll be expected to show up for dinner tonight with the whole family. I mean, there aren't that many people, but family dinner tonight. Tomorrow is cornhole and the big barbecue. Dominic's parents will probably be there. Tuesday should be pretty laid back and everyone will kinda do their own thing; there's a lot to do around the lake house. Wednesday will be the bachelor and bachelorette parties. So, you should be off the hook for that. Thursday is the rehearsal dinner and Friday night is the wedding at the barn. Saturday, we come home."

"Sounds like a busy week. Are weddings in your family always like this?"

She shakes her head. "Maddie and I are the only kids in our family, so since she's the first to get married, it's a big deal."

"What about when you get married?"

She snorts a laugh and her nose scrunches up and it's adorable. "Shit, that'll probably never happen. But in the minuscule chance it does, I'm eloping—no question about it. I hate weddings. All the pomp and circumstance and spending all that money for people you don't even like to eat and drink and criticize the choice of flowers or the bridesmaid dresses or whatever."

"So, are we talking about getting married if anyone asks?"

Callahan shakes her head. "Nah. We're not that serious yet. Maybe discussing moving in together; that would rile Aunt Meredith to no end."

I smile. "Sure. And how did we meet?"

She thinks for a minute. "Hmm. I guess, let's keep things pretty close to the truth, shall we? You and Elliot work together; we can say he set us up on a blind date. It's basically the truth."

"And what did you think when you met me?"

She blushes. "You were way out of my league."

I raise an eyebrow. "Well, you see, that's where you're wrong."

Her expression is amused. "Oh? How do you figure?"

"Because I was a total womanizer. You tamed the beast or whatever."

She laughs and it's a deep, genuinely amused laugh. It's actually pretty great. "I like that. Okay. What about rules?"

I feel my brows press together in confusion. "Rules?"

"Well, yeah. Most likely, my parents will expect us to share a room; sorry about that. But it's a big room. I can take the couch. It's not a problem. And they'll be dancing at the wedding, so we'll have to touch. And if we've been dating for a while, it would probably be weird if we weren't affectionate, right? But we need boundaries. Rules."

I nod in understanding. "Gotcha. I'm not such an animal, that if we had to share a bed, I would attack you or anything. We can share. I mean, wouldn't it be weird if your parents or someone barged in and we weren't in the same bed?"

She bites her lip, considering. "Yeah, okay. That makes sense."

"I have no issues with dancing and I can be casually intimate; hand holding, stuff like that." I quirk a brow. "I'm assuming sex is off the table?"

Callahan blushes and it adds a pleasant glow to her creamy complexion. "That's probably best. Have you ever done anything like this before? You seem oddly calm about the whole thing."

I shake my head. "No, but I like a challenge. This seems like fun, honestly. It might be bad if we didn't seem to get along or—and this is gonna sound shallow—but if you weren't hot. I think I'll be okay."

"And it doesn't bother you we're gonna be faking a relationship?"

I shake my head again. "I don't do relationships, so no."

Surprised, she asks, "Ever?"

"Nope. Not since college."

"And how long ago was that?"

I think back, although I already know how long ago it was. "Eight years."

"So, what, you only date casually?"

I nod. "Yeah, my nana apparently is not pleased with the fact that I don't plan on settling down anytime soon. She keeps saying she wants great-grandchildren. She knows how to lay on the guilt, that's for sure."

"And do you want kids?"

I shrug. "Someday, maybe, but I'm not even thirty, so I'm not too concerned. Have we discussed having kids? You know, in our serious relationship?"

"I want kids, but no, that's not anywhere near where we are."

"Cool. Can we maybe be discussing the possibility of getting a dog?" I ask with a grin.

She chuckles. "Sure. A dog would definitely be an option. When's your birthday?"

"November eleventh. You?"

"March first. And how do you drink your coffee?"

"Black. You?"

"Same." She seems to think of something else. "Tattoos?"

I nod. "One. You?"

She nods. "One."

I smirk. "Do I need to know where it's at?"

Callahan shrugs. "On my hip. Yours?"

"On my ribs."

CHAPTER SIX

CALLAHAN

Jonas and I continue discussing different aspects of our lives and I try to commit it all to memory over the next ninety minutes of our flight. When the pilot announces we'll be starting to make our descent, my anxiety begins to ratchet up again.

When the plane starts to slowly descend, I grip the armrest and close my eyes. The landing is not smooth and I curse under my breath, my stomach clenching. Jonas takes my hand in his and my eyes pop open and he shoots me a reassuring smile. "It's okay. You're alright." And either because an extremely good-looking guy is holding my hand out of comfort or to simply distract me, I don't care, because it works and I instantly start to calm down.

He pats my hand and lets it go. "See, it's over now."

I swallow and blow out a shaky breath. "Thank you."

"Of course. Can't have you freaking out now, can we? What kind of serious boyfriend would I be if I didn't comfort my serious girlfriend while she faces her fears?" His tone is easy and an amused smile plays on his lips.

Once we've been cleared to unbuckle and disembark from the plane, Jonas and I retrieve our bags from the overhead compartments and walk into the airport. As we make our way to the rental car counter to pick up my car, I ask, "Have you ever been to Tennessee before?"

He nods. "Yeah. One year, my grandparents brought me up here for a vacation. We stayed in Gatlinburg and went to Dollywood."

"Oh, okay. Well, the lake house is actually not far from Dollywood; about a half-hour. The house is on Douglas Lake."

When I pick up the keys to the rental and we find the small car I've been assigned, Jonas puts our bags in the trunk and I climb behind the wheel. We make small talk on the way to the lake; about an hour's drive from the airport.

As we get closer, he notices the large lake-front houses dotting the landscape. "So, who actually owns the lake house?"

"Well, my grandparents—my dad's parents—used to own a ton of the land up here and over the years, they sold it off piece by piece. They owned the land the house sits on, but when they passed, my dad and uncle built the house, so they own it jointly. We all use it, and everyone has their own rooms, plus a couple extra for guests and stuff."

"And it's right on the lake?"

"Yep. We have a dry dock for when the lake goes down in the fall and a nice slide and rope swing. You know, all that fun stuff from when Maddie and I were kids. There are woods next to the house, so you can hike and go for walks and stuff. There are ATVs. It's like a complete getaway."

He nods, impressed. "Sounds like it. So, what are your parents like?"

I sigh. "My dad, Alex, is a judge, so he's probably gonna be the hardest one to convince this thing is legit since he's got such a good bullshit detector. But he's pretty cool, for the most part.

My mom, Vicki, is the one who's all about appearances. She's a professional wife; it's like she was made for it. She would have thrived in the fifties. Most likely, the first thing she'll say to me is, 'What, you couldn't put on a little makeup'. It's one of the reasons we butt heads. I'm super low-key and I'm pretty sure my mom sleeps in her pearls."

"So, who are you closest to in your family?"

"Uncle Lance, Maddie's dad. He's an English professor, a total academic. His wife is pretty uptight, but not him. He loves nothing more than sitting around in a moth-eaten sweater with an old book. When I was younger, he and I would sit on the porch for hours reading. He's one of the reasons I wanted to become a librarian. He gave me my love for books."

"So Alex and Lance are brothers?"

I nod. "Yeah, my dad is older, but because uncle Lance is short and bald and super adorable, he looks older. My dad retained all his hair and got all the height. Even though Maddie and I aren't siblings, we might as well be, and we get compared all the time. I'm sure Dad and Lance did, too. And Lance is like me. Dad's like Maddie. They outshine us, I guess."

He grins. "Well, we'll see what we can do about that this week."

I shake my head. "I don't want to draw attention to myself. I don't like to be the center of attention. Ever. I hate it, honestly."

He nods. "Okay, I'll try to remember that."

I quirk my head. "I bet you're the life of the party, aren't you? A real social butterfly?"

"I can be. I like to think I'm whatever I need to be."

"Ooh, a chameleon. Even better."

"So, what's your favorite thing about the lake house? That way, if you go missing, I'll know where to find you."

I chuckle. "Not likely I'll go missing, but I love the porch.

Hands down, my favorite feature of the house. About fifteen years ago, they screened it in and it's sheer perfection now. I've spent so many hours sitting out there reading, I'm pretty sure the cushion on my favorite chair has a permanent imprint of my ass."

He lifts a brow. "Well, it's a nice ass."

I feel myself blush. "Thanks, I guess."

He peers at me as he absentmindedly scratches at the scruff on his jaw. "Callahan, you don't accept compliments or praise easily, do you?"

I shake my head. "Like I said, I don't like to be the center of attention. And getting complimented is not something I'm accustomed to. I feel weird whenever I do."

"Well, that's a shame."

I give him a smirk. "You're used to getting lots of compliments and praise, aren't you? Especially from women."

"Yeah, I guess. I try not to be so cocky it puts people off, but I know I'm confident."

"Confidence isn't a bad thing. I wish I had more of it."

Jonas smiles. "I will say this, though, if you ever need to be put in your place real quick, all you have to do is visit a kindergarten class. They are ruthless. They'll tell you straight to your face you look funny or your hair looks stupid or something."

I laugh. "I'm sure it keeps you humble. Why kindergarten? It seems like there aren't many men teaching younger grades. At least, that's the way it appears."

"No, there aren't. I think a lot of people have this misconception that men can't be nurturing to small children. Don't get me wrong, I don't baby my kids exactly, but I have no issues kissing boo-boos and playing in the 'home' center in my room. And honestly, I'm a big kid. I love that age. It's so much fun. The sheer amount of knowledge kids gain in kindergarten is astounding and I love to watch their little minds work."

I'm quiet for a moment, absorbing Jonas's words. He's confident and somewhat cocky but hearing him talk about teaching, you can tell he's passionate about it and I find it undeniably endearing. "You're a big softy with your kids, aren't you?"

"Sometimes, not gonna lie. Some kids come from terrible homes and don't get any affection or encouragement, and I try to be that for them, even if it's only while they're in my class. I make sure all my kids know they're loved."

I'm truly touched by his care for his students. "That's precious, Jonas. You can tell you love your job."

He smiles. "Summers off don't hurt either."

"I'd say so." A few minutes later, I make the turn onto the winding driveway for the lake house and in spite of everything going on, I feel myself relax a bit when the house comes into view. I gesture to the barn in the field. "That's where the wedding will be held. It's pretty much a barn in name only. It's definitely more fit for events."

When we pull up at the house, Jonas looks out through the windshield. "*This* is what you call a lake house? This is not a house, Callahan. This is a mansion."

"It's really not, I promise. It can be a little intimidating, but it's cozy." I park and he starts to get out of the car and I touch his arm to stop him. "Wait, how long have we been together?"

He thinks for a minute. "Three months? That's long enough we can say we're wild about each other, but not so long we'd be expected to know everything about one another."

I nod. "Okay, that sounds good. And what is your drink of choice? Mine is red wine, specifically a cab or merlot."

"Beer's about it—pretty much any kind of beer. I can do wine, but it's not my favorite. I don't touch liquor. Not since college, anyway."

"Okay. I guess that's enough of a foundation, right? How good are you on your feet?"

He gives me a slow smile. "In what capacity are you referring to?"

Unable to stop myself, I blush for what seems like the twentieth time today. "Wow, you're good. I meant in the aspect of coming up with answers on the fly. We've already squashed the sex aspect of things, remember?"

He holds my gaze. "Yeah, but we're supposed to have had it, right? We're not celibate, are we? Wouldn't it make sense that I'd flirt with my beautiful girlfriend if I'm wild about her?" My blush grows even deeper and a smug smile pulls at the corners of his lips. "Thought so. Although, if you're gonna blush like that every time I compliment you or flirt with you, it might be the biggest tell of all. Otherwise, I'll have to drag you into a closet and pretend to make out with you so you'll have a reason to blush."

CHAPTER SEVEN

JONAS

Callahan's blush is beyond adorable and it even spreads to the tips of her ears. We step out of the car and she opens the trunk and I gather our bags and follow her toward the house.

This is honestly the biggest house I've ever been to in my life. Elliot said she came from money, but man, this is something else. It has white siding with huge stone and wood columns and a large porch facing the driveway. Lots of greenery and flowerbeds flank the porch. "How often does your family use this house?"

"A lot during the summer and we have our big family holidays here; Christmas and Thanksgiving and stuff since it's big enough for everyone."

When she opens the door, I look around at the expansive room. The ceilings have to be at least twenty feet high and I can't imagine what it looks like at Christmas if they decorate everything. Two seating areas with comfortable-looking, over-sized, brown leather furniture play nicely with the exposed wooden beams in the ceiling. The whole room is open to a generous chef-quality kitchen and an equally large dining table.

"Come on, Jonas. There's plenty more to see." Callahan leads me up a set of stairs to a room on the second floor. While not a huge room, it's bigger than the bedroom of my apartment and has an ensuite bathroom and sofa along with a king-sized bed. Okay, maybe it is a huge room. It's decorated in muted earth tones and I'm sensing that's probably the theme throughout most of the house. Callahan looks around. "Well, this is it."

"You weren't kidding, this is a big room."

"You should see the media room."

I snap my head to her. "There's a media room?"

She nods. "Yeah, we all curl up at Christmas and watch movies in our pajamas."

"Wow, what it must have been like to live here growing up. It must've been magical."

She glances out toward the landing and shuts the door and looks at me. "There's something you should know about my family."

I chuckle. "Is it that y'all are loaded? Because that's pretty obvious."

She rolls her eyes. "My family is. I'm not. I've been adamant about making it on my own. I pay all of my own bills, I pay for school on my own, I work a barely above minimum wage job. I work my ass off."

"Your parents don't help you?"

"If I asked, they would. But I don't ask. And it's a point of contention with them. Maddie is happy to take the family's money, hence the huge wedding blowout. But I'm proud of the fact I survive on my own. So, needless to say, I'm a bit of a black sheep with my family."

I study her face. "So, you don't want to be the center of attention, but you're content to pretty much give your family the finger when it comes to their money?"

She sighs. "What can I say? I'm a walking contradiction. Mainly, I want to be able to blaze my own path and if I take my family's money, they feel like they have a say in what school I go to or where I live and I don't want that kind of life. Maddie stayed here and went to school and might not have any plans to work after the wedding.

"She'll most likely pop out a couple of kids and be exactly like my mom. Not that there's anything wrong with that if that's what she wants. It probably makes it sound like I want a lot of things in my life. I don't, but I do want to make all my own decisions. And family money comes with family obligations attached.

"Don't get me wrong, I love this house and I love my family, but I'm not like them. They're content to go to society functions and rub elbows with the who's who. For the most part, that's not me. And my mom doesn't get it."

I nod. "Okay. I get it. Well, I guess I'm glad you're not all uppity. I wouldn't know how to act. I'm definitely not highbrow in any way."

"Well, you sure look like you fit in, so you'll be fine."

I frown in confusion. "Thanks? I can't tell if that was an insult or a compliment. Especially after the way you described your family."

She smiles and rolls her eyes. "I only meant you dress nice and you're charming. It'll go a long way. Trust me, you'll fit right in. They'll probably wonder why you're with me."

I let her last sentence go, but I don't like the way she puts herself down. It's obvious Callahan's intelligent; she's beautiful, witty, and accomplished. Maybe she needs a little more self-confidence?

"So, where is everyone? I figured a lot of people would be milling about and we didn't see anyone when we walked into the house."

"Most likely, they're all out back. We're a little early for supper, so they're probably sitting around drinking on the patio." She steps back out of the bedroom and starts down the stairs.

"Will I need to change for supper?" I look down at my khaki shorts, navy polo shirt, and Chaco sandals.

She shakes her head. "I'm not. Tonight's super casual. What you have on is perfectly fine."

"Okay. I guess it's show time, right?"

"Yep. Ready or not." She stops abruptly and turns to me. "Listen, if this gets to be too weird or you're miserable, you don't have to stay. We can stage some big break up and I'll get you back to the airport."

"I don't scare easy, Callahan. I'm sure I'll be fine." I take her hand in mine and she looks down at our intertwined fingers and blows out a breath.

She nods slowly. "Okay, I just want you to know you have an out if you need it. Also, I appreciate this. Truly. You have no idea." She bites her lip as if she's suddenly nervous.

"I'm sure we'll have a great time. Don't worry. I teach five-year-olds, I'm pretty sure I can handle your family."

"Okay." She starts walking again and we exit out a back door and I'm greeted by the view of a beautiful lake surrounded by lush hardwoods and evergreens as far as the eye can see. I can understand why Callahan likes this place so much; it's gorgeous. As we walk through the yard, she says in a low voice, "The redhead sitting on the other side of the ring of chairs, that's Maddie. The guy whose lap she's sitting in, that's Dominic, obviously. My parents are on the left. Uncle Lance and Aunt Meredith are on the right. I don't see Dom's parents here. They might not be coming until tomorrow."

Her mother notices us and starts walking over and I feel

Callahan tense. Leaning over, I tuck a fallen hair behind her ear and whisper, "Relax. We've got this. See, even right now, it's gonna look like I'm saying something super sweet or dirty in your ear." I'm rewarded with a soft chuckle and when I pull away, the blush is back.

Callahan's mother reaches us a few seconds later. She's what Nana would call "severe-looking". White and in her late fifties, she's slim and about the same height as her daughter with bright blue eyes and sharp cheekbones. Her hair is blonde, cut to her shoulders, and styled in a smooth bob; her makeup is subtle. She's dressed in chic black Bermuda shorts, a white blouse, and wedged sandals. "Callahan, sweetheart, glad you could make it in." Her gaze lingers on her daughter's features, taking in her appearance. "Really, honey, no makeup? We're trying to make a good impression, you know."

I try not to react to what she's said, although I don't understand how she can't see how pretty Callahan is without any makeup and why she'd need any in the first place since this week's not about her.

"Sorry. I can't wear makeup when I fly. It makes my eyes burn too badly." She turns to me, a smile on her face. "Mother, this is Jonas Merritt, my boyfriend. Jonas, this is my mother, Vicki Benson."

I extend my hand to shake hers. "Mrs. Benson, wonderful to meet you. Callahan's told me a lot about you. You have a lovely home. Thank you for having me."

She sizes me up, her blue eyes serious, even as her tone stays friendly. "Yes, thank you. We're happy to have you. Honestly, I was a bit surprised to find out Callahan would be bringing someone with her. We know so little about her life these days."

The woman's last sentence is a bit more pointed and

Callahan pipes up. "Well, Mother, Jonas and I haven't been together long, but I figured now was as good a time as any to introduce him to everyone. But, if you'll excuse us, I think we're gonna make the rounds."

"Of course. Supper's at six. I know you'll probably want to unpack and get settled before then. Jonas, it's a pleasure to meet you. Make yourself at home while you're here, okay?"

I give her mother a warm smile. "Yes, ma'am. Thank you. Nice to meet you as well."

Callahan tugs me past her mom and over to where her father and the remainder of the family are seated. She introduces me to everyone and when we get to Maddie and Dominic, she embraces her cousin enthusiastically and I glance at him. He's white with a ruddy complexion and about five-ten with dark blonde hair and brown eyes. He's fit and good-looking in an unremarkable, WASP sort of way. His eyes trail over Callahan and it appears to be more than a passing glance. He starts to look my way and I turn my full attention to Callahan as if I'm interested in what she's been saying to her cousin.

She's become markedly more relaxed since seeing Maddie; her grin is wide and genuine when she turns to me. "Sorry, Jonas, I got carried away. Maddie, this is my boyfriend, Jonas. Jonas, Maddie." Her cousin shakes my hand warmly in greeting.

I turn and stick my hand out toward Dominic. "Jonas Merritt. Nice to meet you. Congratulations on the wedding."

"Dominic Prescott. Thanks for coming." He grasps my hand firmly, but it's clear by both his tone and his stiff posture that he'd rather be anywhere but here.

I possessively pull Callahan into my side and smile. "Happy to be here." A muscle in his jaw tics and I can't help but wonder if it has something to do with Callahan or the fact that she's with someone. I look down at her. "Didn't you say something about a media room? Do we have time to see it before dinner?"

She smiles up at me sweetly, perfectly playing her role. "Sure. Might not be a bad idea to have a little rest before supper, too, don't you think?" She wiggles her eyebrows and her tone sounds a bit suggestive.

Oh, good job, Callahan. "Sounds perfect," I respond.

She takes my hand and we start to walk away. She hollers over her shoulder to Maddie to say they'll catch up later. I don't miss the way Dominic's eyes follow Callahan. *Douchebag.*

When we get back into the house, we let our hands drop and she turns to me. "Did you actually want to see the media room?"

I nod. "Hell yeah, I do. I've never seen one in real life before. Please tell me it has stadium seating and a huge projector screen, like a movie theater."

She chuckles at my apparent wonder and we walk down to the basement and sure enough, the media room is pretty much like a miniature movie theater. The room is about twenty by thirty and has a projection screen taking up an entire wall. Four rows of, yes, stadium seating with combinations of single recliners and loveseats take up a majority of the space. The windowless room is plush and I can imagine what kind of fun it would be to sit in here as a family and watch movies. I turn to her. "Impressive. What movies do you watch at Christmas?"

"Oh, you know, *Christmas Vacation, A Christmas Story, It's a Wonderful Life, Die Hard.*"

"Nice. Where's the porch? I want to see where you like to hang out."

She nods. "Sure. Follow me." We walk back up to the

second floor and pass through a simple sitting area and out a sliding glass door to a screened-in porch. I can understand why she would like this space. It's quiet and the lake is visible from the porch, but not the patio where her family is sitting. She drops in an oversized wicker chair.

"Is this the chair with the infamous ass print?"

She laughs. "Yeah. In the morning, I'll bring my coffee out here and sit in the quiet. Aside from reading, having my coffee out here is a close second."

"And is this a solo activity, or can anyone join?"

"I don't turn anyone away, but I'm typically up way before everyone else, so I'm usually by myself."

"This is nice. I get why it's your favorite spot."

Smiling, she looks around as if assessing the space with fresh eyes. "Yeah. It's pretty cool." She stands and I'm surprised. I figured she'd want to stay out here longer and she must see it in my face. "I actually do want to rest for a bit and hang up my clothes for the week so they're not so wrinkled."

I nod. "Yeah, but it doesn't hurt if Dominic thinks we're having a little afternoon delight, does it?"

She laughs. "Do people still say afternoon delight?"

I shrug and give her a sheepish smile. "It sounded better in my head."

We make our way back into the house and as we enter her bedroom, she shuts the door. "But to answer your question, no, it doesn't hurt." She lifts her suitcase up onto the bed and opens it and pulls out a few dresses and hangs them in the closet. She pulls out some tops and hangs them and puts a few pairs of shoes away as well.

I ask, "How were you able to fit all your stuff in such a small suitcase?"

"Magic, I guess. I probably won't be as lucky when I pack to go home, though. It's an exact science and somehow never works the same on the trip back. I also have stuff here already, mainly old, comfy stuff, so I didn't have to bring everything."

I also open my bag and Callahan points to the dresser. "The top drawer of the dresser is empty if you'd like to use it and there are plenty of hangers in the closet if you need them. Help yourself."

"Thanks." I pull out my socks, underwear, swim trunks, shorts, and tee shirts and place them in the drawer. I hang up my suit, my nicer shirts, and a couple of pairs of dress pants. "Can I ask you something?"

Callahan looks up at me as she finishes taking some things out of her bag. "Sure."

"What's his deal?"

"Dominic?" When I nod, she says, "Honestly, I don't know. I always thought he was this mysterious, sexy, deep guy, but I don't know if that was actually the case, or only how I built him up in my head. Maddie looks happy, though." I debate whether to tell her Dominic pretty much couldn't take his eyes off her—and not her cousin—while we were being introduced, but decide to leave it. It could be because he hasn't seen her in a long time that he acted that way.

"I guess things must've been pretty good for you to be willing to be with him on and off for four years, though, right? I mean, was the sex that good?"

She blushes and chews her bottom lip. "Honestly, I don't know."

I can't hide my surprise at her answer. "What do you mean, you don't know?"

She looks down. "He's all I know, so I don't know if it was actually good, or that I thought he'd eventually want to commit."

"Oh. Okay."

She returns her gaze to mine, her expression guarded. "What, no comment about that?"

I shake my head. "No. I was just curious." Although that might explain why he looked at her the way he did. If he's the only guy she's ever been with and he thinks she's now with me, it's a territorial thing.

Callahan nods. "Okay."

CHAPTER EIGHT

CALLAHAN

I probably should've been embarrassed to tell Jonas those personal details about my relationship with Dominic, but for some reason, I wasn't. He's easy to talk to, and what else do I have to do this week? After I finish putting my clothes away and toiletries in the bathroom and slide my suitcase under the bed, I pull my phone out and set an alarm for an hour before supper is scheduled to start and slip off my shoes and lie on the bed.

Jonas moves around the room, putting his own things away and once he's done, he asks, "Can I lie down, too?"

I nod. "Of course." He stretches out on the bed next to me, but at least three feet of space separates us and I stare at the ceiling.

After a minute, he asks, "On a scale from one to ten, how weird is it for you to have a guy you only met this morning in your bed?"

I turn onto my side to face him. "Really? That's what you want to know? Not more questions about Dom and me?"

He rolls onto his side as well. "No. I don't care about him. Is it weird for you that I'm here? Or any guy, I guess."

I consider. "It probably should be, but you're easy to talk to, so no, it's not weird. Plus, you can't be too big a weirdo or anything; you've been background checked by the state. You work with kids."

He chuckles. "That's fair. Okay. Yeah, it should be weird, but for some reason, it's not." After a beat, he says, "Okay, I lied; I do have a question."

"Shoot," I say.

"So, he's the only guy? Like for *anything*? And if he broke things off with you eighteen months ago, has there been anyone since him?"

I feel a slight blush creep into my cheeks and I know he sees it, but I answer him honestly. "No, he's it. For everything. I mean, I've kissed other guys, but there hasn't been anyone else for more than that."

He frowns in obvious confusion. "Why not? You can't tell me guys don't hit on you."

I shrug. "Not much. My program at school is primarily women and most of the guys in the program are either too scared of the opposite sex, or they're gay. I don't go out often. I study and work a lot. It doesn't leave a whole lot of time for a social life. What about you? Do you date a lot?"

"Define *a lot*."

I huff out a soft laugh. "Well, I don't know. I don't have much of a frame of reference, so how much do you think you date? Ballpark it for the year."

"Well, are we talking about actual dates or hookups?"

I consider. "I don't know. Do you go on actual dates? Or only have hookups?"

"I mean, yeah, I date. I like going out to dinner and stuff.

Maybe once a month?" He's quiet for a moment in contemplation as he considers my question about hookups.

"Are you performing advanced calculus over there trying to figure things up?" I ask, my tone teasing.

He smiles, amused. "No, but it's more than you."

I roll my eyes. "Well, that's not hard to beat. So, you'd say, you're, what, seasoned?"

He scrunches up his face and laughs. "What am I, fried chicken? What is *seasoned*? I'll put it this way, I have friends I hang out with on a semi-rotating basis."

I nod. "Gotcha. So, you have fuck buddies?"

It's obvious he's surprised by my language, but then tilts his head slightly as if it's an accurate description of things, his expression thoughtful. "I guess, yeah."

Out of sheer curiosity, I ask, "What's it like? I mean, I know my thing with Dom wasn't committed or anything, but to me, it was more than hookup. And for all I know, he was seeing other women the same time as me. What's it like to only have a physical relationship with someone? Don't feelings ever get hurt?"

It would appear he's not put off my question, as he answers without hesitation. "Not on my end. I'm blunt about the fact I don't do commitment. If I get a hint of someone thinking there's more than just sex, I break it off with her."

"Oh, okay. You said the last relationship you had was eight years ago?"

The question gives him pause, but after a beat, he speaks. "Yeah. When I was in college."

And because it's like he's put up some sort of wall, I don't ask any follow-up questions and simply nod. Hoping to move to a safer subject, I ask, "So, would you say this is the strangest date you've ever been on?"

He smiles. "Most definitely. You?"

"Yeah."

"Your mom seems kind of...intense. I mean, she was perfectly polite, but her eyes seem to drill into you and judge every aspect of you."

I sigh. "Yeah, I know. We're not close."

He nods. "I kind of got that vibe."

"She and Maddie are close, though."

"And you're only close with your uncle?"

"Yeah, pretty much. I probably won't get to spend a lot of time with him this week, with everything going on, though. We hang out a lot over the holidays usually. What about you? Family?"

He clenches his jaw but then releases it. "I only have my nana. I've never met my father and my mom and I moved in with my grandparents when I was about three. But then, Mom got on drugs and split when I was in high school."

Shocked by what he's told me, my mouth falls open. I recover quickly and shake my head, my tone sympathetic. "Jonas, I'm so sorry, that's awful."

He smiles, but it's a bit sad and he sighs, resigned. "Part of it, I guess."

"So, what is your grandmother like? Are y'all close?"

His smile turns genuine and his eyes soften. "Yeah. She's great. Feisty, for sure. She lives in a retirement community and loves to tell me all the dirt about the residents. Apparently, there's a huge outbreak of gonorrhea among the geriatric population of Tallahassee."

My mouth falls open in shock. "No way."

"That's what she said. She said they were being forced to attend a safe-sex seminar."

"Wow, that is wild. I guess, good for them; if they can still get it, they should."

"That's exactly what she said." He gives me a lopsided grin. "She's one of my best friends though."

"Wow, you mold young minds and your grandmother is one of your best friends. I'm surprised all the girls aren't banging down your door to beg you to father their children."

He smirks. "How do you know they aren't?"

"I guess I don't. Would you say most of the time, it's you chasing or do you get chased? How do things typically work for you?"

"I mean, I guess I haven't given it much thought before, but probably a bit of both. There's a bar down the street from my apartment. I'm a regular."

"A honey hole? Nice."

He chuckles. "Sure, why not."

"And what normally happens?"

"As in, what, when I pick up a woman? Or a woman picks me up?"

I pull my shoulders up to my ears and drop them. "You picking someone up, I guess. What do you do?"

He considers for a minute and grins. "Definitely the strangest date ever. Do you actually want to know?"

I nod. "Sure, you can teach me a thing or two and maybe when I get home, I'll go out and try your tactics."

"It's more of a show kind of thing than a tell."

I nod. "Okay, so show me."

"I can't do it here. I'd have to be in the right environment."

I raise an eyebrow. "Well, excuse me, I didn't realize it was so scientific. Okay, so show me later, like at supper or something."

"You're sure?"

I nod. "Yeah, why?"

He holds my gaze. "I wouldn't be held responsible for what happens after."

I snort a laugh. "Wow, you seem pretty sure of yourself. Okay. Do or don't, whatever."

Jonas is about to say something, but the alarm on my phone goes off and I sit up and sigh. "Time to face the music, I guess. How do you like your steak?"

He sits up and swings his legs over the bed. "Medium-rare. How do you know we're having steak?"

"My dad won't pass up an opportunity to use the grill. Mom doesn't let him grill out at home much. She says it's something about the carcinogens in the charcoal. She doesn't let him eat a lot of red meat, either. But when we're here, Dad tends to do what he wants. So, we'll have steak. And probably baked potatoes or grilled veggies. My parents are pretty predictable."

"That's nice though, isn't it? Always knowing what to expect?"

I run my hand down my ponytail and stand. "I guess. I think it would pretty nice, if just once, they did something the least bit unexpected, though."

CHAPTER NINE

JONAS

Callahan walks into the bathroom and shuts the door and I get up and stretch and go over to the window to look out toward the lake. Her room has a great view of the water and the woods. A few minutes later, the door opens and I turn. She leans against the frame, arms folded across her chest. I give her a quick smile. "This is a great place, Cal. I see why you love it so much."

Something flashes in her eyes. "Please don't call me Cal."

I nod. "Sure. Sorry. Is there another nickname you have?"

"Callie is fine. No one here calls me that, but Callahan wouldn't fit on my name tag at work, so they went with Callie. Maddie called me 'Hanny' when we were younger. Sometimes, she still does."

"He called you Cal?"

She looks down and nods. "Yeah. I know it shouldn't bother me. It's stupid. But it irks me."

I shake my head. "Not stupid. Callie it is. Although, I might come up with something else I like better."

She folds her arms. "There's only so many things you can get out of Callahan."

"Yeah, but still. I can be creative." I wink and she rolls her eyes and I can't help but smile. "You roll your eyes a lot, you know that?"

"Yeah, I know. If it was an actual exercise, I'd be ripped."

"You done in there?" I gesture to the bathroom and she nods and steps out of the doorway.

"Be my guest."

I walk past her into the bathroom and freshen up and when I come out a few minutes later, Callahan is sitting on the small sofa with a book open in her lap. She looks up. "You ready?"

"Whenever you are," I say. We walk out of the bedroom and down the stairs. "Where is everyone?"

"Most likely, we'll eat outside. Dad likes to eat near the water, so Mom probably set up a whole big spread down near the bank." We stop at the back door and I can see Vicki moving things around on a large table, complete with floral arrangements.

"Fancy."

She snorts softly. "Pretentious, more like. I mean, what's the point of it all?"

Playing devil's advocate, I ask, "I guess if it's what they like, and they can, they should be able to do it, right?"

"Yeah, I guess."

I'm beginning to sense if Callahan's around her family, she's tense. It radiates off her and her posture is rigid. She was completely relaxed up in the bedroom only moments ago.

She opens the door and I follow her out into the backyard. As we get farther into the yard, we can see Maddie curled up in Dominic's lap in one of the large, wooden deck chairs on the patio. Callahan's breathing changes when she sees them and I watch her hands curl into fists but she keeps walking until we're about ten feet away.

She makes a point to not look at them and instead appears to look out onto the water. I step up behind her and lean in and whisper in her ear. "Darlin', if you don't relax, they're gonna think the hour we spent up in the bedroom wasn't a satisfying experience for you. That doesn't make me look like the attentive and caring boyfriend I'm supposed to be, now, does it?" I brush a kiss across the side of her neck and her breath catches. I run my hands down her arms and uncurl her fists.

I step to her side and intertwine our fingers before bringing her hand up to my lips and pressing a kiss to her knuckles. When I look at her, her cheeks are bright pink and she swallows. "Better?" I ask.

She nods slowly and smiles. "Thanks. You're excellent at distracting me, you know that?"

I quirk a brow. "Anytime. I like distracting you. It's fun to see you blush." She elbows me playfully and we laugh.

During supper, we indeed have steak and baked potatoes and Callahan nurses her wine as the dinner winds down I sip a beer. It's one I've never heard of, but it's good; probably some local microbrew or something. We've stayed out of a lot of the conversation, as it has mostly pertained to wedding talk, but she'll lean over intermittently and give me commentary about a certain distant family member they're discussing or to explain a past event that's brought up. She relaxes a bit more once she's had a glass of wine and I'm glad to see it.

Eventually, though, as these things go, I'm dragged into the conversation when Callahan's father asks what I do for work.

"I'm a teacher."

Her uncle Lance perks up. "Really? What grade?"

I smile. "Kindergarten."

"So you play with kids all day?" Dominic asks, his tone laced with what sounds a lot like condescension.

I sit up straighter. "Actually, play is an extremely important way children learn. Unfortunately, due to state regulations and standards, we don't play nearly as much as I'd prefer. Kids learn a lot by playing; usually, more than they do from books. Their brains are wired to retain things through hands-on discovery. So, yeah, I do."

"Wow, must be nice. And you have summers off? Sounds like a cake job."

This guy is such a prick. But I'm not rattled. I simply take a pull from my beer and nod. "Yeah, I do love having my summers free. It allows me to travel." I look at Callahan. "It allowed me to be able to come here with Callie, so I can't complain."

She smiles and I wink at her. I look back at Dominic and he wears a sour expression. After a beat, Vicki says, "Well, that's wonderful you get to teach. It's an admirable profession."

"Thank you."

Maddie, who's been pretty quiet up to this point outside of the wedding discussion, asks, "So, how did y'all meet? Callahan doesn't date a whole lot, or at all, really, so how did you guys end up together?"

I look at Callahan as if to say, *take it away*. She says, "My roommate, Elliot, and Jonas work together. He set us up on a blind date."

"Really, a blind date? I didn't realize people still did those."

She shrugs. "It was kind of a last-minute thing. I had reservations at a restaurant I'd wanted to go to for a month and Elliot was supposed to go with me and bailed at the last minute. And I guess he felt bad because he roped Jonas into showing up in his place."

I interject, "Yeah, except she didn't know I was coming

until right before I showed up. When I walked up on her, she was on the phone with him, giving him hell for abandoning her."

Callahan scrunches up her nose. "I was not using my best language, I'll admit."

I chuckle. "Yeah, there may have been talks of alligators and swamps and what you'd like to do with Elliot's body."

She laughs. "I honestly didn't know you'd heard that part. I thought it all was in my head. But he was my hero. Rescuing me so I didn't have to sit there all alone, surrounded by couples."

"Well, if I'm honest, my motives weren't completely pure. I owed Elliot a favor and he called it in. And then I made him sweeten the pot by doing all my bus duty for the fall semester."

"Wow, a real opportunist," Dominic says with a derisive snort.

I turn to Callahan. "Maybe. But as soon as I saw her, I realized I would have agreed to do it for nothing in return. Elliot had described her to me but didn't tell me how beautiful she was. And when I saw her, I had to take a breath. She had this look of pure murder on her face I found utterly adorable and that was it."

Callahan's expression changes and she looks down into her glass as if she's not sure how she's supposed to react. Maddie doesn't miss a beat. "Oh my gosh, that is such a cute story."

CHAPTER TEN

CALLAHAN

It's not real, Callahan. Jonas is only playing the part to perfection. And damn, he's good. Once supper is done, I help take dishes to the kitchen and offer to wash up, simply so I'll have something to do. Jonas stays to help and I rinse and he loads the dishwasher. I'm quiet and he lets me be, which I appreciate. I think he knows his words hit me, even if I know it's not real.

God, this is only day one. If I'm already struggling with myself, I'm never gonna survive the week. Between his small touches and his whispered words, by the time we go home, I'm gonna be nothing but raw nerves.

It's not real. It's not real. It's not real.

Once the dishes are done and the kitchen is tidied, we walk up the stairs to the bedroom. After I shut the door, Jonas asks, "Is there anything else we have to do tonight?"

I shake my head and drop onto the sofa and he sits beside me. "No. Everyone will do their own thing. The old folks might go down and watch a movie or something. But we're good to chill. I mean, if you want to do something, we can, but I was probably gonna take a shower and read for a little while before going to bed."

"Okay. And tomorrow is the barbecue, right?"

"Yeah, and they'll be a lot of cornhole."

"So, what about before that?"

"Nothing planned that I know of. There's plenty of stuff to do. The boat, ATVs, swimming."

"Do you swim?" Jonas asks.

"No, not since I was younger. I can swim fine, but I don't like to touch the lake bottom. I might put on my suit and sit on the dock and put my feet in, but that would be about it for me. You're welcome to, though. The rope swing's pretty fun."

He asks, his tone curious, "Will they not expect us to sneak away some?"

The thought that I would *sneak away* with anyone is almost comical to me and I nearly smile. I shake my head, unsure. "I don't know, honestly. I think they're shocked to find out after all these years I'm not a lesbian. Since I never dated or brought anyone around, it wouldn't have shocked me if they thought I was."

"So, did they not know about Dominic? And what does Maddie think happened?"

I sigh. "The Benson and Prescott families have always been close. They run in the same circles. Dominic's father and my dad went to law school together. Dom's mother and Aunt Meredith were sorority sisters. So we've always been around one another. He's a couple of years older than Maddie and me and he and I just happened to go to the same college. We started hooking up my sophomore year. He was a senior.

"But since we were away from home, none of our parents ever knew we were a thing. Maddie knows we slept together because we'd both had a crush on him growing up and I was excited to tell her what happened. But Dom wanted to keep things quiet, so I didn't let on that we continued to sleep together while I was in college and grad school. So, for all I know, she thinks it was only the once, or that we were only together for a short time.

"I didn't get to come home one year for our big family Christmas party, because I was working, and Maddie and Dominic reconnected. And she called me a couple of days after that and told me they were seeing each other."

"So, he didn't even have the decency to tell you they were together?" His eyes widen slightly and his tone is incredulous.

"Yeah, he did. When I confronted him about it. We got in a big fight, I don't remember much of what was said. I only remember how crushed I felt. But it was my own fault. He was upfront about what he wanted. But I wonder now if he was only with me until he could have Maddie."

Jonas frowns in confusion. "What do you mean?"

I look down at my hands. "Maddie always had boyfriends. Always dated. That Christmas, though, she'd recently broken up with her boyfriend and she was single when she went to the party. So, Dom finally got his shot with her."

"Can I say something?" When I nod he says, "He's a douchebag. And a prick."

"Yeah, I know. And part of me hates him and hates myself for thinking I meant more to him than I did because he never promised me anything, but I still let myself think he eventually would. And another part of me feels like I'll never be enough for anyone because apparently, I'm only good enough to be someone's placeholder until they can be with the person they truly want. And maybe someday, seeing them together won't hurt as much. But right now, it still does. And I hate that it still does. After everything, I should only be angry, I know that. But, I'm still hurt."

I look at Jonas. "Sorry. Didn't mean to vomit all over you emotionally."

He chuckles. "No worries, I deal with emotions on a daily basis. I don't scare easy." His expression grows serious. "But I'll say this, you are not someone's placeholder, Callahan. Just because that asshole used you and strung you along for four years doesn't mean there's not someone out there who will treat you the way you deserve."

Nodding, I stand. "I'm gonna take a shower." I walk over to the dresser and pull out my pajamas and a pair of underwear and go into the bathroom. Once the shower is hot, I strip down and climb under the spray and tears burn my eyes. I do nothing to stop them, unsure at this point if the wetness streaming down my face is from the shower or my tears.

I know if I was at home, I'd be fine. If I didn't have to see him, I'd be fine. Even knowing that he and Maddie are getting married, I'd still be fine. But seeing him, being around him, it's too much. It hurts too deeply. And I hate him for making me feel something for him. Even after he broke my heart, I still have feelings for him. And for that, I hate myself.

It also hasn't escaped my notice that Dominic hasn't said two words to me since I showed up here. And Jonas is right, he's a prick. He was snide when Jonas talked about his job, which makes me hate him all the more. But my stupid, shattered heart still skips a beat when I'm near him. And it's not fair.

CHAPTER ELEVEN

JONAS

If I needed a legitimate reason to hate Dominic, I now have it. He's a smug, entitled shit, not worth the air he breathes. And seeing what he's done to Callahan, the way he's treated her, the damage he's caused her, makes me want to punch him in the face.

It's no wonder she thinks the way she does about herself. Granted, Maddie's cute, but it's in a different way than Callahan is beautiful.

Maddie's got a bubbly, shiny personality, but to me, that would get old real fast. Callahan is observant and smart and is as understated as Maddie is over-the-top. And given the choice, I'd pick Callahan. She's never had anyone pick her. And that sucks, I know that. I could tell her exactly how much I can relate to her, but I won't. This week's not about me.

But, maybe, by the time she gets home, she'll be in a better place. I plan on being as sweet as possible to her and while it will be a challenge to find the balance between being just flirty and affectionate enough and not too much, since I know there's no sex, I can still treat her well and make her feel wanted; I can do that. But I also don't want to hurt her more than she already is. On second thought, this might end up proving to be difficult by the end of the week.

Callahan is in the shower for a long time, at least a half-hour, and I wonder if she always takes that long, or if she needed some space to be alone with her thoughts. I have my answer a bit later when she comes out of the bathroom with her eyes red and puffy. Even wearing glasses, I can tell she's been crying, but I don't know her well enough to know what she needs, so I don't say anything.

Her hair is wrapped in a towel and her pajamas are a pair of minuscule sleep shorts and a tight tank top. Without a bra. And dammit, she's gorgeous. Her legs are toned and the shorts she wears cut right under her ass and I don't miss how nice *that* is, either. Her tits are full and round and fuck me, her nipples are hard.

There's no sex, Jonas. Don't even think about it.

She sees me looking at her and I quickly avert my eyes. "Sorry about the pajamas; I was expecting Elliot, otherwise I would've packed something a bit more conservative."

I clear my throat and shake my head. "No, remind me to thank him for sending me."

She blushes and sits on the bed. After a moment, she smiles and her tone is light. "Yeah, you're alright. I mean, at least you don't have to pretend to be straight."

"Nope. And he must truly be gay to live with you and see you every day and not want to climb into bed with you."

Her blush deepens but she smirks. "Oh, he does. But it's usually so we can watch *The Bachelor*."

I laugh. "Did you leave any hot water for me?"

She nods. "Oh yeah, there's plenty."

I feign total seriousness. "Oh, by the way, I hope it's not a problem, but I sleep naked. I can't sleep in clothes."

Callahan's face drains of color and she opens and closes her mouth as if she wants to say something but can't find words until she sees the smirk I finally give her. She huffs out a relieved laugh. "That's not funny, Jonas; I almost had an aneurysm."

"I know; it was fun to watch." She throws a pillow at me and I catch it before tossing it back onto the bed. I pull out my own pajamas, a pair of sweats and a tee shirt, and go take a shower.

When I come out, Callahan has braided her hair in a thick rope that hangs over her shoulder and she's curled up in bed reading, her chin resting on one knee. She doesn't look up from her book, so I simply watch her for a moment. She worries her bottom lip between her thumb and index finger. It's not in any way a sexual gesture, but it's still sexy.

After a moment, she looks up from her page and her glasses have slid down her nose and she really does look like a librarian and I can't help but smile. "What?" she asks.

"Oh, nothing. But with your hair in a braid and your glasses perched on the end of your nose, you truly do look like a librarian. I mean, maybe a sexy librarian in that tank top, but still."

She rolls her eyes and pushes her glasses back up her nose and returns to her book. I place my keys, wallet, and pocket change on the dresser and put away my dirty clothes. I dig out my phone charger from my suitcase and plug it up on my side of the bed before crawling under the covers. I run my fingers through my hair, still damp from my shower and scroll through my phone for a bit.

It may be a bit strange to be in a bed with a beautiful woman without there being some sort of sexual activity going on, but it's not awkward with Callahan, which I'm thankful for. This week would probably be going much differently if she was boring, but she's not.

After a while longer, Callahan sticks her bookmark in her book and closes it before setting it on the nightstand. "What are you reading?" I ask.

She turns to me. "*Good Omens* by Neil Gaiman."

"Any good? I read *American Gods* by him."

She nods. "Yeah, I like it. It's different than *American Gods*, but still pretty good."

"Cool. Is that the kind of books you normally read, or do you read other stuff, too?"

"My tastes run the gamut. I can read almost anything, but I prefer fantasy or romance."

I raise my brows. "Romance, huh? What kind of romance? Are you more of a historical romance kind of girl, or *Fifty Shades*?"

She blushes. "I have to admit I've never actually read *Fifty Shades*, but yeah, more along the lines of that."

"So you like full-blown smut? Nice. What would you say is the filthiest thing you've ever read?"

"Oh, wow, that's hard. I've read a lot." Her eyes lift to the ceiling for a beat in contemplation. "Probably this book about a priest and one of his parishioners. God, it was dirty." Color creeps into her face and I laugh. "What?" She asks.

"Oh, nothing. I can see you're picturing some scenes."

Her blush deepens and travels down her chest. "What? No, I'm not."

"You're blushing. It's your tell. I know." I give her a smug smile.

She rolls her eyes. "Whatever."

"Okay, what else?"

"Let's see? The priest one is part of a series, and in the first book, things *conspire* in the church. And then there's another series by the same author about this woman who's in love with the president and the vice president, but they're also in love with each other. They're a throuple." She gives me a wicked grin.

"Oh, God. You read all that stuff and you still don't date or sleep around?"

Callahan gives a little nod in ascent. "Yeah. Like I said, I'm busy."

"Too busy to get busy? Then you are too busy, Callahan."

She laughs. "Probably. But I don't know if I even miss it anymore; it's been so long."

"Then what you had must not have been good. Because when it's good, you do miss it." My tone is even, but I hold her gaze.

"Maybe. I don't know. How long is the longest you've been without?"

I think. "About six months, maybe. Long time ago."

"So, how long do you typically go between hookups now?"

"Is this not weird for you? To talk about this?"

She shakes her head. "No, I'm a naturally curious person. And I'm not a prude, regardless of how much I blush."

"Okay. Probably three days."

"And is it usually with the same woman for a period of time, or all different?"

"Depends."

"On what?"

I shrug. "Different things. If I know I don't have to worry about her catching feelings and we have a good time, I might see her for a few weeks or something, be kind of steady, I guess. But if I think they might get attached, I'll be one and done or go weeks or months without calling her. Probably the only steady I've had in a long time is my friend, Teagan. I've known her since college and she's a good friend and we have a good time together, but there's nothing there."

"So how do you know which way it's gonna go?"

"It's a vibe I get, usually, or the woman will say outright she is or isn't looking for anything and I'm upfront about what I want, so I normally don't have to worry about it."

"Are you not ever worried about you having feelings for someone?"

I shake my head. "Nope."

She examines my face. "Is that because you don't believe in love, period, or you do and you're not willing to get hurt again?"

Her question catches me off guard and I tense for a split second and I know she sees it. "Wow, that bad, huh?"

"I didn't say anything."

She gives me a sad smile. "You didn't have to."

CHAPTER TWELVE

CALLAHAN

I can see on Jonas's face he's surprised by both my question and what I said after, but I simply turn off the light and lie down and roll onto my side. "Goodnight, Jonas."

"Goodnight, Callie." His lamp turns off and I feel the bed shift as he lies down and gets comfortable.

He's been hurt, too. Looks like we're two peas in a pod. At least he's honest, I guess. When he hooks up, he doesn't let things get too far. That would have been nice when I was with Dom. If he'd been man enough to end things when he knew I started falling for him, maybe I wouldn't be so fucked up.

When I wake up, the sun hasn't yet fully risen. I'm still in the same position I fell asleep in, and I slowly get up and stretch and walk to the bathroom to pee and brush my teeth. I pull my old, tattered bathrobe off the back of the bathroom door and open the door quietly, so as to not wake Jonas.

He's asleep on his back with one arm draped above him and

the other resting on his stomach. He's definitely sexy. Overnight, his intentional stubble has turned into the beginnings of a beard and it only adds to his appeal. Sometime while he was sleeping, the covers migrated down around his hips and stretched out as he is, he looks like he could be on the cover of a steamy romance novel. The hem of his tee shirt has slid up his abdomen, revealing about two inches of tan skin. What would that skin feel like under my fingertips? Under my lips? Against my—. *Stop it, Callahan. You cannot sleep with him.* Like he'd want to anyway, but still.

I pick up my phone and book from the nightstand and tiptoe out of the bedroom and gently shut the door behind me and walk down the stairs, missing the creaky third one down and step into the kitchen. I turn on the Keurig and get my favorite mug out of the cabinet and once the machine is ready, I put in a pod and brew my coffee.

Mug in hand, I walk back up the steps and head toward the porch. I sit in my favorite chair and sip my coffee and drink in the early morning light and quiet. It's things like this that make it worth all the shit with my family. Knowing I have a place I can come where I can simply *be* and breathe.

I'm just opening my book when the sliding door opens. I look over my shoulder and see Jonas walking out onto the porch, his own mug in hand. I set my book down as he sits in the chair next to mine. "I didn't mean to interrupt you."

"You didn't. I hadn't even opened it all the way yet. I was caught up in the quiet for a while. Sleep okay?"

He smiles. "Yeah. Probably best night's sleep I've had in I don't know how long. How much did that mattress cost?"

I laugh. "You don't want to know. My parents don't half-ass anything."

"I figured." He sips his mug and his curly hair is mussed from sleep and makes him look that much more handsome. He catches me looking at him and I automatically look anywhere else. "This is nice; sitting out here."

I nod. "Yeah. I usually get about an hour in before everyone wakes up. I've always been an early riser and this became time that was only for me. Time that I didn't have to listen to my parents talk about their expectations or criticisms. Only me, a cup of coffee, and the birds."

"It's nice. At my nana's old house, before she moved into the retirement village, there was a big tree in the backyard. That was my place. I didn't have a tree house or anything, but I'd climb that tree and take a comic book with me and usually a Coke. Nana always bought the ones in glass bottles. She said they tasted better."

"They do taste better," I agree.

He nods. "Yeah."

"So, what do you want to do today? I mean, we don't have to do anything, but it's gonna be way too nice to stay in the house. Especially for July, the weather seems cooler than normal."

He taps the side of his mug with his thumb. "I don't know. That rope swing sounds pretty cool."

I chuckle. "You really are a big kid, aren't you?"

"Most definitely. What do you want to do?"

"Well, I'll sit on the dock and watch you fling yourself into the lake."

"Okay, I like an audience. Will you cheer me on and everything?"

I give him an amused smile. "Well, duh, isn't that part of this deal? You make me look good, I make you look...Well, you look pretty good all on your own. I don't know what I bring to the table for you. But yeah, I'll cheer for you."

His expression grows stony. "Don't do that."

I frown, not understanding. "Do what?"

"Don't act like you're not a smart, beautiful, accomplished woman. Don't belittle yourself, even if you think it's funny, because it's not. You don't need me to make you look good. Darlin', you already look pretty fucking good from where I sit."

I swallow and look down, unsure how to respond to his words. He continues, "I know that's probably a coping mechanism for you, to deflect and be self-deprecating because you don't like praise or compliments or because you think you're less than or whatever, but it stops, got it?"

My chest tightens with emotion. Jonas rises from his chair and squats in front of me and lifts my chin, forcing me to look at him. "Got it?" His brown eyes are warm but serious. When I nod, he smiles. "Good." He goes back and sits in his chair and scrolls through his phone like he didn't possibly say the nicest thing anyone ever has to me.

I go to take another sip of my coffee and find my cup empty and I stand. "Do you want more coffee? I'm headed to fix myself some more."

He looks up at me. "Sure. Thanks." He drains the last of his cup and hands it over. I walk back into the house and down into the kitchen and fix our refills. My dad walks into the room and kisses me on the top of the head. "Good morning, sweetie. Did you and Jonas sleep alright?"

"Yep. Fine."

"Good. We'll fix breakfast in about an hour. I know you've been up for a while, but give some of us who like to sleep past dawn a break."

I laugh. "That's fine. Jonas and I are having coffee now."

"He seems like a nice guy."

"Yeah, he is."

"He makes you smile. I'm glad to see it." I'm surprised by my father's words. He doesn't typically wax poetic about relationships or emotions, so to hear him say something about me smiling is weird.

After a moment, I nod. "Yeah, he does." Because it's true. Jonas makes me laugh and roll my eyes with his shameless flirting. The last of the coffee drips into the mug so I take it. "Well, I'm gonna get back upstairs."

"Sure. Enjoy your coffee." Dad pulls down his own mug and he's placing the pod in the cradle when I walk back up the steps. I head back out the door and slide it closed with my foot and hand Jonas his cup. He's still scrolling on his phone but smiles up at me when he takes his mug.

I sit back down in my chair and open my book and we both sit and sip in quiet for about another half hour until Jonas breaks the silence, his voice low, "*Jesus.*"

I look over at him, alarmed by his tone. "What?"

"You were right; the book about the priest is filthy."

I choke and sputter my coffee down my chin. "You're reading? That's what you've been doing this whole time?"

"Yeah. But I don't know; after what I just read, I feel like I need to go to church, but not this one. Damn."

I flush all the way to my toes knowing what's in the book he's reading. "Why would you read that?" I ask in shock.

"Morbid curiosity, mostly. Damn, Callie, you're a freak, aren't you?" He gives me an impressed nod.

I know I'm still blushing, but I say, "You know, liking to read about something and wanting to do the same kinds of stuff are two entirely different things. I have no desire to have sex on the altar of a church or some of the other stuff that goes on in the book, but it doesn't mean it doesn't do something for me."

"Hey, spoilers. I haven't gotten to a part about an altar." In a lower voice, he asks, "So, what does it do for you?" He gives me a wicked grin.

I narrow my eyes. "Wouldn't you like to know?" But heat

coils low in my belly seeing the expression on his face. *Damn. Fuck. Shit.* I'm in trouble. In a tone I have no clue how I'm able to keep even, I say, "Dad said breakfast would be ready in about an hour. And that was when I went down for the coffee. I forgot. We should probably get ready."

"Oh. Sure. I'm just gonna finish this chapter." He winks at me. "I'll be in shortly. It'll only take me a few minutes to change and brush my teeth and stuff."

I nod. "Okay." I walk back into the house and into the bedroom.

CHAPTER THIRTEEN

JONAS

Seeing Callahan's face when I told her what I was reading was priceless. And although I like to think of myself as pretty adventurous, that book was the epitome of smut and I was impressed by Callie's taste. When I finish the chapter I'm reading, because now I truly am invested in finding out what happens with Father Bell, I get up and go back into the house.

I'm about to knock on the door, but Dominic comes strolling through and I give him a nod and turn the knob and enter, hoping Callahan is changing in the bathroom. Or maybe not; I don't know.

And of course, she's not in the bathroom, and she's clutching a dress to her front, but she's otherwise unclothed. She hisses, barely above a whisper, "What, they don't teach you to knock in Florida?"

I turn and face the wall. "Sorry, Dominic was walking through as I was getting ready to come in, and I thought it might be weird if I knocked. You know, since I'm supposed to have already seen you naked and all."

"Okay, that was smart. Sorry. Since you're here, can you zip my dress? This zipper is being difficult."

"Sure. Can I look?"

"Yeah, I'm decent." I slowly turn around and see she is, in fact, dressed.

I walk around to her back and pull the zipper up. "There you go."

"Thanks."

"By the way," I say, with total nonchalance, "nice polka dot undies."

She spins around. "I was covered. How did you—?"

I smirk. "The reflection in the bathroom mirror. Cheekies. Nice."

She blushes and I can't help but laugh. "You know, I would think with all the smut you read, you wouldn't even be able to blush anymore."

"It's a wonder, huh?" is all she says.

I walk over to the closet. "What's the dress code for today?"

"Something like what you had on yesterday would be fine. Or whatever, really. I'm only wearing a dress because it's cooler." She walks into the bathroom and closes the door.

I pull out a pair of navy chino shorts and a red polo shirt and I quickly change and fold up my sweats and tee shirt and put them back in the drawer. I make the bed and slip on my sandals.

Callahan comes back in the bedroom a moment later and she's re-braided her hair and put on a bit of mascara. "You look great, Callie."

She looks down and smoothes her dress. "Thank you, Jonas. So do you." She notices the made bed. "You didn't have to make the bed, but thank you."

I nod. "I need to brush my teeth and try to do something with my hair and I'll be ready."

"Your hair looks good. It's messy, but it looks intentional."

I run my fingers through it reflexively. "Thanks. I'll only be a minute." I step into the bathroom and brush my teeth and put on deodorant. I put a little water in my hair and then squeeze a bit of gel into my palm a run it through my hair and try to tame the frizz.

Callahan leans against the door frame and watches me. "Do I need to shave? Has my stubble gotten to unkempt instead of scruffy?"

She walks over and and examines my face. She takes her hand and runs it along my jaw. "No, you're good. It's sexy."

I'm caught off guard by her touch and her words, since it's only us here, with no one to perform for. But, not that I mind, honestly. "Thanks. Well, I guess I'm ready then."

"Alright, let's go." We walk out of the bedroom and down the stairs and everyone is starting to file into the dining room and we join them at the table.

The spread is huge. Pancakes, bacon, sausage, eggs, toast, fruit, muffins, and pastries. I drape my arm on the back of Callahan's chair and lean over to her and whisper in her ear, making sure to make it look like I'm being sweet. I run my fingertip down her arm and she leans into me. "Good God, are all your breakfasts this elaborate? There's enough food here to feed twenty people."

I feel her chuckle against me and she turns toward me and says in a low voice, "I told you, my parents don't half-ass anything. That especially means breakfast." She brushes a kiss across my cheek and makes a show of wiping off a smudge of lipstick and she smiles at me. "Do you want more coffee, I left our mugs up on the porch; I can go get them."

I pat her hand. "I'll get them. Would you mind pouring me some juice?"

"Of course."

Breakfast passes pretty uneventfully and everyone appears to be relaxed and we all eat an ungodly amount of food. Alex announces the barbecue will be arriving by three, but everyone should be ready to play cornhole by four and then we'll be eating at six.

Maddie volunteers Dominic and herself to wash up breakfast dishes since Callahan and I did them last night and I don't miss the slight sneer on his face when we all get up. I'm secretly thrilled with this and I ask Callahan if she want to take a walk through the woods before it gets too hot. "Sure, let me run up and put on my shoes and we can go." I lean against the counter to wait for her.

Dominic watches her go. "So, Dominic," I say and his head snaps my direction. His expression says he knows he's been caught leering. "What is it you do for work? I don't think I caught that."

"Investment banker. I figured Cal would've told you."

I shake my head and keep my tone nonchalant. "No. We haven't had a lot of time to talk." I smirk when I see a muscle in his jaw tic. This prick is something else. Ogling his fiancé's cousin in front of her and thinking Callahan would tell her boyfriend anything about him. Wow, what a narcissist. "So, do you like that line of work? I imagine it must be pretty stressful."

Maddie pipes up. "Oh, boy, is it. Dominic's good at his job, though. I just wish he didn't work so many late nights; I miss him."

He turns to her. "I told you, babe, it'll die down after the wedding." *Late nights.* Code for sleeping around?

Callahan comes down the stairs and walks over to me. "You ready?"

I take her hand in mine. "Yep. Let's go, Darlin'." She smiles and we walk out the back door and through the yard toward the woods. "Now, is there an actual trail, or will we need a machete?"

She laughs. "No, there's a trail. Uncle Lance likes to take walks. I think it makes him feel like he's one of those old poets, Frost or Whitman or Tennyson, probably. Especially during the fall. He relishes the chill and the changing leaves and gets this adorable look on his face. But he keeps the trail up, so we'll be good."

She leads us down a distinct cut through some trees and in spite of the humidity, it's nice in the shade. "This is great." I give her a sheepish smile. "I feel like I keep saying that. I probably sound stupid, like I've never been anywhere."

She shakes her head. "You don't sound stupid. It's nice to see things through other people's eyes. I'm enjoying watching you take everything in. It's cute." She looks over her shoulder. "We're far enough away from the house we don't have to hold hands anymore. I don't think anyone can see us."

I find I actually like holding her hand so I grip it tighter. "You never know. Better safe than sorry."

She rolls her eyes and smiles. "Fine."

"So, does Dominic ever smile? For a guy who's getting married, he seems awfully annoyed a lot of the time."

She's thoughtful for a beat. "He's pretty serious, but now that you mention it, he does seem like he's even more so than usual. I don't know."

"He watches you, you know."

She looks at me, her expression confused. "What?"

"When you leave a room, or when he thinks no one sees, he watches you."

She clenches her jaw. "Bastard. I hate him so much."

I nudge her. "Eh, maybe he's jealous and feeling territorial.

Especially since he was your first or whatever and he thinks someone else has you now."

She smiles. "Well, yeah, why shouldn't he be jealous; you're gorgeous. You've got all this amazing hair and you're tall and have those adorable freckles. Not to mention the fact that you're a kick-ass kindergarten teacher. Which, in my book, makes you a total dream boat. You're charming and polite and sweet."

"Well, you sure know how to make a guy feel good."

"All I'm saying is, I'm shocked all the women you see don't fall madly in love with you, with all that going on. You're a catch, Jonas."

"So are you, Callie."

She flushes with the compliment and I expect her to protest or make some self-deprecating comment about herself, but instead, she says, "I am, aren't I?"

"Yes, you are."

CHAPTER FOURTEEN

CALLAHAN

Sometime around two, Jonas mentions wanting to go swim, so he goes up to our room to change and I pull out a couple of beach towels and some sunscreen from the first-floor linen closet. When he comes back downstairs, he's got his swim trunks and a tee shirt on. When I start toward the door, he asks, "You're not gonna change?"

I shake my head. "Nah, I'm not getting in. I told you, I don't like the lake bottom."

"Yeah, but you said you'd put your suit on and sit on the dock. How are you gonna cheer me on while I try to break my neck on the rope swing if you're not right there? Come on, go change. Please?" His tone is pleading and he sounds exactly like the big kid he claims to be.

I roll my eyes and can't keep a grin off my face. "Fine. I'll be right back. There are beers in the fridge; want to take a couple down with us?"

"Okay."

I run upstairs and pull out my ancient bathing suit. It's a black one-piece that's not sexy in the least. Oh, well. But I guess since I'm not trying, it doesn't matter, right? I slip some jogging shorts on over my suit and wrap my hair up into a bun before walking back down the stairs. Jonas stands leaning against the counter with our beers in one hand, the sunscreen in the other and our towels slung over his shoulders. I can't help but smile when I see him. "You look like some kind of summer pack mule. Want some help?"

He shakes his head. "Nah, I'm good."

We make our way down to the dock and I pick up a lawn chair from the patio and carry it down with me. I unfold the chair and Jonas sets the towels and beers down on it and I shed my shorts and take the sunscreen from him and put some on my face and chest, arms and legs. I hand it back to him and he looks at me. "Want me to do your back?"

"Sure, thanks." He rubs some lotion between his palms and applies it to my back, paying special attention to my neck and shoulders. I try not to think about how there's an exceptionally hot guy putting his hands on my body at the moment; even as my skin prickles at his touch and my pulse starts to increase the slightest bit.

Jonas pulls his shirt off and I am in no way prepared for the sight of him and my breath catches. Good lord, he has to be that sexy without a shirt, too? *Fuck me. Shit. No, don't do that. Dammit.* His chest and abs are chiseled and his trunks sit low on his hips and he has that sexy "V" I suddenly can't look away from as he applies sunblock to his face, arms, and chest.

"Darlin', you can't look at me like that. You're already supposed to know what I look like without a shirt, remember?" Damn my stupid blush. Jonas laughs and holds the sunscreen out to me. "Will you do my back?"

"Okay." I take the tube and put a bit in my palms and try to be as nonchalant as possible as I apply the lotion; as if this is something I do every day. Like putting my hands on a man's—

specifically, this man's—body is something I do all the time. His skin is soft and warm and he has freckles dusting his shoulders. His back is muscled and strong. Dammit, why does he have to be this hot? The face and the hair aren't enough? He has to have this body, too? I'm in hell. A hell of my own choosing. I'm gonna combust right here and die of lust. "All done."

He turns to me. "Thanks." He examines my face and gives me a smug smile. He brings his hand up and runs his thumb along my jaw and I stop breathing for a beat. "You had a little lotion there; I got it."

"Thank you." My voice comes out a bit breathy and I'm hoping he doesn't notice. He gives me a goofy grin that tells me he did, in fact, hear the difference in my voice. He jerks his chin in the direction of the rope swing but keeps his eyes on mine. "You think I can do a flip off the swing?"

"I think you're liable to break your neck if you do. It's pretty shallow here." I move the items out of my chair and sit and shade my eyes with my hand.

"I guess we'll have to see." He walks toward where the swing is hooked to the ladder of the slide and takes several steps back as he holds the end of the swing. He takes a running leap and swings out far before releasing the rope and executing a graceful flip into the water. I roll my eyes and shake my head.

"Please tell me he's terrible in bed." I snap my head in the direction of Maddie's voice and see her standing beside me.

"What?"

She sits down on the dock and looks up at me. "Please tell me he has some sort of massive flaw. He can't look that good and be great in bed; it wouldn't be fair."

I give her a little laugh and bite my lip hoping the look I give her comes off as coy.

She raises a brow. "Damn. Well, good job, Hanny. Must be nice."

Her last sentence sounds a little bitter. "Hey, you okay?"

She sighs. "Oh, yeah. I made the stupid decision Dom and I weren't gonna have sex before the wedding and I'm more than a little on edge."

"Since when? I mean, y'all have slept together, right?"

"Of course we have, but I wanted the wedding night to be special, so I said for the month leading up to the wedding, we'd abstain."

"Oh, I see. And it's not going well, I take it?"

"It's just hard, because we're still sleeping in the same bed, but there's no funny business."

I know the feeling. "Well, you can always change your mind. The wedding's only four days away."

"I know, but we've made it this far; I want to hold out."

"Well, good for you. How's he taking it?"

"He's being a big baby about it. I mean, we fool around, but that's it. So he's moody."

"Gotcha." I pick my beer up and twist the top off and take a sip and direct my attention back to Jonas, who's now swimming laps. *I guess he does actually work for that body.*

"So," Maddie says, "you think we'll be planning your wedding next? You and Jonas are so cute together. He's so attentive and kind and that story about how y'all met? Too adorable."

"Oh, I don't know. We've only been seeing each other for a few months. It's early days yet."

"Well, I have a good feeling about you two. Wait and see. I'd love it if we were both happy and married. And then we can raise our babies together, like we were. It would be amazing."

I simply nod and look back out into the water. Jonas climbs up the ladder to the dock and runs his fingers through his hair and smiles at me. Water glistens on his chest and abs and breathing has become nigh unto impossible. And it's in that moment, I get it. How he pulls so many women and why they'd be willing to be with him in any way possible, without commitment. Because he looks at them the way he's currently looking at me. He said how he picked up women was more show than tell and I have a feeling that's exactly what he's doing. *Fuck, he's good.*

He walks over to me and takes my beer and lifts it to his lips and takes a long pull. His eyes don't leave mine and I have to remember to breathe. He winks at me before looking down at Maddie. "Hey, Maddie, how's it going?"

"Pretty good." She stands. "Well, y'all have fun. Mom just texted to say the barbecue arrived and I want to make sure they don't need any help. And Dom's parents are finally here, so I need to go say hi to them. You're playing cornhole, right?"

His eyes return to mine and I can't breathe again. "Sure, Callie and I will play."

Maddie looks at me. "Callahan doesn't play cornhole; she hates it."

I watch as his eyes slowly drop to my mouth and back up. "She might if I ask real nice. But either way, I'll play."

Sweet lord, what have I gotten myself into?

"Cool. See y'all later." She turns to walk away.

He leans down to brace his arms on my chair and looks at me. Water drips off his chest onto my thighs and I fight off a shiver. "You don't like cornhole?"

I struggle to keep my tone neutral. "I suck at it. So, I don't even try anymore. I'm way too uncoordinated. I usually end up tripping and making a fool of myself."

"Would it help if I also made a fool of myself? We can be fools together," he suggests with a grin.

"Probably not. Also, Dad and Uncle Lance are super competitive. Neither one of them played sports much, so cornhole and golf are it. They throw down with it, and I prefer not to get caught in the middle of their pissing contest."

He nods, contemplative. "Hey, you didn't cheer when I went on the swing. I was expecting some critique on my form, at least." His tone is playful.

"Oh, I did; it was all up here." I tap my temple.

He raises one brow and gives me an amused smile. "And what kind of things were you cheering?"

I bite my lip and smirk. "Nothing I can repeat."

He barks out a surprised laugh. "Well, well. Do tell."

I shake my head. "Nope. Can't do it." I glance down and finally see his tattoo just under his right pec.

I instinctively reach to touch it and and then think better of it, but he grabs my hand and places it on his ribs. He leans in to whisper in my ear, his breath hot on my skin. "Darlin', if you're gonna touch me, you can't be tentative about it. Might make someone wonder. You're supposed to know what I feel like under your hands. You're supposed to know what I taste like and what it feels like when we fuck. So, if you're gonna touch, do it. I don't mind."

My breath catches and his words send heat straight to my core and my heart rate ratchets up about fifty beats per minute. He brushes a kiss across my cheek as he pulls back and simply brings the beer back up to his lips and takes a sip and winks at me. He turns the bottle up and drains the rest of the beer. "I probably need to take a shower before cornhole and supper."

I nod, still trying to recover from what he said and the visuals it conjured in my mind. "I'm gonna change back into my dress since I didn't get in the lake. But I'll walk up with you if you're ready to go now."

"Sure." I hand him a towel and he dries off and I try to look anywhere but at him. As we walk and take everything back up to the house, I point out Dom's parents, Lillian and Quincy, and then we and go into the bedroom. While Jonas showers, I change and unwind my hair from its bun and re-braid it. I sit on the sofa with my legs curled up under me and open my book.

The bathroom door opens and Jonas exits in only a towel and my mouth drops open before I can school my features. "Sorry, I forgot my underwear." He walks over to the dresser and pulls open the drawer and fishes a pair out before walking back toward the bathroom. And as he's closing the door, the towel falls and I get a split-second view of his perfect ass.

CHAPTER FIFTEEN

JONAS

Hell yeah, I intentionally dropped the towel as I shut the door. Flirting with Callahan and getting a rise out of her and seeing her blush might be my new favorite thing to do. I probably shouldn't say the things I do to her or look at her the way I do, but honestly, I can't help myself.

She's damn adorable and sexy in the most unassuming way. Even in the super simple bathing suit she had on, I couldn't take my eyes off her. Her tattoo peeked out of the trim of her suit on her hip and I find myself wanting to know what the rest of it looks like.

Nope. Don't go there, Jonas. You've got four days. You can resist the temptation for four days. When you go home, you can call Teagan or whoever and take care of things. Callahan's a nice girl. She doesn't need you to do the same thing to her Dominic did. She deserves better than that. She deserves someone who can love her. Someone who will choose her.

After I come out of the bathroom fully clothed, Callahan narrows her eyes. "Glad to see you didn't forget your clothes, too." She raises a brow and returns her attention to her book.

Simply because I can't resist, I say, my tone playful, "Oh, you didn't like what you saw? Your face sure looked like you did."

She clenches her jaw. "I don't know what you're talking about; I've been reading this whole time."

"Darlin', the mirror says different. I saw you sneak a peek. It's alright. I don't look like this only for myself."

I'm rewarded with a slight blush and she slams her book shut. "Wow, you must think pretty highly of yourself."

I give her a sly grin. "What's the point of not looking when you see something you like? That's why we have eyes. Nothing to be ashamed of. I like to look at you. I've not hidden the fact that I think you're beautiful. The same way you can't hide the fact you think I'm attractive."

She sighs, her tone verging on annoyed. "Yeah, well, it's truly unfair you should look as good as you do. The hair and the face and then all *that*." She gestures to my torso. "I was caught off guard. Give a girl a little warning next time."

I'm surprised by her comment, and I can't help but laugh. "Nah, I get too much enjoyment by driving you to distraction. It's too much fun for me."

She rolls her eyes. "Well, your fun's about to be doubled. Cornhole's getting ready to start. So, yay for you."

"You really won't play? We can be on the same team."

She shakes her head. "Nope. This is all you, buddy. I'll sit on the sidelines and cheer you on."

"Oh, good. Will this cheering be only in your head, like earlier, or will you actually give me sweet words of encouragement?"

She smiles. "Probably a little bit of both."

We walk downstairs and Lance and Alex are standing in the kitchen, having some sort of discussion. Lance looks at us.

"Jonas, Maddie said you're gonna play cornhole. You any good?"

I glance at Callahan and she gives me a *told ya* expression. I nod. "Yeah, I've been known to toss a bag or two. Florida frats are pretty notorious for it. It's right up there with beer pong."

"Good, then you can be on my team. Alex and I have a little wager going and he thinks Dominic can help him win. I thought I was gonna have to get Maddie to play, but maybe you'll be a better choice since I think she'd rather talk with Lillian and Meredith about wedding stuff."

"Sure, I'm in. What's the wager?" *Anything I can do to knock Dominic down a peg.*

"Oh, you know, only a case of Macallan 18."

I whistle in appreciation. "That's quite the prize."

"Are you a scotch man, Jonas? I'd be happy to give you a bottle if we win."

"Oh, no. Don't touch hard liquor, actually."

"Well then, more for me." He gives me a friendly grin and I can understand why Callahan likes her uncle so much. He seems to be a lot more laidback than the rest of her family.

"Yes, sir. But I'm happy to help you win it."

Alex asks, "Which fraternity were you in?"

"Sigma Chi, University of Florida chapter."

He looks surprised. "No shit. Me, too. University of Tennessee chapter. We'll have to share hazing war stories sometime."

I grin. "Sounds good."

"Callahan, I'm willing to overlook the fact you brought a Gator fan into this house only because he's a brother." He winks at her and smiles.

She looks up at me and mock-whispers. "Probably should have mentioned, University of Florida is a dirty word in this family. We're diehard Vols fans."

"Guess it's a good thing I'm so charming. You can forgive that I'm a rival, right?"

She feigns exasperation. "I suppose. But not if you lose Uncle Lance his case of scotch. I might have to reconsider."

"Deal."

Alex scoffs in mock-offense. "Whose side are you on, daughter of mine?"

"Sorry, Dad, looks like I'm sleeping with the enemy, so I think it's more beneficial for me to root for him."

Her father and I both bark out a surprised laugh at her comment and I'm sincerely impressed by her balls. As we walk out to where they've got the cornhole boards setup, I lean over to her. "Jesus, Darlin', might as well have hung a sock on the doorknob with what you said. Good job."

She looks up at me, her voice low. "I told you, I'm not a prude. You're not the only one who can sell this thing."

I hold her gaze. "Is that a challenge?"

"Nope. Only the truth. Now, kick Dom's ass, pretty please?"

"What will you give me for it?"

She grins. "What, my dazzling personality not enough for you?"

"Oh, yeah, but I already get that for free. Are you offering anything as a bonus?"

She thinks for a minute and then gives me a wicked smile. "I'll show you my tattoos. Both of them." I'm caught off guard and my brain glitches for a beat. *Both? She said she only had one. Where's the other one?* I can't come up with a response quickly enough to keep her from laughing. "I wonder, is that what my face looks like when you say stuff to me and I'm thrown for a second? Because if it is, I get the appeal."

Lance hollers, "Are we playing, or are we making goo-goo eyes? Let's go, Jonas. I've got scotch to win."

CHAPTER SIXTEEN

CALLAHAN

For the first time since I met him, I'm shocked to find Jonas speechless and I probably got more enjoyment out of it than I should have. But seeing him think about where my other tattoo might be located made me smile. Because I know he saw at least a bit of the one on my hip. But the other? Well, I'd *really* have to want him to see it. And, honestly, I wouldn't mind.

I shouldn't tease him. I shouldn't play like this. But he's been flirting with me relentlessly since yesterday and I'm so wound up, I can hardly think straight when he's around. So, I wanted to maybe get him back a little. And it wouldn't be the worst thing in the world if he wanted me a little bit, right? It would be nice to feel wanted.

Although, in reality, I don't know what that's like, outside of the context of the way Dominic wanted me. And with the way Jonas treats me and talks to me, I'm beginning to think that's what things are supposed to be like. Even if this thing is fake, it's still feels nice.

Maybe I feel comfortable doing it because I know nothing is gonna come of it. I definitely don't plan on sleeping with him.

And he wouldn't want me anyway; I'm only me and I'm inexperienced. But maybe, by the time I get home, I'll have enough confidence I can get out and date. Because Jonas is right; I should get out more. Not with him, of course; but with someone.

I sit in a deck chair as Jonas, Dad, Uncle Lance, and Dominic play a spirited game of cornhole. There's a lot of trash talk coming from both sides, but I'm pleased to see that while Jonas stays cool and collected, Dominic gets frustrated and the game is not going well for him. And for some reason, this fact brings me such joy.

They play a series of three games and after the first two, it's tied. But during the third game, Jonas sinks the last bag for the win and turns to me, his smile triumphant. Dominic looks like he's ready to commit murder and Dad and Uncle Lance haggle on how many bottles of scotch constitute a case.

Jonas comes over to me and leans down and plants his hands on the sides of my seat. I don't miss how close his hands are to my hips, or the fact his legs are touching mine. He says in a low voice, "Looks like you get to pay up. I expect to see that ink."

I don't acknowledge his statement and I make sure to keep my tone level, even as my skin prickles with his words and the proximity of his hands to my body. "Good game. I think Dominic's face when the last bag went in was my favorite part. You were great."

"I think it deserves a little kiss, don't you? I mean, I won a case of pricey scotch for your favorite uncle and stuck it to your douchebag ex." He gives me a lopsided grin. I roll my eyes and pull his face down to plant a kiss on his cheek. When I pull back, he doesn't move and his eyes drill into mine. "Oh, come on, Darlin'; I thought you wanted to sell this thing."

My heart races as he lifts my chin and brushes a soft kiss

across my lips. It's only for a second, but more than enough to make my cheeks blaze and my breath hitch. When he straightens back up, his eyes travel from mine to my cheeks and ears and back down to my mouth. His lips curl into a mischievous grin. "Breathe, Darlin'," he says softly and winks at me.

I'm still not completely recovered from the extremely innocent kiss by supper time. Jonas must be able to sense I'm off, because after we fix our plates and sit down, he leans over to me. "Hey, did I screw up? Did I cross a boundary? We probably should have talked about kissing on the mouth. I'm sorry, Callahan. I won't do it again." His tone is sincere and his eyes are apologetic.

I turn to him and give him a soft smile. "No, I was caught off guard, is all; I shouldn't have been. I was the one who made the point about selling this. You didn't do anything wrong. And if I'm honest, all the flirting the last couple of days has me a bit on edge. But no, I'm fine. I promise."

He nods, his face relaxing in obvious relief. "You're sure?" he confirms. "You don't seem fine."

I roll my eyes. "Yes, I fine. I mean, it's not every day an extremely handsome man kisses me, but I'm not that delicate."

He smirks. "I see. Well, that's a shame. Beautiful women should be kissed on a daily basis."

I elbow him playfully. "Glad to see you're fine, too."

He gives me a wide, genuine smile. "There she is. I'd prefer to see you giving me shit than being quiet. I don't know what to do with you when you're not being sassy and rolling your eyes. But, I will say, it's nice to know I have an effect on you."

I narrow my eyes. "You like to think you do anyway."

He laughs. "Now, if that's not a challenge, I don't know

what is. Looks like I'm gonna have to bring my A-game for the rest of the week."

"So, what? What you've been doing till now hasn't been your A-game?"

He shakes his head. "I don't think you could handle it," he responds and takes a drink from his bottle of beer.

I hold his gaze. "I think you'd be surprised what I could handle."

Something flashes in his eyes and he swallows. "Don't tempt me, Darlin'." There's an edge to his tone I've not heard before and it makes my pulse jump.

"Why not?" I ask, keeping my tone neutral.

"Because you have rules," he reminds me.

And just like that, it feels as though a bucket of cold water has been dumped on me. Because he's right. *You* have rules. *I* have rules. Not him. I set the parameters for this thing and he's trying to respect them and I'm playing with fire by baiting him.

If what he's been doing up till now is not him at "full strength" or whatever, I wouldn't survive what that would look like. I'd fold like like a cheap suit and let him do wicked, wicked things to me. I nod. "Right; rules. Sorry." I turn to my plate and pick up my fork and dig in.

CHAPTER SEVENTEEN

JONAS

Although I shouldn't want her to, part of me was hoping Callahan would rise to the bait. Another more rational part of me is more than a bit thankful she didn't because I cannot sleep with her. I can't kiss her again either. Nope. I can't break her rules, in spite how badly I want to do exactly that.

I was truthful with her, I don't like to see her quiet and brooding or stewing. It's unnerving because if she's not giving my own shit back to me, I'm at a loss. I want her rolling her eyes and being snarky and playful.

After I'd kissed her she was quiet for a long time, I thought I'd fucked up and it would screw up what we've got going on.

Part of me thinks the reason I'm able to pretend with her and play the part of this doting, sweet guy is because I haven't slept with her. There's a definite attraction for both of us, I know that; but if we got past the flirting and acted on things, I would probably feel like I do after all other women. I got to the end zone, I scored, I've met my goal, I'm done. I'd lose all interest and not be able to keep up this charade for the rest of the time we're here.

Another, possibly more scary notion, would be that if we acted on things, I wouldn't feel that way. And then what would that mean? That I could actually want to have a relationship? That's not me; I don't do that kind of shit. She'd only end up getting hurt. I'm not gonna do that to her. She's been hurt enough. And so have I, for that matter.

After supper, which Callahan and I eat in relative silence following our game of verbal chicken, Maddie comes over to let us know everyone will be gathering around the fire pit in a little bit to hang out and make s'mores. "Jonas, I hate to ask you to work as a guest, but would you care to help Dom move some wood from the shed to over by the pit? Dad and Uncle Alex and Quincy shouldn't be lifting. I mean, if it's not too much trouble. Dom said he could do it all himself, but I don't want him to put his back out before the wedding."

"Of course; I'd be happy to help. Point me in the right direction and I'm on it."

She gives me a relieved smile. "Thank you so much."

Callahan looks at me. "I can show you where the woodshed is." As we make our way over, she says, "We don't have to go down to the pit tonight."

"Why? You don't want to?"

"No, it's not that. I just figured you'd be done for the day. You've gone above and beyond the call of duty for today. You endured family breakfast and a cutesy walk through the woods and cornhole and now supper and hauling wood. I wanted to give you the out in case you needed it."

"I'm good. I knew there'd be lots of stuff to do this week; I'm up for it."

"Okay, but any time you need space or time to chill, that's fine."

I put my hand on her arm to stop her and turn to face her. "What's up? You've been quiet since supper and now you're acting weird."

She looks down and her voice is low, so as to not be overheard. "I know you don't do relationships, so if all this is too much; if it's too hard for you to pretend or whatever, we can chill things."

I lift her chin. "Hey, I'm having a good time. I have fun with you." I look into her eyes. "Is this getting to be too hard for you? The flirting?"

She swallows and blows out a breath. "Not gonna lie, you're shameless and I have a hard time reminding myself it's all for show. And maybe it's because we've had to be on display all day; I'm on edge. When we're alone, it's easier because we don't have to put on or whatever and we just hang out."

"Do you want me to cool it? Dial it back? I don't want to push you. And I don't want to hurt you, Callie. Because you're a nice girl and the last thing I'd want to do is hurt you."

Something flashes in her eyes but it's gone before I can identify the emotion. "I'm a nice girl. Yeah, that's me." She gestures in the direction of a metal shed about fifty feet away. "The woodshed's right over there. I'm gonna go help clean up supper. I'll see you in a bit, okay?"

She doesn't wait for a response and simply turns to walk away and I feel like I've said something wrong, but I don't know what. I watch her walk for a moment before going over to the shed to pull a few pieces of wood into my arms and carry them over to where the fire pit's located. Thankfully, Dominic and I are traveling in opposite directions while we ferry the logs over and I don't have to talk to him.

When there's enough wood by the pit for at least three days worth of fires, I go look for Callahan but I don't find her anywhere outside. I walk into the house and Maddie's standing in the kitchen pouring herself a glass of wine. "Have you seen Callie?" I ask.

"I think she's upstairs. I saw her head that way a little bit ago after we got all the supper stuff cleaned up."

"Okay. Thanks." I head up the stairs and check in the bedroom, thinking she might be reading, but I don't find her there either. I check the porch and find her chair empty. And because I can't think of anywhere else she might be, I walk down to the media room and open the door.

She's sitting in a far chair nursing a glass of wine and the lights are on full blast. I close the door behind me and walk the fifteen feet to where she's sitting and I take the chair next to hers and look up at the screen. "What are you watching?"

"*The Proposal.*"

"Is that the one with Ryan Reynolds and Sandra Bullock?"

"Yeah."

"Can I watch with you?"

She replies, her tone flat, "Sure."

We sit for a while and tension radiates off Callahan and I don't like it. She drains her wine glass before picking up a bottle I didn't know was sitting on the floor and refilling it. "You okay?" I ask.

"Yeah, I'm fine. Why?"

"No reason, but when people sneak away to drink a bottle of wine by themselves, there's usually a reason."

"Nope. Just thirsty."

I nod. "Okay. Is that the reason you haven't looked at me since I walked into the room? Because you're *thirsty*? I get the sense I've said or done something to piss you off and I have no clue what that is."

She takes a long drink of her wine. "You called me nice, Jonas."

I can't bite back a surprised chuckle. "Yeah, you are nice."

She turns to me and her eyes are stony and more than a little hurt. I'm taken aback by the look on her face and feel as though I've caused her pain and I don't like the way something twists in my chest to see it.

"Yeah, but that's all I am. That's all I ever am. A nice girl. 'Oh, Callahan? She's a nice girl, but that Maddie, wow, she's something else with her bubbly personality.' 'Oh, Callahan? She's pretty enough, but have you seen Maddie? She's beautiful.' 'Oh, Callahan? She's a librarian, but did you know Maddie is the youngest vice president in her firm's history?'"

I don't miss the seething bitterness in her tone and I want to shake her because she's still comparing herself to her damn cousin and I can't figure out why. "You say all this like I give a shit what Maddie's like. And you say *nice* like it's an insult. That wasn't my intention and I think you know that. You've got to stop comparing yourself to Maddie. You aren't her. You'll never be her."

She lets out a derisive snort. "Oh, gee, you think?" She starts to tilt her glass up and I take it away from her. "Hey!" She reaches for it, but I down it and set the glass down. Callahan folds her arms and huffs. "I would have given you a drink, you know."

"I know. Callahan, look at me." When she finally does, I say, "You're not Maddie. So, what? But, guess what?" She looks at me expectantly and I continue, "She's not you, either."

"Okay, what's your point?"

I sigh. "You are so focused on what she is and what you think you're not, you can't even see what you are."

"What the hell does that even mean, Jonas?"

"So Maddie's got this bubbly personality. You know what

else she is? Boring. That's all she is. She is gonna do exactly what's expected of her. She's so excited about this big wedding and this amazing life she's gonna have, she can't see what an incredibly narcissistic, vapid asshole she's marrying.

"She's gonna wear the pearls and have the boring kids who will probably play three different sports and two different instruments and need massive amounts of therapy when they grow up. She'll be the head of the Junior League and in ten years—if that—Dominic will be having an affair with his secretary or moved on to wife number two.

"And so, yeah, Maddie's cute. But don't, for one second, think you are not fucking gorgeous. Your eyes change color depending on your mood. When you're upset, like you are right now, they're more gray. When you're giving me shit or you're playful, they have these little flecks of gold around the pupil. And when I flirt with you and I can tell you're turned on, they're dark, like the sky, right after the sun goes down, before full dark sets in. Your hair turns more golden in the sunlight and you have this dimple that pops when you truly laugh. And when you read a book and it's a part you're fully engrossed in, you play with your bottom lip and it's the most adorable and sexy thing I think I've ever seen."

Callahan's cheeks flush pink and her breath catches. I push on. "Can you honestly say you want the life Maddie's gonna have or currently has? You said so yourself, you want to blaze your own path. Could you do that if you had her life? I feel like part of you wishes this was your wedding, in spite of the fact you hate Dominic now. But the fact that she's getting the wedding that should be yours runs all over you."

She looks down and I know I've struck a nerve. "Thought so. But in the same way that you're not Maddie, she's not you, either. You're funny and deep and you're happy to live simply, regardless of what your parents think about it. You care so much about Maddie and her feelings when you could've blown up her life at any point. You could've told her the way you felt about Dominic and what he did to you and it would have crushed her, but you'd rather suffer with it yourself than see her get hurt. Would she do the same for you? I'm guessing not. The fact she knows you slept with him and was okay to date him and marry him tells me all I need to know."

Callahan's eyes are wide and her voice is breathy. "How do you do that?"

I shake my head, unsure of her meaning. "Do what?"

"Know me for two whole days and suddenly pick apart every negative aspect of my life? You make me realize what I haven't been able to see for twenty-five years. I don't want her life. I'd probably end up slitting my own wrists if I was forced to have it."

I nod. "But it still hurts that the guy who's gonna give her the life you don't want wants her, even if you don't want him now. That, and the fact he did what he did to you and doesn't have to pay for it."

She swallows and blows out a breath. "Yeah. Pretty much. And I know it's stupid and it's shallow and I should be thrilled this isn't gonna be my life. Because in my heart, I know I wouldn't have been happy with Dom; he's exactly like them. He wants a wife who's exactly like them. But, I was good enough to fuck, just not good enough to love."

CHAPTER EIGHTEEN

CALLAHAN

Jonas starts to say something and I hold my hand up. "It's okay. I know, eventually, there will be someone who thinks I'm enough. I know that. Deep down, I do. I'm in my feelings is all. I'm sorry I took my bad mood out on you. The 'nice' thing triggered me, I guess. It didn't have anything to do with you."

"You don't have to apologize to me. You're allowed to feel the way you feel. I mean, if I were in your shoes, God, I'd most likely stay drunk the whole week just so I didn't have to remember it."

I snort. "If you weren't here, I probably would be. And then that would be one more reason I'm the family screw-up or whatever. 'Oh, look at Callahan; she must have taken up drinking professionally since she moved to Florida. I've not seen her without a drink this whole week.'"

Jonas smiles. "Well, if for nothing other than to keep you out of the drunk tank, I'm glad I'm here. This is your favorite place, right?" I nod. "If this is your favorite place, it'd be a shame for you to be drunk and miss your favorite things."

"Yeah. I only wish the wedding wasn't here. It feels like this place is gonna be tainted for me now."

"It doesn't have to be," he argues. "This may be their wedding, but we can have a great time this week. Right now, we can go down to the fire pit and flirt shamelessly and make Dominic miserable. We can be goofy and we can laugh and show those boring snobs what we peons call a good time. And when we go home, you'll have memories of the fun time you had with a handsome guy who you just met but who made you realize what an amazing woman you are."

I can't help but smile. "You're a good guy, Jonas. I know you got roped into this, and I'm probably a lot more than you bargained for with all my baggage and drama, but I'm glad you're here."

He waves off my comment. "I told you, I like a challenge. Now, what do you want to do? Do you want to stay here and watch Sandra Bullock and Betty White sing 'Get Low'? Or do you want to stop hiding?"

I laugh. "I mean, that is my favorite part of the whole movie, except maybe when the dog gets snatched by the eagle; but no, I don't want to hide."

He nods and gives my knee a squeeze. "Okay, then. Let's go." He picks up my wine glass and I turn off the projector and grab the wine bottle.

When he sees it's empty, I roll my eyes. "It was half full when I brought it down here, I only had the one glass. You drank half of my other one."

"Okay, but I don't flirt with girls who are already drunk. I'm a gentleman." When I laugh he looks at me, his eyes serious. "I'm not joking; if you get drunk, I'm not gonna flirt with you. I don't take advantage of women."

I sober and nod. "Okay, Jonas. I'm not drunk. I won't be

drunk. Honestly, the last time I got drunk was after Dominic broke things off. I'm not a big drinker anyway."

He nods. "Good to know."

I touch his arm. "Also, I didn't answer your question earlier about the flirting."

He turns to me. "Yeah, and what did you decide?"

"I don't need you to dial it back. I like your flirting. It makes me feel good. I know you're not gonna let me get hurt. Even if we somehow ended up sleeping together, you'd end it. And honestly, I appreciate that about you. Knowing you're so upfront about that would make it easy to not let myself get invested. It would only be for fun."

Jonas is quiet for a minute as he absorbs my words. "Okay. Well, let's go flirt."

I chuckle. "Sounds perfect."

We walk up to the main level and I put the empty bottle in the recycle bin and Jonas sticks my glass in the dishwasher. My mother is coming in as we begin to go out. "Where did you two sneak off to? Maddie was looking for you. Everyone is down at the fire pit."

"We were down watching a movie. We're headed that way now."

My mom nods knowingly. "Oh, well, glad someone is using the media room." She winks at me and my mouth falls open in astonishment.

As we walk outside, I lean over to Jonas. "I think my mother just joked about sex. I must be hallucinating."

He laughs. "If you are, then so am I. Wow, maybe she's not as uptight as you thought."

"Maybe."

When we get closer to the fire pit, Jonas takes my hand in his and I'm thankful I didn't ruin things with my meltdown. And it's probably dangerous to flirt with him, but I like the way it makes me feel, so what the hell? Jonas says in a low voice, "Looks like you're gonna have to sit in my lap."

"There are plenty of chairs."

"Yeah, but how am I gonna properly flirt with you and whisper dirty nothings in your ear if you're so far away?"

I huff out a laugh. "You really are shameless, aren't you?"

"Pretty much. But you like it."

"Yeah, I know."

Dad, Uncle Lance, and Quincy are getting up as we approach the pit. They say something about being too old to hang out with all the young whippersnappers and head toward the house. Jonas sits and pulls me into his lap and wraps his arm around my waist and rests his hand on my knee. I lean against him and he brushes a kiss across my cheek.

Maddie says, "Jonas, I see you finally found Callahan."

"Yeah, she was right where she needed to be. Sometimes you've got to get away for a few minutes."

She smiles. "Yeah, I get that. I'll be glad when the wedding's over and we can go on our honeymoon; I am so ready."

I ask, "Where are y'all going?"

Jonas whispers in my ear, "What do you want to bet it's an island in the Caribbean? Probably Turks and Caicos."

Maddie says, "Turks and Caicos."

I try to bite back a snort. "Oh, wow, that'll be fun."

Jonas whispers, "Told ya. Boring and predictable."

Maddie asks, "So, what do y'all have planned for tomorrow?"

I skim my hand down Jonas's arm to intertwine our fingers as if it's something I've done a million times. He lifts our joined hands to his lips and brushes a kiss across the back of mine. Somehow when I answer Maddie's question, my voice sounds entirely normal, in spite of the way my skin tingles when his thumb rubs over mine. "Nothing right now. We'll probably stick around the house. What about y'all?"

"Well, I have to go for my final fitting tomorrow and hopefully, the dress is perfect and I get to bring it home with me, so Mom and I have to leave pretty early to drive to Nashville. But we'll be back tomorrow evening and then Dominic and I are going out for supper." Her tone turns excited. "Y'all should come out with us. We can double-date. It would be so fun."

Jonas whispers, his nose tracing the shell of my ear, "I'd rather walk on glass barefoot than sit through dinner with Dominic. Tell her we'll be too busy pretending to have copious amounts of torrid, filthy sex."

I feel myself blush. "We'll see. Maybe." I look over and notice the basket with the s'mores ingredients and I look at Jonas. "I'm gonna roast a marshmallow, you want one?"

"Nah, I'll lick what's left off of your fingers."

The thought of him licking any part of me sends heat to places that are not related in the least to my proximity to the fire pit. "Oh, really. You think there will be some leftover? I'm an immaculate eater."

He gives me a slow smile and his voice is low and sexier than it has any right to be. "I think you'll want to leave a little for me. I only want a taste. Don't you want me to have a taste?"

God, yes. Shit. I'm so dead.

I keep my tone level, even as my heart lurches. "Actually, I do." I stand and gather the items to roast and put a marshmallow on a stick. I hold it over the fire until it's golden on the outside and gooey on the inside and go back and sit with Jonas. I slide the toasted marshmallow off the stick and take a large bite, leaving a fair bit on my fingers. I stick my thumb in my mouth and scrape the leftovers off with the edge of my front teeth. I'm about to do the same with my fingers when Jonas takes them and puts them in his own mouth. His tongue swirls around the digits and he sucks the stickiness away.

I nearly gasp and heat pools low in my belly. My thighs instinctively squeeze together and Jonas gives me a smug smile. "You've got a little something right here." He gestures to my lip.

"Oh?" I ask, my voice barely above a whisper.

"Yeah. Want me to get it?" His unspoken questions are clear: *Want me to kiss you? Does that break the rules? Will you be okay?*

I hold his gaze. "Sure, since I can't see it." He takes my chin in his hand and presses his lips to mine. They're soft and warm and full and I have to remind myself not to do anything absurd like start making out with him. He draws my bottom lip between his and suckles it to remove the leftover marshmallow and I almost moan.

He releases it and nuzzles my neck and I press my thighs together and my breathing is a bit ragged. Jonas whispers in my ear, "You're gonna have to quit squirming, Darlin'; it's making it increasingly difficult for me to be a gentleman."

I chuckle. "Sorry, but it's not entirely my fault, you know." I brush a kiss down his neck and Jesus, he smells good. *How can he smell this good after we've been outside all afternoon and evening?* He squeezes my waist and although he doesn't know, it's the most ticklish spot on my entire body and I squirm. "That tickles."

"Noted." He squeezes above my knee. "What about here? Is that ticklish?"

I shake my head. "Nope."

"Good to know. Where else are you ticklish?" He asks, his tone playful.

"Wouldn't you like to know."

"Actually, I would." His voice is a bit husky and makes my skin nearly tingle.

"You might have to find out for yourself." *Good lord, Callahan, what are you doing?*

"Is that a challenge?" He runs the tip of his nose along my jaw.

Danger, woman. Just because your severely neglected vagina is cheering you on doesn't mean you don't need to be smart. Quit it. NOW! And yet, I can't make myself stop. "You said you like a challenge, right?"

"And you call me a shameless flirt."

"What can I say? Maybe you've rubbed off on me." I wiggle my eyebrows and Jonas squeezes my waist again and I squirm. "If you want me to quit squirming, you're gonna have to stop tickling."

His thumb brushes the inside of my knee and his eyes drill into mine. "Do you want me to stop?"

I bite my lip, my heart banging against my ribs. "Not really."

CHAPTER NINETEEN

JONAS

I'm going to hell.

After what Callahan said before we left the media room about *if* we slept together, it's honestly all I can think about. And with her sitting in my lap, I'm thinking of everything I possibly can to keep myself from getting hard, but she's not making it easy.

She feels good in my arms and on my lap and she tasted delicious and fucking hell, why does she smell so good after all day in the summer heat?

If this were a normal date, I'd be hightailing it to the bedroom and stripping her out of this dress and sliding those adorable polka dot panties down her hips. *Shit. Stop it, Jonas. This isn't a normal date. It's pretend. Pretend. Pretend. Don't mess this up for her.*

"Do you want me to stop?" I ask and look into her eyes.

Callahan bites her lip. "Not really."

Danger. Danger.

"What do you want, Darlin'?"

She presses her forehead to mine. "Will you kiss me, Jonas?" Her voice is low and tinged with vulnerability and it pains me to hear it. Like she thinks it's not something I'd be more than happy to do.

I lift her chin until her gaze finally meets mine and I brush my thumb across her bottom lip and give her a soft smile. "Gladly." Because I would.

I slide my hand along her jaw and around to thread my fingers through the hair at the base of her skull and press my lips to hers and she wraps her arms around my neck. The kiss is soft and tender and she seems to melt into me and I can't resist pulling her closer. Her lips part and her tongue tentatively swipes against the seam of my lips and I waste no time deepening the kiss and her fingers tangle in my hair and after a moment, we're both short of breath and she pulls back and gulps air. "Sorry," she says.

I smile. "For what?"

She shakes her head and I can't read the expression on her face. "I'm tired. I think I'm gonna go to bed. It was a long day today."

"Okay, I'll go in with you." She starts to say something, but simply nods and we rise and tell Maddie and Dominic goodnight before walking back toward the house.

When we get into the bedroom, Callahan retrieves her pajamas and walks into the bathroom and shuts the door. The shower starts and I change into my sweatpants and don't bother with the tee shirt.

I check my phone and see that it's after ten and I have a couple of texts from Teagan checking to see if I'm around and after shooting off a quick reply to let her know I'm out of town, I turn down the bed and begin reading the book from this morning. I finally get to the part about the altar and I feel myself blush and get more than a little turned on. Callahan comes back into the bedroom and asks, "What's with your face? Are you blushing?"

I hold up my phone. "I got to the part about the altar. I feel dirty now."

Callahan laughs. "Yeah, just wait. It gets worse, or I guess, better."

"Well, damn."

She climbs into her side of the bed and squeezes the moisture from her hair with a towel before braiding it into pigtails. I put my phone down and roll to face her and prop myself up on my elbow and pick up one of her braids with my free hand. "Cute."

She rolls her eyes. "I don't ever feel like drying my hair and most days, I wear it up, so I braid it or pile it up on top of my head."

"Well, it's still cute."

"Thanks." She looks at me and notices I'm not wearing a shirt. "What, so did you wear a shirt last night so you could see my reaction today when you took it off at the lake?"

I chuckle. "I'm flattered you'd think I'd have that much forethought. But no, I got a little warm last night, so I decided to see if I would be cooler tonight without one."

She nods and lies down, mirroring me. She glances down at my tattoo and brushes her finger across it. "What does your tattoo mean? *Audeamus?*"

Her touch catches me off guard and my breath hitches. Thankfully, she doesn't notice and I recover quickly. "It's Latin. It means 'let us dare'."

"Cool. Because you like a challenge?"

"Yep. What about yours? I know you have one on your hip, but do you actually have another one, or were you only yanking my chain?"

She shakes her head. "No, I have two."

"Can I see? Wasn't that our deal, because I kicked Dominic's ass in cornhole?"

"Okay." She pulls her shorts down on one side, revealing her hip and I see a stack of books with a coffee mug on top with steam drifting up. It's simple, only black ink with some shading.

"I like it. Very librarian-esque. What about your other one?"

She blushes and blows out a breath. "Okay." She tugs her shirt up and lifts her breast, while still staying covered. There's a script of some kind right under the crease of her breast. I let my eyes trail down her waist and would love nothing more than to trace my finger along her tattoo, especially because her skin looks so soft. *Stop it, Jonas. You cannot touch her. You don't get to know what that skin feels like. Knock it off.* I shake the thoughts away and concentrate on the tattoo.

"Is that Elvish? Like from *Lord of the Rings*?" She tugs her shirt back down and nods.

"Yeah." It's part of a quote from Samwise about darkness being a passing thing." She looks down and bites her lip. "I wanted it over my heart, but didn't want it visible, so I figured that was the best place. I hoped someday it would remind me I can be happy and won't always be shrouded in this massive weight of sadness and anger."

I nod. "Nice. And the placement is perfect." I smirk and she rolls her eyes and chuckles.

"Well, we've got tomorrow completely unscheduled. You think we'll survive each other's company without lots of stuff to do?"

"I think we'll be okay as long as we don't go to supper with Maddie and Dominic. I don't know if I can do that."

She shakes her head. "No chance of that. I'm with you about preferring to walk barefoot on a bed of glass. There's almost nothing I'd like to do less."

"I'm glad we're in agreement. I personally plan on finding out what happens to Father Bell, but other than that, I'm wide open."

Callahan laughs. "Sounds good. I'm assuming we'll be fending for ourselves for food all day, too. Since Maddie and Aunt Meredith will be gone all day and as far as I know, there aren't any big meals planned."

I feign indignation. "Okay, well, I'm sure it will be terrible. Having to cook in a gourmet kitchen with exceptional ingredients. It's too much, really."

She rolls her eyes and playfully swats my arm. "Alright, smart ass, do you cook?"

I let out a soft laugh. "Not much. Nana taught me some things, but I'm not great."

"Well, we won't starve, I assure you. There might be leftovers from earlier." She yawns and turns off her lamp and rolls away from me. I turn my lamp off as well and lie down.

A few minutes later, I feel myself starting to drift off. "Jonas?"

"Yeah?" Callahan's quiet for a minute. "What is it, Callie?"

Her tone is hesitant. "Um, will you hold me? Would that be too weird? You know what, never mind. Forget I said anything. Goodnight."

Her words and how she sounds pain me. It's as if she's so starved for touch and affection, she thinks she no longer deserves it. And although I probably shouldn't, because it could complicate things and blur the lines more than they already have been, I say, "Come here, Darlin', I'll hold you." I roll toward her and pull her back against my chest.

She relaxes into me almost instantly. "Thank you, Jonas."

"Yeah, because it's such a hardship having a beautiful woman in my arms. It's torture, for sure."

"Still, you're exceedingly kind. I appreciate everything you've done for me. I know it's a lot."

"Again, it's so difficult to get to spend time with and flirt with and kiss an interesting, witty, sexy woman. I'm gonna need hazard pay for my pain and suffering." I intertwine our fingers and pull her even closer. "Callie, whatever you need this week, I've got you, okay? Don't be afraid to tell me what you want or need. Consider me your personal boy toy for the week."

Her laugh radiates through her back and into my chest. "You could get yourself in trouble with an offer like that."

"It would be good trouble, probably, so it might be alright."

"I feel like I'm taking advantage of you. And I don't want you to feel that way. I shouldn't have kissed you like that earlier. I'm sorry." Her tone is wistful.

I squeeze her hand. "You didn't see me complaining. If I didn't want to, I wouldn't do it. And if you apologize for kissing me, it's gonna make me think you regret it. Do you?"

She's quiet for a beat but then says, "No, I don't regret it. It was a great kiss, but I don't want you to feel like I'm using you. That would be the worst thing and I'd never forgive myself. So, don't let me do that, okay? Don't let me push you or pressure you for the sake of what you think you agreed to for the week."

She's not wrong. It was a great kiss. "Callie, you're not using me. Even if we ended up sleeping together, it wouldn't be because you used me; it would be because we both wanted it. I know it's something we've agreed probably won't happen, but I'm not gonna say if things got physical, I'd be opposed. If it doesn't, I'm not gonna be disappointed either, though, so don't feel like I'm expecting it, because I'm not. Got it?"

"Yeah."

She goes quiet and within moments, her breathing levels

out and I know she's asleep. I should roll away from her, but I told her whatever she needs, and this is what she needs. So while I'm awake, I'm happy to hold her. Plus, she still smells really, really good.

CHAPTER TWENTY

CALLAHAN

Falling asleep in Jonas's arms was almost too much. I can count on one hand the number of times I've fallen asleep with a man. And two of them are since I've been here. The simple act of having someone hold me and pull me close, it's nearly overwhelming. Whispering in the dark before we fell asleep, I could see that's what a relationship—not with Jonas, of course—would be like. Or, at least what it should be like.

I felt so pathetic asking him to hold me. But, of course, he was kind and giving, the same as he's been since I met him. He didn't hesitate to pull me into his arms. And feeling him against me, his warm body pressed against mine, his strong arms wrapped around me, it was comforting in a way that makes me realize how lacking my life is for affection and, hell, simple touch.

It also makes me see how little Dominic actually gave me. The minuscule crumbs of attention he swept in my direction; only enough to keep me available to him. Barely enough to keep me interested until he could have Maddie. He truly is the worst sort of man. He used me. There's no other way to look at it. He got what he wanted, pretty much whenever he wanted it. And when I no longer served a purpose for him, he cast me aside without a second thought.

I *hate* him. And I'm not a vengeful person or someone who holds a grudge, but knowing now how little he must've cared for me, I would love nothing more than to see him suffer a tenth of the pain I've experienced because of him.

The past two days with Jonas have made me realize I want a relationship. I want fun and playfulness and shameless flirting. I want someone to look at me like they desire me. I want someone who whispers in my ear and makes me blush. I want someone who sees me and knows me. I know it can't be Jonas, but someone like him would be nice.

Maybe, when I get home, I'll put myself out there a little more. Hell, maybe Jonas can give me some pointers on navigating the Tallahassee dating scene. Because I know now, I don't want to be single. I want someone to love me. I want someone to build a life with.

As I wake up, Jonas's arm is still draped around me and I feel his hair against my back and he's also hard. I can't help but be impressed by the apparent size of the bulge pressing into my hip. *No, don't be impressed. Don't you dare think about being impressed. Fuck.*

I shake away the increasingly inappropriate thoughts starting to form in my mind and extricate myself from under his arm and tiptoe to the bathroom to pee and brush my teeth and wrap my bathrobe tight around me before quietly exiting the bedroom and leaving Jonas sleeping.

I go through the routine of fixing my coffee and I walk back upstairs and out to the porch. Once I sit down, I realize I've forgotten my book, but I don't want to risk waking Jonas, so I simply sit and sip my coffee for a few minutes and close my eyes and take a few deep breaths.

After about a half hour, I hear the sliding door open, but I don't turn around, assuming it's Jonas. I roll my neck and shoulders and sigh. Hands grip my neck and rub down my shoulders, massaging and kneading. "Well, that's unexpected. But nice. Are you trying to butter me up for something?" I ask with a smile.

"No."

I feel the color drain from my face and I jump up from my chair and turn around. It's not Jonas. "Dominic. What are you doing?" I take another step back, wanting to keep plenty of space between us, lest I get the urge to punch him in the nose.

He shrugs. "I wanted to talk to you."

I fold my arms. "I don't have anything to say to you."

He takes a step toward me. "Come on, Cal. Please?"

I sigh. "What? What do you want to say to me?"

"I wanted to see how you were. I miss talking to you. I miss seeing you. I miss you."

CHAPTER TWENTY-ONE

JONAS

When I wake up, Callahan is gone from bed, which I expected, but I didn't expect I would miss feeling her in my arms. I'm accustomed to women absconding sometime in the night after I fall asleep and it never bothers me. But part of me wishes Callahan would've still been asleep when I woke up. I'd like to know what she looks like when she sleeps. Does her face look relaxed? What does she look like without her glasses perched on her nose? Does she sleep with her lips pursed or slightly parted?

But then, I shake the thoughts from my head, because I can't be thinking like that. I swing my legs over the edge of the bed and stand and stretch and go to the bathroom. I pee and brush my teeth before donning a tee shirt and preparing to go down to fix some coffee and go sit on the porch with Callahan. I glance over at the nightstand on her side of the bed and notice she's left her book. I pick it up, planning to take it to her before going to make my coffee.

When I open the bedroom door, the sound of voices streams in from the porch. *Maybe Lance came up to have coffee with Callie?* But I stop short when I see who's on the porch with Callahan. I don't want to eavesdrop, but I know she doesn't want to be out there with him—I can tell from her body language alone—and I want to be able to step out if I need to, so I stay out of sight, but within earshot.

Dominic says, "I miss you."

Oh, you are a bastard. God, I hate this fucker.

Callahan snorts. "You miss me? What's that supposed to mean? You've said exactly zero words to me since the day I called you and we had it out about you and Maddie. You've not said so much as a hello to me since I got here."

"I know. I didn't want to talk to you in front of Maddie, I was afraid she might read something into it. But I still wanted to talk to you. I've wanted to talk to you since you got here. You look fantastic. Especially right now."

Callahan's tone is sharp. "You don't get to talk about how I look. Now, if you'll get off my porch, I don't want to associate this space with you. This is my space and Jonas will be out here soon, and I'd prefer he didn't find you here."

Dominic huffs a laugh. "What are you doing with that guy anyway?"

"What do you mean, *what am I doing?* I'm spending the week with my boyfriend; spending time with him. That's what couples do."

"Yeah, but he's not your type, Cal. What are you doing with a guy like that?"

"What's that supposed to mean, *he's not my type,* a *guy like that?*"

"I looked him up, Cal; he dates a lot. There are pictures of tons of women on his social media profile. And he seems to have a noticeably specific type. And you know what I didn't find? Any photos of the two of you."

Shit, I didn't even think about social media, but this guy looked me up?

"What's it matter to you, Dom? I don't even have a Facebook or Instagram or any of that. What do I care who Jonas dated before me? And when you say that he has a 'specific type' are trying to say I'm not pretty enough? Because if I didn't know better, you sound jealous."

Score one for Callie. He is jealous.

Dominic scoffs. "Jealous? Of that loser? I don't get jealous."

"Oh, really? Then why would you look him up? Because from where I stand, it looks like it's eating you up that I actually brought someone with me. You probably thought I'd come here and pine for you while you fawned over Maddie. You thought I'd still be so broken and hung up on you. And you can't stand the thought that someone else might want me. Is that what you thought?"

"No, I just can't see you with a guy like that."

"A guy like what? A sweet, kind, caring, attentive, sexy, strong man? Why, because I don't warrant that? I'm not good enough for that?"

"That's not what I'm saying. I wonder what this guy's after. Does he know how much money your family has? Is he after some sort of payday?"

Callahan's tone is cold. "Yeah, because that's the only reason anyone would ever want me, right? For my family's money. It can't be because someone simply cares about me or wants to spend time with me or just plain wants me, right, Dom?"

"I don't want to see you get hurt."

"*You* hurt me. *You* broke me. *You* used me."

"I never used you."

"Bullshit. You had me for four years. You'd call and I'd come running. I was so in love with you, it didn't matter that you'd kick me out of bed after sex every single time. I was so in love with you, I let myself be willing to accept the crumbs of time and attention you deigned to toss at me. I was so in love with you, it didn't matter that you wouldn't even acknowledge me in public. I was so in love with you, I let myself think that someday, in spite of all the ways you showed me exactly how little you actually cared for me, you'd eventually come around and I'd be the one you chose. I'd be good enough, pretty enough, just plain *enough* for you. That you would want me, not only at night, not for a quick fuck whenever you wanted, not to simply satisfy yourself. That you'd want me."

"I do want you, Cal."

Her reply is icy. "You might not want someone else to have me, but you don't want me. And now that I'm all fixed and moved on, you can't stand the thought that someone else actually wants to be with me.

"You don't want me. You only want somewhere to put your dick. I know Maddie's cut you off for the past month. Did you think to yourself, 'huh, well, Maddie's gone for the day, I'll see if Cal's got five minutes for me'? I mean, is that still about all you're good for, Dom? Or have you figured out how to last longer than that?"

Oh, shit, Callie; hit him where it hurts.

"Go fuck yourself, Callahan."

"Oh, I do, frequently. And you know, I'm a hell of a lot better at it than you ever were."

Well, that's a nice visual. Thanks for that, Darlin'.

Dominic's tone is venomous when he speaks again. "You're something else, you know that? I bet this guy didn't even have to try with you. You were so desperate, you were willing to put out on the first date just to have someone touch you. You've always been so pathetic and needy; hoping for anyone to give you just the least bit of attention. I bet you were on your back for him five minutes after you met."

"Yeah, because that's all I'm good for, right, Dom? To fuck? Even if that were the case, at least he looks me in the eye when he does it. He doesn't kick me out of his bed. He pulls me to him at night and whispers in my ear. He wants me. He chose me. He's willing to be seen with me in public. He's sweet and he's kind and he's sexy in a way you could never begin to be."

God, this guy is terrible. Would Callie mind if I punch him in the face?

"You only wanted me until the Benson girl you were really after was available. What was your plan? You'd string me along and keep me complacent enough I wouldn't want anyone else in the event that Maddie married someone else; you'd have me as a backup? That way, you could still be a part of the Benson family. You could have access to the Benson money?"

"I don't need your family's money; I've got plenty."

"Yeah, but you and I both know *Benson* money and *Prescott* money are two completely different types of money. Do you actually love Maddie, or is this a merger for you? To further your own ends."

"Of course I love Maddie. I've always loved her."

"Then fucking act like it, Dom. If I wasn't so worried about hurting Maddie, I'd tell her exactly who you are. And hopefully, someday, she'll realize that all on her own. But if you ever speak to me again I'll tell her who you are and I'll tell her you tried to sleep with me three days before the wedding."

"Like she'd ever believe you."

"Want to find out? I'm happy to call her right now." After a beat, she says, "Try me."

CHAPTER TWENTY-TWO

CALLAHAN

I level Dominic with the most threatening glare I can muster. "Try me." A muscle tics in his jaw, but he doesn't respond. "Get out of my way," I demand, and he steps to the side. And in spite of my racing heart during my confrontation with Dom, I can't be anything other than proud of myself for the way I handled things.

I walk past him and into the house and stop short when I see Jonas. His expression is sympathetic which, somehow, makes me deflate. I know there's no way he didn't hear every awful thing Dominic said and the shit that I made up to make myself feel better in that moment. He starts to say something and I hold up my hands and push past him into the bedroom. I run into the bathroom and close the door right before the tears start. I sit in the floor in front of the sink with my knees drawn up and sob into my folded arms.

I don't know if they're tears of sadness, anger, embarrassment, or from simple adrenaline, but I can't stop.

There's a knock on the door and Jonas's voice is muffled through the wood. "Callie, are you okay?"

"Go away."

"Come on now, Darlin', you know that's not my M.O. I'll stand right here and talk to you, but I'm not going anywhere. I'd prefer to look at your face, but I'll stand on the other side of this door all day if you want."

Through my tears, I say, "I don't want you to see me like this; I already feel pathetic enough. I don't need your pity, Jonas."

"Callahan, open the door. Please." His voice is soft and coaxing, as if he's trying to calm a scared or wounded animal. Which, I guess at this point, is a pretty accurate representation of the situation.

I sigh. "It's not locked." I don't look up as he opens the door. He sits on the floor in front of me and rubs his hands down my arms, trying to comfort me.

We stay like this for a long time, I'm not sure how long. But after a while, my sobs subside and Jonas says, "Man, I hope I'm never on the ass end of one of your verbal beatdowns. You sure know how to tear a guy down."

In spite of myself, I snort a small laugh. "How much did you hear?"

"Probably about all of it. I was coming to bring you your book before I went down to get coffee. But after that, I don't know if I need any. Man, Callie, you were ruthless. It was incredible."

"Pathetic, more like."

"Hey, look at me." I glance up at him over my knees and he wears a serious expression, his brow furrowed. "Why would you say it was pathetic?"

I shrug. "Because of all the stuff I said. I didn't want you to hear all that stuff about what I was willing to put up with. He wasn't wrong when he said I'm desperate for someone to give me attention. And all that stuff I made up about you and me, it makes me feel that much more pathetic. I wish you hadn't heard any of it."

"Well, I'm glad I did. And do you honestly believe I give a fuck what you said about me? All of it made me look real good, as far as I'm concerned, so don't be sorry about that. And as far as the other stuff goes, everyone has periods in their lives they wish they could go back and redo or take out. Trust me, I know I do.

"But we can't change the past. And do you think if you could, you'd actually want to? Knowing how he treated you has made you realize what you don't want in a relationship. And your douche-ometer is in tip-top shape now." I can't help but smile and he continues, "But man, Callie, what I would give to know what his face looked like when you were tearing him down. It was beautiful."

I sniffle and huff out a soft laugh. "It was pretty good. This vein in his forehead kept popping out and I thought, for sure, when I said I was gonna call Maddie, I could almost see the dollar signs fading away in his eyes."

Jonas laughs. "You were brilliant. Attacking a guy's ability in bed? You sure know how to cut deep."

"I might feel a little bad about that if it wasn't true."

His eyes widen. "Well then, no wonder you don't miss sex if that's your whole experience. Jesus, Callahan. And did he really kick you out of bed and not look you in the eye?"

I flush with embarrassment and the tears start anew. "Like I said, pathetic."

"Pathetic for him; not you. The fact that he had a gorgeous woman in his bed and had no clue what to do with her, that's pathetic. And for four years, no less? Damn, he's a stupid bastard."

"Yeah, pretty much."

He squeezes my arms. "Come on. Get up and get dressed."

I frown in confusion. "Why?"

"Because we're going out."

I sigh. "Jonas, honestly, I don't feel like leaving this spot right now, let alone the bedroom. I don't want to see him."

"Oh, I don't either, but if we don't get out of this house for the day, it's highly likely Dominic will have a nice black eye to wear for his wedding photos. We're going out."

He hops up and tugs me up from the floor. "Come on, it'll be fun. We can go do touristy stuff and make a day of it, and by the time we get back, we'll be so exhausted, we'll have no choice but to come back and go straight to bed."

I look at him. "Why are you being so nice to me? You don't owe me anything. All I've done is make you see what a fucked up mess I am and you've continued to comfort me and make me feel better. I don't get it."

He brushes a tear off my cheek with the pad of his thumb. "Because it's what you need. I told you last night I'm here for you in whatever capacity you need from me this week. And right now, getting you out of this house and distracting you is what you need." He takes my chin in his hand and looks into my eyes. "And part of me says if I don't get you out of this bedroom, I'm gonna be forced to show you what sex is truly supposed to be like."

Heat floods my entire body and my breath catches. He gives me a slow smile and drops his hand and turns to walk back into the bedroom.

I stand there for a minute, unable to move, absorbing his words. When I finally snap out of my daydream of what it would be like if Jonas and I did have sex, I wash my face and take my braids down, revealing waves, which honestly, aren't terrible. I slip a hair tie onto my wrist in case my hair gets on my nerves and swipe on a bit of mascara.

When I come into the bedroom, Jonas has already changed

into shorts and a tee shirt and has his sandals on. I dig through a dresser drawer and pull out an old comfortable pair of cutoff denim shorts and a tank top. I slip back into the bathroom to get dressed and examine my reflection. Yep, that's me, plain old Callahan.

Jonas looks up from his phone from where he sits on the sofa and smiles. "Your hair's down. Wow, I didn't realize how long it is. It's pretty."

I tuck it behind my ears. "Thanks. I'm ready when you are."

He stands and pulls a ball cap from his bag and puts it on backward and I'm picturing what he looked like in college when he was in a fraternity. And I don't know what it is about a guy in a backward cap that makes them look that much more sexy. Damn. Jonas touches my arm and I'm brought back to myself. He has an eyebrow quirked, as though he can read my thoughts. "Let's go, Darlin'."

I roll my eyes and pick up my purse and phone and we walk out of the bedroom and down the stairs. My parents are sitting at the kitchen table eating and Dad hollers, "Oh, y'all are just in time for breakfast, come on and eat."

I smile. "Thanks, Dad, but Jonas and I are gonna do touristy stuff. He's only been to this area once before, so we're gonna go have a fun day. Don't wait up."

Dad nods. "Y'all have fun. Traffic and crowds will be outrageous with the holiday, so good luck."

When we get outside, Jonas asks, "Want me to drive?"

I frown. "You don't have a clue where you're going."

"Well, I figure you're not gonna let me get lost. But if you prefer to drive, it's fine."

I dig out the key to the rental car and hand it over. "Have at it. If you want to fight traffic, be my guest. After this morning, I'm probably better suited to the passenger seat anyway."

He gives me a wicked grin. "So you're okay if I drive? And you're okay to sit back and let me take charge?"

Sweet lord, this guy is gonna be the death of me.

I hold his gaze. "Do you need directions? Because I normally drive myself everywhere."

"I heard you mention that earlier. I've never needed directions before. I'm an experienced, safe, and reliable driver. Usually, people who ride with me claim it's a pretty fun time."

"Oh, I'm well aware of how *experienced* you are. But in my, albeit limited, experience, no one can drive my car like I can." How I'm able to keep a straight face, I'll never know.

He closes the distance between us and runs the knuckle of his index finger along my jaw and whispers in my ear. His breath is hot on my skin and sends a shiver down my spine. "I'd love nothing more than to watch you drive your *car*. I'm sure that's a sight to behold. But driving with someone else can be just as much fun; you just haven't ridden with the right person. I'd be happy to drive you almost anywhere. In the car, in the bed, in the shower, on the porch." He brushes a kiss on my neck before pulling back.

My cheeks burn and heat pools low in my belly and my voice comes out breathy. "You had to make it dirty, didn't you?"

"Yeah. I like seeing what it does to you. And you like it; I can see it in your eyes. They're that dark blue color. Much better than the grayish-blue from earlier. I don't like that one as much."

"Yeah, me neither. It's not fair, though, how you can read me the way you do. How do you do that?" We climb into the car and he starts the engine and turns around in the driveway before slowly making his way down to the road.

"I don't know; you're like an open book, honestly. I know it might sound a bit on the nose or whatever since you're a librarian, but it's true."

I look down at my hands. "I don't know about that. No one else in my life knows me like that. You're freakishly perceptive. It's not fair. You've seen me at what could ostensibly be my lowest points and you know exactly what to say to fix me."

He huffs out a soft laugh. "Callie, you didn't need fixing. I only made you take a look at things from forty thousand feet instead of four. All you've seen for all these years is what your family sees and now you see the bigger picture."

I swallow. "Want to hear something truly pathetic? A definite bad, bad, realization?"

He frowns in confusion. "Sure."

"If you weren't here and I hadn't had that mental breakdown yesterday that you helped me work through, I probably would've slept with Dom. I know that's terrible and part of me wonders if that had happened, would it have kept happening at every family gathering when Maddie wasn't around? And would I be somebody's mistress for the rest of my life, still surviving on crumbs?"

He squeezes my hand, his expression serious. "Well, if for nothing else than to save you from five terrible minutes, I'm glad I'm here." He winks and I burst into laughter.

"It probably is terrible. Think how miserable Maddie is gonna be for the entirety of their marriage. Yikes."

He nods. "See, there it is, big picture. You're learning, Darlin'."

CHAPTER TWENTY-THREE

JONAS

As we continue driving away from the house, Callahan asks, "So, what do you want to do?"

I consider and tap my fingers against the steering wheel. "What is something your family would never, in a million years, be caught doing because it's so far beneath what they would consider a good time?"

She laughs. "Well, that's a lot of stuff actually, but if we're talking about tourist-type stuff; hmm. let's see." She thinks for a few minutes. "I've got it. We're going to the strip. It's gonna be a nightmare because of the holiday, but it's something no one in my family would ever do. So, yeah, head toward Gatlinburg. We can park somewhere between Pigeon Forge and Gatlinburg and take a trolley. It's only a couple of dollars, but it'll be way cheaper than parking."

"Trolley, okay. And then what?"

"Mini golf. My dad would die."

I nod approvingly. "Perfect. Okay, what about food, because I'm starving."

She points at a gas station about a mile ahead. "Stop there."

"For food? Callie, I can't survive on a bag of chips and a candy bar."

She rolls her eyes. "Trust me; it'll be worth it."

I pull into the gas station parking lot and we enter. Callahan pulls me toward the back of the store, where there's a short-order, fast-food grill. She turns to me. "Do you like fried bologna?"

"Sure. With lettuce, tomato, cheese." She nods and orders us each a sandwich and we also get a couple of snack-size bags of chips and some sodas. When our sandwiches are ready, we take them back to the car and I open mine up. "Holy hell, this is not a slice of bologna; this is a log between two slices of bread."

She laughs. "Well, at least you won't be hungry for a while."

We eat our sandwiches and chips and toss the trash into a nearby can. "Man, that was so good. How did you know about this place?"

"Well, you know how *not* like my family I am?" I nod and she continues, "So, once I started driving and we'd come up to the lake for the summer, I made it a point to do something at least once a week that would appall my family. I happened upon this place one day when I was getting gas. I have no clue what their health inspection rating is, and for that alone, it made it worth it to me. I've yet to get food poisoning, so they must do alright."

"So, you've been giving your family the finger for a long time, not only since college."

She shrugs. "I guess. As you can imagine, I wasn't overly rebellious or anything. I mean, I was a virgin until I was twenty, so you know, not a big surprise that I also wouldn't do drugs or drink before I was legal or other stuff a lot of people do when they're in high school. But this, this was how I rebelled. That, and the tattoos. I'm still not sure my parents know I have them. Maddie knows about the one on my hip, but no one else knows about the other one."

"Well, I like your tattoos. Especially the other one." I smirk.

She rolls her eyes. "You only like that one because you'd like to see my boobs."

I laugh. "Well, yeah, I wouldn't turn it down, but seriously, I like what it means to you. It's awesome, really. You got it after things went south with Dominic, right?"

She nods. "Yeah. I spent the week between Christmas and New Year's that year completely wasted, as well as the next couple of months after I moved to Tallahassee. But after I crawled out of my hangover, I went and got it done. Because I was in a dark place, but I thought I'd eventually come out of it and now, I guess I have, for the most part, and it's my war badge or whatever."

We continue to make small talk until Callahan tells me to turn onto a highway and after about an hour of bumper-to-bumper traffic, she directs me to turn into a parking lot. "The trolley stop is right there and it will take us to Gatlinburg. There's a separate trolley when we get there, but we can get to pretty much anywhere in Pigeon Forge and Gatlinburg via trolley. And public transit is frowned upon by the Benson family, so all the more reason to do it, right?"

We get out and walk over to the stop and wait. Fifteen minutes later, the bus pulls up and we pay our two dollars to ride and walk toward the back of the trolley. With no seats available, we're forced to stand and hold on to a pole as the vehicle makes its ascent up the mountain. It makes a few more stops and many people get on, forcing Callahan to stand directly in front of me. She turns and looks up at me over her shoulder. "Sorry it's so crowded."

I smile and lean down to whisper in her ear. "I'm not gonna

complain about you standing close to me. You're welcome to get even closer." The trolley hits a pothole and she's jostled and nearly loses her balance, so I brace my hand on her waist to keep her upright.

"Thanks," she says.

"Anytime."

We start to approach the first stop in Gatlinburg. "Is this where we need to get off?" I ask.

"Yeah, we have to change trolleys. This one will go back to Pigeon Forge. And then it's a few stops ahead where we'll get off for the strip."

We switch busses, this one more crowded than the first, but we manage to find some standing room mid-way back on the vehicle as it crawls its way up the busy street to the next stop.

A guy behind us rises from his seat, ready to disembark, and bumps into me, making me press closer to her. I grip her waist tighter to keep us both standing and inadvertently slide my pinky under the hem of her tank top. I can't stop myself from brushing the digit across her skin and Callahan lets out a breath and leans back into me. I whisper, "Your skin is really soft." And it is. And her hair smells good. And her being so close is not helping me maintain my ability to not want her.

"That tickles."

"So show me how to make it not tickle." I keep my voice low—a challenge—fully expecting her to bat my hand away since there's no one around here to pretend for. But to my utter surprise, she moves my hand lower on her hip and my thumb brushes along the waistband of her shorts. I lean down and run my nose along the shell of her ear. "You smell good, too."

She chuckles. "I probably won't by the end of the day; after we've walked around and gotten covered in sweat and exhaust." She stands up straighter. "This is us."

We make our way to the front of the bus and when it pulls

up at the stop, we hop off. "Okay, miss rebel, where are we headed?"

She rolls her eyes. "Well, do you want indoor or outdoor mini golf?"

"Let's do indoor. It would most likely be cooler, right?"

She nods. "Yeah, and it's got blacklight in places, so extra not Benson-approved."

I laugh. "Even better. Lead the way."

We make our way through the crowd, and Alex was right, it's a lot. I stick close to Callahan as we walk up the sidewalk. "Man, I knew Gatlinburg was a big tourist attraction, but you don't think of a small town in Tennessee being this crowded. It's wild."

She nods. "Yeah, you should see it in the fall, though, when the leaves start to change. It's worse than this. But, honestly, it's always crowded, regardless of the time of year."

When we get to the mini golf place, we pay for our game and pick our clubs and wait for our number to be called to get started. "What color ball do you want?" Callahan asks.

"Blue," I say without hesitation.

She laughs. "Blue ball, okay."

I smile. "Now who's making things dirty?"

She grins. "I couldn't resist. I'll get blue, too, so we can both have blue balls."

I burst out laughing. "You're really not a prude are you?" We walk over to a bench and sit while we wait.

She shakes her head. "Nope. I don't know, you'd think I would be with my family and my limited experience, but maybe reading all those smutty books has made me not care."

I lean over to her. "Well, you know what they say; it's those quiet ones you have to look out for. Especially nerdy book-worms. They turn out to be freaks."

She rolls her eyes. "I'm certainly no freak. I think I'm probably pretty vanilla, although I don't have a frame of reference for *that* other than what I've read. But even reading about stuff doesn't necessarily make me want to do it."

I raise a brow. "So, what is the wildest thing you have done?"

"Please, you think Dom is adventurous at all? No. So nothing. Nada. He was a methodical, by-the-book kind of guy."

"So, what drew you to him?"

She gathers up her mass of hair and drops it absentmindedly. "Believe me, I've been asking myself that question since he broke things off. He was always around and he's good-looking. And I used to think he was charming and intellectual, but in reality, he's not. And honestly, I've never felt like I was good enough for him, simply because of my baggage about Maddie, so when he showed interest, I was shocked and he didn't have to try. Like, at all."

I nod. "I believe that." She blanches and I quickly elaborate. "Shit, that sounded bad. I didn't mean to sound like I think you're easy. I only meant that from the way it looked this morning, he acted like if he said he missed you and wanted you, he thought you'd hop into bed with him. Regardless of the fact you were with someone."

She clenches her jaw. "Yeah. Pretty much. Because that's what it's always been like between him and me. He says jump and I say okay." After a beat, she asks, "What about you? Are you wild and adventurous?"

"I think it depends on what you consider wild and adventurous," I reply with a smirk.

She rolls her eyes and elbows me in the ribs. "Come on, what's the craziest thing you've ever done? Or are you a prude and can't talk about it?" Her tone is challenging.

I shake my head and smile. "You actually want to know?"

She nods and gives me an expression that says, *well, duh.* "Yeah. Make me blush."

I laugh. "That's not hard to do, Callie."

"So do it then. Tell me about some wild encounter you've had."

I think for a minute and then lean over to her. "Okay, so it might not be wild, but it was definitely risky. I was on a date with this girl and things were going well, so she invited me back to her place. We get there and we start making out in her kitchen. It's getting pretty hot and then the front door starts to open, so she shoves me down onto the floor. I'm thinking, 'oh, shit, she's got a boyfriend' or something and I'm thinking I'm dead, for sure. But it was her dad; which, I don't know, maybe that was worse.

"But anyway, so I'm sitting on the floor while she has this full-blown conversation with her dad, but I'm just tipsy enough I'm not exactly thinking with my big brain if you know what I mean." Callahan chuckles and I go on. "So, this girl is wearing this short skirt and I know her dad can't see me, otherwise, I would've been busted already, so, while she has a conversation with her dad, I start running my hand up her leg. And I think, for sure, she's gonna kick me or something, but she actually shifts her body like she's encouraging me."

Her mouth drops open. "No. In front of her dad?"

I nod. "Yeah, so I'm doing my thing and she's enjoying herself, but somehow manages to not give anything away at all, until the end when she lets out this little yelp and her dad asks her what's wrong. She tells him she thinks she saw a mouse over in the corner. He goes to investigate and she sneaks me into her room while his back is turned."

Callahan laughs. "That's pretty good. Did her dad catch you?"

I shake my head. "No, but, man, knowing he was there, made it hot."

"Because you like a challenge."

"Yeah, probably."

CHAPTER TWENTY-FOUR

CALLAHAN

A few minutes later, our number is called for us to start our game and we step up to the first hole. I ask Jonas, "Have you played a lot of mini golf before?"

He nods. "Yeah, tons. Nana and I used to go all the time when I was younger. What about you?"

I shrug. "Some, but probably not as much as you."

"Well, ladies first. Show me what you've got," he says and gestures to the starting point.

"Alrighty then." I set my ball down and line up to make the putt. I draw the putter back and hit the ball and it goes over a small hill and around a post and comes to rest a couple of feet from the hole. I walk over and easily knock it in the rest of the way.

I pick the ball up and Jonas shakes his head. "You lied. You've played a lot. That was a par four. And you probably could have made it in one."

I smirk. "Beginner's luck, maybe."

"Uh-huh. I'm sensing I'm about to get hustled."

"For you to get hustled, there would have to be some sort of wager. And I'm not that good." I really am, but I'm not about to tell him that and I want to see if he rises to my bait and issues some sort of flirty challenge to me. Because at this point, I'm so wound up from all the flirting and stuff these past few days, I would love nothing more than to let Jonas get me naked. Although it's a bad idea, I don't know if I'm necessarily thinking with my big brain right now, either.

"So, are you saying you want to make a bet?"

I shrug and keep my tone nonchalant. "Like I said, I'm not that good, so you'd probably win anyway."

"Well, I like making wagers when I think I can win, so okay."

Sucker. Looks like he is easier to read than I thought. "Alright, so, what are your terms?"

He comes over to me and moves my hair off my shoulder and leans in. "If I win, you tell me about a fantasy you have."

There it is.

Man, that was easier than I thought it was gonna be. I nod. "Okay. I can do that."

"And if you win?"

Heat climbs up my neck, but I hold his gaze. "If I win, I tell you about my fantasy and if you like it, we act it out."

He stands up straighter and his eyes search mine, his expression unsure. "Callahan, come on."

"What, you suddenly don't like a challenge?" I ask, a teasing lilt to my voice.

"What about your rules?"

I splay my hands, aiming for casual. "What about them? Who's to say what I fantasize about would violate my rules?"

He scoffs. "Well, what the hell kind of fantasy could it be if it's not gonna break your rules?"

I lean in and keep my voice low. "If I recall, when we were on the plane you asked if sex was off the table and I said it would probably be best. So, last I checked, that leaves a lot of other things *on* the table." His mouth falls open. "And saying something 'would be best' doesn't necessarily make it a rule. So, there may not be any rules to begin with." His brain seems to glitch for a moment and he opens and closes his mouth as if he's trying to speak but nothing comes out and I laugh. "So, you in or not?"

He swallows slowly and blows out a breath. "Darlin', I'm tempted to throw this game, if only to find out what goes through that mind of yours."

I laugh. "No, you can't do that. You'd have to actually try or else it's not fair. Either way, you'll hear about the fantasy, but if you want, you can take my terms and I can take yours; if that gives you more incentive to try."

He considers this for a moment before his eyes come back to mine. "Are you sure about this?"

I look down because although he's flirted with me and stuff, I'm thinking now it could only be because of people being around and maybe he wouldn't want to do anything. And why would he? I'm just me. I'm not adventurous or experienced. And now I feel stupid. "I mean, we can forget it. It's fine. Let's play."

He examines my face. "Callie, what happened? Right then, in your mind? What was that?"

Dammit, how does he do that? "Nothing, Jonas. Stop trying to read me. I'm fine. Let's play."

His expression is hard. "No, tell me. Right now. I swear—."

"Excuse me?" We both turn to see an older couple. The man says, "I'm sorry, can we play through?"

Jonas smiles at them. "Of course, sir; I'm so sorry." He tugs me over to the side so we're no longer in the way and looks at me. "Well?"

"Well, what, Jonas?" I ask, exasperated.

"Tell me what went through your mind. Because I know you weren't just thinking some shit about I can't possibly want you or you're not good enough or anything remotely close to that."

My cheeks immediately burn with embarrassment. "Stop it."

"Stop what, Callahan? It's not my fault I can read you. You broadcast what you're thinking like you're wearing a billboard; it's not my fault I know where to look. And all because I asked if you were sure about something, you assume it means I'm not open to it? I only wanted you to think. To be sure. And I swear, I'd love nothing more than to strangle Dominic for the way he's fucked up your sense of self-worth.

"I know he said all that stuff this morning about seeing a lot of women on my social media page, and he's right; I do typically have a type. Easy. And you're not, so if that makes you mad, I'm sorry. I like that you're not easy. I like that I don't know if I'm gonna get to sleep with you. It's fun. We play and we flirt and I like it. You give me shit and I like it. I like teasing you and making you blush and I like seeing you turned on. I like holding you and touching you and I sure as hell like kissing you. I think I've made it pretty damn obvious how attractive I think you are.

"So don't take my wanting to check in with you as me not wanting you. Because, Darlin', you are extremely desirable and I'd love nothing more than to show you what it's like when someone has you for more than five minutes at a time. Five minutes isn't even enough time for me to tell you all the things I'd love to do to you."

My breath catches and Jonas steps closer to me and my pulse increases. He tucks my hair behind my ear and his eyes travel from my own down to my mouth and back up and my knees go watery under his gaze. He gives me a smug smile. "I'll take your wager. Original terms. If you want to act out your fantasy, you're gonna have to beat me. And, like I said, I'm pretty good." He walks back over to the tee and sets his ball down and putts and sinks it in one stroke. I look at him, surprised. "Looks like you're the one getting hustled, Darlin'." He winks at me and we move on.

———

By the end of the seventeenth hole, it's tied and as we walk toward the last, Jonas says, "So, last hole. It's all tied up. What do you think is gonna happen?"

I shrug. "I don't know. Could go either way. But how did you get so good at mini-golf? You said you played a lot when you were younger?"

He gives me a lopsided grin. "Yeah, but what I didn't tell you is that I take my students every year as a math exercise and I still go about once a month with Nana, so I may have fudged a little. I figured you were probably a lot better than you let on and I was curious to see what you'd do. I knew you'd expect me to challenge you."

I can't keep a wide grin off my face. "And here I thought I was so clever. Dammit. It's not fair. How do you do that?"

He smirks, his tone cocky. "Just that good, I guess. Plus, like I said, if you know where to look, you're easy to read." He looks me up and down. "I'm curious how far that extends."

I narrow my eyes. "You might never know."

He laughs. "Yeah, but it'd be fun to try."

I put my ball on the tee and look at him. "Does that mean you're trying?"

He holds my gaze. "Do you want me to?"

My stomach knots up and I bite my lip, suddenly nervous. And yet, I can't stop myself from asking, "And if I did?"

His expression is serious. "You'd have to be sure, Callie. I've told you what I'm capable of and what I'm not, so you'd have to know what you're agreeing to. It wouldn't go anywhere. Most likely, once we get back to Florida, you might never hear from me again. I don't want to mess you up like Dominic did, though, so if that's even a remote possibility for you, I need to know. Because I was honest last night, I don't want to hurt you, Callahan. I think we'd have a lot of fun, but I'd rather not if there's a chance you'll get hurt."

I nod, letting his words settle in and return my attention to my ball. I look down at the hole and calculate the best angle at which to strike it. Once I've decided, I pull my putter back and hit the ball, but I don't hit it with enough force and it doesn't travel as far as I thought it would. It ends up taking me three more strokes to get the ball in because of a windmill and once I finally sink it, I'm pissed at myself.

Jonas sets up and makes the hole in three, beating me by one stroke. He comes up to me. "Did you throw the game?"

I scoff. "No, I didn't throw the damn game; I'm too competitive for that. Although, I was probably distracted by everything you said, so it's most likely still your fault. But you won. Fair and square."

He chuckles. "Wow, touchy. Remind me never to play you in anything with real stakes." He takes our clubs and balls over to the desk and comes back to me. "Okay, what's next on the tourist Callie agenda?"

I think for a minute. "Ice cream?"

He smiles. "Okay. Want to split a sundae?"

"Hot fudge or caramel?"

"Whichever. I like both."

I nod. "Okay." We walk down to the ice cream stand and I order a hot fudge sundae and while we wait, I look at Jonas, and I find my mind wandering again to what it might be like if I went to bed with him. How different he'd be than Dom. Because in only the last three days, I've been more turned on by him than in almost all of the four years I was sleeping with Dominic and I realize what a piss-poor lover he truly must be and it almost makes me pity Maddie.

"Callahan? Did you hear me?" I shake away my thoughts and focus my eyes on Jonas. He wears a smug, knowing grin and holds our sundae in his hand. "You alright, Darlin'?"

I nod. "Yeah, why?"

He chuckles and holds the spoon out to me and I take a bite. "Oh, nothing, it looks like you were thinking about something pretty intently."

I blush. "Nope, only thinking about how I should have kicked your ass at mini-golf. But I didn't realize I was playing with Happy Gilmore. I was swindled."

He takes a bite and laughs. "Sorry, Darlin'. But you're good, too. I know your family doesn't play, so how'd you get that way?"

"Well, I come here or go to Pigeon Forge and play by myself whenever I come up. I'd always wanted to play when I was little and we'd drive through the area, you know, if we were going to Dollywood or something and I always thought it looked like it was fun. So, it became part of my rebellion."

We walk around Gatlinburg for a few more hours, visiting shops and simply talking and being goofy. We stop for some sodas and walk a bit farther and pass a drugstore. I stop and turn to Jonas. "Do you have condoms?"

He chokes on his drink and I wait for him to calm down. "What?"

I roll my eyes. "I'm not saying yes, but, you know, be prepared and all that. Do you have any?"

He shakes his head. "No, I honestly wasn't thinking it would be a remote possibility this week."

I give him an amused smile. "You mean, you, of all people, who hooks up all the time, weren't prepared for that? I'm truly shocked."

He gives me a sheepish smile. "Okay, so you want the truth?" I nod. "So, when Elliot called me and asked me to do this, he said you were nice and pretty. But he's gay, so I thought his definition of pretty and mine were probably different. And nice usually means boring, so I thought for sure I'd be miserable this week. Plus, I had almost no time to pack and would've had to go get some anyway."

I narrow my eyes. "I don't know whether to be flattered or offended."

He laughs. "Well, I'll just say, I was pleasantly surprised by who you turned out to be. But you're not on anything? I mean, I'm always careful and I'm clean, if it matters."

I sigh and look down. "It's not about that, I mean, not all of it. But Dominic refused to ever use anything and I had a pregnancy scare a couple years back and so I just like having control over this. Sorry. I have an IUD now. I got it after my scare."

Jonas closes his eyes and lets out a heavy sigh. "Can I please knock his teeth out? He does't need those, right? I hate that guy."

"You and me both. So, I guess I need to make a stop then."

He shrugs. "Your call. But if we stop, I want to get some candy. Maybe we can watch a movie tonight when we get back to the house?"

I nod. "You hoping you'll get to make out in the media room?"

He laughs. "I mean, it wouldn't be the worst thing. And I'm pretty sure your mom already thinks we had sex in there, so why not?"

CHAPTER TWENTY-FIVE

JONAS

By the time we eat supper at a hole-in-the-wall pizza place and stop for candy and, yes, condoms, and take the trolley back to the car and fight traffic to the house, it's nearly eight-thirty.

When we get up to the bedroom, Callie tosses the bag onto the sofa and says, "I'm gonna take a shower; I'm wiped out."

I give her a wicked grin. "You need any help? I'm an excellent shower helper."

She rolls her eyes. "I'm good. I'll holler if I need you."

When she goes into the bathroom, I read for a bit, but realize I'm thirsty. I knock on the bathroom door. "Callie, I'm gonna get a bottle of water. You want one?"

"Yes, please."

I walk downstairs and pull a couple bottles of water from the refrigerator. When I shut the fridge door, Dominic is standing on the other side. I do my best to keep my features neutral and turn away.

"I don't know what you're playing at with Cal."

I stop and pivot to face him and set the waters on the counter. "I'm sorry, *playing at?*"

"Yeah, you think you can worm your way into this family? Make a quick buck? I know about you."

I keep my tone even. "Oh, really, and what is it you think you know?"

"That you come from an unknown father and a junkie mother and she didn't even want you."

I could be mad at what he's saying, but none of it is untrue and I've come to terms with my family, so I don't let it get to me. And I'm shocked he didn't dig up the stuff from college, so him bringing my parents into things is basically nothing. "Yeah, and what's your point? Callie knows all that."

"I'm guessing her parents don't. They'll never let her be with someone like you."

"I honestly don't think Callahan gives a whole lot of thought to what her parents want for her life. She's gonna make her own way in the world; with or without them."

"Someone like you could never understand what she needs; could never be enough."

I laugh. "Why, because I'm not someone like you?"

He scowls. "Exactly. You're trash."

I let my grin widen. "Trash I might be, but at least I'm not jealous."

"Jealous of what, you?"

"Yeah, because I've got what you thought you'd always keep back for yourself. You thought you could have Maddie and Callahan would always be there for you, just in case. And you're pissed she's finally over you and found someone who knows exactly what she needs. And the thought of someone else having her and kissing her and fucking her, it just runs all over you, doesn't it? At least I know how to please her. Five minutes isn't even enough time to get her naked if you do it right."

His face turns crimson and he grabs my shirt. "Careful,

Dom; I'm sure the offer is still good for Callahan to call Maddie. I'm sure she'd be real interested in how you treated her all these years. I'm sure her parents would enjoy knowing how you used her, too. All that Benson money you're so concerned about, it wouldn't be anything you needed to worry about anymore."

"Jonas? Everything okay?" Callahan's voice sounds from the foot of the stairs, her tone tinged with concern.

I smirk at Dominic and he releases my shirt. "Oh, yeah, Darlin'. I was about to fall and Dom was nice enough to help make sure I didn't. He's a real pal." I pick the bottles of water back up and meet her on the steps. I take her hand in mine and kiss the back of it.

She tucks my hair behind my ear and her expression is full of worry. "You okay?"

I nod and we walk up the stairs. When we get back into the bedroom, I ask, "How much did you hear?"

"From the part about him accusing you of wanting my family's money. I'm sorry he said all that stuff. He's an asshole."

I level her with a gaze. "Do not apologize for him. I know where I come from. I'm not ashamed of that. I'm not either of my parents. He's just a jealous, elitist snob."

She nods. "I know. But you don't deserve to be treated that way over me because it's not what you signed up for."

I give her a wink. "Nothing I can't handle, Darlin'."

She bites her lip. "You were pretty brilliant, too. What you said to him? Masterful." She makes a little *chef's kiss* motion and I can't help but laugh. I hand her a bottle of water and I open my own and take a long drink.

"I'm gonna go take a shower. I'm pretty beat, too."

Callahan sighs. "Yeah, this was, like, the longest day. The beginning and end were pretty rough, but the middle turned out okay."

I nod. "The middle part was perfect. I had a great time today. Thanks for letting me be a tourist."

She gives me a sweet smile. "Anytime."

I pick up my sweats and walk into the bathroom and start the shower. I stand under the spray and let the hot water wash all the sweat and grime and tension away.

If for no other reason than making Callahan recognize how much better off she is without Dominic, I'm glad I came. She deserves so much better than the likes of that prick. Not me, because I can't be what she needs, either, but definitely better than him. And in spite of what I told Nana about settling down, I don't know if I'll ever be able to do that. Not after everything that happened in college. I don't know if I'll ever be able to get past it.

I take a few minutes to trim my stubble to a less grizzly length and wash the shavings down the sink. When I come out of the bathroom, Callahan is asleep, her book laying on her chest. Her head is lolled to the side and her glasses have slid down her nose. *I guess she really was tired.* I walk over to her side of the bed and pick her book up, making sure to keep her place with her bookmark and set it on the nightstand. I pull her glasses off her face and fold them up and set them on top of her book.

I look down at her, seeing her for the first time without her glasses and I realize she's as beautiful in them as out. I watch her sleep for a moment and can't help but smile. Her braid falls across her chest and her eyes flutter under her lids and her lips part slightly as she huffs out a small breath.

I turn off her lamp and walk around to my own side of the bed and climb in and read for a few more minutes before my eyes start to grow heavy. I plug my phone up and turn off the light and lie down. And simply because I want to feel her against me, I pull Callahan into my arms. She shifts and settles and her breathing deepens again.

———

When I wake up, I realize Callahan is still in bed, but she's awake. Pleasantly surprised, I pull her closer and nuzzle under her ear. "You're still in bed? I figured you'd be on the porch."

"Yeah, but I didn't want to risk another run in with Dominic. I'm sure Maddie's back and it's not an issue anymore, but I didn't want to chance it. Now, is that something in your pocket, or are you just happy to wake up next to me?"

I chuckle. "Sorry."

She laughs and snuggles closer to me. "No, you're good. This is kind of nice. You're warm, you know that?" She wiggles herself against me and I grip her waist.

"Darlin', you remember what I said the other day about squirming and me being a gentleman? I'm not gonna be able to be a gentleman much longer with you wiggling your ass like that."

"Sorry, I'll stop. I just had to give you a hard time. Pun intended." We both laugh and simply lie in bed for a bit longer and she's right; it is nice. After a beat, she says, "I don't want to go to the bachelorette party tonight. Can you think of a reason I can't?"

"I mean, you can tell Maddie the thought of being more than five minutes away from my magic penis is too much for you."

"Well, now, that's a new one. Is it actually magic?" Her tone is amused and I can't help but smile.

"Compared to what you've had, I'm sure. But as the standard, maybe better than average."

She laughs. "Well, I'll consider it. Maybe you can come

rescue me halfway through? I'd prefer not hang out with Maddie's sorority sisters. Most of them are exactly like Maddie and my family; obsessed with money and fashion and status. They're all gonna be drunk and expect me to keep up and I like the prospect of you flirting with me more than the prospect of being drunk, so I'd rather not have to explain that to them."

"I like the prospect of flirting with you, too. Sure, I can do that."

"Perfect. We can come back and watch a movie and maybe I'll let you feel me up."

I snort. "That would be something. I might think about that all day. Except not right now. Right now, I need coffee."

"You and me both. I laid here for thirty minutes waiting for you to wake up."

"You could have woken me up. I wouldn't have minded."

"Nah, I liked listening to you sleep. And you're a good snuggler, so I hated to stop."

CHAPTER TWENTY-SIX

CALLAHAN

Jonas and I finally get out of bed and brush our teeth and I put on my robe and he pulls on a tee shirt, which, I almost hate to see. We make the bed and walk downstairs and I turn on the coffee maker, since it looks like even with me sleeping in, we've still beat everyone else out of bed.

I open the cabinet to get a coffee mug and see none on the bottom two shelves. I stand on tiptoe to try to reach one on the third shelf and Jonas comes up behind me. He presses himself into me as he pulls two cups from the cabinet and I have a momentary thought of what it would be like if he bent me over the counter and fucked me and I flush with the mental image.

He runs his free hand down my waist and my breath catches and desire shoots to my core. When he sets the mugs down, he looks at my face. "What's that face about?" But his smirk tells me he can read me, damn him.

My voice is a bit breathy. "Nothing."

He nods. "Your eyes say otherwise."

I narrow my eyes at him. "Stop that. You don't get to read me like that whenever you want."

He reaches past me to start a cup of coffee. "But you make it so easy, Darlin'." He kisses me on the cheek and chuckles and hands me the full cup of coffee before starting one for himself.

I turn to face him and run my finger along his jaw. "You shaved."

"Just a trim." He catches my hand and kisses my palm before dropping it. He reaches around me to get his cup once it's finished and presses himself against me and I have to remember it would be bad form to get naked in this kitchen right now. I'm in the process of wrapping my arms around his neck when Maddie's voice breaks through the quiet.

"Come on, Hanny, if y'all are gonna do that, you should take it somewhere else. Some of us would still like to have coffee this morning. I mean, it looks like it's not a huge priority for you, but I'd love to have some caffeine." My head snaps to my left and she's standing there with her hands on her hips with a smirk on her face.

"Sorry, Maddie," Jonas says with a smile. "Don't know what got into us." He takes my hand and tugs me back up the stairs.

"Callahan?" Maddie hollers and I stop and watch Jonas's ass as he climbs the stairs. "We leave at eight. Dress to kill, okay?"

I paste a smile on my face and glance back at her. "Sure. I'll be ready."

I walk the rest of the way up and join Jonas out on the porch and sit in my chair. I see my book on the table. "You didn't have to get my book," I say. "But I appreciate it."

"Sure. I know you like to read with your coffee, so I thought it couldn't hurt."

I cut my eyes at him. "Look at you, being all sweet and stuff. If I didn't know better, I'd think you were trying to get in my pants."

He laughs over his mug and looks at me. "That's up to you, Darlin'."

I give him a playful smile. "So you say, but it seems like you have a vested interest."

"Oh, yes; I think we've established that already."

I sip my coffee. "It's gonna be a late night tonight. If you don't want to come get me, you don't have to. I know you wanted to finish that book."

He digs his phone out of his pocket and taps the screen and hands it to me. "Put your number in and I'll text you and if you need me, I'll come and make a scene." I smile and take his phone and put my number in and hand it back. He taps on the screen a few more times and returns it to his pocket. "I sent you a text so you'd have my number."

I nod. "Perfect." My phone vibrates in my robe pocket and I dig it out and check the screen and laugh. "Boy toy? Really?"

He shrugs. "You knew who it was, so it must work for me."

I read for a bit while I drink my coffee and end up finishing my book and coffee about the same time and set them down. I look over at Jonas who is staring out toward the water. He looks peaceful and I simply watch him for a minute until he senses my eyes on him. "What?" He asks.

I shake my head. "Nothing. You're exceptionally good looking. And you have a great ass."

He smiles. "Well, thanks. Yours is pretty nice, too."

I stand, planning to go fix myself another cup of coffee, but Jonas pulls me into his lap. I let out a surprised squeak. "Well, this is nice." I lean against him and he rests his hand on my knee.

He nuzzles my neck. "I wanted to see if you wanted a better memory of this porch than your fight with Dominic."

I furrow my brow in feigned confusion. "Dominic who?"

He smiles. "Worked already? Damn, I must be good."

"Yeah. But you could give me a little incentive."

He raises a brow. "Incentive for what, Darlin'?"

"You expect me to want to go to bed with you when all I've had is one kiss and a whole lot of flirting? I mean, granted, the flirting has been extremely excellent, but—."

He covers my mouth with his and the kiss is deep and searing and possessive. He runs his hand up the outside of my thigh and around my hip to my ass. I fist his shirt to bring him closer and moan into his mouth as my heart pounds.

When he breaks our kiss, my chest is heaving. My cheeks flush as I try to gulp in air. "Well."

He takes a sip of his coffee and I try to remember my own name or any pertinent information about myself, because at this moment, all I can think about is that kiss.

"I'm gonna get more coffee. You want some?" I ask.

"I'll go with you." I climb off his lap and he gives my ass a playful slap as I grab my mug and we walk back down to the kitchen and fix another cup of coffee.

"What are you feeling like for breakfast? I'm not sure what everyone else is doing, but I can make some eggs and bacon and toast. Keep it simple."

He nods. "Sounds good to me. I'll help."

"Thanks. Want to get the stuff from the fridge and I'll get the cookware?" He nods and we begin moving around the kitchen and I pull out a baking pan for the bacon and Jonas lays slices down on the pan before sticking it in the oven. "Scrambled or fried?"

"Either."

I nod. "Scrambled it is. With cheese or no?"

"Cheese, please."

I grab some half-and-half and some shredded cheddar from the fridge before coming back over to crack some eggs into a bowl, add a bit of half-and-half, and whisk with a fork. While we wait on the bacon to get far enough along to start the eggs, I hop up onto the counter and sip my coffee.

"So," Jonas begins, stepping between my knees, "what do you want to do today? You'll have to start getting ready by, what, seven, to leave?"

I nod. "Yeah, probably. Since it will be late when I get back, we could go ahead and watch a movie today, or we can go out on the boat."

He glances out the window. "It's probably gonna rain."

I look outside. "It's clear."

He takes a sip of his coffee. "Yeah, it is now, but I smelled rain. Give it about an hour, it will be pouring."

"Okay, so I know impending rain has a smell, but they're not forecasting it and it's not even all that humid out."

He shrugs. "Call it a super power. I'm telling you, in an hour, there's gonna be rain."

"Well, movie day then?"

He rests his free hand on my hip and brushes his thumb along the waistband of my pajama shorts. "Sounds good to me." He leans in and whispers in my ear, "Does the media room door have a lock?" My heart lurches and heat climbs up my neck at the thought of what his question might imply.

I set my mug down and drape my arms around his neck. "You planning on doing something that might require one?"

He gives me a wicked grin. "Thought I might incentivize you some more."

I laugh and nod, contemplating. "Well, that could be interesting."

"Darlin', interesting is nowhere near the right word. That's a sad word compared to what it could be."

I run my fingers through his hair. "You seem pretty sure of yourself."

"Always." He sets his mug down and tilts my chin and presses a kiss to my lips.

"Lord, y'all can't help yourselves, can you?"

Both our heads snap to the direction of Maddie's voice and Jonas steps back a respectful distance. Maddie, Dominic, her parents, his parents, and my parents are all standing there dressed for the day. I don't miss the murderous look on Dom's face which makes me want to laugh. "Y'all going somewhere?"

Aunt Meredith says, "Madison and Dominic have their final dance lesson and last meeting with the wedding planner. Quincy, Lillian, Lance and I are also going for a dance lesson. Your parents are going for moral support and then we're all going to lunch."

I nod. "Well, y'all have fun. We'll be here."

Maddie smirks. "I think we know where y'all will be."

"Madison! That's enough," Aunt Meredith scolds.

My mom winks at me as they all leave and again, my mouth falls open. I look at Jonas after the door closes. "My mother winked at me again. I swear, I don't know what to think about that."

He steps back between my knees. "Well, you said you'd like it if they did something unexpected. Looks to me like you got what you wanted."

I consider and laugh. "Yeah, I guess I did. It's just weird, because I've always thought of my mom as this stick in the mud. Maybe I was wrong. Sure as hell wouldn't be the first time."

"Did you see the look on Dominic's face?" Jonas asks with a grin.

I frown in mock-confusion. "Dominic who?"

He laughs and gives me a kiss. "Exactly."

CHAPTER TWENTY-SEVEN

JONAS

After breakfast and cleanup, Callahan and I stay in our pajamas and take along some snacks and drinks to last us a while and head toward the media room. Just before we go down the stairs, I nudge her and gesture out the window. Sure enough, it's pouring rain. Her mouth falls open and I laugh.

"That's quite the trick," she says as we close the door to the media room and she searches for the remote.

"I lived with my grandparents; they were old school. Taught me a lot of stuff like that."

"Oh, really, what else?" She comes up with the remote and sits down beside me.

"Well, they lived on a farm, so a lot of animal husbandry, gardening, vehicle maintenance, plumbing, electric."

She nods, her expression impressed. "Well, looks like I know who to call the next time I need a lightbulb changed."

I chuckle. "It might cost you."

"I'll keep that in mind." She scrolls through several streaming services on the screen. "What do you feel like watching?"

"Doesn't matter to me." *I don't plan on watching anyway.*

"Okay, is there a specific genre you prefer?"

"Anything but rom-com. I mean, unless it's got Matthew McConaughey in it. Otherwise, action or fantasy."

She nods. "Okay, so we have *How to Lose a Guy in Ten Days*. We have *The Hobbit*. We have *John Wick*."

I consider. "Not feeling much like watching a puppy get killed today, thanks. Kind of a mood killer, if I'm honest. I've never seen *The Hobbit*. Let's go with that."

"Well, that was easier than expected."

"What, you expected a fight? I mean, I can shoot down all those choices if you want, but I figure you want to watch it anyway, so why not?"

She laughs and shakes her head. "I would have gone with any of them. They're all good. And the dress Kate Hudson wears in the movie is gorgeous. I've always loved it. But I like the dwarves in *The Hobbit*. Graham McTavish is my favorite."

"Is he the guy from *Outlander*?"

Her expression is surprised. "You know about *Outlander*?"

I nod. "Oh, yeah. I love it. It's got everything. Action, time travel, love, history. I went back and read all the books after I watched the first season and found out it was a book series."

"Wow. I was not expecting that. But yeah, Graham McTavish is in *Outlander*; he played Dougal."

"Glad I can keep things interesting for you."

She quirks a brow. "I thought you said interesting was bad?"

"Only in the sense of what I had planned. Otherwise, interesting is good."

She nods. "Gotcha. Want to get the light? I'll start the movie."

"Sure thing." I hop up and turn off the overhead lights and

dim lights on the walls come up. "Damn, your family really doesn't half-ass things, do they? It's like a legit theater."

I see her shrug, even in the muted light and I sit next to her. "Some parts of it are nice. But other parts, not so much. Sometimes, I wish I could be like everyone else."

"You are like everyone else. You're normal. Like what we did yesterday, that was normal people stuff. And the fact you didn't have to think all that hard about what a 'normal' day as a tourist looks like, tells me you are incredibly normal."

"Yeah, I guess."

"And when you get married someday, are you gonna do dance lessons and have all this stuff?"

"Nope. Not a chance. I'm thinking Vegas. I'm not gonna tell my parents; I'll just show up at Thanksgiving with a husband." I laugh and she smiles. "You think I'm joking?"

I shake my head. "No, I don't. That's exactly what I would expect you to do. Although, is it actually what you want, or do you only want to give them the finger?"

She lets out a soft sigh. "Maybe a little of both. But if, someday, I get married, and I let my parents in on things, it would turn into what Maddie has and I don't want that. I don't like to be on display, which, I know, is sort of ironic considering what we're doing this week, but still. I don't like to draw attention to myself. If I get married, I want it to only be me and him. That's all that matters."

I nod. "Yeah, I get that. I mean, you could always do a Vegas wedding and let your parents throw you a reception. There's so much going on; the bride and groom are only a fraction of the event, even if it's supposed to be about them. You'd have to dance and cut the cake, but otherwise, everyone else does stuff and you get to chill. People come and say hi and give you money; it's not all bad."

"You sound like you speak from experience. Have you been married before?"

I shake my head. "No. Not married." I turn my attention to the screen. I don't want to get into my own stuff, and I'm pretty sure Callahan can sense it, because she doesn't press me.

She doesn't press me even though she must know something happened in my past. She doesn't push. She doesn't pry. And for that, I'm thankful. She's a good woman and someday, she's gonna make some man truly happy. I wish I could say it could be me, but it can't.

"Hey."

I turn to her. "Yeah?"

She smirks. "I never did tell you about my fantasy."

My heart rate spikes and I swallow and try to keep my tone level. "No, you didn't. Do you still want to?"

"A bet's a bet, right? And you won, fair and square. So if you want to hear it, I'll tell you."

"Sure."

She nods and folds her legs up under her, getting comfortable. "Alright, so have you ever seen the movie *Fear*?"

I try to think. "Is that the one with Mark Wahlberg?"

She nods. "Yeah, so I think I was about twelve the first time I saw that movie, which was way too young, but whatever. And I never noticed anything other than the first time they have sex, which to a twelve-year-old was pretty hot. But when I went back and watched it when I was older, probably about sixteen or something, I noticed the rollercoaster scene and it was... enlightening. And so, that's been the fantasy; to fool around on a roller coaster. Not so much the psycho boyfriend who carves my name in his chest or anything like that but the rollercoaster part was pretty hot."

I nod. "Yeah, that's pretty good. I'd have to go back and

watch it, but I get the appeal. You would almost have like built-in vibrations with something like that."

Even in the dark, I can see her blush. "I didn't think about that part. That's even better."

"Well, doesn't Dollywood have rollercoasters? We could go make it happen for you." I give her a sly smile and quirk a brow.

She rolls her eyes. "They did it in the dark. I'm not about to do something public like that in broad daylight."

I lean toward her. "Does that mean you'd be willing to do something in public as long as it was dark?"

She laughs. "I'm not saying that, either. Dollywood is a major family attraction." She's struck by a thought, one brow tilting up. "Although, they do have a ride that's almost completely dark since it's indoors." She shakes her head and smiles. "Nope. Not happening."

"Well, damn. Here I thought I'd get to help you out."

She grins, her tone playful. "Sorry, it's only a fantasy."

I tilt my head. "But yesterday, you said if you won, we'd fulfill it. How did you plan on doing that?"

"I don't know. I probably would've chickened out."

"Nah, you wouldn't have. You're not a chicken. You're brave."

Callahan shakes her head. "Not brave. If I were, I wouldn't have let Dominic string me along all those years. I wouldn't have needed someone to be here with me so I didn't look like a loser. I would've just showed up and told Dom to fuck off."

"Well, you did that yesterday, so I think you're good there."

"So did you," she says.

"Yeah, I did."

CHAPTER TWENTY-EIGHT

CALLAHAN

I turn my attention back to the screen and watch as the dwarves bust in on Bilbo's supper and can't help but laugh. *I get you, Bilbo. I don't like my supper interrupted either.*

Jonas pulls me to his side and I snuggle into him and wrap my arm around his waist. I'd love to know what happened to him, but if he wanted to tell me, he would, so I don't pry.

He runs his finger along my arm and plants a kiss on the top of my head. I sit up. "Going somewhere?" Jonas asks.

"Nowhere. I'm just taking off my robe. I'm getting a bit warm snuggled up next to you. You're plenty warm enough, so I don't need it." *I mean, that, and it puts your hands closer to my skin.*

He nods and I lean back into him and drape my legs over his knee. He puts his arm back around me, his hand resting on my hip, his fingertips brushing against the strip of skin between my tank top and shorts. He takes my hand in his and lays mine palm up on my leg and drags his fingers slowly up and down my palm and fingers. Between his fingers brushing against my hip and my hand, it's ultra-sensual and my heart rate starts to increase.

Good lord, he's not even really touching me and I'm already getting turned on? Either he's that good, or I'm that starved.

I lean my head on Jonas's shoulder. "Is it difficult for you?"

"Is what difficult?"

"Well, you said you go about three days between hookups. Is this difficult? Since it's been longer than that and the fact that I'm drawing this out and you don't know for sure what will happen?"

"No, Darlin', it's not difficult. Because I love foreplay. And this is pretty nice as far as foreplay goes. And I know if or when I do finally get you naked, you're gonna be begging me to fuck you."

My breath catches. "Well, that's a pretty bold statement."

He huffs a soft laugh. "Callie, I think we've established I'm a pretty bold guy."

I chuckle. "Oh, yeah. I'm aware."

"Is this difficult for you?"

"Incredibly," I say with a laugh.

He chuckles and plants another kiss on the top of my head. The hand on my waist begins a sweeping motion up toward my ribs and he hits a ticklish spot. "That tickles."

And just like he did yesterday, he says, "So, show me how to make it not tickle."

A challenge.

I keep my tone nonchalant. "Put it somewhere else." Knowing full well if I issue my own sort of challenge, he'll take the bait because he knows I want him to.

"Did you have a specific place in mind, Darlin'?" *God, yes. Everywhere, please.*

"Not really, just not there."

"Okay. Higher or lower?" I almost want to laugh, because I

know he wants me to be blunt and tell him what I want, but I like that he knows I like to play, and he's willing to go along.

"Lower." He moves his hand down to my hip and his thumb brushes just under the waistband of my shorts and I try not to picture him taking them off of me. I exhale slowly and have to turn my hand over to stop him from stroking my palm, because it's becoming too much.

"So, do Bilbo and the dwarves get the treasure from the dragon?"

"Sorry, you have two more movies to watch before you find that out."

"Darlin', I think I've watched about all of this movie that I can."

I can't keep the smile off my face. "Oh? Something else you'd prefer to do?"

He nuzzles under my ear and brushes kisses down my neck, scattering goosebumps along my arms. "There are several things I'd like to do more than watch this movie right now."

"Oh, and what's that?" I try to keep my voice even, but it's difficult with his lips and tongue and breath on my skin.

He stops and takes my chin in his hand, forcing me to look at him. "Do you want me to show you?"

And whether out of sheer curiosity to know what it's like to have another man's hands on my body; ones that, judging by the way he flirts and seduces, can be nothing less than expert. It could be that I feel wanted and it's nice. Or, it could simply be I'm more than a bit horny after over eighteen months with no one but myself for satisfaction. And, honestly, at this moment, any of these are good enough reasons for me.

I hold his gaze. "Yes, Jonas. Show me." I expect him to kiss me like he did this morning; deep and possessive. But instead, it's a soft, tender kiss, his lips full and warm.

I wind my arms around his neck and pull him closer to me,

my hands tangling in his curls as he deepens the kiss. He seems to devour me, claim me, and after a moment, I'm short of breath and wet heat pools between my legs and I press my thighs together trying to generate friction.

Jonas wraps his arms around me and pulls me fully into his lap. I break our kiss and shift so I'm straddling him and he pulls my face back to his and claims my mouth. His kiss is demanding and greedy and damn, how have I gone my entire life without having someone kiss me like this?

He grips the back of my neck with one hand and wraps his arm around my waist with the other and pulls me closer to him. His mouth travels down my cheek and neck and my chest heaves as I try to catch my breath. He nips at my collarbone and shoulder and grips my ass and grinds himself against me and I can feel that he's hard and I can't bite back a soft moan as I get just enough friction to make me want more.

"I like that sound, Darlin'. What other sounds I can get you to make?"

My voice is breathy. "Maybe you'll get to find out." I grip his face and return to kissing him, which honestly, might be my new favorite thing in the whole world.

His hand trails from my neck down my arm and settles on my waist. He brushes his thumb under the trim of my tank top and it sends a shiver down my spine. I expect him to run his hand up my shirt or try to remove it, but he doesn't. I expect him to grope and run his hands all over me and possibly try to get me naked and have sex, but he doesn't. It's as if he's content to simply kiss and brush my skin lightly with soft touches that are driving me wild.

And, sweet lord, the kissing. If he fucks like he kisses, I'm done for. I'll be ruined for the rest of my life. No one will ever compare. Foreplay, indeed. Damn it all to hell; I will end up sleeping with him. It's a foregone conclusion at this point.

Then the thought hits me: If I do this, will I be able to give it up? Because that's the price. I can have him but I can't keep him.

He's honest about what he's willing to do. He's been upfront about what he's able to give. And commitment, even for more than a few weeks, if that, isn't possible. And I would have to be alright with that. *Most likely, once we get back to Florida, you might never hear from me again.*

Three more days. That's all I might have him for. Three days to flirt and play and yes, fuck. Is that enough? Can it be enough? Enough to get under him and over him?

As bad as it sounds, I want to find out. And damn the consequences.

CHAPTER TWENTY-NINE

JONAS

Damn, Callahan can kiss. How on earth Dominic could kiss this woman and be content to have her for five minutes at a time, I'll never know. I don't want to stop. As much as I want to do more with her, and fuck, how I do, this is quite nice all on its own.

I can tell Callie expects me to simply move right along and feel up every inch of her, but in truth, I'm enjoying the simple act of kissing. Maybe it's knowing I still have three days with her and I can take my time and make this good for her. Because after what she's been through, that's the least she deserves. And that's all I can do for her.

I can make her feel wanted and I can make her feel good. And even if she decides to do more would be too much for her, I'll respect her decision and enjoy getting to do only this. I can't remember the last time I simply made out with a woman. I'd forgotten how nice it can truly be.

She feels incredible in my arms and under my hands and I could almost forget for a moment this thing we've got going isn't real. And I don't know what to think about that. I don't feel things for women. Not anymore. But if I could, I would want it to be someone like Callie. She's the exact right kind of woman I would want; the kind I should want. But I can't let myself do that. She'd only end up hurt. That's all I'm good at for the long-term: hurting women. And so, I don't do long-term.

Callahan breaks our kiss and pulls back, her chest heaving. "Damn, Jonas." She shakes her head.

I rub my thumb along her now swollen bottom lip. "What, Darlin'?"

Her brow furrows in confusion. "I don't even know. I didn't know people could kiss like that. I know that makes me sound as inexperienced as I am, but still. What did you do, major in kissing in college?"

I can't help but laugh. "No, only a minor. You're no slouch, either, Callie; just so you know."

She chuckles and presses her forehead to mine. "I need to breathe for a minute."

"Sure. We've got time." I drag my mouth down her cheek and neck to her collarbone and flick my tongue over the hollow of her throat.

"You keep that up, I'm still not gonna be able to breathe."

"You want me to stop?"

"God, no."

I laugh and trail kisses across her chest and she arches her back. *Still easy to read, Darlin'.* I run my hand up her ribs and cup her tit through her shirt and brush my thumb across her nipple and it rises to my touch. I lower my mouth to flick my tongue over it through the fabric and she gasps, her fingers fisting my hair.

I move to tug her other nipple between my teeth and Callahan hisses. She leans back and begins to shed her tank top and I stop her. Her expression is questioning and I run the back of a finger along her jaw and hold her gaze. "I'm not ready to see you yet. I want to take my time and enjoy taking each piece of clothing off you slowly. I wasn't lying last night when I said five minutes wasn't even enough time to get you naked if you do it right. But I'm not doing that unless I can spread you out and show you what it's like to be fucked like you're supposed to be. To taste and tease and truly give you something worth remembering."

Her breath catches and her throat bobs as she swallows. She nods slowly, absorbing my words. "Well, you make a compelling argument. And you paint quite the picture." After a beat, she gives me a slow smile. "Care to give me a little more incentive?"

I laugh and pull her mouth back to mine. "Gladly, Darlin'."

We end up spending the next couple of hours simply making out and it is a test of my considerable strength and will to not go ahead and get her naked. By the time we leave the media room, we're both overheated and sporting swollen lips. Callie's face, neck, and chest are red from my stubble and I'm pretty sure I'm physically dying from needing a release.

When we get back to the bedroom, I say, "I'm gonna take a quick shower so I don't have to take one later."

She smiles knowingly. "Sure. Will it be a cold shower, you think?"

I raise a brow. "Care to come find out for yourself?"

She shakes her head and tries not to laugh. "Nope. I'm good. You enjoy, though."

"Are you laughing at my pain?" I ask, trying to bite back my own laugh.

"No, not at all. It's actually pretty impressive. Not the pain part; I'm sure that's not fun. But the fact that you can make out for well over two hours and not...just..." She makes a sound like some kind of explosion and opens her hands miming said explosion and I can't help but finally laugh.

I shrug. "It's definitely a challenge. But kissing you is fun, so I'll survive. I'm still gonna take a shower, though. Try not to think about me while I'm naked and rubbing soap all over my body."

Her eyes narrow. "How do you know I've not been picturing that all week?"

I smile. "Well, I was assuming you had been, but thanks for the confirmation."

She rolls her eyes. "You are shameless."

I walk into the bathroom. "Yeah, but you like it," I say over my shoulder.

CHAPTER THIRTY

CALLAHAN

After Jonas takes a shower, we go down and reheat some leftover barbecue and eat. I start yawning and he laughs. "Tired?"

I nod. "Yeah, I think I'm gonna have to take a nap to even make it halfway through Maddie's party."

He raises a brow. "Need someone to cuddle you?"

"I'm definitely not opposed, but you don't have to. If you'd rather read or watch TV or something, that's fine."

He rolls his eyes. "You think I'm gonna turn down an opportunity to have a beautiful woman in my arms? Not happening."

I shrug. "Suit yourself."

We clean up our dishes and walk back up the stairs to the bedroom. I turn down the covers on the bed and Jonas strips down to his boxer briefs and my mouth falls open. "That's not fair. You can't lie here with me half-naked and expect me to nap."

"I don't want to wrinkle those clothes. I have to wear them out later when I come rescue you or whatever. I'll be good if you will." He gives me a smug smile. "And I think we both know I have superior self-control."

I narrow my eyes. "Fine." I tug my shorts down and stand there in only a pair of panties and my tank top and Jonas's eyes go wide.

"Callie, that's playing dirty."

I bat my eyelashes. "I don't know what you're talking about. You have superior self-control, remember? Shouldn't be a problem for you, right?" His jaw clenches and I almost want to laugh, but I keep my expression neutral.

"Fine," he says and we climb under the covers. I put my glasses on the nightstand and lie on my side. Jonas pulls me toward him and I can't help but smile, because in spite of us goading one another, he's still willing to snuggle up to me and it's adorable.

I roll over to face him and rest my head on his chest and throw my leg over his. "You're cute, you know that? Especially when I surprise you with something I do. You should have seen your face when I dropped my shorts," I say and run my fingers down his ribs.

He looks down at me. "You're cute, too. Can you see at all without your glasses? When you look at me, am I blurry?"

I shake my head. "No, you're pretty clear. It's stuff any farther away I have trouble with. If I wanted to read, I'd have to hold the book pretty close and forget making out anything more than about ten feet in front of me."

"Well, I can see you alright."

I chuckle. "I'm glad for that, I guess."

"I've not seen your eyes without your glasses. I saw your face the other night when you'd fallen asleep and I took them off so they didn't get damaged, but I haven't seen your eyes open without them."

"And? What do you think?"

He brushes a hair off my forehead. "I think you're beautiful either way."

"Thanks. Sometimes, I think about getting Lasik or something, but I'm freaked out at the idea of someone cutting into my eye with a laser. So, I'll keep wearing glasses, I guess. I occasionally wear contacts, but not too often, and I can't wear them for longer than a few hours because my eyes dry out, but I have them."

"Probably the only good thing about you not wearing your glasses right now is that I can do this and not have to worry about my nose smudging them." He rolls us until we're both on our sides and he kisses me deeply and desire coils low in my belly. With everything we did earlier, I'm so on edge, if he got anywhere near my vagina, I'd probably climax immediately.

I run my hands down his chest and abs and around to his ass, which I've wanted to get my hands on for days. It's strong and muscled and feels amazing under my touch. I throw my leg around Jonas's hip and pull him into me.

He trails his fingers up the outside of my thigh and grips my hip. I move my mouth down his neck and chest and tug his nipple with my teeth and he lets out a soft hiss. I run my fingers along the waistband of his underwear and he snatches my hand away. "Nope. That's not part of the incentive make-out package. If you decide you'd like to upgrade, you'll be handsomely rewarded, but until then, hands off the merchandise."

I chuckle. "Got it. Thanks for the clarification."

I finally do sleep for about an hour before I have to start getting ready for Maddie's bachelorette outing. Jonas is still napping, so I climb out of bed and throw my hair in a messy bun and jump into the shower, quickly washing and shaving all pertinent areas of my body before drying off and climbing out of the tub and wrapping myself in a towel.

I turn on my curling iron and while it heats up, I walk into the bedroom and notice Jonas is up and dressed and his eyes follow me across the room. "Darlin', that's cruel."

I wink. "Sorry, I forgot my underwear." I pull my bra and panties from the dresser and my dress and shoes from the closet and walk back into the bathroom and drop the towel as I shut the door. I can't wipe the smirk off my face as Jonas speaks through the closed door.

"Oh, Callie, that was dirty."

"Well, you did it first. Payback is a bitch, *Darlin'*." The sound of his laughter grows faint as he walks away from the door.

I don my tight, black mini-dress with wide shoulder straps and a low scoop neck and style my hair until I have large curls cascading down my back. I do a simple winged liner and thick mascara and dark, red lipstick. I examine my appearance and find that I like the way I look. What will Jonas think when he sees me? I'm dressed what I would consider to be sexy, and I can't help but hope he'll want me when he sees me. Because although I can't keep him, I've determined I will have him, and it will be tonight, because I'm dying and I want him so badly I can't think straight.

I give myself one last look in the mirror and spritz on some of my favorite perfume and open the door. Jonas looks up from his phone and does a double take, which makes me blush. "Do I look okay?"

He stands and walks over to me. "Darlin', okay is nowhere near the vicinity of where you are. You look hot. I'm tempted to follow you to that bar so no one gets any ideas about who you're coming home with tonight."

My blush deepens under his compliments. "Well, I'll text

you, because I'm not staying at this thing any longer than I have to." I hold Jonas's gaze. "I have other, more pressing, plans for tonight."

He sticks his hands in his pockets. "Oh, really? Anything I might be interested in?"

"I think you'll be interested in what I have on under this dress," I offer.

He smirks. "That so? Are you telling me you want me to take it off you, Callie?"

I look him up and down. "That's exactly what I'm saying, Jonas."

His eyes drill into mine. "Is that all you want me to do; take it off? Or do you also want me to do more than that?"

My heart races at the thought of *more*, but I don't take my eyes from his. "Definitely more."

His expression softens. "And you're okay with that? And what it would mean? And what it wouldn't?"

"I wouldn't say I was if I wasn't."

He nods. "Okay. Just wanted to be sure."

I put my hand on his chest. "I know. And I appreciate you being so adamant about consent and stuff. It makes me feel safe."

He takes my hand and brushes a kiss across my palm. "I want you to feel safe. And wanted. And I want to show you a good time."

I huff out a soft laugh. "Oh, I have no doubts about you showing me a good time." I bite my lip. "If you fuck half as good as you kiss, I'm sure it will be an extremely memorable next few days." And knock me over with a feather, Jonas blushes. Like, all the way to the tips of his ears and down his chest and my mouth falls open in shock. "Are you blushing? Actually blushing because of something I said? Now, that's a first. Mark it down, Callahan made Jonas blush."

He laughs. "It's not an unheard of thing. Nana makes me blush quite a bit when she talks about all the elderly people getting it on."

I burst out laughing. "I bet your nana is a hoot."

He nods. "She is."

I check Jonas's watch and frown. "I don't want to go but I guess I have to." I sigh and walk over to the closet and pull out a small beaded clutch. I shove in my phone, lipstick, ID, and credit card. "Walk me down?"

He nods and we leave the bedroom to walk downstairs. Maddie is waiting in the living room, sipping a glass of wine.

"Hanny. About time. You look pretty. Are you ready?"

"Yep. Is the Uber on its way?"

Maddie says, "I got a limo. All the other girls got picked up in Knoxville; they're coming to get us and then we're headed out. They should be here in a minute. I talked with Taylor a few minutes ago and they were pulling in on the road. Jonas, what are you getting up to tonight? I'm sure you could crash Dom's bachelor party if you wanted."

I snort and try to cover it up with a fake cough. He answers casually, "Actually, I've got some reading I've got to get done tonight. Getting ready for the new school year and all that." He winks at me. "I brought work stuff with me but Callie's kept me pretty busy this week. But I've got to get this book finished."

"Oh, really? What book is it?"

I look at Jonas, interested to see how he's gonna spin a smutty priest book. He says, "It's a religious studies book." I try not to laugh at his explanation.

Maddie doesn't appear to notice my efforts to keep my features neutral. "Huh. I wouldn't think you would be able to bring religion into the classroom."

"We aren't, but I still like to study up in case I have a

student with specific religious observances or something like that."

I'm actually impressed with his ability to think on the fly. Maddie nods. "Wow, that's considerate of you. Well, Hanny, I guess we better go. I think I see the limo pulling in. Jonas, don't study too hard."

I turn to him and wrap my arms around his neck. "I hope you study real hard."

He pulls me to him and brushes a kiss down my neck and whispers in my ear, "Oh, I will. I'll also be thinking of all the ways I can get this dress off of you, too. And all the places I plan to kiss and lick and touch. Try not to miss me too much, Darlin'." Heat rushes through every inch of my body and I blow out a shaky breath. Jonas kisses my forehead before turning me around and giving me a playful slap on the behind. "Have fun, ladies."

CHAPTER THIRTY-ONE

JONAS

I was not prepared in the least to see Callahan in that dress. Although she still looked like her beautiful self, she also looked confident and sexy and I keep checking my phone every ten minutes to see if she's texted me to come get her.

After what she said, I can't think of anything other than what it's gonna be like when we get back here tonight and I'm nervous in a way I haven't been in longer than I can remember. I don't know if it's because we've basically had four days of foreplay and there's a lot of buildup or if it's something different. I don't want to think about what the *something different* might be.

I walk down to the kitchen to grab a beer in an attempt to calm myself down a bit. Callie's mother is in the kitchen making a sandwich. And the sight of a woman like Vicki Benson making a simple peanut butter sandwich strikes me as odd. She looks up at me. "Good evening, Jonas. How are you?"

"I'm doing well, Mrs. Benson. How are you? Did you enjoy the dance lesson today?"

She smiles. "Please, call me Vicki. It was fun to watch

anyway. Dominic seems to be a bit on the clumsy side on the dance floor, but I'm sure they'll get everything worked out before Friday. Are you on your own tonight?"

"Yes, ma'am. Maddie stole Callie away for the night but it's alright. I hope she has fun."

"Callahan seems happy."

"I hope she is."

She levels me with a gaze. "You seem to make her much happier than she's been over the past five years. I can see it in her eyes. She's not been appreciated and treated the way she should have been before now."

Vicki knows about Dom? Well, damn. "I'm glad I can help her be happy."

"You appear to be happy, too. I mean, I understand I don't know you well at all, but the way you look at my daughter and the way you seem to care for her overjoys me as her mother. I don't want to meddle, of course, but I hope we've not done anything that might scare you off coming around in the future."

"No, ma'am. Your family is great. I've felt very welcomed here this week. I appreciate you all making me feel so at home."

"It's been our pleasure. To see Callahan smile and laugh the way she has since you all got here has truly been a blessing. So, thank you, Jonas."

"Of course. Your daughter is an exceptional woman."

She smiles warmly. "On that, we can agree. Well, I'll let you get back to your evening. Have a good night."

"You as well, Vicki." I watch her take her sandwich down a hallway and I open the fridge and take out a bottle of beer and open it and think about the fact Callahan's mother probably knew about Dominic. I'm sure Vicki was hoping someday, Dominic would step up and do right by Callie, but looks like she also wasn't fooled by him. Good for her.

Once I finish my beer, I put the bottle in the recycle bin

and walk back upstairs and sit down on the sofa with my phone to read.

After about an hour, I'm utterly shocked by the part of the book I just read and shoot off a quick text to Callahan.

> Jonas: I got past the part in the book about the sacramental oil. I am SHOOK!

My phone vibrates a moment later with a response.

> Callahan: Right?! I hope you're not getting any ideas about that. That is not on the table.

I laugh and send a quick response back.

> Jonas: No worries about that, Darlin'. How's the party?

> Callahan: Sweet lord. Am I actually the same age as all these girls? I feel like a chaperone. And Maddie is 3/4 wasted. She's gonna be so hung over tomorrow. I don't know how she got so drunk so fast.

> Jonas: You're not drunk, are you? I'd hate to have to not get you naked because you're too tipsy.

> Callahan: Nope. I'm not risking you not taking this dress off and seeing what's under it by getting smashed.

> Jonas: I'll happily smash with you.

> Callahan: Good lord. [Eye roll emoji].
> Although, yes, please.

> Jonas: Do you need me to make a scene yet?

Callahan: Keep it in your pants. Give me
about another hour?

Jonas: Sure. Drop a pin and I'll be there.

Callahan: Sure thing. See you soon. XOXO

CHAPTER THIRTY-TWO

CALLAHAN

After receiving that text from Jonas, I'm still nursing my first glass of wine, watching the clock. When would it be acceptable for me to text him to come get me without it seeming like I'm too eager? I'm filled with nervous anticipation for what the night holds and I can't get him off my mind.

Maddie and her sorority sisters keep trying to get me to do the shots a lot of people keep buying for us in honor of Maddie's bachelorette party, but I find the possibility of Jonas getting me naked a lot more appealing than any drink at this moment.

Maddie's maid of honor, Taylor, picked a bar smack dab in the middle of Pigeon Forge. Luckily, for a Wednesday night, it's not too busy, but the girls are all gonna be sorry tomorrow. I've never seen so many shots and cocktails being dropped off at one time.

Maddie, whose dark red curls are pinned back from her face and her makeup is starting to smudge from sweat, is the drunkest of all. Is she only enjoying herself, or is it something more? She stumbles over and plops down next to me. Her skirt is riding up and, at this point, is barely covering her ass.

"Hanny! There you are." Her voice is slurred and she throws her arms around me. "I'm so glad you're here. I thought after everything that happened, you'd never want to speak to me again."

I chuckle and brush her hair back off her shoulders. "What do you mean, Maddie? I wouldn't miss your wedding."

She leans into me. "That's because you're a good person, Hanny. If I had been in your shoes, I don't know I could be as sweet as you."

Confused, I ask, "What are you talking about?"

"Dom. If I had been you, I don't think I could have showed up."

My stomach drops, unsure where she's going with this conversation, but I suddenly don't like it. "What are you talking about, Maddie? What about Dominic?"

She's apparently not too drunk to see the look of confusion on my face, though. "Oh, come on. You think I didn't know y'all were screwing all those years?"

My cheeks flame and my throat goes dry. "You knew? You knew what he did to me? And you still agreed to be with him? To marry him?"

"Well, yeah. I was ready to settle down and it's a good match."

My eyes burn with angry tears. "Maddie, how could you do this to me? Do you know how badly I've been hurt by Dominic? I thought all these years you didn't know. That if you did, you'd never be with him after what he did to me."

She rolls her eyes. "Oh, come on, Callahan. You have a great guy now. What do you care?"

"What do I care? I'm supposed to be okay with the fact that

my cousin, who is like a sister to me, was okay with me getting my heart ripped out and stomped on? Because at least it's a good match for you, right? Does Dominic know you knew about us?"

She snorts. "Please. No, he didn't know I knew. He's not the brightest, you know. He's handsome, but not a lot going on up top. Not real good in bed, either, but I guess you know that. Good thing I've got a good vibrator, right?" She laughs.

"So how did you know about us?"

"I came up to visit you at school a few times and would call you and Dom to see if either of you were available to go out to eat or something. It didn't take much figuring out when you were both conveniently busy at the same time. And I saw you going into his apartment and come out a little while later looking like you'd been fucked." My face burns with humiliation and rage and I pull my phone out of my purse with shaky hands.

Callahan: Come now. 911. Please.

I drop a pin at my location and send it to Jonas, his response almost immediate.

Jonas: On my way.

I turn to Maddie, who's starting to nod off. I stand and pick up my bag from the table and go wait at the bar for Jonas. I order a glass of wine and sip it as I try not to cry knowing that Maddie knew. She knew everything and she didn't care. I feel like a complete fool.

Jonas arrives about twenty minutes later and comes up to me at the bar. When he sees my face, his expression turns concerned and he takes my chin in his hand. "What's wrong, Callie?"

I shake my head. "Can we go, please? I can't be here anymore."

He takes my hand. "Of course. Are you safe? Did someone hurt you?"

I snort. "Not physically." When he opens his mouth, I hold up my hand to stop whatever he's getting ready to say. "I'm fine. Honestly, I just can't be here anymore."

He nods. "Do we need to pay your tab?"

"No, it's all on uncle Lance's card."

"Okay. Let's go. Do you need to say goodbye?"

I try to keep my anger in check. "No."

He examines my face and his jaw clenches at the sight of whatever expression I wear. "Alright, Darlin'. Let's go home."

I nod and we walk out of the bar. He opens my door and I climb into the car and he gets behind the wheel, but doesn't start the engine. "Do you want me to ask?"

"Not yet. Please, Jonas. I need to wallow for a minute."

"Okay. Do you need wallowing music? I've got a hell of a playlist."

I look at him, my expression skeptical. "You have a playlist specifically for wallowing?"

He shrugs. "I mean, I call it my big sad playlist, but sure."

I smile in spite of myself and what just happened. "Actually, no. Do you have any rage music? Because that might fit better."

"Yikes. Rage. Sure. I can do rage." He taps his phone screen and plays some heavy metal and I nod.

"Thank you. That's perfect. Who is this?"

"It's Slipknot."

"Awesome. Can we go home?"

"Sure."

I'm quiet on the way home and Jonas doesn't pry and doesn't try to get me to talk, which is strange for him in my experience, but I appreciate him giving me a few minutes to process what happened. When we get to the house, we walk in and I'm thankful no one is in the living room. Jonas puts his arm around me as we walk up the stairs and into the bedroom.

I slip my shoes off and plop down on the sofa. He sits beside me and doesn't say anything. But because I know he'll have some sage words of advise and he'll help me work through this like he has everything else this week, I figure, what the hell.

"Maddie knew." He turns to me and I elaborate. "About me and Dom. She knew everything. She's known the whole time. And honestly, she might be worse than him in all this."

His brows knit together in confusion. "She knew? And she's fine with what he did?"

I blow out a breath. "I guess. She said she was ready to settle down and he's a *good match*. Fuck. She's diabolical. She even made a joke about him being terrible in bed. Which if I wasn't so thrown by everything she said, I might have laughed along with her about. But she doesn't care that I got hurt."

Jonas shakes his head in shock. "Does Dominic know she knows about y'all?"

"Apparently not. Somehow she figured it out and would come up to school to see me and also to visit with Dom and because we were both busy at the same time she put two and two together. I guess I shouldn't be surprised, but I thought I meant more to her than that.

"I should probably want to cry and be angry, but honestly, I guess this isn't even the weirdest thing that's happened this week, so maybe I can't process it yet. I don't know if I can look at her or speak to her again."

He takes my hand and gives it a squeeze. "Yeah, it might not sink in for a while. What are you gonna do if Maddie doesn't remember what she said? Didn't you say she was super drunk?"

My eyes go wide and I nod. "Wasted. I'll be shocked if she's not puking already. Her voice was all slurred when she was making her confession."

"So, what will you do?"

"Fuck if I know. I can't pretend like she never said anything."

He smirks. "Or, you can."

"What do you mean?"

"Well, what if she only remembers bits and pieces of what she told you or what if she thinks it was all some kind of drunken dream? You could be exactly the same as you've always been to her and it will drive her crazy thinking maybe she confessed, maybe she didn't."

I roll my eyes. "I don't know. I think it would be easier to never see, speak to, or acknowledge their existence."

He nods. "Yeah, but if you do that, she's gonna think you're still affected by it all."

"I am."

"Sure, but she doesn't have to know that. Let her think you could care less. You are the better person because at least you're not settling for some marriage that truly is a merger from what you said Maddie told you. That's not what you want. I know you. You want the real deal. And just think how miserable they're both gonna be. Seriously. They deserve each other."

CHAPTER THIRTY-THREE

JONAS

Callahan nods. "Yeah. So what do we do about the wedding?"

I give her an *isn't it obvious* expression. "Darlin', we go to the wedding. We dance and we laugh and eat cake and if I'm exceedingly lucky, you'll sneak away with me for a mid-reception quickie and it'll still last longer than five minutes."

She bursts out laughing. "Okay. Deal."

I raise my brows in surprise. "Really? Even the quickie part?"

She gives me an amused smile. "Especially the quickie part." Her face falls. "This is *so* not how I saw tonight going."

I nod. "Yeah, but that's okay."

She worries her bottom lip between her teeth. "Thank you, Jonas."

I tilt my head in confusion. "For what?"

She blows out a breath. "All week, you've supported me and helped me work through all my issues and honestly, I can't remember a time in my life where I felt as attractive and special as I have this week. And you've made me realize that someday

I'll find someone who'll treat me right, because I deserve it. So, thank you.

"I feel like by the end of the week, you're truly gonna need some sort of hazard pay for all the free therapy you've given me. If you ever decide to get out of teaching, you'd make an excellent shrink."

I shrug. "I double majored in psychology and elementary ed, so I took a lot of psych classes. Sometimes I feel like teaching is being a therapist. All these little people have big emotions and I try to help them work through them."

She smirks. "And here I thought you minored in kissing."

I laugh. "That, too." After a moment, I ask, "So, what do you want to do? It's still early enough we can go down and watch a movie or we can go and make a fire in the fire pit or we can put on our pajamas and chill."

Callahan shakes her head. "None of that was on my agenda for tonight."

"I know. But I understand if you'd want to reconsider what we had planned because of what happened with Maddie."

She scowls. "Why, so she can ruin something else in my life? I'm not gonna let her ruin my night anymore. I'm so done with letting them affect me and cause me so much turmoil. I'm better than that." I can't keep a wide grin off my face. "What?" She asks with a frown.

I shake my head. "Nothing. It's only, this is the first time all week where you haven't been concerned about what someone else is doing or how it's gonna affect you. You are finally thinking about what you want and what you deserve. It's great to see, Callie."

She shrugs. "I've wasted enough of the past five years being miserable. I don't want to be miserable anymore. I want to be happy. You made me see I deserve it. So, if my ego gets too big, it's all your fault."

I laugh. "I'll gladly take the blame if it means you're happy with yourself."

She rises from the sofa and walks over and locks the door and I sit up straighter, my heart giving a little lurch. She comes back to stand in front of me. "Jonas, would you like to get me naked now?"

I take her hands in mine and look up at her. "Is that still want you want, Callie? We don't have to. And I don't say that because I don't want to, so don't get in your head like I know you're prone to do. You've had an emotional evening, and I'm cool if this is not something you're up for." And as much as I've thought about taking her to bed, especially this evening, I'd much rather her be in a good place emotionally. I don't know what to think about that. The fact that I have this gorgeous woman standing in front of me, asking me to get her naked and I'm more worried about how she's feeling?

What the hell is wrong with me? Snap out of it and take this dress off her. Jesus.

She rolls her eyes. "Listen, I didn't put on this fancy underwear so nobody would take it off of me. I promise, you'll like it."

I chuckle. "I'm sure I will." I consider. "If you thought you were bringing Elliot with you, why did you have fancy underwear?"

"I've had these a long time. Been saving them for a special occasion. They've been in that dresser for years. Even before Dominic, so don't think I bought them for him; I bought them for me. They make me feel pretty, but I've never had occasion to wear them. So you should feel special."

I nod. "Got it. Well, I'm flattered you want me to see them. Even if you're not gonna be wearing them too much longer."

She smiles. "That's actually a good thing. The thing about lingerie; it's not made for comfort. So the sooner I'm free, the better." She bites her lip. "I mean, not too soon. I was kind of hoping you'd take your time and all that."

I tug her down into my lap. She hikes her dress up a bit as she straddles me and I have to remind myself to, indeed, take my time. I'd love nothing more in this moment to rip this dress off of her, but she deserves better than that.

I run my hands up her arms and grip her face. "Oh, I'm most definitely gonna take my time, Darlin'. You're too beautiful for me to not want to savor this. I want this to be good for you, Callie."

She bites her lip, her expression apprehensive. "I want it to be good for you, too, Jonas, but what if..." She trails off and blushes before finding her words. "What if I'm not? I mean, I know you've had a lot more experienced partners. What if I'm terrible?" She looks down, as if embarrassed.

Something in my chest tightens at the way views herself and how horribly she's been treated. She still has no clue how sexy and beautiful and amazing she is. I lift her chin. "Callahan, I'm not here to compare you to other women. I don't do that. I love women. And I love sex; I'm not ashamed of that. But if I didn't want to do this, I wouldn't be here in this moment with you, trust me on that. I'm here right this moment because I'd love nothing more than to get you naked and make both of us feel good. And I know there's no way you're terrible."

She rolls her eyes. "Oh, really? How can you know that?"

I smirk. "What was it you said earlier, if you fuck half as good as you kiss? That goes for you, too, Darlin', because, damn, you can kiss."

She blushes and her eyes trail down my face and stop at my mouth before coming back up to hold my gaze. Callie takes off her glasses. "Would you like to kiss me now, Jonas?"

CHAPTER THIRTY-FOUR

CALLAHAN

I take my glasses off and set them on the window sill behind the sofa. "Would you like to kiss me now, Jonas?" I ask, my heart racing.

"Fuck, yes." He grips my face and crashes his mouth against mine. It's not tentative. It's not tender. It's hungry and claiming and demanding and I melt against him. I wrap my arms around his neck and pull him closer, wanting him against me, hating all these layers between us.

Right in this moment, I wish I had told him to get me naked and get on with it, because after everything that happened this afternoon, this single kiss has rekindled the embers of the fire he started earlier and now, it's a blazing inferno.

He trails his lips down my cheek and neck and his mouth is hot and wet and when I feel his teeth graze my collarbone, it sends goosebumps down my arms. "You smell good, Callie. You taste good, too. Do you taste good everywhere, Darlin'?"

His words send heat coiling through my belly and I grind myself against him, needing friction in the worst way. Jonas tugs the straps of my dress off my shoulders and brushes kisses across them. He slides his hands down my back and grips my hips as he moves himself against me, hard and impressive, and I can't bite back a soft moan at the even minor sensation.

I tug his shirt over his head, needing to feel his skin under my hands. I run my fingers down his muscled chest and abs and grip his waist. God, he feels good. He's warm and strong and damn, is he beautiful. And tonight, he's mine. Even if it's fake. Even if, in a few days, I never see or hear from him again, he's given me something this week no one else ever has. He's made me feel desired and special and sexy. And for that, if nothing else, I'll be forever grateful for him.

He brings his mouth back to mine and seems to devour me. My heart is pounding and the need building in me is so acute, I'm not sure I'm gonna survive. He breaks our kiss and we're both short of breath. "God, Callie, do you know how bad I want you right now?"

I wiggle my hips and smirk. "I think I have a pretty good idea."

"Stand up." His voice is low and husky and sends a jolt of anticipation through me.

I obey and he rises from the sofa. He comes behind me and gathers my hair and settles it over my shoulder. He kisses the back of my neck and lightly drags his fingertips down my arms. "Jonas, you're killing me."

He huffs a soft laugh. "That's the plan. Just you wait. But I'm enjoying this, so you don't get to rush me." His teeth nip at a sensitive spot on my shoulder and I let out a soft gasp. "All these little noises, Darlin'. I can't wait to hear what you sound like once you truly get going."

"Why don't you hurry up and find out?" My voice is shaky and I'm so on edge, my thighs press together and I'm so wet already, I can feel it soaking into my panties.

He chuckles. "Nah, I'm having too much fun." The zipper

of my dress slowly descends and a shiver runs through me. I start to pull it off my shoulders and he stops me. "No. Don't take this away from me. I've been thinking about this all evening; unwrapping you like a present."

I drop my hands to my sides, but I don't like not being able to see him so I start to turn around. "No. Not yet. Stay just like that, Callie." His voice is soft, but commanding and I freeze. He pulls my dress off my shoulders and kisses my back as he slides it down. He takes his time tugging the dress off my body and my skin prickles as his fingers brush against my hips.

The fabric pools around my feet and I worry my bottom lip nervously between my teeth. I'm not used to being on display like this and I don't know how to act. Jonas whistles appreciatively. "Damn, Callahan, you've got a fine ass."

I can't help but chuckle, even as I blush. "Turn around, Darlin'. Real slow. I want to enjoy this." My heart rate picks up as I slowly turn to face him. He's standing a few feet away and I can't read his expression. His eyes travel the length of my body and I start to feel self-conscious and look down at myself.

I'm wearing a sheer, dark blue, lace bra and panties that leave exactly nothing to the imagination. Jonas closes the distance between us and lifts my chin until I look into his eyes. "Don't you look down. I couldn't say anything because I was speechless. You are exquisite, Callahan. Fucking incredible. Don't ever forget that, you hear me?"

I flush with his compliment and give him a tiny nod. He presses a soft kiss to my lips. "Absolutely gorgeous, Darlin'." He gives me a smirk. "Now, get on the bed."

My heart lurches and desire shoots to my core. "Wait," I say.

His expression changes to concern and he drops his hand from my face. "Okay. Did you change your mind?" There's no anger or anything other than genuine inquiry in his tone.

I let out a snort of surprise. "No. I just wanted to undress you. It's not fair you got to do a whole big production of getting me half naked and I don't even get to take your pants off? What kind of fair is that?"

He looks relieved and smiles. "Oh. Okay." He drops his hands to his sides and gives me a smug smile. "Have at it."

I take a step back and reach down to unbuckle his belt and brush kisses down his chest and stomach as I unbutton his shorts. Jonas lets out a slow exhale as my mouth moves across his skin. I tug his shorts past his hips and they fall to the floor. I rise to my full height and assess him, my eyes lingering on his hips and the sizable bulge in his boxer briefs. "Hey, my eyes are up here, lady." His tone is playful and I blush as I drag my eyes up to his face.

"You look pretty incredible, too," I say with a smirk.

He pulls me to him and his hands grip my face and he claims my mouth. His kiss is searing and steals my breath. I wrap my arms around his waist and he walks us back toward the bed.

When the back of my knees hits the edge of the mattress, I break our kiss and sit down on the bed and scoot back toward the headboard, pulling Jonas down with me.

CHAPTER THIRTY-FIVE

JONAS

Callahan and I lie facing each other for a long moment and honestly, I'm a bit hesitant to truly get underway because then it will eventually be over. I meant what I said to her; she's is exquisite. And I've seen my share of women, but Callahan, with her unassuming sexiness and vulnerability, makes me want to completely worship her and show her exactly how desirable she is.

I run my fingers down her arm and up her ribs and across her stomach. I trail them lightly across her hip and down the outside of her thigh. She lets out a soft huff and I feel the goosebumps as they pop on her skin.

"If you don't do more than just touch me like that, I'm about to combust."

I give her a soft smile. "Then I've got you right where I want you."

"Well, I know where I want you. And touching my arms and ribs and anywhere but where it matters is killing me." Her voice is a near whine and I'm loving it. I want to draw this out and make her understand what pleasure truly is; until she's begging.

"And where do you want me, Darlin'?" I take her hand and brush a kiss across her palm and up the inside of her arm and she lets out a soft breath.

"Jonas, I want your mouth and I want your hands and I want your cock. Please?"

My dick jerks at her words. "And where do you want my mouth?"

"Everywhere."

I quirk a brow. "You can't be more specific?" I lean down and brush a kiss across her stomach. "Here?"

"No, not there."

I smirk and look at her. "Higher or lower?"

She huffs. "Higher."

I roll us until she's beneath me and I kiss her lips. "Here?"

She shakes her head and her eyes are dark. Darker than I've ever seen them. "Higher or lower?"

"Lower."

I trail my mouth down her neck and chest and run my tongue under the lace trim of her bra and she inhales sharply as I rub my lips over her nipple through the fabric. It hardens under my touch and I flick it with my tongue and Callahan gasps and arches her back. I pull the cup of her bra down and swirl my tongue over the stiff peak and tug it between my teeth, making her hiss as she tangles her fingers in my hair.

I kiss my way over to her other breast and roll the nipple between my fingers before drawing it into my mouth. "Shit, Jonas." Callie's words come out in a moan and it might be the best way she's ever said my name before. Her bra is one that closes in the front so I unlatch the clasp and her gorgeous, full tits fall free.

And because I've wanted to do it since I first saw it, I can't stop myself from running my thumb over her tattoo. "Perfect tattoo placement, for sure." She gives me a shy smile and I lower my mouth again and continue to tease her; licking, nipping, and sucking until she's nearly panting. She pulls my face back to hers and her kiss is frenzied and desperate. I trail my hand up the inside of her thigh and when I get to her panties I almost lose it. "Jesus, Darlin', you're soaked. Is that for me?"

She nods. "You like?"

"Damn, Callie, I'm liable to come right now. God." She bites her lip and gives me a soft smile.

I grip the back of her neck and cover her mouth with mine as I thumb her clit through her panties and Callahan huffs into our kiss. I move the fabric to the side and work the swollen bud in lazy circles as she writhes against my hand and lets out a soft moan a beat later as I slide two fingers into her slick folds. Her hips buck as I stroke her inner walls and within seconds she's rocking her hips, grinding against my hand and her breathing has turned shallow.

She's perfect—so fucking perfect—and I can't get enough of her. The way she feels around my fingers. The way she sounds. The way she moves against me. The way her chest heaves. The way her mouth falls open with a soft sigh as she comes; almost as if she's surprised it's happened.

I gentle my movements and withdraw my hand and want nothing more at this moment than to feel her fall apart on my tongue, the ache in my balls be damned. "You feel so good, Callie. Can I taste you?"

"Yes. God, yes," she replies with a jerky nod, her breathing still labored.

Smiling, I kiss my way down her neck and chest and stomach and hook my thumbs into the sides of her panties and drag them down her hips and off her legs and I drop them on the floor. I look at her, fully exposed to me and have to remind myself to breathe. I want her so badly, but I want her pleasure more than my own in this moment. I want to make this so good for her; to show her what making love is supposed to be like.

What? No. Not that.

Callahan says my name, her tone nervous, and I shake the thoughts from my mind. "Sorry, you're just so beautiful. I wanted to look at you for a minute."

She flushes with the compliment and it travels down to her chest and torso and makes her skin almost glow. God, she is beautiful. And although I can't be what she needs for longer than this week, for tonight, I can call her mine.

I kiss and nip my way up her inner thighs as I hook her knees over my shoulders and Callie lets out these little squeaks that are immensely enjoyable to hear. But then, I lick a lazy line up her pussy and flick my tongue over her clit and her gasp sounds even better. And Jesus Christ, if I thought she felt good, she tastes even better. She's earthy and a bit sweet and I could just drink her up. Planning to do exactly that, I work my tongue in slow circles and draw her clit into my mouth. I'm rewarded with a soft *fuck* from Callahan that makes me smile.

Sliding my tongue lower, I explore her more fully and can't bite back my groan as I lick into her pussy, her flavor even more strong and fuck, I could happily camp here for days. But as much as I could do that, I want to feel her wrapped around my cock almost as badly. Bringing my fingers back into the mix, I thrust into her as I suck her clit between my lips. Her hands tangle into my hair; pushing, pulling, using my face for her own pleasure as she lets out low moans that have me grinding my hips into the mattress. Thankfully, seconds later, she's arching her back and clenching around my fingers, her cry a ragged huff as she orgasms.

She falls back onto the bed, her breathing labored and I kiss my way back up her stomach to her breasts and her mouth. She tries to turn away when I kiss her and I take her chin in my hand. "I love the way you taste, Darlin'. Have you not ever tasted yourself before?" She blushes and shakes her head. "Oh, you're missing out. You taste sweet, Callie. Can I kiss you?" After a split-second hesitation, she nods and I kiss her, so she can see that she does, indeed, taste perfect. She wraps her arms around my neck and deepens the kiss. After a moment, I pull back. "See?" She gives me a small smile and I lift a brow. "Condoms?"

She gestures to her left. "Nightstand." I roll over and sit up and open the drawer and pull out a condom. I stand and start to pull down my underwear and Callahan says, "Wait."

I turn and look at her expectantly. "Can I do it?" she asks, her expression curious.

Nodding, I hand her the condom. "Sure." She comes to the edge of the bed and tugs my boxer briefs down and my dick pops free and I have to take a deep breath. Callie rips the foil wrapper and proceeds to roll the condom on and I blow out a sharp exhale as her hands touch my cock. Once she gets it on, I make a quick adjustment and crawl back onto the bed.

I tug her hips down the bed and thank fucking God, I'm finally able drive my cock inside her and sweet merciful lord, she's perfect. She gasps, her nails digging into my sides and I'm forced to take several calming breaths because she feels too good already and I can't, after all this, blow in one thrust.

When I'm sure I'm in control, I pull out and slide back in; a slow, agonizing drag that's the best kind of torture. Callahan rocks her hips, moving with me, and I stand corrected because *this* is the best kind of torture. She pulls my mouth to hers and kisses me before pressing her forehead to mine, her breathing already shallow again. "Fuck, you feel good, Jonas."

Unable to even form words in this moment, I huff out a

sharp exhale and take her hand and kiss the palm. Intertwining our fingers and gently pinning her hand above her head, I look into Callie's eyes as we move together and I watch her face for a while as she loses herself in the moment and it's a glorious site. Her eyebrows press together and her nose scrunches and these soft puffs of air fall from her lips.

And somehow, despite all the women I've slept with in the past, this is different and I don't know how, but it is. It scares me a little because I feel like I *know* Callahan. I have to believe it's more than simply the time we've spent together this week, although that's likely a contributing factor. I can read her, sense her mood, know what she needs.

Like right now, in this moment, I can tell she's getting close again. Her breathing is becoming ragged and she reaches down to work her clit and after a couple of minutes, her pussy clenches around me and I'm unable to hold back my own release. She cries out and I follow right behind her with a deep, shuddering grunt.

I collapse next to her, my own breathing coming in short bursts as I come back to myself. I rack my brain trying to figure out what's wrong with me, why I'm so out of sorts all of a sudden.

Rolling onto my side, I look at Callahan, who has a sleepy smile on her face. "God, I'm gonna sleep so well tonight."

I can't help but laugh. "Glad to be of service."

She rolls over to face me. "Is it always like that for you?"

I prop myself up on my elbow and look at her more fully. "Like what?"

She searches for the right words. "I don't know how to describe it because good or great or fucking amazing all fall woefully short."

I laugh. "I don't know. But yeah, it was great." *No. Not like this. Ever.*

A few minutes later—after I'm sure my legs won't give out
—I walk into the bathroom to discard of the condom and clean
up. Callahan's voice follows me. "You have a fine ass, too.
Damn."

"Glad you like it, Darlin'."

When I come back to bed, I'm also tired, in spite of the nap
Callie and I had this afternoon. When I check my phone, it's
well after midnight, so I'm not surprised I'm so beat.

She walks to the bathroom and when she emerges a few
minutes later, I say, "Stop."

She looks at me, confused. "What?"

I hold my hands up like I'm framing a shot and say, "I want
to remember you, exactly like this. Naked and sated and your
hair falling down past those amazing tits. Fucking beautiful."
Because I do want to remember it. Forever.

Shit, Jonas. What are you doing? Stop it. This isn't you.

She blushes and rolls her eyes before climbing back under
the covers. "Well, you sure know how to make a girl feel good."

"Only the truth, Darlin'."

"Well, still, you did." She gives me a sexy grin and pumps
her eyebrows. "Really, really good."

I smile and lean over and drop a kiss onto her bare shoulder. "Anytime." I turn my lamp off and lie down and Callahan
does the same. I pull her into my arms and curl my body against
hers and something in my heart clicks into place.

Shit. I'm so fucked.

CHAPTER THIRTY-SIX

CALLAHAN

I wake up as I have for the past three mornings, with Jonas's arm draped around me. Except this morning, we're both naked, reminding me of what happened last night. It wasn't a dream. Thank God, because I would not have wanted to wake up. Five minutes. Jesus. How did I ever think I was only worth five minutes of someone's time and attention?

Jonas's breath is hot on my back and his hair tickles my shoulder. He feels so good against me, I don't know how I'll ever sleep alone again. I roll over in his arms and watch him sleep. His long, dark lashes rest on his cheeks and he looks younger than his age when he sleeps. His face is relaxed and his dark, curly hair is wild. Freckles dust his cheeks and he has some on his eyelids I hadn't noticed before.

He's so handsome. And that's not even a strong enough word for what he is. It almost hurts to look at him, he's so good-looking. Knowing I only have two more nights with him, although they're sure to be fabulously, earth-shatteringly amazing nights, I'm still dreading this ending. Because I don't know that it will ever be like this with anyone else.

Jonas *knows* me; which is insane when I consider I met him less than a week ago. But he reads me and is almost able to see what I'm thinking most of the time. And last night, when everything happened with Maddie, he was the only person I wanted with me. I don't know what this is, but I'm probably gonna pay for it when I get home. What did I tell myself yesterday, *damn the consequences?* Looks like there will be some. But I'll be fine. Because I have to be.

I roll back over, intending to get up and Jonas pulls me closer to him. "Not time yet. It's too early." His voice is husky from sleep and so damn sexy, I'm more than happy to stay exactly where I am.

I chuckle. "It's broad daylight. I have a feeling we slept pretty late."

"Well, it was for a good reason." He nuzzles my neck and brushes a kiss just behind my ear and it sends a shiver down my spine.

I snuggle back against him. "Yes, it was." His hand trails up my waist and cups my breast. "That's nice."

He chuckles. "Yeah, it is."

Reaching back, I run my fingers down his thigh. "What do you want to do today? We have the rehearsal dinner tonight, but other than that, we're free."

He nips my earlobe and it sends goosebumps down my arms. "I can think of a few things I'd like to do."

"Do any of them involve getting out of this bed?"

"Not really."

I breathe a soft laugh. "I might be persuaded."

His fingertips inch down my stomach. "Well, I look forward to trying to persuade you."

I'm about to put my hand on his to show him how he can *persuade* me, when there's a knock on the bedroom door. "Callahan?"

Jonas whispers in my ear, "Is that Maddie?"

I sigh. "Yeah. What do I do?"

"Pretend like she's not there?"

Maddie's voice comes through the door. "I know you're in there. I can hear you. Can I talk to you?"

"Just a minute." I get up and grab my glasses and my bathrobe from the back of the bathroom door and wrap it around me and tie the sash tightly before going over to unlock the door and stepping out of the bedroom.

Maddie looks terrible. Her skin is sallow and her hair has something in it I'm hoping is not vomit. I look at her and keep my tone even. "What?"

"I was worried. You left the party last night without telling anyone."

Reminding myself that I'm supposed to appear as though nothing is amiss between Maddie and me, I shrug. "Sorry, I came down with a headache and I had Jonas come pick me up. Did y'all have a good time?" And somehow, when I ask the question, it doesn't sound like, *did you have a good time breaking my heart.*

"Yeah, except I'm massively hungover. I think I puked up most of the booze and I remember almost nothing after those first couple of shots." I guess I should be happy she doesn't remember last night; even if, for a second, I thought she might be coming here to apologize for everything.

"Those shots will get you." After a beat, I ask, "Was there anything else?"

"Well, Mom, Lillian, Aunt Vicki and I are all going to get mani-pedis. I wanted to see if you'd like to come."

Like I'd willingly go anywhere to do anything with her after what she did. Not gonna happen.

"Actually, I brought everything to do my own nails and I was gonna do them tonight after supper. I think Jonas and I are gonna have a lazy day. My headache is still not all the way gone, so we'll probably just chill today. Thanks for the invite, though. I hope y'all have fun."

Her face falls. "Oh. Okay. Well, if you change your mind, we're going to that place out on the highway. We're gonna go to lunch after; call me and we'll tell you where we're going. I feel like I haven't seen you at all this week and I thought it might be fun to catch up. I miss you, Hanny."

Anger bubbles up in my chest and try to keep my features and tone neutral. "Sorry, Maddie; you've been busy. There's been a lot going on."

"Yeah, but all you've done is spend time with Jonas."

"Well, he came with me, so of course I'm gonna spend time with him. He doesn't know anyone here, I'm not gonna abandon him to go run off."

"Well, he can hang out with Dom and Dad and Uncle Alex and stuff so you can go with us."

I clench my jaw so hard my molars ache and I'm about to say something I'll probably regret when the bedroom door opens and Jonas steps out beside me, dressed in his sweats and tee shirt. "Sorry to interrupt, ladies. Callie, I'm gonna go get some coffee, want me to bring you a cup?" I look at him and give him an appreciative glance.

"I'd love that. Thank you."

He plants a kiss on the side of my head. "Sure thing, Darlin'. Be back soon."

Once he's moved past Maddie, I look back at her. "Sorry, Maddie. Maybe we can catch up some other time. Like I said, this headache is still pretty gnarly, so I'm gonna lie in bed and hope it goes away."

She sighs. "Okay. Well, call me if you change your mind."

Fat chance of that. "I will. Have fun."

I step back into the bedroom and shut the door and blow

out a breath as I sit on the bed. Bitter, hot tears come to my eyes and I do nothing to stop them. Jonas comes back into the room a few minutes later, two cups of coffee in hand. He sets the mugs down on the nightstand and crawls into bed with me. He pulls me into his arms and I bury my face in his neck and cry the tears I couldn't last night. Tears of anger and sadness and humiliation. In spite of the fact Dominic was the one who used me, Maddie's actions hurt more. And the fact that she doesn't remember confessing everything to me makes it so much worse. It makes me feel small and dirty and worthless.

Jonas doesn't say anything; he simply holds me and rubs my back comfortingly. Eventually, once my tears start to subside, I pull back and look at him. "Sorry," I say with a hiccup.

He takes my face in his hands and his eyes are soft and his expression is tender. "You don't have to apologize to me. I'm sorry you had to face her again so soon. I'm sorry she doesn't remember everything. I know that had to be hard for you."

I nod and bite my lip. "It's not fair. And not that I want Dominic or their life, because I don't, you know that, but still."

"The fact they get to be happy knowing how much pain they've caused you and it doesn't seem to affect them at all?"

I nod again and a tear rolls down my cheek. "I didn't do anything to deserve how they hurt me. How can they live with themselves? If it was me, I wouldn't be able to eat or sleep or do anything for thinking about wanting to make things right with the person I hurt."

He brushes my tears away with his thumb. "I know. You didn't deserve what happened to you. And someday, they'll get theirs. It might not be in some big act of retribution or something like that, but still. Maybe Dominic will get toe fungus and Maddie will have to live with him and treat his nasty feet. And maybe their kids will be hideous."

In spite of everything, I can't help but laugh and Jonas gives me a lopsided grin and presses a kiss to my forehead. "There she is. Able to laugh in spite of her pain."

I wipe my eyes and nose with the sleeve of my robe and shake my head in disgust. "How am I gonna get through today and tomorrow? If she talks to me, the whole time, I'm gonna be trying not to slap her."

He pushes a stray hair off my forehead and tucks it behind my ear before he slides his hand down the side of my neck to settle on my shoulder. He gives it a supportive squeeze. "Well, you'll have me to distract you and we'll people watch at the wedding and you can give me all the juicy gossip on all of your family members. And whenever you need a big distraction, I'll steal you away to make out in a corner."

I smile and nod. "I like that plan. You can't leave my side at all. I don't want to chance being alone with Maddie."

Jonas pulls me to his side and plants a kiss on the top of my head. "Deal. Consider me your shadow."

I lift one brow. "Does that mean you'll be pressed against me all the time? I might like that."

He chuckles and nods. "I think I might like that, too." After a beat, he asks, "So, coffee?"

I turn and lift our mugs from the nightstand and hand his over before taking a sip of my own. I sigh. "What do you want to do today? Did we ever decide?"

He shrugs. "Lady's choice; you know I'm down for whatever."

Right at this moment, I want nothing more than for Jonas to distract me with some incredible sex. I take a long sip of my coffee and put my drink down and stand. "You know, I think I need a shower."

He sets his own mug on the nightstand and smiles. "And would this shower be big enough for two, you think?"

I walk over to the bathroom and drop my robe and look at

him over my shoulder. "Only one way to find out." I start the shower and feel Jonas come up behind me, already naked. "That was fast."

He chuckles. "You don't have to invite me twice." He moves my hair off my shoulder and kisses my neck and I let out a slow breath. I set my glasses down on the sink and tug Jonas into the shower with me. I direct the spray so it's not hitting us in the face and I wrap my arms around his waist and pull him to me and lay my forehead on his chest. He rests his chin on the top of my head and rubs my back. "You alright, Darlin'?"

I sigh. "No, not really, but I will be."

He lifts my chin and his eyes search mine. "Anything I can do to help?"

I give him a sad smile. "Just you being here is enough." After a beat, I smirk. "An orgasm wouldn't hurt, though."

He laughs and nods. "I think I can help with that."

I raise a brow. "Oh?"

He nods and presses his lips to mine. The kiss is tender and sweet and makes me feel like I'm gonna have so many regrets after this week is over. But, I guess, that's "next week" Callahan's problem. "Right now" Callahan is gonna enjoy this while she can.

I deepen the kiss and press Jonas against the shower wall. I run my hands down his chest and abs and break our kiss. "Okay, seriously, what do you do to have these abs? Because you eat like a normal person. Do you work out all the time, because *damn*."

He laughs. "I do workout, actually. Not this week, obviously, but usually. I run and do a lot of CrossFit-type stuff. And I normally eat a lot cleaner than I am this week."

I shake my head. "Well, it's distracting, you looking like this."

He wiggles his eyebrows. "You like that I distract you."

"You're not wrong about that, but man, you're too perfect. You have no scars or weird moles or anything like that. Other than your tattoo, which is freaking sexy, you are unmarred. Normal people aren't like that."

"That's not true."

"Oh? Because I've seen all of you. You are the perfect specimen of the male form."

He looks away for a moment, then takes my hand and places my fingers about three inches above his left ear, his eyes coming back to mine. "You feel that?" I rub the area in question.

"Yeah, what is that?" It feels slightly raised and I frown in confusion.

"A scar." When I attempt to pull his head down, he doesn't resist and lets me get closer to examine the area. It looks to be about a four-inch scar that travels from his ear back toward his neck.

I let his head go and ask, "What's it from?"

"A car accident."

"Oh, wow. Was it bad?"

"Yeah. So, see, I'm not perfect. What about you? You don't have any scars or anything."

I scoff. "You mean, besides the ones you can't see?"

He holds my gaze. "Callie, don't do that."

I chew my bottom lip, feeling more vulnerable in this moment than I would like. "Those *are* the only ones I have. And nobody but me can see them, I guess."

He lifts my chin. "I see them."

I sigh. "I know. And it kills me. How do you do that; have me so figured out? It's weird."

He shakes his head and blows out a breath. "I don't know. I don't understand it either. Guess you're just transparent."

I bite my lip. "Only to you"

He runs his finger along my jaw. "Well, I like what I see."

I roll my eyes. "Oh, you like all my damage? I'm sure it's such an attractive feature."

"I like that you're working through it so you can be happier with yourself and your life. I think when we got here, part of you was still hung up on Dominic, but you're not anymore. When we got here, your self-worth was in the toilet. Now, you know what you deserve. It's been nice to watch you grow."

I smile. "It's all your fault. Like I said, when I get a big head, you'll have no one but yourself to blame."

Jonas laughs. "I'll gladly bear that burden." He wiggles his eyebrows. "And I can show you a big head."

I roll my eyes and laugh and swat him playfully and he grabs my hand and kisses my palm. His lips travel to my wrist and his tongue flicks over the tender skin on the inside and my breath catches and need pools low in my belly. "You know, you do magic things with that tongue of yours."

He nods and looks into my eyes. "Would you like me to work some magic now?" I shake my head and he quirks a brow. "Then what do you want?"

"Well, considering we've got about ten minutes of hot water left if my calculations are correct, I want a superb, but speedy distraction. Because I actually do need to shower."

He laughs. "That so? Well, let's not waste any more time then." He grips the back of my neck and claims my mouth with a deep, searching kiss and turns us so I'm against the wall. I crook my leg around Jonas's waist and he grips my hip and presses himself against me and I moan into our kiss.

He moves his mouth to my neck and reaches his hand down and uses the pad of his middle finger to circle my clit and I tangle my hands in his hair. Needing more friction, I rock my hips against his hand, my breathing turning ragged after what seems like seconds.

"Do you want me to go get a condom?"

I shake my head and pull his mouth to mine. "No, it's fine."

He takes my chin in his hand and looks into my eyes. "Are you sure?"

I nod. "Yeah, but thank you for letting me make the decision."

"Of course." He kisses me and lifts my leg higher. My exhale is sharp as he slams into me.

"Fuck," I say, almost breathless.

His thrusts are hard and relentless and the base of his cock rubs my clit with each movement and after only a few minutes, my pleasure starts to build and build and build until I can't hold back any longer and I grip his shoulders as I cry out with a gasp as my climax overtakes me.

"God, Darlin', I love to hear you come." He drives his hips into me furiously until a moment later he bucks one last time and pulls out with a soft grunt just before streams of cum shoot toward the shower floor to be washed down the drain.

After a moment, as our breathing calms, he slowly releases my leg and brushes a soft kiss across my lips. "Sufficiently distracted?"

I laugh and nod. "Yes, thank you."

We hurriedly wash up and just before the water turns chilly, I shut it off.

CHAPTER THIRTY-SEVEN

JONAS

After we get dried off and dress for the day, it's after eleven and we're both starving. When we start down the stairs, I ask Callahan, "You like grilled cheese?"

She nods. "Who doesn't?"

"Well, I'm about to make you the best grilled cheese you've ever had in your life," I tell her with a wide grin.

One of her brows lift skeptically. "You realize it's grilled cheese, right? Not a whole lot of ways to perfect it. It's pretty perfect on it's own."

I shake my head. "Oh, ye of little faith. Just wait."

She chuckles. "Alright. I patiently await the world's best grilled cheese."

When we get to the kitchen she hops up on the counter next to the stove and watches me move around the room. She anticipates some of the items I'm searching for and points them out or tells me where to locate them. I pull out a non-stick skillet and set it on the stove and turn it on medium. While it heats, I take two slices of bread and spread mayonnaise on them. "I don't like mayo," Callie says and scrunches up her nose.

"It's okay. You won't taste it. Promise."

"Alright, I'm trusting you. But I'll tell you if it's gross, because I despise mayonnaise."

I chuckle. "I have no doubt you will." I lay the side of the bread with the mayo face down in the skillet and layer on a couple of thin slices of sharp cheddar cheese and sprinkle a bit of salt on them. I spread mayo on the remaining two slices of bread and place them mayo side out on top of the melting cheese.

Callahan looks down in the skillet. "That's it?"

I nod. "That's it. But, I promise, it's good. I lived all four years of college on almost exclusively grilled cheese."

She laughs. "Spoken like a true frat boy. I'm sure there was also pizza and beer, too, right?"

"Yeah, but grilled cheese was cheaper."

She nods. "I gotcha. Well, I can't wait to try this remarkable Jonas Merritt grilled cheese."

Once the sandwiches are ready to flip, I turn them over and turn off the heat. "Now we wait."

"Well, what will we do while we wait?" Callie pulls me between her knees and wraps her arms around my neck.

"Well, I can't do too much in the three minutes it'll take for the sandwiches to be done, but I can do this." I trail kisses down her neck.

"Good lord, don't y'all ever stop?" Maddie's voice rings out from the direction of the front door.

I whisper in Callahan's ear, "Sounds like somebody's jealous. Looks like those five minutes she gets aren't a lot of fun for her."

Her laugh vibrates against my chest but when she turns her

face toward Maddie, her expression is flat. "I thought y'all were going to lunch after your nail appointment?"

"We were, but Mom forgot her wallet, so they wanted me to run back and get it so she can get a drink at the restaurant."

"Well, have fun," Callahan says, her tone lacking any sort of emotion.

Maddie's expression turns concerned. "Something wrong, Hanny? You seem off."

She tenses against me and I squeeze her hip in reassurance. "Nope. I'm fine."

"You sure? You seem like something's bothering you."

"No, just this headache. It's still nagging me a little."

She examines Callahan's face. "Well, I think Mom has some migraine meds if you need them."

She shakes her head. "I'm sure I'll be fine. It'll go away."

"Alright. Well, y'all are coming to dinner tonight, right?"

Callahan nods. "That's the plan."

Maddie smiles. "Perfect. Okay. Well, feel better." She walks out the door and Callie slumps against me.

"I don't know if I can do this; pretend like everything's fine. I just want to punch her. And I'm not a violent person, but I'm so angry, Jonas." Her expression is pained and she blows out a breath.

I nod. "I know. I'm sorry. Do you want to skip dinner tonight? I'm sure we can find other, more fun activities to do." I wiggle my eyebrows and she rolls her eyes and chuckles.

"Probably shouldn't. My parents will expect me to be there and I'm sure the food will be great, so I hate to pass it up. Promise me we'll sit as far as possible away from them."

"Deal." I pull a couple of plates down from a cabinet and serve our sandwiches. We sit at the large dining room table and I watch as Callahan takes a tentative bite of her sandwich and then her eyes go wide. After she swallows, she says, "You can't taste the mayonnaise. This is good. Do you normally cook for the women you hang out with?" *No. Never.* I simply shrug and she smirks. "I guess they aren't usually there to eat anyway, right?" For some reason her thinking of me being with other women bothers me.

For fuck's sake Jonas, stop it. This is not the time to be having some sort of weird glitch.

"No." I try to keep my features even so she won't see her words have affected me.

What is wrong with me?

CHAPTER THIRTY-EIGHT

JONAS

The rest of the afternoon and evening thankfully pass by without event and after a delicious supper at an upscale steakhouse, Callie and I are lying in bed but there's still a lamp on so we can see one another. I'm on my back and her chin is resting on my chest and I'm twisting her ponytail around my fingers. "Is this weird for you?" she asks.

"Is what weird? Lying like this? No, it's actually pretty comfortable, except your chin is kinda pointy."

She rolls her eyes. "No, I mean this; this whole thing. I know it probably wouldn't have been if there was no sex, but since there has been, is it weird since we're still spending time together and stuff? Since this is not something you do with the women you hookup with."

I can't help but chuckle. "No, I don't normally spend a week straight with a woman. And so as far as that goes, yeah it's a little strange, but I'm having a good time. It's not every day I get to hang out with a beautiful woman in a huge house on a lake. It's like a great vacation. Best one I've been on in a long time, actually. Is it weird for you?"

She shakes her head, her expression unsure. "I don't have anything to compare it to, so this whole week's been a little weird for me. But I'm having a good time, too. I know tomorrow is probably gonna be a little crazy, so if I don't get to say it, I truly appreciate everything you've done for me this week. You've been an excellent fake boyfriend and someday, if you decide to actually get into a real relationship, you'll be great at it."

For some reason, her words make me feel like she's already beginning to say goodbye even though we still have two more nights and it makes my chest tighten at the thought of leaving her. I swallow and nod, trying to keep my emotions in check. "Well, if I need a letter of recommendation, would you care to write one?"

She laughs. "Absolutely. I'll sing all your praises."

"Perfect." After a beat, I ask, "What's the schedule for tomorrow?"

She thinks for a moment. "Well, you and I don't have anything to do until the actual wedding. There will be a lot of caterers and other vendors in and out all day. The wedding starts at five, followed by a cocktail hour and dinner. Dancing and cake; all the standard stuff. I'll need to start getting ready by about three-thirty."

"Okay. Well then, that gives us most of the day to *not* see Maddie and Dominic."

She smiles. "Yes. And I'm hoping she's too busy during the wedding and reception to acknowledge me at all. Maybe when-ever they do the bouquet toss is when you can steal me away for that quickie."

I let out a soft laugh. "I can definitely do that. Although, you don't want to see if you're the next one to get married or whatever?"

She mimes making herself gag. "From *this* wedding? No,

thank you. It would probably be cursed. I don't want any of their energy rubbing off on me. If I had my way, I'd never have to see either one of them ever again," Callahan replies with a yawn.

"Sleepy, Darlin'?"

"I shouldn't be, but this week has made me lazy, so yeah."

I nod and pull her glasses off her face and fold them up and put them on my nightstand and turn off the light. Callie rolls onto her side of the bed and I pull her against me and press a kiss to that sensitive area just under her ear.

Her question rings back in my mind. *Is this weird?* Yes. Weird because I'm enjoying it way more than I should. Weird because I'm dreading getting on the plane Saturday to go home. Weird because I don't want to let her go. What does this mean? That I have real feelings for a woman? I haven't had feelings for any woman since...Well, since Leah. And I don't want to think about her. It hurts too much. Even after eight years.

CHAPTER THIRTY-NINE

CALLAHAN

Jonas is already awake when I come to and he's kissing my neck. "Oh, that's nice." My voice is husky from sleep and he's running a hand up my thigh. "Exceptionally nice. But can I brush my teeth first?"

"Nah, we won't kiss."

I scoff. "What fun would that be? I like kissing you. I don't want to deprive myself of that pleasure."

He sighs. "Yeah, that part is pretty nice. Alright."

We both hop out of bed and go into the bathroom and race to brush our teeth. He stands behind me and reaches around me to dip his free hand into the front of my shorts. As he uses his fingers to search out my clit, I brace myself on the sink and concentrate on finishing my task. I can't stifle the moan that wells up my throat and I back up and wiggle my ass against him and he slides a finger into my pussy.

Knowing my dental hygiene is a lost cause at this point, I hurriedly rinse my mouth and toss my toothbrush onto the sink and round on Jonas who is spitting his toothpaste into the basin. I push him against the bathroom wall and grab his face and kiss him deeply. His hands skim under the hem of my tank top before he tugs it over my head and pulls my mouth back to his.

I trail my hands down his chest and abs to his pants and I slip my hand inside and wrap my fingers around his cock and stroke him until he's hard and he lets out a soft groan. I kiss my way down his chest and stomach and drop to my knees. I tug his pants down his hips until his dick pops free and I take him in my mouth.

Jonas exhales sharply and I swirl my tongue around the head of his cock and work my hands and mouth together and his hips buck, driving himself deeper and he lets out a soft, *shit, Darlin'*, that makes me chuckle as his fingers tangle into my hair.

When my tongue flicks the underside of his cock, he hisses. "Callie, stop." When I don't, a few seconds later, he wraps his hand in my ponytail and tugs me back to my feet. His brown eyes look almost black and they're hot and full of want. He crashes his mouth against mine and backs me against the bathroom counter. He yanks my shorts down and they fall to the floor.

He cups my breast and rolls the nipple between his fingers and I let out a soft, *fuck me*, and I'm not sure if I'm requesting or only commenting on how good this is.

He huffs a laugh. "Happily." He pulls back and holds up one finger. "Don't move." He runs back into the bedroom and I hear him open a drawer and then slam it a second later. He's ripping the condom wrapper with his teeth as he comes back and rolls it down before he even gets back to me. "You made quick work of that," I say with a smile.

He kisses me and then turns me around to face the mirror. "Hold on to something, Darlin'." Heat surges through me with his words as he nudges my legs farther apart. He grips my hips and I gasp as he slams me. I hang on to the edge of the sink as he drives into me over and over and my breathing turns ragged and a strong orgasm begins to build inside me.

Jonas tugs my ponytail. "Look at me, Callie." I look up at the mirror and our eyes lock in our reflection. Seeing him like this makes things more intense and when he reaches around to work my clit, my climax swiftly finds me with shuddering gasps and my pussy clenches as I let go.

Several strong thrusts later, Jonas finds his own release and lets out a guttural groan and drops his forehead to my back. After a moment, he trails kisses across my shoulder blades as he pulls away from me.

Well, looks like I got to find out what it was like to have him bend me over a counter and fuck me. Definitely did not disappoint.

After we get cleaned up and dress for the day, I start gathering up all my dirty clothes from the week. "Want me to throw your stuff in with mine so you don't have to do laundry when you get home?" Jonas looks unsure and I laugh. "It's only laundry, not a declaration. It's not a big deal, I don't have enough for a full load, but if you want to wait till you get home, be my guest."

After a moment, he shrugs. "Sure. Okay, yeah." He pulls his dirty clothes from his suitcase and I pull the hamper from next to the dresser and he tosses his things in.

I nod. "Okay. Be right back."

"I'll go with you. I'm gonna fix some coffee and go out to the porch. Want a cup?"

I smile. "Thanks, that'd be great." I carry the basket down to the laundry room and find my mother pulling a load of towels from the dryer.

She smiles at me. "Getting a head start on packing?"

I nod. "Yeah, thought I'd go ahead and toss a load of laundry in so we don't have to do any when we get home."

As I pile the clothes into the machine and add detergent, Mom says, "Jonas seems like a good man, Callahan."

"Yeah, he is."

"And you're happy?"

I smile and nod. "I am."

"I like seeing you happy, sweetheart. You haven't been in a long time."

I'm surprised by my mother's statement. Because that's what it is. It's not a question. "I don't know; I guess."

She examines my face as if she's trying to see something there. "Can I say something to you?"

I brace myself for whatever she's about to say, because typically, whenever my mother wants to *say something* to me, it's some sort of criticism of my life. I nod. "Yeah, sure."

"I know for a long time, you probably thought this would've been your day. And for a while, I thought Dominic might do the right thing by you and be a good man."

My mouth falls open in shock and my cheeks flame with the knowledge that my mother knows about Dominic and me; at least in part. Mom gives me a sad smile. "A mother knows when her daughter's heart's broken, honey. I watched you pine for that boy for years and then while you were in college, I saw the glances between the two of you and how you all would sneak off together during functions.

"But then, that Christmas, when he and Maddie began dating, and I saw you at New Years, I knew you were hurting. And then, when you moved, I figured that was part of the reason. I wish I'd had words for you back then to tell you that you'd been saved a greater heartbreak, but I get the feeling you know that now."

I look down and nod. She closes the distance between us

and lifts my chin and gives me a genuine smile and brushes a stray hair off my face. "But seeing you this week, with Jonas, it's the happiest I think I've ever seen you. You're laughing and smiling and I've got to tell you, it's nice to see you happy. I hope you and Jonas won't stay away simply because you might have to see Maddie and Dominic together. Because I can tell by the way he treats you, Jonas is ten times the man Dominic is."

"Yeah, he is."

She smirks. "Looking the way he does surely doesn't hurt, either. He has quite the nice butt."

I blush. "Mother!"

She laughs. "What? I have eyes. And so do you. I've seen you watching him. You practically salivate when he's around. And don't think I don't notice how late you've been sleeping. If I had a man that handsome in my bed, I'm sure I'd struggle getting up, too."

"Good, lord, Mom. I'm not talking about this with you."

She chuckles but then her eyes soften. "All I'm saying is, good for you, honey. But I'll tell you this, I've seen the way he looks at you, too. He's the real deal, Callahan. Don't let him get away. Especially if you think you might truly care for him. Men like him, genuine, kind men, they're hard to find."

My chest tightens because regardless of the fact I care for him, it doesn't matter. After today, I go back to *only* being me and he goes back to *only* being him. And I'll most likely never see him again. But I simply nod. "Well, I'm gonna get back out there. Jonas made us coffee and he's waiting on the porch."

"Sure, honey. Go; have fun."

I feel strange after my conversation with my mother, because it's probably the best conversation we've ever had. But I truly can't believe she knew about Dom and me. Was there anyone who *didn't* know? Sweet lord.

I slowly walk up the stairs and out onto the porch and sit in my chair. Jonas is on his phone, but looks up when he sees me. "Don't tell me this house has a whole wing for laundry? Did you have to go through a secret passage or something? You were gone a while."

I chuckle and shake my head. "No, it's normal laundry room, thank you. I ran into my mom; we were talking."

He nods. "Well, you don't look too worse for wear, so it must have not been too bad."

I sigh. "No, it was actually good."

He smiles. "That's great."

I nod. "My mom thinks you're hot."

He snorts a laugh. "Well, thanks, Vicki. What else did she say about me?"

"That you're kind and genuine."

He rolls his eyes. "Well then, she obviously doesn't know me too well."

I level him with a gaze. "You told me not to do that, so you don't get to do it either."

"Do what?"

"Be self-deprecating. Because you are a kind and genuine person. You've been extraordinarily kind to me this week. You agreed to come here, knowing next to nothing about me and you stepped up and have been exactly what I needed this week." My chest tightens with emotion I don't want to reveal, lest I tell him how sad I am this thing is ending; even if I know it's what I agreed to. "You've made me feel smart and attractive and sexy. You've helped me realize I deserve to be happy and I hope someday, I can repay the tremendous kindness you've shown me this week." I look down at my hands. "You're a good man, Jonas, and someday I hope you find someone who makes you feel the way you've made me feel this week. I'm truly thankful for everything you've done for me."

I look over at him and he's looking down into his mug, his

elbows on his knees. "You don't owe me any thanks, Callie. I'm glad I came. You're an amazing woman and I'm glad you now know what you're worth, because you're priceless, Darlin'. And there's a guy out there who will see that and he's gonna be able to make you as happy as you deserve to be."

I try to swallow the lump that's formed in my throat at his statement and I think to myself, *I wish it could be you.*

CHAPTER FORTY

JONAS

Callahan is quiet for a while following our conversation and I
don't press her to talk, because honestly, I don't know what to
say. Everything I said was true. She's amazing and she's priceless. And someday, she will find a man who will make her
happy. And it can't be me, although a huge part of me wishes it
could. All I would do is hurt her, because with me, people get
hurt.

When I look over at her, she's staring out at the water and
her jaw is clenched and although I shouldn't, I reach over to her
and run my finger along her cheek. "You okay?"

She nods and although she smiles, it doesn't reach her eyes
and the color is the grayish-blue of when she's upset. But I don't
question it, even though I'm pretty sure it's the first time she's
lied to me all week.

She stands. "I'm gonna go switch the clothes over to the
dryer. They should be ready."

"Want some help?"

She shakes her head. "No, it's only laundry. One person
job, really. I know the caterers and stuff are gonna start arriving

soon, so it'll be a little crazy in the kitchen after that. I'm probably gonna make myself a sandwich. Want one?"

"Sure. Thanks."

After lunch, Callie is stacking our plates and glasses to take down to the kitchen. "Want to go for a walk? We have enough time before we have to start getting ready. Might be the last peaceful moment we have before the wedding."

"Okay," I agree. We walk down the stairs and she deposits the dishes in the sink and we walk out the back door toward the woods. I want to take her hand in mine, but she has them shoved in her pockets as if she doesn't want me to. As if she's trying to put space between us. *Probably smart.* "What time does the flight leave tomorrow?"

"Seven-thirty. So we'll have to leave around five."

I can't hide my surprise. "In the morning?"

She nods. "Yeah, so I was gonna say my goodbyes to my parents tonight, and if you want, we can leave tonight and stay at a hotel next to the airport so we don't have to get up so early."

"No, that's okay. I don't mind to get up early. And I can drive to the airport so you can sleep on the way if you want."

She rolls her eyes. "Last I checked, I've woken up before you almost every morning this week." I almost want to breathe a sigh of relief that she's finally giving me attitude, because that, at least, feels normal. I don't like this weird tension between us. I know it has to do with us leaving tomorrow and I wish I could comfort her about that, but we both agreed to this thing and the ending was part of it. Bad as I now don't want it to.

"Oh, I'm well aware of how we woke up this morning. It was great." I poke her in the spot on her waist I know is ticklish and she huffs a laugh.

"That tickles."

"I know. That's why I did it."

"I know." She's quiet for a moment but then says, "I think Elliot is gonna owe you way more than one semester of bus duty. And he owes me a whole month of dish duty."

I chuckle. "Maybe. But he was right, he said I'd have a good week, and I have, so who knows?"

"What reason did he give you for this week; why he couldn't come? He didn't explain it to me, only said he couldn't make it."

"I don't want to get him in trouble; you have to live with him."

She turns to me and quirks a brow. "Was it something stupid? I mean, not that I'm not glad he did it, but if I didn't have a good week, would I have been pissed at him?"

I duck my head and grip the back of my neck. "Probably. He told me he got invited to a party by this hot guy and didn't want to turn him down."

She nods and frowns, considering. "Yeah, that tracks. Can't blame him, I guess. At least he sent me the perfect guy to stand in for him. And besides, he probably would've blown my cover the first night by giving my mother tips on her floral arrangements."

I can't help but laugh. "Probably."

She sighs. "So, plans when you get home?"

I shrug. "Go visit Nana. I usually try to see her at least once a week. You?"

"Not much. I go back to work on Tuesday, so I'll probably hang around the house and read, do some grocery shopping. You know, boring grown-up stuff. Standard Callahan Saturday night."

I nod. "Sounds nice."

She rolls her eyes. "Sounds boring. Isn't that what you said nice was code for?"

I sigh. "Yeah, but you're not boring."

"I am when I'm not ensconced in so much drama. You only think I'm not boring because of everything that's happened this week. Otherwise, I am entirely boring."

"Well, if you're boring, then so am I."

"Jonas, you are the least boring person I know. You go out all the time, you have this adorable relationship with your grandmother. You work out so you can look like some kind of Greek god. You give insightful advice to women you barely know. And you're fantastic in bed. You are not boring, my friend."

"I'm not Greek," I deadpan.

She's caught off guard by my comment and laughs. "Well, you know what I mean. You are the epitome of not boring."

"Okay, well, if you think you're boring, do something about it," I suggest.

"Like what?"

I sigh. "I don't know. Get another tattoo. Get a piercing. Go skydiving. Take a risk. Do something crazy. Be impulsive. I know that kind of goes against the whole librarian persona, but I also know you don't mind to do something because it might piss off your family, so I feel like you've got it in you."

She nods. "True. Okay. Maybe I will." She smiles wickedly and it's not a look I've seen on her and it takes me by surprise.

"Oh, no. I don't know if I like that look."

"Want to help me do something evil?"

I stare at her in disbelief. "Oh God, Callie, what are you planning?"

"Something entirely vengeful and deserved. Will you be my partner in crime, Jonas?" She wiggles her eyebrows menacingly and I can't help but laugh.

I sigh. "Well, I did tell you I was here for you this week in whatever capacity you needed. If you need a partner in crime, I guess that falls within the parameters. Sure. I'm guessing you have something planned for Maddie and Dominic? It's not illegal, is it?"

She rolls her eyes. "No, of course not. But, it is perfect. We'll have to wait until dark."

"Okay. I'm in."

She throws her arms around me. "Thank you. Although I would have had to give you shit if you chickened out, Mister I-like-a-challenge." I pull her to me and press a kiss to her lips. "What was that for?"

I shrug. "You looked like you needed to be kissed."

"Well, I hope you still think that later after I put my evil plan in place."

I laugh. "I'm sure I'll think so even more by then."

I'm glad she seems to be in better spirits. I know tomorrow is gonna be weird and hard and I have to pretend to not be affected when I tell her goodbye, because I already know I will be. But I don't have a choice, because hurting Callie is the absolute last thing I'd ever want to do in my life. And if I stayed with her, if I gave her hope that we could be more than what we are for this week, she'd end up hurt.

CHAPTER FORTY-ONE

CALLAHAN

I know I'm acting weird. Jonas knows I'm acting weird. But neither of us is talking about the fact that I'm being weird, because we both know why. We both know I lied earlier when I told him I was okay. At this point, I've given up on the fact that he can read me. And sometime during our walk in the woods—right about the time I came up with my mostly harmless plan of revenge—I resigned myself to the fact that I'm gonna be hurt tomorrow when we part ways. But for now, I can pretend I won't be and I've gotten good at putting up a front, even if he'll see through it. But maybe he'll choose to ignore it. So, for this last night, I'm gonna enjoy myself and enjoy Jonas.

I can cry about things tomorrow when I get home. I can be sad it's over, even if I'll never be sad it happened. I can drink a shit-ton of wine and watch sappy movies and swear to gut Elliot if he tells Jonas how much this week affected me.

Checking my phone, I turn to him. "It's after three, we should probably start heading back. I need to get the laundry folded before I have to start getting ready." I drop my hands to my side and he takes one of mine in his own.

"Sure."

We start walking back toward the house and when we come in the back door, there's a crowd of people bringing in racks of food and cases of alcohol and Aunt Meredith is directing where everything should go. I step around different workers and into the laundry room to pull the clean clothes from the dryer and place them back in the basket before going upstairs.

I notice the shower is running in the bathroom and I debate for a moment about going to get in it with Jonas, but decide against, since I actually do need to take care of the laundry and get most of my stuff packed up before we go down for the ceremony.

I start folding Jonas's and my clothes, separating them into piles, when on a whim, I take the shirt he slept in the first night and stick it under my pile of clothes. Childish to steal his shirt? Probably. Okay, definitely; but I don't care. If I never see him again, I at least want some sort of reminder of what could arguably be the best and maybe the worst week of my life by the time it's all said and done.

I pile my things in my suitcase, hoping everything fits, and miraculously, it does. Jonas comes out of the bathroom with a towel wrapped around his waist and I have to remind myself not to stare and to breathe because being near him steals most of the breaths I try to take.

I softly clear my throat and gesture to his pile of clothes. "All your stuff is there; I'm gonna take a shower."

He nods. "Thanks. I guess we probably need to be completely packed tonight, huh?"

"Yeah, that's my plan. It's gonna be a late night and with us having to leave so early, it's not looking like we'll get much sleep."

I step into the bathroom and start the shower and pull my

hair up into a bun so it doesn't get wet. I shower quickly and shave and as I'm washing my face, Jonas sticks his head into the bathroom. "Callie?"

"Yeah?"

"Your dad asked me to go help move a few things for the wedding. I didn't want you to think I ran off."

I can't help but chuckle. "Well, if I haven't scared you off by now, I wouldn't expect you to abandon me before zero hour."

He laughs. "Yeah, probably not. I'll be back soon."

"Alright." I rinse my face and turn off the shower and dry off and wrap my towel around me. I dig out my old set of hot rollers from under the sink and plug them up. I pull on my bathrobe and go into the bedroom and pull on my underwear.

Returning to the bathroom, I pat on some face moisturizer and put in contacts since there will probably be photos taken of me tonight and I'd prefer to not have the glare from my glasses show. I proceed to section my hair and wrap the pieces around the rollers. After I'm done, I put on my makeup and go a bit more heavy on the eyes than I would typically wear.

Once I'm satisfied my face is suitably made up, I pull on my dress. It's a knee-length, thin, convertible dress that can be worn in many different configurations. It's a dark forest green that I've always felt compliments my skin tone and hair color. I decide to wrap and tie the dress so that it's one-shouldered and don't bother with a bra, since the way I have it wrapped gives me plenty of support.

I check my hair and find all the rollers have cooled and I begin to take them down. I back-comb the roots to give myself a bit of volume and finger comb the curls and shape them until I'm happy with the end result; which, to my mind, looks almost like something out of old Hollywood. At the last minute, I decide to pin one side off my face with a gold clip and step back to look at my reflection. I can't help but be pleased by the person I see in the mirror as I swipe on a bit of lipgloss.

I pull my shoes from the closet, a pair of nude wedge sandals, and slip them on. For jewelry, I've kept it simple with only a pair of diamond stud earrings my parents gave me and a wide hammered gold ring on my right middle finger.

I check the time on my phone and it's after four-thirty but I don't see Jonas's suit hanging in the closet, so I assume he's already ready to go. I start to head toward the door and as I reach for the knob it turns and Jonas steps in. He stops in his tracks when he sees me.

His eyes travel the length of my body and when he doesn't say anything, I instantly grow self-conscious and I try to swallow the lump of nerves that's formed in my throat. "You're gonna have to give me something to go on here, Jonas. Does the dress look funny? I had a bit of trouble getting it wrapped properly and I'm worried it looks wrong. I can always fix it differently. I probably should've gone with a different configuration." At this point, I know I'm rambling, but I can't help it.

He steps closer and takes my face in his hands and gives me a kiss to stop me from talking. "You're stunning. You caught me by surprise is all. They say the bride is supposed to be the most beautiful woman at any wedding, but Darlin', you've got her beat by a mile."

I blush and roll my eyes. "So, it's okay?"

He nods. "Yes, you look beautiful."

I bite my lip. "Thank you." I step back and look at him, for the first time taking in his well-tailored navy blue suit with a crisp white shirt and burgundy tie. His dark curls are stylishly messy and his stubble is trimmed to an intentional, sexy length. "Jonas, you look incredible. I mean, not that you don't always look handsome, but you in a suit? I'm a lucky girl tonight; you're hot."

He gives me a lopsided grin. "Thanks." He quirks a brow. "You're not wearing your glasses?"

I shake my head. "Not tonight. I'd prefer if there are photos of me taken tonight, that you're actually able to see my eyes, not a glare from a flash."

"Well, you look amazing, Callie, seriously. I'm not gonna be able to take my eyes off you."

I blush. "Well, I'll consider that a compliment. The feeling is mutual." I hold up my lipgloss. "Would you care to put this in your pocket so I don't have to take a purse down? I'm not bringing my phone, so I hate to carry a purse for only this."

He takes it from me and slides it in his pocket and holds out his hand. "Shall we?"

I take a deep breath. "Let's do it." Just before we leave the bedroom, I say, "We need to stop by the kitchen. Hopefully no one is down there."

He gives me a puzzled look. "Okay."

I wiggle my eyebrows in what I hope is a maniacal gesture. "It's all part of my evil plan."

He nods and rolls his eyes. "Right, the plan. How silly of me. Care to let me know what I'm gonna be involved in?"

I shake my head. "You'll have to wait and see."

He turns to me and searches my eyes with a soft smile. "Let's see, I've seen what color your eyes are when you're having fun, when you're upset, and when you're turned on. But when you're mischievous, your eyes are almost an icy blue. I don't know what to think about that."

I sigh. "Who knows? I guess it's like my own personal mood ring. Just be glad this icy blue stare isn't directed at you," I say in my most menacing tone and narrow my eyes, but I can't hold on to the seriousness and we both crack up.

"Oh, God, I hope that's never the case. I have a feeling you're about to do something truly heinous."

I feign total innocence and dramatically clutch my chest. "Who, *moi*? Why, soft, sweet, wholesome Callahan, do something wicked? Perish the thought."

Jonas laughs. "Well, rest assured if your career as a librarian ever goes sideways, you could definitely make it on the stage. That was a pretty good performance."

CHAPTER FORTY-TWO

JONAS

Callie and I walk down the stairs and into the kitchen and she tells me to stand watch while she digs around in a cabinet. I can't help but laugh at how sneaky she's being, but honestly, it's nice to watch her let loose and do something that might be a bit out of her comfort zone. All the tension from earlier appears to have left her and I feel myself relax as well.

"Okay, let's go." She walks up to me with a small paper sack in her hand. I look down at it and she shakes her head. "All in good time."

"Alright; you're the boss."

She smirks. "I'll remember that later."

I brush a kiss down the side of her neck and she leans into me. "You smell good enough to eat, Darlin'." Whatever perfume she wears, I'm never gonna be able to smell it again and not think of her. And I don't know whether that's a good thing or a bad thing. Oh, who am I kidding? It's a good thing. Everything about Callie is a good thing. Even if she can't be *my* good thing.

She lets out a soft sigh. "Do you think they'd notice if we

skipped this thing? I'd much rather do other things tonight." Her tone is suggestive as she tucks a hair behind my ear.

I bring her hand to my lips and kiss her palm and the inside of her wrist. Her breath hitches and her eyes fall closed. "How about this," I say. "Whenever you're ready to bail, you give me some kind of signal and we'll go. I love wedding cake, though, so if it can be after that, I'd appreciate it."

Her eyes pop open and she lets out a surprised laugh. "I'll try." After a beat, she frowns. "Fine. I like wedding cake, too. And there's no telling how much money they spent on the cake alone, so it has to be good, right?"

"Has to be. Your family doesn't half-ass things, remember?"

She rolls her eyes. "Yeah, yeah. Okay, but after cake, no promises."

"Alright. But, not even one dance? Dancing is fun." I nudge her playfully.

She huffs. "You've gonna end up talking me into staying for the whole thing, aren't you?"

I give her what I hope is a charming grin. "Well, can you blame me? Look at you; you're beautiful. It would be a crime not to show you off."

A blush creeps into her cheek and she smiles. "Jonas, thank you for being here with me. I would probably be miserable if you weren't." Her voice is low and her eyes are soft.

I don't trust myself to be honest and tell her there's nowhere else I'd rather be in this moment and no one else I'd rather be with. That I'd love to freeze time and stay right here, forever, with her. But I can't say any of that, because Jonas Merritt doesn't say those kinds of things. Not in a long, long time. So, instead, I brush a soft kiss across her lips and tug her out the front door.

We start making our way up to the barn and Callie stops in front of a black Audi sedan. "What are you doing?"

She looks around furtively. "Planning." I watch her open the passenger door of the car and then the glove compartment.

"Callie, what are you doing? Who's car is this?"

"Keep watch. I'm making sure it's the right one."

I glance around and seconds later, Callie shuts the glove compartment and then the car door, but I notice she no longer has the paper sack. "What did you do?"

She wiggles her eyebrows. "Nothing yet. I just wanted to make sure it was Dom's car. Because that's the car they're taking when they leave tonight."

"I don't know if I find this vengeful side of you scary or sexy," I say with a laugh.

"I hope sexy. But we have to go. Can't be seen around the scene of the crime more than necessary. And the wedding is starting in ten minutes."

We walk up to the barn and find our seats next to Callie's parents. Vicki turns to her daughter. "Well, don't you both look lovely. I was beginning to wonder if you were gonna miss the wedding." She lifts one brow suggestively.

Callie leans over to Vicki. "I tried to convince him to let me keep him locked away tonight, but he wouldn't go for it. Said he just *had* to take me dancing." They both laugh softly and I'm glad to see mother and daughter in a good place.

A few minutes later, soft music starts and Dominic and several groomsmen enter from a side door and stand next to the officiant. The bridesmaids make their way up the aisle, six in all, followed by two adorable little flower girls and a ring bearer, all appearing to be about four-years-old.

The music changes and the officiant signals for all guests to stand and everyone does and we turn to face the back of the barn, where Maddie and Lance are standing. Maddie looks pretty, but the expression on her face is not one of a woman overjoyed to be getting married. I can't resist leaning into Callie and whispering in her ear, "Look at her. She doesn't look like a woman super excited to be here. And what I said about you being the most beautiful woman here still stands." I squeeze her hip and she lets out a soft sigh. But since I can't see her face, I can't determine if it's sad or indifferent.

When we sit back down, I drape my arm over the back of her chair and brush my thumb absentmindedly across her shoulder. She leans into me and I take her hand in my free one and intertwine our fingers. For the first time, I look at the bridal party, since I don't want to be looking at Dominic or Maddie and I scan the faces of the bridesmaids, in their identical pink dresses. My eyes land on the bridesmaid to the left of the maid-of-honor and she's staring right at me. And she looks familiar.

I lean over to Callie. "Who's the girl next to the maid-of-honor?"

She looks at me and whispers in my ear. "I don't know her. I only know her name is Abby. She's one of Maddie's sorority sisters."

My heart lurches and I know why I know her. I've not seen her in eight years, and she would have been about sixteen the last time I saw her. Abby. *Leah's sister.*

Callahan squeezes my hand. "Everything alright?" she asks, her expression concerned. "Do you know her?"

I give her a smile. "Yeah, fine. I used to know her sister."

She nods but doesn't ask any additional questions. Soon, the officiant is doing the whole kiss-the-bride bit and everyone claps.

CHAPTER FORTY-THREE

CALLAHAN

Okay, so Jonas knows one of Maddie's bridesmaids. Or, according to him, one of Maddie's bridesmaid's sisters. Small world, I guess? But he looks rattled and I don't know what to think about that, considering he's been so cool and collected all week. Not even when Dominic cornered him or when we've had our little flair-ups, have I seen him like this.

But I don't have time to dwell on the thought, because Maddie and Dominic and the bridal party go back down the aisle and all the guests are instructed to go to the tent setup next to the barn for the cocktail hour.

Jonas and I walk over and I pick up a glass of wine and he gets a beer and we make small talk with my parents and I don't get an opportunity to ask about Abby or why he's acting strange. He keeps running his hand through his hair and he's antsy. I don't know what to think since I've never seen him nervous or anxious, but I can tell he is. Before we sit down for supper, I finally pull him to the side. "Are you okay? You seem off."

He gives me a quick smile and squeezes my hand and runs

his fingers through his hair again. "Oh, yeah; I'm fine." But I can tell he's not. I don't know if I can push him if he doesn't want to talk about this, since that's not what this thing is and it'll be over tomorrow anyway, so does it actually matter? So, instead, I simply nod and return his smile and we go sit at our table and eat our catered dinner and Dad and Jonas talk about all the shenanigans they got up to in their fraternity days and he finally seems to relax and then, so do I and we enjoy ourselves.

Once the cake is cut, Mom and Dad get us each a slice and we nibble our pieces and Jonas leans over to me. "See, the cake is good. Aren't you glad we didn't skip it?"

I lean even closer and keep my voice barely above a whisper. "I mean, I can think of some equally great things to do with you, but it's alright."

He raises a brow. "Oh, really? What did you have in mind?"

I hold his gaze. "Do you want me to tell you or show you?"

He smiles. "Show. Definitely show."

"Well, finish the cake you wanted so bad and I will."

He smirks and pushes his half-eaten slice away. "You know, I don't think I want cake anymore."

"Are you sure? It might be all gone when we get back."

"Have you seen you? Yes, I'm sure."

I laugh and turn to my mother. "We'll be back soon. Have Dad save me a dance, okay?"

Her eyes travel from Jonas to me and she nods knowingly and winks. "Sure, honey. See you later."

In spite of the blush creeping into my cheeks, I take Jonas's hand in my own and tug him toward the edge of the tent and as we pass the bar, I snatch an open bottle of champagne. We head back toward the house and I tip the bottle up to my lips and take a swig of the bubbly. When we get to Dom's car, I stop and hand the bottle to Jonas and he takes a sip of the champagne. "See, when you said *equally great things*, I assumed you meant there would be kissing and heavy breathing involved."

I laugh and glance around and make sure no one is looking. "Oh, there will be. I want to go ahead and take care of this. Keep watch?"

He nods and I open the door to Dom's car and pull out the bag I left under the seat. I pop the trunk of the car and Jonas gives me a quizzical look. I pull out the can of tuna from the bag and his eyes go wide. He whispers, "Callie, what are you gonna do?"

I smirk. "I'm gonna drain this can of tuna into the trunk of his car. They shouldn't notice the smell until they get back from their honeymoon in two weeks. You know, after the car has sat at the airport the entire time and baked in the July heat. It's not illegal, but it will be awful and it might take them a lot longer than that to figure out where the smell is originating from."

He looks surprised and nods. "Sufficiently evil. I like it."

I mime a little bow and pop the lid on the can and I start to pour the liquid into the trunk when Jonas stills my hand. "Wait, aren't they gonna put their suitcases back here when they leave tonight? If they open the trunk, they'll smell it."

I frown. "I didn't think about that. Shit."

He thinks for a minute. "Put the whole can under one of the seats. You barely popped the top on it and the smell won't get out that quick. It will smell a lot worse, too."

I shut the trunk and nod. "Okay. Fair." I stick the open can under the passenger seat of the car and make sure nothing is amiss when I slam the door and Jonas and I run toward the house. I'm laughing hysterically by the time we make it inside. I shut the door and lean against it. Jonas sips from the bottle. "I didn't think you liked wine."

He shrugs. "Champagne is fun and I knew it would be the good stuff."

I nod and pluck the bottle from his hand and turn it up and take a couple of long sips. When I pull the bottle back down, I say, "Thank you for not trying to talk me out of being petty and giving me some wise shit about being the bigger person and all that crap."

He laughs. "No, I'm all for a bit of revenge; especially in this case. If I were you, I probably would've done a lot worse."

I turn the bottle back up and drain it and some of the champagne spills out of the corner of my mouth. I start to wipe it away and Jonas stills my hand and swoops in to lick the droplets off my chin before claiming my mouth with a searing kiss. I wrap my arms around his neck and pull him closer, deepening the kiss as heat shoots to my core. He grabs my hips and tugs me into him before he snakes his hand down to squeeze my ass. His mouth moves down my cheek as he nips and licks my neck and bare shoulder, sending goosebumps down my arms and torso and I can't bite back a soft moan.

I drop the bottle to the floor and tangle my hands in his hair and pull his mouth back to mine. Jonas nudges my knees apart with his own and runs his hand up my thigh and he teases his fingers under the trim of my panties starting at my hip and moving toward my pelvis.

When he thumbs my clit, I gasp into his mouth. I run my hand down his chest and undo his belt and the button of his pants and slip my hand into his underwear and stroke his already hard cock. "Is this for me?" I ask with a playful smile.

He huffs a laugh. "Yes, Darlin'." He grips the back of my neck and covers my mouth with his as he pushes my panties to the side and slides two fingers into my pussy and my hips buck with the sensation. My heart pounds with my building pleasure and if this is the last time I get to be with him, I want him now.

I want to chase the high that he gives me. And although my heart wants him for longer, tonight is all I get and I'll take it.

"God, Jonas, I need you." My words come out in ragged huffs.

He pulls away from me and turns to tug me up the stairs, both of us practically sprinting. When we get to the top, he turns to go into the bedroom and I stop him. "What?" He asks, his expression confused.

I slip my shoes off and tilt my head toward the porch. "Will you give me a good memory in my favorite place? Something to look back on?" My chest tightens with the emotions I'm trying to tamp down and all the words I'm not saying. *I wish it wasn't over. I wish you could be mine. I wish you wanted me to be yours.*

Jonas gives me a soft smile. "Of course." He leads me out the sliding glass door and shuts it behind us. Faint music streams from the reception, but I can't make out what it is. The sun is starting to make its descent behind the trees and I simply watch it go down for a minute, trying to memorize this moment, to keep it in my heart forever.

Jonas wraps his arms around me from behind and rests his cheek on the side of my head and presses his lips to my temple. When he pulls them away, his warm breath ghosts across my skin as he runs the tip of his nose along the shell of my ear. "This is beautiful. It'll be a great memory to have."

I turn around to face him and look into his eyes. In the waning sunlight, they're almost golden and I want to remember them forever; this wonderful man who's given me so much this week. He's helped me finally realize I deserve to be happy. He's made me feel beautiful and wanted and valued. He's made me laugh and dried my tears and shown me what true passion is. And for everything he's given me, I will forever be thankful.

Jonas lifts my chin and presses a kiss to my lips and it's as though a switch flips in me. The need that was building only moments ago, comes roaring back to life and I deepen the kiss and push his jacket off his shoulders and down his arms. It falls to the floor and I unzip his pants and shove them down his hips, along with his boxer briefs. I push him down into a chair—*my* chair—and stand in front of him. "I want to remember you every time I sit in this chair. How good you make me feel. Everything you've given me. I never want to forget this week, Jonas."

He pulls me closer and slides his hands under my dress and up my thighs. He hooks his fingers in the waistband of my panties and tugs them down, his eyes never leaving mine. Once they're on the floor, I step forward and he hauls me into his lap and I hike my dress up around my waist and straddle him, his cock immediately pressing against my entrance. I shiver at his nearness and Jonas grips my hips, guiding me down onto his shaft.

I roll my hips, adjusting to him, and he lets out a soft groan. I take his face in my hands and look into his eyes as he holds me in place and drives up into me, the thrusts powerful and deep and nearly stealing my breath but I don't take my eyes from his. Not when my breathing turns into shuddering gasps. Not when my climax starts to build. Not when Jonas places my hand between us for me to work my clit. Not when I cry out hoarsely with a powerful orgasm that rips through me suddenly. Not when Jonas digs his fingers into the flesh of my thighs as he bucks his hips one last time, finding his own release.

My eyes don't leave his until he brings his forehead to mine and presses a tender kiss to my lips. So tender, in fact, it makes my heart ache.

CHAPTER FORTY-FOUR

JONAS

The sun is fully set when Callie and I step into the bedroom to hurriedly clean up and head back to the reception. "We don't have to go back if you don't want to," I say, knowing she wasn't wanting to stay at the reception in the first place.

She shakes her head and smiles. "No, you promised me dancing and I told my mom to have Dad save a dance for me, so I'd like to do that. Hell, I might never get married, so this may be the only time I get to dance with him at a wedding." We leave the bedroom and walk down the stairs and out the front door.

"Okay, well, let's go dance then. Are you any good?"

She quirks a brow. "Isn't the guy supposed to lead?"

"Well, yeah, but I want to make sure I don't need to be concerned for the safety of my toes."

She rolls her eyes. "I'm alright as long as I have a good partner. Can you dance?"

I nod. "Yes, actually. My nana made me learn. She said I was gonna be a gentleman if it killed me."

"Man, I like your nana. She did a good job with you."

I sigh. "I didn't make it easy on her or my grandad. I was a punk in high school after my mom left."

"Well, I think you turned out alright. Does she know what you're doing this week? That you've been my knight in shining armor?"

I shake my head. "I called her after Elliot talked to me about coming and told her I had to help a buddy from work who was in a bind but I didn't have time to go into details."

We make it to the tent and I pull Callahan out to the dance floor right as a slow song is starting. I pull her to me and rest my hand on the small of her back and take her hand in my free one. She snakes her other arm around my shoulder and grips the back of my neck as I guide her around the floor. "When you tell her the story, maybe try to make me sound a bit less pathetic than I truly was."

I look into her eyes. "We're not on that again, are we? You were never pathetic, Callie."

She gives me a sad smile. "Oh, I was. Honestly, when I got on the plane to come here, I was thinking it would have been preferable if the plane actually crashed and then I wouldn't have had to come."

"Well, I'm glad it didn't; I was on that plane."

She chuckles. "I remember. I don't feel pathetic now, just so you know. I'm glad I came and finally got over Dominic once and for all. I don't know if I'll ever be able to look at Maddie the same again, knowing what she did, but I'm not gonna let it ruin my life. I'm better off and they truly deserve one another.

"And I know I've said it a lot, but thank you. For every-thing." She bites her lip. "And I do mean *everything*. It's been a great week and it wouldn't have been nearly as good without you. You could make a career out of something like this. Show up for weddings with sad girls and help them work through all their issues and by the time you're done with them, they're definitely not sad anymore."

I laugh. "I think the state might frown on a kindergarten teacher being an escort. And besides, I don't know if I could do this again."

Callie gives me a puzzled expression. "Why not?"

"Because this was a pretty perfect week and I don't know if I did something like this again, it would ever be as good. And, honestly, I think I only want to remember this one."

She nods. "Oh, okay."

I feel a tap on my shoulder and Alex is standing next to us. "May I cut in? Vicki and I are getting ready to turn in and I wanted at least one dance with my girl."

Callahan smiles and I pass her off to her father. "I'll be over at our table." She nods and I walk over to the bar to get a beer and sit at our table and watch Callie and Alex move around the dance floor. She laughs at something he says and I can't take my eyes off her; she truly is the most beautiful woman here. I'm sad knowing this is almost over but I don't know what to do about it because I can't be what she needs. I can't be a boyfriend. She's too good for me and I don't know if she knew what I've done—saw all my damage—that she'd look at me the same way she does right now. I know she thinks she has scars you can't see, but so do I.

My thoughts are interrupted by a tap on the shoulder and my heart lurches when I see Abby standing in front of me. "Jonas?" she asks, her tone unsure.

"Abby."

She looks relieved. "I thought that was you. May I sit?"

I swallow the lump in my throat and nod. "Sure. How are you? Small world, seeing you here."

She smiles. "I know, right? What are the odds? I'm doing well, thanks. Looks like you are, too. Your girlfriend's pretty."

I glance back at Callahan who is still dancing with Alex. "Yeah, she is."

"Listen, I told Leah I thought I saw you."

Nervous and tense, I reflexively run my fingers through my hair. "Oh?"

She nods. "Yeah. She asked how you were. I told you looked happy."

I look down at my hands. "How is she?"

Abby touches my arm and I look up at her and she wears a wide grin. "She's married. And expecting her second baby."

My eyes go wide and I can't help but smile. "Really? So did they end up getting married? Wow. That's amazing." And I find I mean it. All I wanted for Leah was for her to be happy, even if she couldn't be happy with me.

"And she's walking. One of the perks of being married to a physical therapist is twenty-four-seven access to therapy, I guess. She'll probably never run any marathons, but it's amazing, Jonas."

My eyes burn with unexpected tears. "Seriously? Abby, that's unbelievable. Oh my God. Since when?"

She smiles warmly. "A couple years. She's worked her ass off and it's been an uphill climb, but yeah."

"I've never forgiven myself for what happened but I'm glad she's doing so well. Honestly. And kids. Wow. I know she wanted babies so badly. I'm glad she's happy."

Abby nods. "She is. And she's happy you seem to be doing well. I know things between you and Leah didn't end the best way, but I'm glad I got to tell you the good news. But I'll let you get back to your night."

"Abby, thank you. I'm glad you came to talk to me. I'm happy to hear Leah's doing so well. Give her my best?"

She nods and stands. "Sure."

I sit, staring at the beer bottle in my hand for who knows

how long when Callahan touches my cheek, bringing me out of my daze. "Hey, you okay?"

I take a deep breath and nod. "Yeah. I'm fine."

I can tell she doesn't believe me, but doesn't push it. I don't know whether to be relieved or sad about that. And I don't know if I'd tell her if she did ask. Although knowing Leah is doing so well fills me with joy for her.

"I guess we should say our goodbyes to my parents. They're getting ready to turn in and since we'll be leaving so early, I won't see them in the morning."

"Oh, sure." I rise from my chair and walk over to Alex and Vicki on the dance floor. Callahan hugs both her parents and Alex shakes my hand and Vicki pulls me in for a quick hug.

"Thank you for being so good to her, Jonas. I hope we'll be seeing more of you."

When she pulls back, I simply smile because I don't want to lie and tell her mother I'll see her again. "Thank you for having me this week. It was wonderful to meet you all. Your daughter is an amazing woman and I know a lot of that has to do with how y'all raised her."

Callahan and I make our way back to the house and up the stairs to the bedroom. We shower and get ready for bed and I've been quiet since we came up and I know she notices because I'm nothing if not chatty typically. "Do you want me to ask?" Callahan inquires when we climb into bed.

"I don't know," I say honestly and look down at my hands.

She nods. "Well, I know this week, the whole listening and advice thing has been pretty one-sided, but I can be a good listener. I know I didn't major in psych or anything, but I can be a sounding board if you need it. Because I know you're not okay. You've not been okay since you saw Abby."

My head snaps to her and she rolls her eyes. "I'm sure you're not as easy to read as me, but you've been agitated and on edge since you saw her. And if you don't want to talk about it, I get it, but if you do, I'm here. Even if it's not tonight. Whenever. It's an open-ended invitation. It's the least I can do for you after everything you've helped me work through this week."

I let out a heavy sigh. "I was engaged to her sister, Leah."

After a moment, when I don't elaborate, Callie simply nods. "Well, we should get some sleep. Early morning tomorrow."

"Yeah." We turn off the lights and lie down and Callie rolls to face me and I pull her into my arms and in only a few minutes, she's sleeping soundly, her head on my chest. I listen to her and wonder if I told her what happened, would she look at me like I look at myself when I think about what I did? With disgust and regret. Would she still see me as the good guy she thinks I am?

Part of me would love to tell her, to unburden myself of this secret from my past. To have her tell me I'm not a terrible person, even if I am. To have her look at me the same way she has all week, with her eyes warm and caring. But all that would most likely change if she found out. It's the reason I don't let myself get close to anyone. Teagan knows, but only because she was there. And at this point, Teagan's probably a crutch. She's comfortable and I don't have to worry about her judging me, and we love each other in our own ways, I guess, but not how I loved Leah and not how I could see possibly loving Callie if I let myself.

CHAPTER FORTY-FIVE

CALLAHAN

I'm jolted awake by the sound of my alarm clock and I know I'm gonna be dragging ass all day simply by how long it takes me to climb out of bed. Jonas is already up; which I find strange. He's dressed and has a cup of coffee in his hand. "How long have you been up?"

His thumb taps the rim of his mug. "Couldn't sleep. You were snoring."

I scoff and shove my glasses on my face. "I do not snore."

He chuckles. "I know. Only giving you a hard time. I made you some coffee." He gestures to the nightstand where my favorite mug sits.

"Thank you." I sip my coffee as I move around the room, gathering up my things. I change quickly and shove my pajamas into my suitcase and zip it up. I walk into the bathroom and brush my teeth and don't bother with makeup and I redo my braid.

I try not to let myself think about the fact that in a few hours, I'm gonna say goodbye to Jonas and I might not ever see him again. It's probably a good thing we're in a bit of a rush this morning, since it doesn't give me much time to think.

When I come out of the bathroom, Jonas has all our stuff piled together. "Are you ready? It's almost five."

I nod. "Yeah." He starts to make the bed and I stop him. "The cleaners are coming tomorrow, they'll change all the sheets and stuff; we don't have to."

"Oh, okay. Really is like a vacation, huh?"

"Yeah, I guess." We quietly make our way down the stairs and out the front door and to the car. I pop the trunk and we put our bags in. I climb behind the wheel and Jonas gets in the passenger seat and looks at the house one last time before I turn around in the driveway.

We don't talk during the drive to the airport or while we're waiting to board or while we sit on the plane. And I don't know whether to be okay or devastated by this. I want him to flirt with me and make me blush, but all that's over now, I guess. I'm so preoccupied with the fact Jonas is not speaking to me and I'm not speaking to him, I don't have the chance to get anxious about takeoff.

When I can't stand the silence anymore, I finally say, "Tell me about your nana."

Jonas looks caught off guard. "What?"

"Tell me about your nana. I can't stand this; us not talking. It's driving me bananas. Tell me about your nana. I feel like that's a safe topic, right? You already know pretty much everything about my family. Your nana, I know she's feisty, but what else?"

He thinks for a minute. "She met my granddad when she was sixteen. He worked at the soda fountain and she was on a date with another boy but she said when he took her order and she ordered a cherry soda, he gave her extra cherries, and it won her over. She was the first woman in her family to graduate high school and go to college. She was a librarian."

Curious, I ask, "Really?"

He nods. "Yeah, she still is. She works a couple days a week over at the little library on Park Avenue. I don't know she actually does a whole lot. I know she still does the preschool story time. It's her favorite thing."

I can't hide my shock and my mouth falls open. "Your nana is Dorothy?"

He nods, surprised. "You know her?"

"Yeah, I work with her." I laugh. "She said she had a grandson who was a catch. She tried to set me up with you."

He shakes his head, amused. "Wow. I can't believe this. She said there was a nice girl she worked with she wanted me to meet."

"I'll have to tell her we met and you're a wonderful guy." Something flashes in his eyes, but I can't read the expression. "What's that face about?"

He shakes his head, a mask of indifference taking its place. "Nothing, just thinking about something she said to me a few weeks ago."

"Oh. Well, tell her I said hi when you see her. Are you gonna take her to Cracker Barrel?"

He nods. "Yeah."

"She loves that you do that, you know. It's the highlight of her weekend."

He blushes. "Yeah, I don't get to see her as much as I'd like. She's pretty busy for her age. All the bingo and cards and trips with her friends and the library."

"Don't forget the safe-sex seminars," I add.

He covers his face with his hands. "Oh, God. Don't remind me about that."

I laugh and I'm thankful it seems like Jonas and I can still talk, even after everything that's happened.

When the plane lands a short time later, I find I'm not as anxious, probably because I'm thinking about the goodbye that's getting ready to take place. As the plane rolls to a stop and we're released to exit, Jonas takes my bag down and sets it on the ground and our hands brush as I grip the handle and my heart lurches. It's the first time we've touched all morning and it makes me ache. I miss him already, even though he's standing right next to me.

We walk through the airport and out the door and he pulls out his phone. "Did you drive?" I ask.

He shakes his head. "No, I took an Uber."

"Well, come on, I'll give you a ride home."

"No, I don't want to put you out."

I roll my eyes. "Jonas, I'm not taking no for an answer. It's the least I can do. Let's go." He sighs and follows me to my car. I unlock it and he puts his things in the trunk with mine.

I pull out on the highway and he gives me directions and in about twenty minutes, I pull in at his apartment. When I park, I don't know how to end things. And I knew it would be awkward, but this feels weird. I've spent the last week with him and after everything we've said and done, this is the first time I've been at a loss with him.

He turns to me. "Do you want to come in?" His tone is hopeful and I don't know what to make of that.

I shake my head. "No, I don't think I can do that." His disappointment is evident and I elaborate, my heart pounding. "Honestly, it's not that I don't want to, but if I do, I'm gonna want to sleep with you. And if I do that here, I'm gonna start thinking all the things I didn't let myself think this week." My cheeks burn with my words as they pour out. "It would be way too easy to let myself fall for you, Jonas, and I *just* got over one guy who I wasn't enough for and I don't know if I could survive it again. So, no, I can't come in."

He's quiet for a moment as he absorbs my words. After a beat, he nods. "Okay, But can I say something?"

And because I would honestly listen to him read the phone book at this point to keep him talking to me, even if I already feel like I know what he's gonna say. *If I could pick you, I would. I'm sorry I can't be what you need. You're a great girl.* But I brace myself and nod. "Don't think you're not enough. For anyone. Least of all, me. Because you are." He steps out of the car and I pop the trunk and let his words sink in.

What does that even mean? *Least of all, me?* Obviously, I'm not enough for him if he's simply walking toward his apartment without so much as a goodbye or glance back over his shoulder. And now, I don't know whether to be pissed or depressed. Before it's over, I'm sure I'll be both. I shift my car into gear and drive home.

I make it home fifteen minutes later and Elliot is in the kitchen frying bacon. He turns to me, a smile on his face. "Hungry?"

I shake my head. "No, just tired. I'm going to bed."

When I'm almost to the hallway, he pipes up, "Stop."

I freeze and turn and look at him. "What?"

"I want to hear about your week. Was it as bad as you thought it was gonna be? Did Jonas show up?"

"Yes."

"Yes to which question?"

"Both. Dominic was still a prick and tried to sleep with me a few days before the wedding. Good news is, I'm over him. Bad news is, I have another guy I have to get over now. So thanks for that, El."

His face falls. "You slept with Jonas? I didn't expect that."

Anger wells up in my chest. "What did you think was

gonna happen? We were together for a whole week and had to pretend to be dating. You've seen what he looks like. I hadn't had sex in eighteen months. It was like putting a big, juicy, ribeye steak in front of a starving person and telling them to look and smell, but don't touch or taste."

He quirks a brow. "So how was he?"

"Fucking phenomenal. But he doesn't do relationships. And I knew that when I slept with him. I knew it would only be until we got back. But then he asked me to come in when I dropped him off and I had to tell him no. I had to tell him if I slept with him here, it'd be too easy for me to fall for him, but the truth is, I already did. But I can't put myself through that again. Not when I did it for four years."

He comes around the counter and hugs me. "I'm sorry, Callie."

I shake my head. "I'm not sorry; it was an amazing week. I'm only sad it ended. And Jonas is a great guy, even outside the sex. He helped me realize things about myself I hadn't ever seen before. He made me see I want a relationship and what I deserve. It would be terrific if it could be with him, though.

"Oh, and you know Miss Dorothy at work?" Elliot nods. "Jonas's grandmother. So, the grandson she was trying to set me up with. It was him." His mouth falls open in surprise. "Yeah, I know. I was shocked, too." I sigh. "I'm tired, though. We didn't get in bed until late last night and had to leave at five. I'm going to bed."

CHAPTER FORTY-SIX

JONAS

It would be way too easy to let myself fall for you. As I walk into my apartment, Callie's words replay over and over in my mind. She did what I couldn't, which was end this. I would have happily brought her into my place and taken her to bed and stayed all day. And it would have been unfair to her. She truly is brave.

I can't believe she knows Nana. That's wild. And Nana's words from one of our last conversations run through my mind. *You need someone smart and kind, but who will still call you on your bullshit. Find someone with a pretty soul, not only a pretty face.* Dammit if that's not Callahan, but still, I can't be what she needs. I'm not good for her. I would hurt her. I know she thinks she's not enough and it kills me. And I know what I said before I got out of her car probably confused her, but it was all I could say without spilling how I truly feel about her.

If I did that, I would have to tell her I stayed up all night last night, simply listening to her sleep and feeling her in my arms because I didn't want it to end. I would have to tell her about Leah and what I did, because that's the only way I could truly know if she could want to be with me.

I take a few minutes to unpack, thankful I don't have to do laundry since Callie did it yesterday. I put everything away but notice I'm missing a tee shirt. *Probably got left behind.* Oh, well, I guess. Once everything is put away, I strip out of my clothes and crawl into bed and try to sleep. But not having Callahan in bed with me, I'm at a loss. I wrap my arms around a pillow, which is a piss-poor substitute for a beautiful woman, but I can pretend.

The next day, I'm on my way to pick up Nana for supper and I can tell I'm not in a good mood. I miss Callie. All day, I've found myself wondering what she's doing. What her hair looks like today. What she's wearing. I had to stop myself from texting her several times today. Because if I do that, I'm no better than Dominic. Not letting her go and dragging this out when she's been clear about what she wants. I don't miss the irony in all of this, considering I told her I end things with women when they get too attached. And, this time, I'm the one who's attached. Although, it sounds like Callie might be, too.

And maybe that's the worst part of this. The fact we truly want one another and I can't let myself want her because I would have to be honest about myself and if I do that, I'd have to be in a position where she could reject me and I don't know if I can handle it.

I get out of the car at Nana's and walk up to her door and knock. She answers a few minutes later with a smile on her face and hugs me. "Jonas, sweetheart; so good to see you."

"Good to see you, too, Nana." I walk her to the car and make sure she gets in alright and then climb behind the wheel.

When we pull out of her parking lot, she says, "So, tell me about the big favor you had to do for your friend that took you away for a whole week."

I sigh. "Well, Nana, you might not believe me if I told you. It's a wild story."

"Oh, is there drama? You know I like drama."

"Some. Not my drama, but yeah." I give Nana the rundown of my week and I don't miss how her eyes go wide when I tell her about Callie giving Dominic hell, but I leave out the part about me sleeping with Callie. I tell her about running into Leah's sister and how well she's doing. As I pull in at the restaurant and park, I turn to Nana. "You want to hear the craziest part of all of this?"

"Of course."

"You know her. The girl who's ex got married."

"I do?"

"Yeah. Did you miss anyone at work last week?"

"Well, Callie was out on vacation. She said she had to go to her cousin's wedding." I nod and Nana grabs my arm in surprise. "Callie? You were with Callie?"

"Yep."

"You were with Callie all week?"

"Yes."

"And what did you think about her?"

"She's great," I admit.

"That's all? 'She's great'? She's wonderful, Jonas. She's exactly the kind of girl you need. She's smart, she's pretty, she's kind."

I nod. "I know all that, Nana. She's also way too good for me."

"Oh, hush; she is not."

"You should see what she comes from; the kind of money her family has. She's way out of my league."

Nana scoffs. "Bullshit."

"Nana."

"Jonas, Callie is the least materialistic person I know. And something tells me you already know that. If you like her, you should tell her that."

I shake my head, defeated. "I can't, Nana."

"Why not?"

I look down, and try to swallow the lump in my throat. "Because I would have to tell her what happened with Leah and if I do that, she might not want me. I'd rather not have her at all than find out she can't be with me after what I did."

Nana pats my hand. "Jonas, you were so young when all that happened."

I protest. "I was twenty-one. That's not that young."

She levels me with a gaze. "Son, when you're eighty-one, everything is young. Listen to me. You are not the same person now you were then. I've never seen you drink more than two beers at any given time. You made a mistake. Granted, it was a costly mistake for both Leah and you. But from what you said, she's doing much better, right? Isn't that what you said her sister told you? She's happy and she's married with children? And she's walking now. My goodness, that's amazing."

I nod and Nana continues. "You've made yourself pay for this mistake for the last eight years. You've kept yourself miserable and unable to commit because you're afraid to let anyone in because you're a coward. You'd have to be vulnerable and risk letting yourself get your heart broken again. Do you honestly think Callie couldn't get past what happened?"

I grip the steering wheel and watch as my knuckles turn white. "I don't know," I answer honestly. "But she's so good, Nana."

She pats my cheek and her eyes are kind. "You're good too, Jonas. You made a stupid mistake; a mistake you'll never make again. I know that; you know that. You have paid dearly for your mistake. And I think you ought to give Callie a chance to make up her own mind about you." She lifts a brow. "I'm happy to put in a good word for you. She loves me."

I find myself laughing in spite of how sad I am. "I know she does. But no, don't tell her anything. Please?"

Nana sighs. "Okay. If that's what you want."

CHAPTER FORTY-SEVEN

CALLAHAN

When I unpack my bag and pull out Jonas's tee shirt, I bury my nose in it, even though I know it's not gonna smell like him since I washed it. But I still sit on my bed and cry into his shirt and sleep in it every night. I've sworn Elliot to secrecy about how upset I am Jonas hasn't called or texted. But I can't bring myself to text or call him because as soon as I do, I'll fall back into the same type of relationship I had with Dominic and I refuse to do that to myself again.

As I went back to work the Tuesday after I returned from Tennessee, I told Miss Dorothy I'd met her grandson and I was surprised she didn't try to pry about how I'd met him or what I thought about him. She merely said, "Oh, really? That's nice." Definitely not what I expected from her after the way she tried to set me up with him. But, I guess it's possible she's moved on from trying to find someone for Jonas.

My days all pass the same way anymore, especially since classes have started again. I grill Elliot when he gets home from work to ask about how Jonas is doing but he says he seems fine, and I don't know whether to be happy or sad about that. I mean, I definitely don't want Jonas to be miserable, but would it kill the guy to be affected? I guess I shouldn't be surprised, though, since Jonas isn't affected by women. He does what he does. And I guess I should actually be thankful he's not calling me, because I don't know if I'm strong enough to not answer his calls. And I know if I heard his voice, I definitely wouldn't be strong enough to tell him no if he asked me to come over.

I go to work at the library then go to class and work on my dissertation. Repeat. Five days a week. I should go out and try to date, but truthfully, I don't know where to start. I don't want to date casually; I want a relationship. I know I have to go out with men to get to that point, but I don't have the energy after work and class. And bad as I hate to hope for it, I find myself hoping Jonas will decide he wants something and call me.

I took Jonas's advice and got another tattoo and it will forever remind me of the time I spent with him. I look down at the inside of my left wrist where Jonas would always brush a kiss that made my heart race. But no one but me would ever know what it signifies, because it's a pretty common tattoo.

I haven't had the nerve to tell my parents Jonas and I "broke up". I'll have to tell them before Thanksgiving, since I'll be going home for that, but I can't yet. My mom sent me a photo she took at the wedding of Jonas and me dancing and I lost it. It was after we'd snuck away to the porch and come back and he's looking down at me and his expression looks genuine. And part of me knows it was. In spite of the fact it was fake, parts of it were real. The conversations we had. The way he made me feel. The attraction. You can't fake those things.

But I saw that photo and cried for two hours. And the worst part is, I'm not sorry about what happened. I could never be sorry I met Jonas or the time we shared. I'm only sorry it ended. I'm sorry that, once again, I wasn't enough for someone. And I know I'm probably throwing myself a pity party at this point, but I feel like it's allowed. Who's gonna tell me I can't?

At night, I lie in bed at night and don't sleep. I miss Jonas's arms around me. I miss his warmth and his hair tickling my back. I miss his stubble and his freckles and his eyes and his smile and his kiss. God, how I miss his kiss. I miss his abs and his ass and hands and, yes, his cock.

But more than all that, I miss how he could read me. I miss how he seemed to always know exactly what I needed to hear, even if it wasn't what I wanted to hear. No one has ever been able to perceive me the way he can. I don't know that as long as I live, anyone ever will again. I miss the way he'd flirt with me and make me laugh and roll my eyes. And maybe I'm just transparent, but I honestly think it was only him. There's no logical reason that after one week of knowing someone, I should feel his absence as acutely as I do. And yet, here I am, entirely forlorn.

The week before Halloween, I had plans to go to a study group with a few of my classmates and once we finished up, the only guy in my group, Russ, asked if I wanted to go get drinks. I figured, what the hell, it's Friday night and I never go out and Russ is cute, in the way that nerdy guy librarians are cute. Roughly five-ten with pale, freckled skin and dirty blonde hair, a runner's build, and chiseled jaw. I'm pretty sure he's gay, so even if I don't hit it off with him, I might be able to hook him up with Elliot. I followed him to a bar I'd never been to before and park in the lot next to the building. We walk in together, laughing about something the instructor had said in our last class and sit at the bar. "There's no way he wasn't high," Russ comments.

"Oh, most definitely. But, still, he made some good points about the dewey decimal system."

Russ laughs. "But that wasn't even what the topic of today's discussion was supposed to be. At least he's hot. So I suppose he can be forgiven."

Definitely gay.

"So, Russ, are you seeing anyone?"

He narrows his eyes. "Honey, you know I'm gay, right? Wasn't the comment about the instructor being hot enough to give it away?"

I laugh. "I figured that. I have a roommate. He's hot, exactly your type, I think. He's a teacher. Granted, he teaches second grade, but still."

He looks impressed. "Do tell. I've always been a hot-for-teacher type."

We both order a glass of wine and when they come I sip mine. "Well, Elliot is twenty-eight. He's good-looking. Tall, gorgeous brown eyes, dreadlocks down to his shoulders . Fit, but not obsessive about it. Sweet."

He nods. "Okay, I may have to get his info. So what about you? You're super cute, why don't you have a boyfriend?"

I sigh. "That's a loaded question. I was seeing a guy on and off for four years, but he was only with me until he could get with my cousin. He broke my heart. I was super pathetic and when it came time to go to their wedding, I didn't have a date, so I tried to rope Elliot into going with me. He was gonna pretend to be my boyfriend so I didn't look like a loser but when it came time to go, he bailed and got this guy he worked with to go with me.

"And let's just say, the guy he set me up with helped me get over my ex in so many, many ways. It was supposed to be fake and it was, but a lot of it felt real. So I'm still kind of stuck on him. But he doesn't do relationships and I knew that.

"When we got back, he invited me in to his place, but I told him I was in danger of falling for him and I wasn't gonna go from one guy who couldn't or wouldn't commit to another and we've not spoken since. And that was three months ago."

Russ nods. "Well, I don't know if it's any consolation, but there's a guy at the back of the bar who hasn't taken his eyes off you since we walked in." I start to turn around and Russ grabs my arm. "Don't look. Go to the bathroom and take your hair down out of this bun and put on some lipgloss. Take off this frumpy sweater and then come back to the bar. Then, you look at him."

I roll my eyes. "Russ, I bet he's not looking at me."

He levels me with a gaze. "I'm telling you, Callahan, he's looking at you. He's sure as hell not looking at me. He's with a woman and hasn't taken his eyes off you. Now, go and do what I said."

I frown. "If he's with another woman and he's looking at me, he's probably a sleaze ball anyway. Why should I want him?"

"Because their body language isn't screaming 'date' or 'couple'. Most likely, they're just friends."

I sigh. "Fine. Watch my drink."

He smiles. "You've got it. Now, go get sexy and come back."

CHAPTER FORTY-EIGHT

JONAS

After my conversation with Nana about Callie, I've been giving what she said a lot of thought. And maybe she's right; I am a coward. I don't want to tell Callie what happened and have her look at me any different than she did before. And I miss her. I've tried to be with other women and when it comes down to it, I can't do it. It feels wrong.

It makes no sense whatsoever, but there it is. Women whom I would've happily jumped into bed with prior to meeting Callahan don't do it for me. They don't feel right under my hands, their kisses don't feel right and the only woman I've slept with since her is Teagan and it was weird the last time. Actually, weird is generous. I cried like a baby after and told her about Callie. Definitely not my finest manly moment.

I'm *this* close to calling her, but I don't know if she'd answer my call at this point since it's been a few months. I ask Nana and Elliot about her and they says she seems fine, which I should probably be happy about.

Teagan is back in town tonight and we're out at the bar, but I'm not gonna sleep with her. She's too good a friend to keep having bad sex with her. She's telling me about her job as a high school guidance counselor and all the things high school kids get up to today. She's in the middle of another story when I notice the door to the bar open and a man and woman enter and sit at the bar. My heart lurches when I realize who the woman is. *Callahan.*

Callahan. With a date? They're laughing and having drinks. *Shit. I'm too late.* I can't take my eyes off her. Her hair is up in a bun and she's wearing a cardigan. She must have had to work today. What is she doing here? God, this hurts. She looks so beautiful.

"Jonas, are you even listening to me? I spinning some comedy gold over here." Teagan nudges me.

I glance at her. "Oh, sorry. Tell it to me again."

She sighs. "It won't be as funny the second time." She follows my gaze. "Ahh. I see. Who is she? Oh, shit, is that her?" I simply nod. "So, what are you waiting for?"

"She's with someone, Teag. I'm too late. I fucked up and waited too long."

"So, call her tomorrow. Tell her. You're not you, Jonas. You haven't been yourself since you got back from that wedding. And shit, if any guy ever looked at me the way you're looking at her, I might have to rethink my stance on marriage. I haven't seen you look at anyone like that since Leah. You've got it bad, huh?"

The guy sees me looking at Callie and says something to her. He touches her arm and gestures to her hair. She nods and gets up and I watch her walk toward the bathroom.

Teagan touches my arm. "That guy is gay. He watched this other guy go by and he checked him out. I bet she's not *with* him. Maybe they're just friends. Go, man, go. Right now."

"What do I even say?"

Teagan rolls her eyes. "I don't know; maybe the truth? That

you're in love with her? If you love her, you need to tell her about Leah. If she cares about you, it won't matter."

I stand and run my fingers through my hair and walk toward the bathroom. It seems to take forever and my heart is pounding, my palms sweaty as I stand in front of the women's bathroom. It's a single, so I'm not worried about someone else coming out. I wait for what feels like an eternity for Callie to open the door.

The knob turns and suddenly, she's there. She's taken her hair down and shed her sweater. Her expression registers shock as she looks at me. "Jonas?"

My mouth is suddenly dry and I can't form words because I've forgotten how breathtaking she is and the only word I can say is, "Hi".

She barks out a surprised laugh. "Hi? That's all you've got?"

I finally find more words. "Sorry, Darlin'. I forgot how beautiful you are. It caught me off guard."

She blushes and my heart turns over seeing it. I had forgotten how sexy she is when a blush creeps into her cheeks. Callie tucks her hair behind her ear. "So, did you need something? Or is it your habit to corner women in a bar bathroom?"

I shake my head and clear my throat. "Are you with that guy?"

She lifts a brow. "Define *with*."

I sigh. "Is he your date?"

"No."

"So, can you ditch him?"

She squares her shoulders. "Why would I want to do that? I'm having a good time."

I plead. "Callie, please? I just want to talk."

She must see something in my expression that gives her pause because she nods. "Okay, let me tell Russ goodbye." I watch her go to the guy at the bar and tell him something and he smiles and nods. I glance at Teagan and she gives me a thumbs-up and a huge grin. Callie comes back over to where I stand at the entrance to the bar and slips her sweater back on. "Where do you want to go?" She asks.

"My place is only a couple miles away."

She chews her bottom lip in indecision but finally nods. "Did you drive?"

I shake my head. "I came with a friend. She drove."

Callie pauses for a moment. "She's not gonna be mad you left her?"

"No. She told me to go."

She looks confused but simply says, "Okay." She digs her keys out and hands them to me. "Do you care to drive?"

"Not at all." I open the passenger door of her car and she climbs in and I shut it before coming around and sliding behind the wheel and drive the five minutes to my apartment. We don't speak and the tension is thick in the confines of the car. When I park, all I want to do is pull Callie to me and kiss her, but I don't.

We exit the car and I hand her keys back to her before pulling out my own. I swipe us into my building and walk around the corner to the end of the hall where my apartment is located. Callie's visibly nervous and I wonder if she doesn't trust me to be alone with her, or if maybe she doesn't trust herself.

When we get inside, I toss my keys in the bowl on the table next to the door and turn on a lamp. Callie sets her purse down on an end table and looks around. "This is a nice place, Jonas. It's exactly what I would picture you'd have. Decidedly modern, but comfortable."

"Thanks. Can I get you something to drink? I have beer and beer."

She chuckles. "Beer is fine."

I pull two bottles of Stella Artois from the fridge and open them. I hand one to her and she takes a long pull. "You cut your hair," she comments as we sit on the sofa. She takes a seat on the opposite end, as far away from me as she can get while still actually sitting on the sofa.

I nod and run my fingers through my hair. "Yeah, I always cut it when school starts. I'm due for another one in a few weeks. How have you been?"

She sighs. "Fine. Busy. School, work, homework. Same old. You?"

Besides missing you? "Oh, you know. Kindergarten is pretty much the same every year. Cute kids, crazy parents."

Callie bites her lip. "So, what did you want to talk about?" Straight to the point. Gotta admire that about Callahan. She's nothing if not direct.

I blow out a breath. "I miss you."

She takes a pull from her beer. "Sure looks that way. I haven't heard from you in three months, Jonas." Her tone is frustrated. "And I doubt if we hadn't run into each other that I would've heard from you at all.

I nod. "I know. It's not for lack of trying on my part. I pick up my phone nearly every day wanting to call you or text you but I haven't been able to work up the courage."

Surprised she asks, "You needed courage? For what?"

I look down. "To tell you something." She waits patiently as I find my words. "About Leah," I say finally.

"Your fiancé?"

"Ex-fiancé, but yes." She nods and I take a deep breath and I struggle to even start. I open and close my mouth several times trying to find the words.

Callie scoots closer and touches my arm and her eyes are soft. "It's okay, Jonas. You don't have to tell me."

"No, I do. I need to tell you. Because I want to be with you, Callie, but you need to know what I did. Because after, you might not want to be with me; I mean, if you wanted to in the first place." I'm so nervous, my mouth is dry and I take a swig of my beer.

She looks taken aback. "You want to be with me? What are you saying?"

I sigh and look at her. "I want to be with you, Callahan. I want a relationship with you. I miss you and I haven't been able to stop thinking about you since we got back from the wedding. But there are things you need to know. Things that might affect your decision to want to be with me."

"You don't do relationships, Jonas. Not in eight years."

I nod. "I know. And there's a reason for that."

"And it has to do with Leah?" Callie asks.

"Yes." My chest tightens with emotion, knowing what I'm about to reveal may doom me with Callie, but if she doesn't know, I can't build an honest relationship with her and it's the thing I want most. "You remember when we were in the shower and you said I didn't have any scars and I showed you the one on my head?"

"You said you got it in a car accident."

I nod and lick my lips nervously. "Yes. Leah and I has been to a party and we'd both been drinking. This was back when I drank a lot. I didn't have a problem or anything, I just liked to drink. I had recently turned twenty-one, so, you know, it was legal and I binge drank on the weekends.

"I don't know if you've ever noticed, but I don't drink more than a couple of beers at most now and you know I don't do hard liquor." She nods. "Well, Leah liked to drink, too, and she was blitzed and I'd had quite a bit to drink, but my apartment was only a few miles away and I'd driven it plenty of times before when I was buzzed. But that night, I had no business driving. And Teagan, one of our friends— that's who I was with tonight, actually. But anyway, Teagan tried to take my keys and I wouldn't give them up; I told her I was fine."

I look down at my hands. "But I wasn't fine. I drove the car into a tree going eighty. I have no memory of the wreck and I was so drunk, I never hit the brakes."

Callahan's inhale is sharp and I continue with the worst of it. "Leah was paralyzed from the waist down. Other than the gash on my head and a bad concussion, I walked away without a scratch. I still don't know how that happened, honestly.

"She was in a coma for two weeks and when she woke up and couldn't move her legs, she blamed me; which, of course, she should have. It was my fault. I tried to be there for her after, but Leah couldn't forgive me because they told her she probably wouldn't be able to have children after the accident and she wanted to be a mother more than almost anything. And I couldn't forgive myself for taking that away from her.

"She started going to physical therapy after some surgeries to try to regain the use of her legs and she fell for her physical therapist. I guess he was who she needed, which I get; I couldn't help her. And the fact I was pretty much unscathed was a constant reminder since I was fine while she was irreparably damaged.

"She broke things off with me and she ended up marrying him. Abby told me at the wedding. I hadn't seen her since everything happened with Leah. But she said Leah was able to have kids and she's actually started to be able to walk again."

After a moment, I finally look at Callie. Her expression is sympathetic. "So, she got a happy ending and you've, what, punished yourself for eight years?"

"She was paralyzed; t was my fault."

"It doesn't change the fact that she cheated on you, Jonas, or the fact she *chose* to get in the car with you. She was obviously okay enough after everything to move on and find someone to be happy with. But you've carried this with you like your own personal penance all this time. Depriving yourself of happiness. You made a mistake. But you're not that person anymore, are you? You've never driven drunk again, have you?"

I shake my head. "I've never been drunk since that night."

She nods. "See? You're never gonna do anything like that again. Hell, you won't even flirt with a woman who's had too much to drink. Did you honestly think this would make me not want you?"

I shrug. "I still haven't forgiven myself."

"Why?"

"Because I ruined her life."

"No, you didn't, Jonas. I'm not saying what happened isn't awful, but she's happy. She's been happy this whole time. You're the only one who's been miserable. And so, let me get this straight. You've refused to be in a relationship all this time because you were afraid of telling someone what happened?

"You were so afraid to let yourself be vulnerable and let someone see your own damage, you'd rather be alone than allow someone in—Mister I-Love-a-Challenge? As long as it's not to challenge yourself, I guess. Sound about right?" She doesn't attempt to hide the bitterness in her tone. "You let me think you didn't want me all because you didn't trust me to see past what happened *eight years ago?*" Anger flashes in her eyes and I start to say something, but she holds up a hand. "I'm not finished, Jonas."

Tears well in her eyes and her voice grows shaky and it makes my heart ache. "You saw every bit of my brokenness and it still wasn't enough for you to trust me. And then we come home and you invite me in here after you had to know I had feelings for you. And I was the one who had to end it after you made that big statement about how if you get a hint of a woman catching feelings you'd drop them."

I nod and hope she sees the regret in my eyes. "I know; I was selfish. I didn't want to be like him. I didn't want to hurt you like Dominic did. But after you dropped me off, I realized I was exactly like him for asking you to stay. And I hated myself for it. I should've told you about Leah that last night at the lake. I knew I had feelings for you, but I was so overwhelmed by running into Abby at the wedding, I couldn't think and I was afraid you wouldn't want me when you found out what I'd done. I'm sorry, Callahan."

CHAPTER FORTY-NINE

CALLAHAN

I absorb everything Jonas has said and it's not a question of me wanting him. I've not stopped wanting him since the first day we met. I can't fault him for a mistake from his past, regardless of what happened. He's punished himself enough all these years. "Why me, Jonas?" I finally ask.

He frowns. "What do you mean?"

"Why me? Why do you want me, when you've hooked up with all those other women? Why, suddenly do you want me? We both know I'm not anything extraordinary or special. I'm just...me."

He stares at me in disbelief. "You think you're not extraordinary? You're amazing and smart and sexy and you were the first person in eight years I've remotely had a connection with that wasn't purely physical."

I look down. "You don't know that. It's only because we spent so much time together. You saw me when I was vulnerable and got to know me. Who's to say it wouldn't be that way with someone else?"

He sighs in exasperation. "Dammit, Callahan, I don't want

anyone else. I want you. You know who the last person I slept with was?"

I honestly don't know if I want to know the answer but I simply shake my head. He blows out a breath. "It was Teagan. She and I have known each other since college and she's a good friend, but there's never been anything between us beyond only the physical."

"Okay? Why are you telling me this?"

He flushes and I'm caught off guard. "Because, the last time I slept with her, I cried. Because I felt like I'd cheated on you. We weren't together and even though I had no reason to feel that way, it felt wrong. Everyone since you has felt wrong. Not that there's been anyone else, but still, to even talk to another woman or kiss another woman. It felt wrong, Callie."

"You cried during sex?" I ask, surprised.

"*That's* what you took from everything I just said?" He deadpans.

I give him an apologetic smile. "Sorry, I'm shocked is all."

He rakes his fingers through his hair. "I've known since I first met you there was something different with you than with anyone else. You remember when we were telling the story at supper that first night and I said that when I saw you, I realized I would have done it for nothing?" I nod, thinking back. Jonas swallows. "I was truthful. When I saw you talking on the phone with Elliot and I realized you were the girl he was sending me to 'rescue', I thought, 'damn, she's cute and she's angry and it's adorable'. I really did have to take a breath when I saw you. I was so thrown by you. I can't tell you what it was, it was just...you."

My chest grows tight hearing him say this and I look down at my hands. I remember thinking that night he was a good actor and it would have been nice to actually have someone see me that way. I bite my lip as my eyes burn with tears. Jonas lifts my chin. "And then I talked with you and I can't explain it; it was easy. I've never talked with a woman the way I was able to talk to you. And I wanted to see you smile and roll your eyes and blush. I wanted more than anything to make you understand how beautiful and amazing you are. My whole goal for the week was to make you feel wanted and sexy. I truly didn't think I would have feelings for you. I never expected that."

He gives me a soft smile and continues, "And then, that night, when you asked me to hold you, something cracked in me. I hated hearing how sad you were. I would have done anything in that moment to make the pain go away for you."

My cheeks burn with humiliation. I felt so pathetic that night and even more after Jonas had taken pity on me by holding me. He squeezes my hand. "And no, it wasn't out of pity, so don't be thinking that. I've never pitied you, Callie." When my mouth falls open because he's almost read my mind, he quirks a brow. "You're still easy to read, Darlin'."

"Anyway, when I woke up the next morning, and you were already up, I missed you. I missed having you in my arms. It was an entirely new feeling for me. Normally, when I sleep with a woman, and she falls asleep, if I wake up and she's gone, I'm thankful. I know, that makes me sound like a shit, and, historically, I have been.

"Then the night when we had sex the first time, and fell asleep after, I knew then I had feelings for you. I was terrified. And I thought it would go away. But it hasn't, Callie. My feelings for you have only gotten stronger."

My chin quivers with barely contained emotion and the tears roll down my face and Jonas swipes his thumbs across my cheeks. I struggle to speak but finally find my words. "I thought I was crazy. I thought I had imagined all of it. I thought it was all one-sided and I felt so stupid. I wanted so badly to tell you I didn't want it to end, but I knew it was what I had agreed to and I knew I would've rather had you, truly had you, for only a few days than not at all. I knew I would be sad after and I was prepared for that.

"And then, when you asked me to stay that day we got back; it hurt so bad. Because I wanted to say yes. But then I realized I would have been no better off than when I was with Dominic and I couldn't go through that again. And you told me to not think I wasn't enough for someone, least of all you, and I was so confused."

Jonas nods. "I know. I'm sorry I couldn't tell you how I felt then. I still wasn't sure I could tell you about the accident and I knew if I couldn't tell you about that, then I had no right to tell you I had feelings for you. I couldn't build something with you on half-truths."

He blows out a breath and his eyes search mine. "Callie, I'm in love with you. I don't want anyone else. I want you. Only you. For as long as you'll put up with me. I want to have dinners with you and breakfasts with you and wake up with you and go to bed with you. I want to see your eyes change with your mood and take care of you when you're sick. I want to find out how many kids you want and I want to be the one to give them to you. I want to watch you become the sexy librarian you were meant to be. I want you to spend time with Nana and listen to her tell you all my embarrassing stories. I want to watch you blush on a daily basis when I flirt with you. I never want to be without you again. These last three months have been the worst in my life. If you want Vegas, I want you to have that. If you want a big wedding, have it. Or, if you never want to get married, that's fine. I only want to be with you, whatever that looks like."

My breath catches at hearing his declaration and my mouth falls open. "Jonas, I don't know what to say to all that. What are you saying?"

He huffs out a soft laugh. "I'm saying, I don't want to half-ass this. I want a commitment. A long one. Preferably for the rest of our lives."

I can only sputter. "Marriage? Are you crazy?"

He smiles. "Probably. But I'm crazy about you, Callahan."

"What if you change your mind? What if you decide you like someone better? Someone more interesting or pretty. What if you get bored? We only spent a week together. That's not enough time to know if you want to be with someone forever, Jonas."

"As far as those questions go; not gonna happen. I've been in a committed relationship before. I like it, contrary to what I've shown of myself over the past eight years. I was ready to get married back then, even at twenty-one. I know what love is, Callie. I love you. And yeah, we spent a week together. And then I was without you for three months and I never want to do that again. I was so miserable. Weren't you miserable?"

I nod. "Yeah, I was."

He smiles and then his expression grows serious. "I know I don't come from the best background, with my mom and stuff. I know your family has expectations of you and if that's a concern, I get it."

I scoff. "I think you know me better than that. I think things like excessive wealth and good breeding only serve to give people an excuse to be assholes. I mean, look at Maddie and Dom. Both wealthy, both assholes. I don't want someone who thinks that kind of stuff is paramount. Besides, my parents have met you; they love you. Mom's already asking about Thanks-giving and Christmas."

He looks surprised. "You didn't tell them we broke up or whatever?"

I shake my head and give him a sheepish smile. "No. They

were so happy I'd found someone, I didn't want to burst their bubble and I liked pretending. Pathetic, I know."

He gives me a lopsided grin. "Nah. It would make it sound a lot better if we eloped. They'd think we'd been together this whole time. Looks a little less impulsive probably."

"Jonas, be serious. What you're suggesting sounds crazy."

"So, is that a no?" His tone is neutral, without any disappointment, as if he's genuinely curious.

Is this real? Jonas loves me? Wants a future with me? Wants forever with me? Is that something I want? Jonas, forever? Maybe.

"No, it's not a no," I say with a smirk. "I might be open to being incentivized."

His expression is jubilant. "How much incentive do you need, Darlin'?"

I love hearing him call me Darlin' and I realize how I've missed it more than I even thought possible. I grip his face and press a soft kiss to his lips. "Take me to bed and keep me there until I say yes?"

He chuckles. "Gladly."

FALLING INTO FOREVER

SUMMER LOVIN' BOOK 2

AUTHOR'S NOTE

Dear Reader,

Falling Into Forever deals with themes surrounding infidelity (not with main characters), addition, parental abandonment, pregnancy (not with main characters), and homophobia. Certain scenes and situations may be triggering or disturbing for some readers.

CHAPTER ONE

JONAS

If you'd asked me a year ago where I'd be today, I could pretty much tell you exactly how my evening would play out. If Teagan was in town, we'd go to the bar, have some drinks, come back to my place and have no-strings-attached sex. If she wasn't around, I'd find someone else to spend my evening with. Always no strings, never letting myself actually get close to anyone. For the past eight years, this has been my life. Ever since the accident my senior year of college where I stupidly drove drunk and caused my then fiancé, Leah, to lose the use of her legs.

I loved Leah, but after the hurt I caused her, she couldn't forgive me and ended up beginning a relationship with her physical therapist while we were still engaged. She married him and I recently found out she's begun walking again and even has a couple of kids. Which, honestly, I'm overjoyed about for her and the happiness she was able to make out of the misery I caused her.

Truthfully, I couldn't forgive myself either, and when Leah broke things off, it severed something inside of me. Knowing how

I'd hurt her and then her cheating on me felt like this gaping wound that wouldn't heal. I leaned into the guilt and pain and decided I wasn't gonna let myself get hurt again, or worse, hurt someone else. But it's probably more accurate to say I didn't want to allow myself to be happy again. I wouldn't have relationships ever again. What was the point? I simply shut my heart down.

I dated with abandon, hardly more than an eight-year string of one night stands, with the exception of Teagan. And in spite of the fact I eventually wanted kids and a family, I couldn't bring myself to tell another person what I'd done to Leah and the pain I caused her. I couldn't let my guard down enough to allow myself to be vulnerable. As my nana says, I was a coward. She wasn't wrong.

Enter Callahan. Like a wrecking ball, she completely demolished me in the best way possible. She was only supposed to be a favor for a friend. I was supposed to show up and be her fake boyfriend for her ex's wedding. It was only supposed to be for a week; no feelings, just flirting and pretending.

And in truth, I tried to keep it that way; I really did. Somehow, though, over the course of the week we spent together, I was gone; I totally fell for her. But because I was scared of her telling me she couldn't get past what I'd done to Leah, I let her go. I let her think I didn't have feelings for her, even though I was completely in love with her.

And for months, I didn't call her, even though it was the only thing I wanted to do. I tried to go back to my regular life. I tried to hook up with women, just as I'd always done, but I couldn't even do more than kiss another woman. Even with Teagan, who's always been a reliable good time, I couldn't do it. I cried and felt like I'd cheated on Callie, even though it was absurd.

Then, she happened to walk into the bar where Teagan and

I were getting drinks. She was with a guy and I thought, for sure, I was too late. But I finally spoke with her and she came home with me and I told her how I felt and what I done. She was angry and hurt I'd let her think I didn't care, but thankfully, she told me she still cared, too.

And now, she's back in my arms and I want to pinch myself for how good it feels, how right. I take her glasses off her face and set them on an end table before I brush a kiss across her lips. It almost aches to kiss her, the way my heart feels.

Callie deepens our kiss and I'm reminded just how much I love to simply kiss her. And although I really didn't plan on saying everything I did when I spouted my declaration of wanting lifelong commitment and undying love, I certainly don't regret any of it because it's all true. I love her and I don't want to be without her.

She shifts in my lap and straddles me and moves her mouth down my cheek to my neck and runs her hands under my shirt and sighs against me and rests her head on my shoulder. "I've missed you, too. I don't think I told you that." I wrap my arms around her and simply hold her for a moment, thankful to have her in my arms again, because it feels right. *She* feels right. I don't know how long we stay like this, but after a while, she pulls back and looks into my eyes and the smile she wears is playful. "Guess what?"

I smile. "What?"

She quirks a brow. "I got another tattoo."

I nod, surprised. "Really? What is it?"

She tilts her head, the gesture almost mischievous, her long mane of strawberry-blonde hair falling over her shoulder. "Do you want me to tell you or do you want to find it? Might take you a little while. You know, if you do it right."

Unable to keep a wide grin off my face, I run my hands along her jaw and look into her dark blue eyes. "I'd very much like to take my time discovering it." I press my lips to hers and all I want in this moment is for it not to end. Our kiss turns rapidly turns hungrier and Callie drags her mouth back down my cheek and neck and my pulse races. She tugs my shirt over my head and trails her lips across my chest and I grip the back of her neck and claim her mouth. The kiss is deep and passionate and after a moment, I have to come up for air.

I push her cardigan off her shoulders and it falls to the floor and I'm just beginning to work my hands under her shirt when the front door opens. Both our heads snap that direction and we see Teagan standing in the doorway. Her expression is apologetic as she closes the door. "Shit. Sorry, I just came to get my stuff. I didn't think y'all would be out here in the open."

Callie looks at me expectantly and I make the introductions. "Callie, this is Teagan, one of my best friends since college. Teagan, this is Callahan."

Callie nods and looks at Teagan. "Did he really cry?"

Teagan's eyes flit to me and I shrug and she nods. "Yeah, he did. He wouldn't shut up about you. I swear, if he hadn't come to talk to you at the bar, I was gonna track you down myself. I was done hearing him bitch about missing you. Glad to see y'all made up."

She drops the couch and I scoff. "Teag, we're a little busy here." Callahan snorts in amusement.

Teagan waves me off and looks at Callie. "Sorry if this is weird, but I wanted to tell you, Jonas really does love you. I knew as soon as I saw him the last time he was different. And I'm happy he's finally found someone. From what he said, you're really great. Well, I'll be on my way."

"Wait, Teagan," Callie says. "Have you eaten?" She looks at me. "Have you?"

I shake my head and she nods. "Me, neither, and I'm starving. I skipped lunch at work and then had class and study group. Teagan, want to join us for supper?"

Teagan looks taken aback. "It wouldn't be weird?"

Callie waves off her concern and stands. "Please, I took a man I didn't even know to watch my ex marry my cousin and lived with him for a week. I think this is right on par for Jonas and me. Besides, I want to hear what Jonas was like in college and stuff. I mean, if it's not too weird for you."

Teagan looks at me as if she's not sure how to answer. I can't help but laugh as I pick my shirt up off the floor. "Pizza or Chinese, ladies?"

They both answer, "Pizza".

Once the pizza arrives, we sit at my kitchen table and while this should be awkward, given my history with Teagan and my current relationship with Callie, it's not. They're both relaxed and laughing—mostly at my expense—and I'm thankful they're getting along. Teagan swallows a bite of her pizza and turns to Callie. "So, your cousin married your ex after she knew y'all had been together for four years and how badly he treated you?"

Callie nods. "Yeah. I still haven't spoken with her since the wedding. She doesn't remember that she told me that she knew. But, apparently, she wasn't the only one. My mom knew."

I look at Callie. "Your mom told you she knew? She alluded to me the night you went out with Maddie, but she told you she knew?"

She nods as she swallows a bite. "Yeah, the day when I did

our laundry. She told me I looked happy and she knew I hadn't been in a long time." Her eyes soften. "She told me she thought you were the real deal and ten times the man Dominic was." Her expression turns suggestive. "I could've told her that was true in many, many ways."

Teagan snorts. "Come on, y'all, I'm eating."

I can't help but laugh and Callie turns to her. "So, why did y'all never do more than hookup? I mean, not that I'm tore up about it, obviously, but after all this time, I would think y'all would just be together."

I look at Teagan and shrug as if to say, *go for it.* She takes a sip of her beer. "Well, Jonas and I have known each other for ten years. And I don't have to tell you he's fun and we've always had a good time together.

"But I don't ever plan on getting married or having kids. I knew eventually Jonas would. I watched him with Leah and knew, even after what happened, he'd eventually want to find someone to build a life with. And honestly, I don't like Jonas romantically. He scratches an itch for me. Granted, he's really good at it, but we're just friends. So, you don't have to worry about me going *Fatal Attraction.*"

Callie laughs. "Okay. I can respect that."

As we clean up supper, Teagan is gathering her stuff and Callie looks at her. "You were supposed to stay here tonight, right?"

She nods. "Yeah, but we weren't gonna have sex. Last time was weird, with him crying and all. I was only gonna sleep."

I sigh. "Thanks, Teag."

She shrugs. "Well, it's true."

Callie asks, "So, where are you gonna stay?"

"I'll probably get a hotel. I come into town about once a month to see my parents, so this just happened to be when I was in town."

"You don't have to go anywhere. Jonas and I can go stay at my place."

Teagan protests, "No, I don't want to put y'all out."

Callie looks at me. "I have the same kind of mattress at home as my bed at the lake house."

I smile. "Nuff said. Teagan, stay. I'm going to Callie's. I haven't had a decent night's sleep since I got back from the wedding." I don't mention that it might also have to do with the fact that I haven't slept beside her since the wedding and I truly think that's a big factor as well.

Teagan shrugs. "Works for me. Thanks."

CHAPTER TWO

CALLIE

I really like Teagan. I should find her intimidating or be jealous of her, given her history with Jonas, but I don't. Once supper is over and we've cleaned up, Jonas gathers some clothes and toiletries into a backpack and we bid Teagan goodbye. He follows me home in his car and we arrive about fifteen minutes later.

I love Jonas. I don't know when it happened, but sometime between the lake house and now, I was a goner and I don't want to have another day in my life without him in it. Forever. I owe Elliot so many days of dish duty.

When we walk in the door, Elliot is sitting on the couch watching a movie. He glances up at me and does a double take when he sees Jonas. "What did I miss? When did this happen?"

I shut the door and tug Jonas toward my room. "We ran into each other. We're getting married. I'll fill you in later. I have plans right now. You might want to put on some head-phones or something, El." I hear Elliot laugh as I pull Jonas into my bedroom and slam the door.

I turn on the bedside lamp and Jonas gives me a lopsided

grin. "Really? I figured you'd need more incentive than that; I haven't even taken my pants off yet."

I push him down onto the bed and straddle him. He settles his hands on my hips and I give him a slow smile. "You're gonna take them off; don't worry." I take his face in my hands and search his warm brown eyes. "I love you, Jonas. You've never been a man of few words, by any means, but your speech was pretty compelling. And although I should be completely thrown by everything you said, I'm not. It's always been different with us, I think. You've known how to read me since the day we met. I've never understood it, but I love it. I hope someday you're as transparent to me as I apparently am to you. Knowing that you see me—you know me—that's all I've ever wanted. And you do it so well."

I sigh. "After how screwed up I was because of Dominic, I never thought I was worth anything more than what he gave me. I thought I was only good enough to sneak around with, to be someone's dirty little secret. You made me see I'm worth so much more. You made me feel valued and I can't thank you enough."

Jonas brushes a kiss across my lips, his expression hopeful. "You'll really marry me?"

I smile and nod. "Yes, Jonas; If you'll have me." After a beat, I add, "Now you can take off your pants."

He laughs and wraps his arms around me and buries his face in my neck. "Damn, Darlin'; this has turned out to be a great day."

I pull my glasses off and set them on the nightstand. "Um, I hope it's about to be a great night, too. I told Elliot to find some headphones. Don't make a liar out of me now."

Jonas pulls back and slides his fingers around to the back of my neck and into my hair. "Yes, ma'am." His mouth crashes against mine with a scorching kiss that immediately makes need coil low in my belly and only grows stronger as he trails his lips down my cheek and neck.

He shoves my sweater off my shoulders and it falls to the floor as I yank his shirt up and pull it over his head. I let my eyes travel down his torso, quickly reminded exactly how gorgeous he is. "Sweet lord, I forgot how beautiful you are."

Jonas chuckles and tugs my tank top over my head before unhooking my bra and sliding it down my arms. He sighs. "You, too, Darlin'." He runs his thumb over the tattoo under my left breast, making goosebumps scatter down my chest. "Still the perfect placement." I pull his face back to mine and claim his mouth and his hand skims up my ribs to cup my breast and I moan into our kiss as his thumb grazes my nipple.

He wraps his arms around me and rolls us over and I scoot further back onto the bed, pulling him with me. Wasting no time, he unbuttons my jeans and I lift my hips as he tugs them and my panties down my legs and tosses them on the floor. He shakes his head and smiles as he takes me in. "Don't know if I'll ever get over seeing you like this, Callie. All beautiful and splayed out for me."

I blush as his eyes travel down my body. "You gonna make me be naked by myself here?" I ask.

"For a minute maybe." He plants his knees on either side of my hips and leans down to brush a kiss across my lips. I start to unbuckle his belt and he grabs my hand and when he sees the question in my eyes, his grin turns positively wicked. He takes my hand and places it on my stomach, then slides it lower. "You know, ever since you had that fight with Dominic and he told you to fuck yourself and you said that you did frequently, I can't tell you how many times I've thought about you doing that." My mouth falls open in surprise and the flush deepens on my face and chest and Jonas leans in to whisper in my ear. "Make yourself come for me, Darlin'. Can you do that?"

My breath hitches and my pulse quickens at the thought of him seeing me masturbate but honestly, I'm not ashamed. The thing I've come to know about Jonas, even after only the few times we slept together is, he loves to watch me climax. I don't know if he was like that with other women, but every time we were together, I always felt his eyes on me as I'd come and it's sexy, so the thought of him watching me bring myself pleasure sends heat straight to my core.

I close my eyes and let him guide my hand to my pussy and I slip my fingers between my slick folds and search out my clit, sighing as I begin to get into a rhythm. I work it in lazy circles and after only a few minutes, my breathing turns ragged. His tongue flicks over my nipple and I gasp and grip the back of his neck as I rock my hips against my hand, a moan falling from my lips as my pleasure starts to build. "Shit, Callie, that's sexy." I pull his mouth to mine as my orgasm rips through me with a soft sigh.

CHAPTER THREE

JONAS

Watching Callie come is one of my favorite sights. Watching her make herself come? That's a whole other animal. Part of me expected her to be shy about it or refuse me, but she didn't and it was beautiful. Definitely lived up to the hype in my mind. Once she opens her eyes, her hands reach for my belt and she starts working to get it undone. I let her and my eyes trail over her body. "So, where's this other tattoo?" I roll her on her sides trying to locate it.

She laughs as she tugs my jeans down my hips. "Fuck me now; find it later, Jonas."

I chuckle. I can't argue with her logic. "Condom?"

She shakes her head. "No, I don't have any. Are you still clean?"

"Yeah, of course."

"Then don't worry about it."

I stand and drop my jeans and underwear and Callie's eyes drag down my body. "Damn, I'll never get used to the sight of you. I'm a lucky, lucky woman."

I climb back onto the bed and settle myself between her

thighs and take her face in my hands. "I'm the lucky one, Callie. Thank you for reminding me how good love is. I thought I wasn't built for it anymore, but you showed me how much I missed it."

Her expression softens. "I love you, Jonas."

"I love you, Callahan." I claim her mouth and grip her hip as I enter her. God, I've missed this, the way it is with her, the feel of her under me.

We begin to move together and Callie rocks her hips, driving me deeper and for a while, it's languid and easy, simply enjoying the feel of one another, the rightness of it.

Callie takes my face in her hands and her eyes search mine. "Make me yours, Jonas. Forever?"

I kiss her palm. "Forever, Darlin'." She pulls my face to hers and soon, the kiss turns desperate. Our movements follow suit and my thrusts quickly grow faster, harder. Our breathing becomes labored and I press her knees back farther, slamming into her even deeper and she grips my shoulders, her nails digging into my skin.

"Fuck, Jonas. I'm so close. Don't stop." Her words come between ragged gasps and my own release starts to build. It's all I can do to hold off until she clenches around me and cries out. I finally give myself permission to let go and my balls draw up as my hips buck with one last thrust and my own climax tears through me with a shuddering, deep grunt.

I collapse beside her and pull her into my arms. "God, I've missed this," I say, as my breath comes back to me.

She nods against my chest. "Me, too." She traces light circles over my chest with her fingertips and I look down and finally see her tattoo on the inside of her wrist.

I pick up her hand and turn it so I can see it better. It's tiny, about an inch square but fairly detailed. "A bird?"

"A dove."

"What does it mean for you?" I ask, because she wouldn't have gotten it if it didn't mean something.

"It's you."

More than a bit surprised, I look down at her. "What?"

She brings her eyes to mine. "Your name. It means dove. If anyone asked, I was gonna tell them it meant I was at peace with my life, since doves signify that, too; but it's you. I got it to remember you. I thought I'd never see you again after everything happened, and I wanted to have part of you with me forever. So, yeah."

My chest tightens with emotion. "Callie, that's...Wow. I don't know what to say."

She chuckles. "You, at a loss for words? That's new."

I brush a stray hair from her forehead. "You're amazing, you know that? Truly, Callie."

She sighs. "So you say." She yawns and I reach over to turn off the lamp and snuggle down with her in my arms.

When I wake after one of the best nights of sleep I've had in months, Callie is still curled up next to me. I carefully exit the bed without waking her up and find my underwear and slip them on. I quietly exit the bedroom and find the bathroom down the hall and once I finish in there, I walk toward the kitchen and take in the space. It's tidy and open and large for the size of the house; which appears to only have two bedrooms. I set about making a pot of coffee and search for the mugs while I wait for it to brew.

A few minutes later, while I'm pouring a cup for Callie and myself, Elliot walks into the kitchen and pauses when he sees me. "Well, damn; Callahan wasn't lying. You're hot. I mean, I knew that, but shit."

I chuckle. "Good morning to you, too, Elliot. Want some coffee?"

He shrugs. "Sure." I pour him a cup and hand it over. "So, y'all are back together?"

I nod. "Yeah." I sip my mug and then remember the guy Callie was with last night at the bar. "Oh, you might want to talk to Callie about the guy she was with last night; I'm pretty sure he's gay. Good looking, too."

He smiles. "Oh, really? Well, alright. So, was she serious? Y'all are getting married?"

"Looks like it."

He sobers considerably. "Jonas, don't hurt her. You didn't see what she was like after Dominic or after the wedding when she got home. I don't like having to watch her cry like that and console her. She doesn't deserve it."

I nod. "I know; I'm not gonna hurt her. I love her, Elliot. I know you've never seen me in a relationship, but I was engaged before. I almost got married. I've done commitment before, I just hadn't met anyone since then who made me want to do it again. Not until Callie. And I know what Dominic did to her. He's an asshole. You have nothing to worry about."

He sips his coffee and slowly nods. "Okay. Well, I guess congrats. When's the big day?"

I shrug. "Didn't really get that far last night."

He smirks. "I think I know how far you got last night."

I roll my eyes and I'm about to say something when Callie comes padding into the kitchen in my missing tee shirt. "Morning, Darlin'. Nice to see my shirt found a good home. Looks better on you anyway." I hand over her mug and she takes a small sip.

She smiles and wraps an arm around me. "Morning. Yeah, I totally swiped it at the lake." We both laugh.

Elliot turns to her. "So, Jonas said you might have a guy for me?"

Still a bit sleepy, she looks up at me, confused. "The guy you were with last night; he's gay, right?"

Understanding dawns and she nods and looks at Elliot. "Yeah, Russ is gay. I told him about you. I'll get you his info. He's really cute."

He smiles. "Perfect."

I refill my mug and pull Callie back to the bedroom and we climb into bed, curled up as we drink our coffee. She asks, "Did you sleep okay?"

I kiss the top of her head. "Best sleep I've had since we got back from the lake."

"Me, too. I think I missed sleeping with you more than anything. I'd forgotten how much I loved that part of things."

"Yep. It's pretty great. Do you have to work today?"

She shakes her head. "No, I worked last Saturday, so I'm off today. I either work Monday to Friday or Tuesday to Saturday."

"Well, lucky for me. So, what do you want to do today?"

"Not leave this room."

I chuckle. "Great idea. What else?"

"Call my parents. Tell them. Maybe. Are we crazy, Jonas? I mean, for real? It's insane, right? We've essentially only known each other a week. We only spent a week together and haven't seen one another in three months. It sounds absurd."

I look down at her. "Maybe. And if you want to just be together a while—date and stuff—we've got time. I'm not gonna change my mind, though. I love you, Callie."

She sighs and gives me a soft smile. "Would you mind if we wait a little while? I feel like we didn't even get to date, you know? I want to see what it's like to be with you outside of just a week at the lake house. I want to experience the everyday normal you. But I honestly don't think anything is gonna change my mind, either."

I shrug. "Sure. Of course. I plan on spending the rest of my life with you, so take all the time you need, Darlin'."

Relieved, she smiles. "Okay, I will." Callie takes a sip of her coffee. "Not to change the subject, but you know you have to come to Thanksgiving with me at the lake, right? Do you think your nana would like to come as well? Do you normally spend Thanksgiving with her?"

I nod. "Yeah. I'd say she probably would. She loves you and I'd love to get you back out onto the porch." I wiggle my eyebrows and Callie rolls her eyes.

CHAPTER FOUR

CALLIE

Being back with Jonas feels like no time has passed. We spend nearly the whole day in bed making up for the time we lost and by late afternoon, we're both starving and finally drag ourselves out of the bedroom to find something to eat. As I'm searching through the cabinets and fridge I turn to Jonas. "Looks like we're out of almost everything. I normally go grocery shopping on Saturdays but I was a bit busy today," I say with a smirk. "So we may have to order something. I know you like to eat clean and since we had pizza last night I don't know what you want to do."

He thinks for a minute. "Got any rice? And did I see some veggies in the freezer? Do you have any eggs?"

"Yeah, I guess. What are you thinking?"

"If you've got some soy sauce and a couple other seasonings, I can make a quick stir fry and fried rice."

I nod, impressed. "You're gonna cook?"

"Well, yeah; unless you want to."

I shake my head. "Nope, you already volunteered yourself, so have at it. I'll go see if Elliot's gonna eat with us or what." I walk to the living room where I see him watching TV, but with headphones on. I tap him on the shoulder. "El, you can take off the headphones," I say, laughing. "We're fixing supper. Jonas is gonna make a stir fry and fried rice. Want to eat with us?"

He shrugs. "Sure." He pulls me down beside him on the couch and says in a low voice, "So, how do you feel about him being back?"

I smile and blush with satisfaction. "It's amazing; like no time has passed. I love him. I can't believe it, and I know it's crazy, but he's it. He's the real deal."

He searches my eyes. "Okay. I just want you to be happy. It probably is crazy, but what do I know about straight love? If you decide you need me to move out, can you give me plenty of notice? I mean, I assume you're gonna live here, right?"

I shrug. "I mean, it would make sense, but I don't think Jonas knows it's my house. But I'll make sure you get a heads up."

"Okay. Well, I'm gonna go make sure my headphones are charged for later."

I roll my eyes. "You don't have to do that. We can restrain ourselves, you know."

He quirks a brow. "Please, I've seen the man in only his undies. You better not."

I laugh. "Yeah, it's pretty great." I return to the kitchen to find Jonas stirring a pot on the stove. I wrap my arms around him from behind. "Elliot's gonna eat with us."

"Okay. Tomorrow, you're gonna come with me to supper with Nana, right?"

I hop up on the counter next to the stove. "Of course. It will be strange to see her outside of the context of the library, though."

He sets the spoon he's using onto the stove and comes to

stand in front of me and settles his hands on my hips. "Well, I can't wait for her to see you."

I wrap my arms around his neck. "What did you tell her when you got back from the wedding? Does she know everything?"

He quirks a brow. "Not *everything*. She thinks you're a badass for what you said to Dominic when y'all had your fight. I also told her I had a great week with you and she's tried to get me to call you for weeks because she said you were exactly the right girl for me. And she wasn't wrong.

"A few weeks before I met you, she was giving me shit about all the girls I dated and said they were bimbos. She told me I needed to find someone who was smart and kind and who would call me on my bullshit. She said to find someone who wasn't *just* a pretty face, but who had a pretty soul, too. She was right. And when we were on the plane ride back and I found out you were the girl who Nana wanted me to go out with, that conversation with her flashed in my mind. And I knew right then I'd found exactly that, but I was too much of a coward to tell you." He presses his forehead to mine. "I'm sorry I cost us time that we could've had together. I hate it so much."

I take his face in my hands. "We can't change what happened; neither of us is perfect. I'm just happy we ran into each other last night. When I opened the bathroom door and saw you standing on the other side, I nearly pulled you in there with me and locked the door."

He gives me a wide grin. "Damn, Darlin'; that would've been hot."

I laugh. "Yeah, it would have. But I think we did alright anyway. It still turned out to be a good night."

He gives me a soft kiss. "You're not wrong." He steps back to the stove and I hop down from the counter.

"I'm gonna go take a quick shower. How long do you think before supper is done?"

Jonas does some quick mental calculations. "About twenty minutes. Plenty of time for you to get clean so I can dirty you up again later."

I go up on my toes and press a kiss to his cheek. "I look forward to it."

———

While Jonas and I lie in bed later, he's dragging his fingers down my back and I'm trying not to nod off because I don't want today to end, even if he'll still be here tomorrow. "Darlin', you can barely keep your eyes open. Want me to turn off the light?" Jonas asks and I hear the smile in his voice.

I shake my head. "I don't want to go to sleep. I'm afraid today has been a dream and if I let myself go to sleep, I'm afraid you won't be here when I wake up."

"I'm not going anywhere, Callie. Count on it. I'll be here when you wake up. Promise."

I nod. "Okay. Oh, what do you want for your birthday? It's in a few weeks, right?"

"You remembered?"

I tap my temple. "It's all up here. I remember everything. Do you have any traditions?"

"Not really. Nana usually makes me a cake, but last year, I think it was really hard on her. Her arthritis is getting really bad, so I almost want to tell her not to."

"Maybe I can help her. What kind of cake does she usually make you?"

"A pineapple upside down cake. It's my favorite."

"Okay. I'll see if she'll let me assist her, do the hard parts."

He kisses the top of my head. "You're sweet. But be warned, Nana can be a bit of a control freak in the kitchen."

I chuckle. "I think you forget I work with her. I know how feisty she is. So other than a cake, what do you want?"

He thinks for a minute. "To spend time with you."

"Well, that's a given. Anything specific you'd like to do?"

"Oh, Darlin', don't ask unless you mean it."

I laugh. "That good, huh? Hit me with it."

"You talking about pulling me into a bar bathroom earlier sounded like a lot of fun."

"Well, maybe. If you're a really good boy."

He laughs. "What kind of good are we talking? Good good or *bad* good?"

"We'll have to see, won't we?"

On the way to pick up Dorothy for supper, my mother calls.

"Hey, Mom."

"Hey, sweetie. I know it's still a few weeks out, but I wanted to see if Jonas would be joining us for Thanksgiving? Just working on the menu and want to plan accordingly."

"Yeah, he's coming. His grandmother might also join us if it's alright? She's his only family and I know he won't want to leave her all alone on the holiday."

"Oh, of course. That's perfectly fine. Maddie and Dominic are spending Thanksgiving with Quincy and Lillian, so we'll have plenty of room. Do we need to make sure there's a ground-level room available for her?"

"Yes. She's pretty spry, but she's still in her eighties, so that'd be great. We're gonna have supper with her now. I'll confirm with you as soon as I know, okay?"

"Sounds good. I'm glad we'll get to see you and Jonas this year. I look forward to a lot of holidays with the two of you."

"Me, too, Mom. Well, I've got to go. I'll let you know about Dorothy."

"Okay, bye sweetie."

I disconnect the call and turn to Jonas. "My mother is very excited about you coming for Thanksgiving."

He chuckles. "What, was she afraid they'd scared me off or something?"

I smile. "I think if you didn't come back, they might have thought that. But on the bright side, Maddie and Dominic won't be there. I'm sure they will be for Christmas, but at least this one holiday, we'll get a reprieve."

Jonas sighs. "Thank heaven for small favors, I guess."

"No joke. We'll need to find out if your nana will be coming. I'll need to book the flight pretty soon."

"Oh, sure. Let me know how much I owe."

I shake my head. "No. Going home is the one thing I let my parents spring for. They usually end up using their credit card miles anyway, so it probably does't actually cost them anything." After a beat, I add, "I don't know if I told you or not, but the house I live in, it's mine. Elliot rents from me."

He nods. "Okay. Well, that's kind of convenient. If and when we move in together, we already have a place. We can even talk about Elliot subletting my place if you want."

"Well, I promised him I'd give him plenty of notice if we needed him to move. But honestly, he's a great roommate, so I'm good with him staying. I like having the income; it really helps so I can work at the library."

"Well, I can pitch in with the mortgage, especially if I don't have a place."

"Oh, the house is paid for."

His brows press together in confusion. "What do you mean

it's paid for? How's that possible on your income at the library? Even if Elliot is paying you rent, there's no way."

"Well, I had a trust and I bought a house. It was a great deal and was a good investment."

"You had a trust? I thought you didn't take your family's money?"

"It's not theirs, it's mine. My grandparents left it to me, and I had to do something with it or forfeit it, so I bought a house. It was one of the stipulations. It couldn't be a frivolous purchase. It had to be something that would have a good return on investment. The neighborhood has really prospered in the last year and the value of my house has almost doubled. So, if I choose to sell, I'll make money."

He looks surprised. "Well, that's a lot of information. You sounded almost financial for a moment."

I roll my eyes. "I've always made good financial decisions. Maybe not always good personal decisions, but I've always been good with money."

"I hope the personal decisions you're referring to don't include me."

I swat him playfully. "You know what decisions I'm referring to. You've always been a good decision. Best decision I've ever made."

CHAPTER FIVE

JONAS

Over the next several weeks, Callie and I spend every possible moment together outside of work and school and I've essentially moved in with her and Elliot. Which, on the bright side, he and I carpool to work and it saves us both on gas.

We enjoyed a wonderful Thanksgiving with Callie's family and Nana loved the lake house. I was surprised to see the lake was gone and Callie told me it drops in the fall but will rise again in the spring. It was great that Maddie and Dominic weren't there for that visit, even if they will be when we visit tomorrow for an extended trip at Christmas.

Nana is not joining us this time, and we celebrated with her a few days ago. She and one of her friends from the retirement community are traveling to the Keys for about six weeks and she's excited to get to be at the beach and relax.

"Jonas, are you packed yet?" Callie comes into the bedroom and is clearly frazzled, judging by how fidgety she is.

I look up at her. "Yeah, pretty much. What's wrong? You seem on edge."

"I'm really not looking forward to being with Maddie for a

whole two weeks. I really thought they'd only get to come up for few days, but no, they're both off. Isn't it great?" Her tone tells me she thinks it is, in fact, not great.

I sit on the bed and pull her down beside me. "Callie, you're gonna be fine. I'm gonna be there and if things get hard, we can always sneak away. You know I'm really good at distracting you." I give her a kiss on the side of her head. "Besides, if you need a diversion, we can always tell your parents we're getting married and don't plan on having a wedding. That ought to rile everyone sufficiently."

She sighs. "Yeah, I guess there's that. Although, I haven't decided about the wedding part yet."

I'm surprised to hear her say this, because the way she talked the week of Maddie and Dominic's wedding, she was adamant about not having one of her own. "Oh, really? What are you thinking, Darlin'?"

She shrugs. "I don't know. My parents and I have been in a really good place since the summer and I feel like when I originally talked about eloping, it was mainly out of spite. Now, I'm thinking, it might not be so terrible to have my dad walk me down the aisle and have our family there. I know your nana will want to be there and I'd hate to take that away from her. Maybe we can do things down here, though, and only have immediate family and friends? Mom, Dad, Nana, Elliot, Teagan. Keep it simple?"

I consider and nod. "Could work. I already told you, it's whatever you want."

Callie leans her head on my shoulder. "I know that's what you said, but I don't want to make all the decisions myself. I want you to help; it's supposed to be your wedding, too."

"The only thing I care about is that you'll be there. It's my only requirement."

I feel her nod against me before she sits up. "There's probably something you should know."

"What?"

She lets out a heavy sigh. "If we tell my parents, they're gonna insist on a prenup. I don't care about one, but I know them; it's gonna be front and center for them."

I expected this, knowing what kind of money Callie comes from, so I simply shrug. "Well, it's smart of them to want that for you. I don't have an issue with it. I know your family has money and I definitely don't. If I were your parents, I'd want to protect you from the likes of street trash like me."

She rolls her eyes. "Jonas, you know I don't care about any of that. You know I don't care about their money. I don't want it and I don't need it." Her expression grows serious. "And you are not street trash. Don't ever let me hear you say anything like that again. It's completely disrespectful to your nana. I could give a shit about where you came from. Your nana didn't raise you to be ashamed of where you came from. She raised you to be a confident gentleman and that's who I fell in love with."

I nod. "Yes, ma'am. But seriously, I'll sign whatever. As long as I get you, I could care less what kind of paperwork is involved. I'm only getting married once, Darlin', so if I have to be all fancy and legal, I'm down."

I take her face in my hands and look into her eyes. "We don't have to get married if you don't want. That's always an option, too. If you feel like you don't want to go through the hassle or have to deal with your family on stuff."

She shakes her head. "No, I want to marry you. I love you. I love the idea of being married to you. Having a super sexy, amazing, loving husband. It's the dream, really. I want it. You know me, I hate being the center of attention and I hate how my family's money complicates things."

"Okay. Then let's do it. The whole deal. Prenup, official

engagement, wedding or court house, whatever you want. As long as I get to put a ring on your finger and call you mine forever, I don't care how it happens." She smiles and I continue, "Speaking of rings, do you want to go look sometime?"

"We don't need to; I have a ring. Well, my mother has it, but it's been mine since I was a little girl. It was my great-grand-mother's. It's from the 1920s."

I nod, impressed. "Do you like it?"

"Yes. It's beautiful. Art deco with this really intricate fili-gree work and I've always looked forward to getting to wear it."

"Well, I'll tell you, Darlin', you're making this whole thing way easier on me than I ever thought possible. I'll have to come up with something else to get you as an engagement gift."

"Jonas, *you* are the best gift. I don't need anything else."

I smirk. "Surely, we can think of *something*."

A slight blush colors her cheeks. "Oh, I'm sure you can come up with something. You're nothing, if not creative."

I brush a soft kiss across her lips. "I love I can still make you blush. I hope I never stop being able to do it."

She smiles. "Don't ever stop flirting with me and I think we'll be good."

"Promise, Darlin'. Flirting with you is one of my favorite things to do." After a beat, I ask, "What time is our flight tomorrow?"

"Eleven. So we'll get in town sometime after lunch. Are you sure you're ready for two weeks with Maddie and Dominic?"

I shrug. "I'm ready for two uninterrupted weeks with you. I'm ready to see what Christmas looks like for the Benson crew. I can't wait to curl up with you in the media room and watch *Die Hard* on the big screen. I can't wait to have coffee with you on the porch. I can't wait to take walks through the woods with you; maybe see some snow. I can't tell you the last time I saw snow."

She chuckles. "You're such a romantic. It's adorable. Not likely it will snow. Tennessee doesn't actually get a lot of snow. And even though the lake house is kind of in the mountains, it's still not at a super high elevation. Snow on Christmas?" She thinks for a moment. "It's probably been at least five years since that happened. But, who knows?"

I quirk a brow. "Can I tell you something else I'm looking forward to?" When she nods, I give her a mischievous smile. "I also can't wait to flirt with you in front of Maddie and Dominic and make them uncomfortable with our shameless displays of affection. I know that's really petty, but for some reason, I get so much enjoyment out of it."

She laughs. "Me, too."

I run my fingers through her long hair. "Feel better than you did when you walked in here?"

She nods. "Of course. I always feel better after you've worked your psychobabble magic on me."

I scoff in mock disdain. "Psychobabble? That's offensive."

She elbows me playfully. "Oh, really? You, offended? I'm pretty sure it takes more than that to offend you. I did say it was magic, so doesn't that make it better?"

I poke her in the waist where she's most ticklish and her body folds into my touch and she squeals. "Ooh, I like that sound, Darlin'; what else you got?" I continue to tickle her and she squirms away from me.

"Jonas, stop; it's too much," she says between fits of laughter.

I grab her face and kiss her soundly. "God, I love you. Did you know that?"

She reaches up to grip my wrists. "Yeah, I did, actually.

You're not so bad yourself. Thank you for talking me down. I love you for that."

I press my lips to her forehead. "Anytime, Darlin'."

CHAPTER SIX

CALLIE

We pull into the driveway at the lake house at two PM on the day before Christmas Eve. Thankfully, I don't see Maddie and Dominic's car in the driveway, so I relax a little. Jonas parks the rental car and shuts off the engine and takes my hand and kisses my palm. "Callie, it's gonna be alright. I know you're tense; you have been since we pulled onto the road for the house. It's two weeks; we'll be fine. We don't really even have to interact with them."

I nod. "I know. I just don't know if I'll ever be able to look at her and not want to punch her teeth out. I shouldn't still be bothered by this. I'm over Dominic; you know that. I shouldn't still be hung up on what she did."

He sighs. "I know it's easy to think that, but with family, I think it's different. She's always been like a sister to you and you've always kind of had her on a pedestal, because she's 'perfect', or whatever. And you've found out she's as flawed as everyone else. And no one can hurt you quite like family, so it's completely normal that what she did is still affecting you. Hopefully, someday, you'll be over it enough to at least be able to have a civil conversation, but it's okay if right now, you can't. I'm here, Darlin'; whatever you need."

I pull his face to mine for a quick kiss. "I know. And I love you so much. If I start to get childish or petty, can you rein me in please?"

He shrugs. "I can try but I know you. Once you've hit your limit, I've seen what kind of verbal damage you can do. Might not be a bad thing, though, if you actually had it out with her. She might not remember telling you what she did, but you could always bring it up. In front of your entire family, preferably. I'd give almost about anything to watch that go down."

I roll my eyes. "Yeah, not happening."

We exit the car and Jonas gets our bags out of the trunk and we walk up the sidewalk to the front door. When we get into the house, Jonas takes in the space and his mouth falls open and he shakes his head in disbelief. "Damn, Darlin', I knew your family would do it up right, but this is something else. The big kid in me is jumping for joy right now."

I chuckle and try to see things through his eyes, because this is what I'm used to. Next to the fireplace, there's an elaborately decorated, eighteen-foot-tall tree. Festive garland is draped over all of the doorways and archways. "Yeah, it's pretty nice. The tree down in the media room isn't as big. It's usually my favorite, because it's movie-themed."

My father enters the room from a hallway and pulls me in for a hug. "Hey, Dad."

He gives me a kiss on the cheek. "Hey, sweetie. Glad you finally made it." He turns to Jonas. "Did y'all have a good flight?"

Jonas sets our bags down and shakes my dad's hand. "Pretty good. You know Callie, not big on flying, but she did alright." He winks at me and I can't keep the blush off my cheeks.

If by *alright*, he means he grabbed my face and made out

with me as the plane was landing to distract me, yeah, I did just fine.

"Good to hear. Looks like Florida ended with a pretty good season."

Jonas nods. "Yeah, and your boys are definitely gonna have to work on their offense. It's a bit sad, Alex."

Dad chuckles. "Yeah, there's always next year."

I roll my eyes. "Dad, you say that every year."

He shrugs. "I mean it every year, too."

"Where's Mom? I want to make sure our gifts got here."

He gestures downstairs. "She's putting the final touches on the tree in the media room. But I'm pretty sure they did. No clue where she put them, though."

I nod. "Okay, I'll go down and see if she needs help."

Jonas starts up the stairs. "I'll take our bags up. I'll find you later, okay?"

"Sure." I head down to the basement and find my mother hanging the last few ornaments on the tree. "Hey, Mom. Need any help?"

She turns to see me, a smile on her face. She comes over to me and throws her arms around me. "Callahan! I'm so glad y'all made it. How was your flight?"

I return her hug and then shrug. "You know me, I hate flying. Good thing Jonas is good at distracting me."

She chuckles. "I'm sure. How are things with you all? Do I need to be thinking about getting your ring out of the safe deposit box?" She quirks a brow.

I blush and bite my lip. "I'll keep you posted."

Her eyes light up. "Really? Oh, Callahan, that's wonderful."

I nod. "Jonas is a wonderful guy. He's practically moved in with Elliot and me and I thought it would be awkward, but it's not. I love him, Mom."

She smiles. "Well, not that I condone living together before marriage, I honestly think it's smart these days. You never know someone until you live with them. You need to know if he leaves his dirty socks lying around or doesn't put the toilet seat down."

I laugh. "Not too much to worry about there. Jonas lived by himself for all those years. He's pretty tidy. And his nana raised him right. He's never left the seat up."

"How is Dorothy? We really enjoyed having her at Thanksgiving. She's a hoot."

I nod. "Yeah, I love her. She's good. She's down in the Keys with a friend of hers. Jonas and I are gonna miss seeing her for a few weeks, but she's happy she went." Remembering the gifts, I ask, "Did our presents get here? Dad said he thought they did, but he wasn't sure where they got to."

She nods. "Yeah, I put the box in your room. I didn't open it, because I wasn't sure if you'd already wrapped everything."

"Okay. Well, I'm gonna go unpack. What's the plan for the next couple days? Same as every year?"

"Yeah, you know us, nothing if not predictable. We do love our traditions."

"You're not totally predictable, Mom. Not anymore. You really surprised me the week of Maddie and Dominic's wedding with all your innuendo and you telling me you knew about him and me."

She sighs. "Well, it was good to see you happy. And as far as Dominic goes, I'm just glad Maddie's prenup is ironclad."

I can't hide my surprise hearing my mother's comment. "Has something happened? Surely things can't be that bad yet? It's not even been six months since the wedding."

She waves away my question. "Not that I know of. But knowing how badly he treated you, I can't imagine he treats

Maddie any better. Speaking of prenups, you know if you and Jonas get married, he'll have to sign one."

I let out a sigh. "Yes, I'm aware. He and I have talked about it. He knows it doesn't matter to me, but he's fine with it."

She looks pleasantly surprised. "Oh, well. Okay. Things are really serious, especially if you've already discussed that."

I nod. "Jonas and I have discussed everything. We have a very open and honest relationship."

She smiles. "I'm glad. And I'm really glad to see you happy, honey. Honestly."

"I am happy, Mom."

CHAPTER SEVEN

JONAS

When I get upstairs to the room Callie and I share, I'm flooded with all the memories we've had in this room. All the talks, all the kisses, the first time we had sex. I love this room and it will always hold a special place to me, since this is where we fell in love.

I set our bags on the bed and notice the box on the sofa. I assume it's the box of gifts Callie had shipped so we wouldn't have to check a bag when we traveled. I start unpacking my suitcase and take my toiletries to the bathroom and put them away. I hang up my clothes in the closet and put away my other clothes in the dresser.

I hear the bedroom door open and see Callie walk in. She looks at me and then sees the box on the sofa. "Oh, good. There it is."

"Hopefully everything arrived unscathed from transit."

"I don't think I got anything that could get damaged, I just wish we hadn't had to buy for *everyone*. I can't tell you how much I hated buying a gift for Maddie and Dominic. It's stupid." She picks up the box and sets it in the floor.

I nod and walk over to where she stands. "Yeah, but your family isn't huge and if we buy for everyone but them, they'll think it's because you're affected by their relationship."

Her lip curls into a snarl. "That's because they're narcissists."

Ever since Callie found out Maddie knew about her relationship with Dominic and was complicit in her heart getting broken, she's had this underlying current of rage where Maddie is concerned. I don't worry about how she'll act around Dominic. She's already said what she needed to say to him. But Maddie, I do worry about.

Maddie drunkenly confessed to Callahan she knew Callie and Dominic had been seeing one another for four years, and when Dominic pursued her, in spite of him still being in a quasi-relationship with Callie, she went for him. Callie was heartbroken by her cousin's betrayal and she's still not over it. So I do my best to help her work through it, although part of me wishes it would all come to a head, so she'd feel better about it.

I nod. "Yeah, they are. They're never gonna feel like they did anything wrong. And so, you letting them affect you the way it does isn't gonna hurt them. It's only gonna hurt you. So, I honestly think you need to find some time while we're here to have it out with Maddie. You'll feel better and then I won't feel like I have to watch you like some kind of ticking time bomb, afraid you're gonna go off on her at any moment."

Callie's nostrils flair in anger. "I don't need you to watch me. I'm fine. I don't even want to talk to her or ever see her again."

I can't bite back a soft laugh of annoyance. "Oh, yeah, you're fine alright. You forget I can read you. I know you're barely holding it together right now and they're not even here. If you'd just have it out, you'd feel better. I know you would.

Were you not relieved after you finally told Dominic off once and for all?"

When she doesn't answer me, I continue. "I feel like, at this point, you're only *not* having the confrontation you need with Maddie for the sake of your parents or her parents. You've always cared more about other people than yourself. And trust me, I love that you're such a considerate person. But if you don't fix this for yourself, you're the only one who's gonna be miserable, not them. And I don't want you to be miserable, because then I'll be miserable. And I'd rather us have a good time while we're here. I want you to be relaxed and fun and sassy."

I pull her into my arms and for a moment, her posture is rigid, as if she's not wanting to give up this fight, even with me. But then, she finally relaxes against me and lets out a heavy sigh. "I'm sorry. I know I'm eventually gonna have to talk to her and tell her how she hurt me. But part of me feels like even when I do, she's not gonna care."

I take her face in my hands and search her eyes. "Yeah, it's always a possibility. You've said Maddie's always been the golden child. She's probably never been told she's done anything wrong in her life. And she might not react or she might be defensive and try to turn things around on you, but at least you'll have made peace about things within yourself.

"And I'm sure it's probably sad for you to think about not being on good terms with Maddie again. I know y'all have always been close and I know not talking to her and having her in your corner has taken a toll on you.

"But you've got to come to some sort of peace within yourself. I don't want it to be like this every time we come here. You love this place and I don't want it be tainted for you. To make it to where you don't want to come here and it cause issues with your family, all because of her."

Callie nods and I see a tear roll down her cheek. I wipe it away with the pad of my thumb. "Darlin', I don't want to have to dry your tears the whole time we're here. Not that I'm not willing to do it, but I'd rather you be happy while we're here."

She sniffles. "I know. I'll be fine. Maybe Maddie will say something to push me over the edge and I won't have a choice. But I don't know if I can bring it up. I don't want this place to be ruined either. I already have bad memories on the porch, I don't want them other places, too."

I quirk a brow. "I thought I erased all those bad memories for you? Do we need to go back out there right now? I'm happy to try again."

She chuckles. "No, I'm good. You did a really good job."

I lean in and brush a kiss on the side of her neck. "You know, I can do a good job right now, too, even it's not on the porch. I'm really good at distracting you. Or, have you forgotten?"

I pull back and her cheeks are flushed and she shakes her head. "No, I know exactly what kind of distraction you're really good at providing me. Too bad we don't have time."

"How much time do we have, I can always make it work."

Callie laughs. "Twenty minutes, maybe. Dad needs help to move wood for the fire pit."

I run my thumb along her bottom lip. "Twenty minutes? I only need half that and it'll still be really good."

"You're quite persuasive, you know that?"

"So, is that your way of telling me you want me to take your mind off things for a few minutes?"

"It's my way of telling you I'm more than happy to let you try."

"Oh, Darlin', I don't have to *try*. I'm happy to simply *do*." I sit on the sofa and pull her down with me. She wraps her arms around my shoulders and runs her fingers through my hair.

"You're too good for me, Jonas. Are you sure you wouldn't rather have someone who's not such a wreck?"

I trail kisses down her neck as my fingers skim under the hem of her sweater and across the skin of her waist. Her breath catches as my hand moves up her ribs. "I'm not even gonna dignify that with a response, Callie. I'm a little busy at the moment." I brush my thumb across her breast and the nipple rises to my touch under the lace of her bra. "Oh, there it is."

Callie claims my mouth and shifts so she can straddle me. She grinds herself against me and my dick instantly gets the memo. She works my shirt up over my head and I grab her ass and pull her into me. I take her glasses off her face and set them on the window sill behind the couch and look into her blue eyes, currently gone dark with lust. "Your eyes are my favorite color right now."

She smiles. "Well, you're doing a pretty good job, so I'm not surprised." I start to tug her sweater over her head and she stills my hands.

"What, Callie?"

"Listen," she whispers. I do and then I hear it. A knock at the door. We both slump. "Every fucking time." She sighs and grabs her glasses as she rises from my lap and I pull my shirt back over my head.

CHAPTER EIGHT

CALLIE

When I open the door, I already know who I'm gonna see, but I'm still not prepared. I try to keep my features even, although, inside, I'm on edge from the anger always sitting under the surface whenever I'm around Maddie anymore and the fact Jonas and I were interrupted.

"Hey, Maddie."

"Hey! I wanted to come say hi, since we just got here. Especially since we seem to keep missing each other on the phone. I feel like I haven't spoken with you in months. And since we didn't get to come to Thanksgiving, I couldn't wait to come see you."

I nod. "Okay. Well, hi. Jonas and I were unpacking."

She smirks. "Yeah, your face says that's what y'all were doing. I know better. I can't wait to tell you all about our honeymoon. I'll have to show you all the pictures."

"Maybe later. I'm still trying to get everything unpacked and need to make sure the gifts we brought are still in good shape. I'll talk to you after while, okay?"

As I turn to go, she puts her hand on my arm. "Callahan, did I do something? It feels like you don't even want to talk to me anymore —like you're avoiding me and I don't know why. Or is it something else?" In a lower voice she asks, "Is everything okay with you and Jonas?"

I clench my jaw. "Jonas and I are fine. Perfect actually. You interrupted us, so if you'll excuse my annoyance, being cock blocked isn't necessarily my favorite thing." My words come out harsher than I intend, but as far as things go with Maddie, I'm barely holding on.

Maddie's face flushes and her mouth falls open as if she can't believe what I've said. "Oh, well. Um. Sorry. You guys are coming to the party tonight, right?"

"Yeah, of course."

She nods, unsure what else to say. "Okay, well, I brought that cab you like, I thought we could share the bottle later. Might be kinda fun, like old times." Her tone sounds hopeful.

"We'll see, Maddie. Jonas and I haven't really gotten to see each other much lately with work and my school schedule, so we're hoping to make up for lost time over the next few weeks."

Something flashes in her eyes. "I haven't seen you since my wedding. You've seen him pretty much nonstop since who knows when. From what your mom said, y'all are practically living together. What is wrong with you, Callahan? Are you mad at me?"

Barely contained rage bubbles up in my chest. "Maddie, I can't talk about this right now. I might in the future, but for now, I really don't have anything to say to you. I don't want to hurt you, I don't want to fight, I just can't talk to you about this right now. It's Christmas and I'd prefer to keep things peaceful."

She frowns in confusion. "Callahan, what happened? What did I do?"

I hear Jonas's voice behind me, edged with concern. "Callie, you okay?"

I call over my shoulder, "Yeah, I'm fine." I look at Maddie. "If you can't remember, I don't really want to bring it up. You probably never meant to tell me what you did and I need time to get over it."

"Well, how am I supposed to know how to fix things if I don't even know what I did wrong?"

I huff a soft laugh. "Maddie, I don't know if it ever can be fixed. I just need space."

Stunned by my words, she finally nods. Her voice is low and sounds pained. "Okay. Well, if you do want to talk, I'm around." She backs away and walks across the landing to her own room and shuts the door.

I turn to go back into my own room and shut the door harder than is really necessary and Jonas looks up at me from the book he's reading on the sofa. He closes his book, his expression confused. "Why didn't you go ahead and talk to her? She outright asked you what she'd done."

I shrug. "I don't know. She started in on us spending time together and sharing a bottle of wine like old times. I just got so angry."

"Well, you should've talked to her. I know you said you want things to be peaceful for Christmas, but I'm telling you, that's not gonna be how it is with all this animosity between you and Maddie when she doesn't even know what she did."

I sigh. "I know. But I don't even know where to start."

He stands and walks over to me and kisses the side of my head. "Darlin', I know better than anyone what can happen when you get really drunk, and I know what I did. I can't imagine if things had happened and I had no clue, how much worse I'd feel learning the truth. Don't keep her in the dark about this. She's gonna stew and so are you and no one is gonna have a peaceful Christmas until this is resolved." After a beat, he adds, "Did you really tell Maddie she cock blocked us?" His tone is amused and I roll my eyes.

"Yeah, I did. It was true. And not for the first time with her. I think I just wanted to catch her off guard."

He laughs. "Caught me off guard, too. But you know I like it when you talk dirty." I playfully elbow him and he says, "I guess I better go help your dad. Don't need him pulling anything trying to prove he's a youngin' any more. And I probably should show up Dominic."

I nod. "Don't overexert yourself. I have plans for those hands later."

He smiles. "I can't wait to hear what those are." He brushes a kiss across my lips. "Go down, have a glass of wine, calm down."

My brows raise in surprise. "Are you telling me to drink? If I do that, you won't flirt with me. You know which of those things I'd prefer."

He rolls his eyes. "I didn't tell you to get shit faced. I said have *a glass*, Darlin'. Take the edge off. Make it so you can stand to be in the same space as Maddie." He considers. "On second thought, don't drink that much, I don't know how much it would take for you to be able to put up with her. Later, I'll help you work out this pent up aggression."

"Is that a promise?"

He kisses my cheek. "Always. After the party tonight, we'll come back up here and I'll make you feel really good."

I quirk a brow. "I'll hold you to it."

"Is that a challenge, Darlin'?"

I shrug. "Guess we'll see, won't we." I blow out a breath and lean into him. "Thank you." And I know he knows I'm thanking him for more than simply the earlier distraction and the promise of great sex later. It's for him, being here with me. For loving me. For telling me what I need to hear, even if it's not what I want to hear.

"No thanks needed."

CHAPTER NINE

JONAS

After Callie's run in with Maddie, I hated to leave her alone, but I know this is something she's gonna have to work through on her own. No amount of, in my opinion, good advice is gonna fix them or bring their issues out into the open. So, instead, Dominic and I simply haul wood to the fire pit, much like we did back in the summer.

For a split second, I debate mentioning to him that Maddie knows about him and Callahan's relationship and how long it was. But I can't stand the guy, for one, and another, I'm not about to tell Callie I got involved in her squabble with Maddie by bringing Dominic into the mix. I value my balls too much. Because I've seen Callie give someone a verbal lashing and I don't want to be on the receiving end of one of those.

After we get done hauling wood, I head back up to the bedroom to take a quick shower and find Callie sitting on the sofa reading, in her bathrobe, her hair wrapped in a towel. "Damn, Darlin', give a guy a little warning when he's gonna find you like that. It's almost too sexy for words."

She sips her glass of wine and rolls her eyes. "Keep it in your pants."

I stop in my tracks. "Callie, you alright?" Her tone is not playful. It's more annoyed and it has me worried because it's totally out of character for her.

"Yeah, I'm fine."

"No, you're not. What happened?"

"Nothing."

I squat down in front of her. "Callahan, what happened? You're not fine. What's going on, Darlin'?"

"I had too much wine. Maddie was going on and on about her honeymoon and crap. I'm sorry. I'm pissed at myself."

I let out a small sigh of relief. "Is that all?" I sit next to her on the sofa. "Callie, I'm not mad, if that's what you're worried about."

She frowns in confusion. "But you've always said you won't flirt with me or anything if I have too much to drink. I'm pretty buzzed. I figured you'd be pissed."

I shake my head. "No. If you get drunk, I'll bring you to bed and tuck you in and I won't have sex with you, but you still seem pretty levelheaded as of this moment. I'm not gonna get mad at you. I'd prefer you not feel like you needed to get drunk to endure a party with your family, but I know with things the way they are with Maddie, you're a bit on edge."

"Can I ask why you've always been so adamant about the 'not flirting with a drunk woman thing'? I know you're big on consent. Is it only that?"

I shrug. "Some of it. Plus, I feel like if a woman is drunk, she's not gonna remember what she did and I always like a woman to remember what fun she had with me."

Callie rolls her eyes, but this time, it is playful. "Well, no worries. I'm pretty sure, I'd remember everything if we went to bed right now."

"Well, that's good. Because I intend on taking you to bed later. Want me to finish that wine for you?"

She hands it over and I sip it. "Damn, this is pretty good. And I don't even like wine. Is this the wine Maddie wanted you to share with her?"

She nods. "Yeah. It's my favorite and she knows it."

I sigh and level her with a gaze. "Darlin', I don't know if I can handle a whole two weeks with you avoiding talking to Maddie about what she did. You're gonna have to hash this out with her. You can't avoid her for the rest of our lives. Please tell me you're gonna have it out with her before we leave to go home."

Her jaw clenches. "I can't promise that, Jonas."

"Well, what if I said I'd make it worth your while?"

Her eyes narrow. "What are your talking about?"

"What if I said that until you get things squared away with Maddie, I will sleep beside you, but not sleep *with* you?"

Her hands ball into fists. "You can't do that. What kind of fair is that? Simply because you don't want me to whine and be pissy and drink too much?"

I nod. "Yeah, pretty much. If you're miserable, I'm miserable. I don't want to spend my winter break miserable, Callie. I love you and I want to enjoy this time we have together, but I can see that until you have it out with Maddie, it's not gonna happen."

She laughs, but it's hollow. "I think you forget who you're dealing with. I've gone a whole lot longer without sex than you. I could basically make a career out of it."

I shrug. "Be that as it may, you and I both know you're having really good sex now, compared to what you were having before. You also know I have excellent self control."

Her nostrils flair and she jumps up off the couch and goes into the bathroom and slams the door. *Great, Jonas. Go ahead and piss her off more.* My goal is truly not to piss her off, but to make her confront Maddie. I know she's gonna feel a lot better when she does and so will I.

I rise from the couch and go into the bathroom and Callie doesn't look at me while she's drying her hair. *Definitely pissed.* I start the shower and once it's warm, I strip down, but don't miss her glancing at me in the mirror as I enter the shower. *Definitely pissed, but she still finds me attractive.*

Once I'm washing my hair, I hear the toilet flush and I'm hit with freezing cold water. I gasp and move out of the spray. "What the hell?"

I hear Callie laughing. "You want to play, I can play."

"Callie, that's low."

"Yeah, well, you threatening to withhold sex is low, too, Jonas. Simply because I don't work on your timeframe, doesn't mean you can dictate to me when I'll do what."

I quickly finish washing up and step out of the shower and dry off and wrap myself in a towel. "You think I want to withhold sex from you? It's a punishment for me, too."

"Then why even threaten it? You don't do shit like that."

I sigh. "I just really want you to have it out with Maddie already. I thought I'd give you some incentive."

She quirks a brow as she curls her hair. "Negative reinforcement doesn't really work for me."

I trail a finger down her neck. "How about positive reinforcement? Does that do anything for you?"

She moves away from my touch. "Jonas, I'm not a dog or a child you can punish or reward." Her tone sounds bitter.

"I know that."

"Then act like it. If you have sex with me, don't put conditions on it. I don't need the head games."

My stomach drops. I didn't consider how she was treated before and how it still might be affecting her. *Fucking Dominic.*

Once she sets the curling iron down I take her chin in my hand. "I'm sorry. I didn't mean to do that to you. I won't do it again. Forget what I said, okay?"

She sighs. "I'll talk to Maddie. I will. I need to do it in my own time, though"

"Okay. Forgive me for being an ass?"

She nods and presses a kiss to my cheek. "Of course."

CHAPTER TEN

CALLIE

During the party, I greet my parents' country club friends and Dad's work colleagues whom I've not seen since the last Christmas party. I introduce Jonas to everyone as we make the rounds.

As usual, he looks entirely dashing in a charcoal gray suit and black button down and black tie. He winks at me from across the room as he talks with a law clerk who works for my father. And in spite of our earlier spat, I can't keep my eyes off of him.

"You know, it's totally rude to eye fuck someone from across the room." My head snaps to my right and I'm shocked to see Clint Branch, an old family friend.

Clint hasn't changed at all, from what I can see. His warm olive skin is clear and smooth and his almost black eyes take me in mischievously. He's dressed in a tailored navy suit and festive bow tie. His normally close-cropped black hair is a bit longer and more messy than I've ever seen it, but he's still as handsome as ever.

My eyes go wide and I can't keep the blush from my

cheeks, but I smirk. "Not when you know what he looks like out of those clothes. It's entirely warranted, trust me."

He laughs and pulls me in for a hug. "How are you? I haven't seen you in, what, three years?"

I return his hug. "I know, it's been way too long. How are you? What are you up to?"

He shrugs. "A little of this, a little of that."

I laugh. "So, still being a spoiled shit? Nice."

He nods, amused. "Yeah, pretty much. So, the guy? Yours?"

I nod and look at Jonas. "Yes, actually. Jonas. He's a kindergarten teacher."

Clint arches a brow. "Shit, he doesn't look like any teachers I had in school. I might have paid more attention if they looked like that. Good for you."

"Thank you. I am very lucky."

"How did y'all end up together?"

"You wouldn't believe me if I told you. It's a totally crazy story."

"Ooh, well you know I love me some crazy. Spill."

I glance around. "You can't tell anyone." I can tell Clint's intrigued and I know he'll keep my secret, as I've had several of his over the years. He mimes crossing his heart. "Okay. So, you know how Dominic and I were a thing for years?" When he nods, I sigh. "Well, I didn't want to come to the wedding without a date and let him think I was still hung up on him, even though I was. My roommate was supposed to come with me and be a stand-in boyfriend, but he decided pretending to be straight for a whole week was gonna be too much for him.

"He and Jonas work together and Jonas owed him a favor and Jonas figured, what the hell? A free trip to the lake and all he had to do was pretend to be my boyfriend and if it made Dom a little jealous or whatever, even better. And for a few days, we were playing the part, flirting and stuff. But, then it wasn't play." I raise a brow suggestively.

His mouth falls open. "No shit. So, y'all have been together since then? That's crazy."

I shake my head. "My parents think we never split up. But Jonas didn't do relationships, and I knew that when we were together at the wedding, so when we got home, we went our separate ways."

He frowns. "So, is it still pretend?"

"No, for three months, we were both miserable. I thought he didn't care, because I knew he didn't do relationships. He had a past relationship that kind of did a number on him, and he thought I wouldn't be able to accept what happened. But we ran into each other around Halloween and he told me he was in love with me. And here we are."

"Well, Callahan, I tell you. That is quite the story."

I nod and sip my wine. "So, what about you? Boys? Girls? Who's got your fancy these days?"

He sighs. "No one in particular. But, if you hadn't told me he was yours, I was so gonna make a run at Jonas."

I laugh. "You wouldn't be the first guy to try."

"Does he have any brothers or sisters who look that good?"

I shake my head. "Only child, that we know of."

"That's a damn shame."

I laugh. "I can see why you'd think that. So, where are you living now?"

Clint sips his drink. "DC. I'm working with a PR firm for Halston Bailey."

"The senator? How'd you swing that?"

He nods. "Yeah. Dumb luck, actually. I didn't even know who he was, but I was at a bar and made a crack about an ad that came on. It was truly terrible, by the way. And the guy next to me says, 'Oh, you can do better?' And you know me, I'm nothing if not an arrogant shit, so of course, I say, 'Definitely.' But I didn't see the guy's face until after, and it was him. I was mortified. But he told me to put my money where my mouth was and offered me a job if I could come up with a good campaign for him. And I did."

"Wow, Clint, that's amazing. So, are you liking it?"

He quirks a brow. "I like DC. Lots of parties. Lots of beautiful people."

"So, how long are you in town for? Are you staying at your parents' place up here?"

"Yeah. I fly back the day after New Years."

"Well, we'll have to get together. I think Jonas and I might try to go to Dollywood and see the lights while we're here. You know how I love that."

He nods and I notice Jonas coming over. I pull him to me and introduce Clint to Jonas. "Jonas, this is one of my oldest friends, Clint Branch."

They shake hands and Clint shakes his head as his eyes take in Jonas. "Damn, you're even prettier up close. Callahan, do they just breed them different in Florida or something?"

I laugh. "Not sure about that, but he's alright."

Clint turns to Jonas, "So, Jonas, tell me, is Callahan a better kisser than she was when we were kids? Because she used to be really bad at it."

"Clint!" I flush with embarrassment.

Jonas looks at me confused and I roll my eyes. "Clint and I used to practice kissing when we were younger. We both had a crush on Zeke Cooper. And he also had a crush on, what was her name? Audrey Fisher?"

Clint sighs. "Yeah, Audrey Fisher. Shit, she had a great set of tits."

Jonas laughs. "I see. Well, I definitely don't have any

complaints about Callie's abilities. Kissing or otherwise." He winks at me and I blush.

I sigh, exasperated. "Clint, it's so nice to see being in politics hasn't changed you. You're still as charming as ever."

Jonas turns to Clint. "Politics? What do you do?"

"PR for Senator Halston Bailey."

I see something flash in Jonas's eyes but it's gone just as quickly and I can't read what emotion it is. "Oh, really? Is he as pompous as he looks in interviews?"

Clint shrugs. "Not as far as I've seen. He gave me a job, so I can't really complain. He's a fair boss."

Jonas nods. "Well, maybe tell him to do something about trying to get the teachers' union legislation passed?"

He nods. "I can definitely try." He glances across the room and sees someone. "Listen, I'm gonna make the rounds. Come see me sometime this week. We can all do lunch, okay?"

"Sure. Good to see you, Clint. Merry Christmas."

He waves to us as he walks across the room. I turn to Jonas. "What was that about?"

"What was what about?"

"Your face. When Clint mentioned Senator Bailey."

"Nothing. I just never really liked him." He sips his beer and doesn't meet my eye.

"Is that all?"

He pulls me to his side and kisses the side of my head. "Yeah. He used to be a state congressman in Florida. Did a terrible job. Still don't know how he got to where he is on his record."

I get the feeling he's not being entirely truthful, but I don't understand why he'd lie or what he's lying about, so I drop it for the time being.

CHAPTER ELEVEN

JONAS

Halston Bailey. A name I hoped to never hear again for the rest of my life. I knew at some point, I probably would, simply due to the nature of politics. And I'm pretty sure Callie knows I wasn't totally honest with her. But I need time to figure out how to tell her about *that* part of my past. Until then, I'll try to forget the scum bag exists.

The party winds down around one AM and Callie's a bit tipsy, so I take her up to bed and help her get changed and take her makeup off. "You sure you don't want to seduce me, I'd be real easy right now."

I braid her hair, because I know she prefers to sleep with it that way. "No, Darlin', I'm sure. You look like you had fun tonight, though. Your friend, Clint, seems nice."

"Yeah, he is. I haven't seen him in a couple years though. I forgot how much fun he is."

"So, he's bi?"

She nods, her eyes heavy. "Yeah, although, he doesn't really look at gender. It's more, he looks at the person. He's sweet, though. Not bad for a first kiss."

I huff a soft laugh. "Nice." I finish her braid and drop it over her shoulder. "All done."

She runs her hand down the corded strands and turns to me and smiles. "Thank you."

"Anytime. So, what's the plan for tomorrow? Y'all do anything special on Christmas Eve?"

She blinks slowly, struggling to think, and I'm realizing she's either more intoxicated than I originally thought, or she's simply exhausted. And with the late hour, it could go either way. "Hmm. We have family dinner tomorrow night and we'll go down to the fire pit to roast chestnuts."

I can't hide my surprise. "Seriously, chestnuts? For real?"

She nods. "Yeah. Dad and uncle Lance have done it since they were kids. I don't like them, but they still insist on doing it every year. I don't know if anyone actually eats them, but it's tradition."

I plant a kiss on her shoulder. "Well, you know how I feel about the fire pit. I can't wait to snuggle up to you next to the fire."

She turns off the lamp and lies down and I curl my body around hers and in moments, she's out. Unfortunately, I'm not so lucky and I'm not able to clear my mind enough to settle down and sleep until sometime around four AM.

When I finally drag myself from bed, I look at my phone and see it's after nine, which is pretty late for me, but I pull on my sweats and a hoodie and make the bed. I head into the bathroom to splash a little water on my face and brush my teeth. I know Callie will probably still be out on the porch, so I head downstairs to make myself a much needed cup of coffee.

Steaming mug in hand, I step out onto the porch and see

Callie and Lance are in some sort of debate. Callie stands to let me have her seat and I pull her down into my lap. "Ooh, you're still warm. I forgot to bring a blanket out with me. I was about to go in, but you'll do."

"Jonas, what are your thoughts on *A Christmas Carol?*" Lance asks. And much like Callie described him back in the summer, he's wrapped in an ancient cardigan, looking exactly like the college professor he is.

I take a sip of my coffee. "Book or movie?"

Callie looks at me. "Best adaptation. The book stands on its own merits, but we're having a debate about which television or movie adaptation did the best to capture the spirit of the work."

I smirk. "I see what you did there." She winks at me and I think for a moment. "Well, that's quite the topic to delve into before I've had my coffee, but if I had to choose, I'd probably have to say the Muppets version is pretty good. Michael Caine plays a pretty convincing Scrooge."

Lance chuckles. "Not bad. See, I'm of the opinion that the more non-traditional *Scrooged* is the best."

Callie interjects. "And I say that it shouldn't count, because it's not the actual story."

I consider. "Well, I think the argument can be made that retellings still retain the *spirit* of the story. And *Scrooged* still gets the message across about what the holiday should really be about. So I say it definitely counts."

Lance smiles, clearly vindicated. "I knew there was a reason I liked you, Jonas."

Callie frowns in mock dismay. "You're supposed to be on my side."

"Nah, you'd hate it if I agreed with you on everything." I lean in closer and whisper in her ear. "If we never disagreed on anything, we'd never get to make up after and have really good make up sex." She blushes and elbows me playfully. I look back at Lance. "So, how are things at the university?"

He waves his hand and scoffs. "Kids have gone soft. I miss the days where you gave the syllabus, and if the students didn't read it and go by it, and they failed, it was their fault, not mine. Now, I'm expected to explain it line by line, it seems."

I chuckle. "Yeah, I know what you mean. I know kindergarten's not college, but even with kids that young, a lot of the parents coddle and hover and don't even let the kids make their own mistakes and you can always tell when the parent has done the project for the kids. I don't look forward to what college will be like when this generation of students gets there."

Lance drains the rest of his mug. "Alright, y'all, I'm headed in. My old bones can only handle the cold for so long. Callahan, I've got some books for you. They aren't the terrible stuff you read. You might actually learn something from these."

Callie quirks a brow. "Uncle Lance, how do you know I don't learn stuff from those terrible books I read?" They laugh and he shakes his head. "Thanks, though. I'll get them sometime. Anything I might actually like?"

He considers. "There's an Erik Larson you'll probably enjoy."

She nods. "Okay. I'll check it out."

"Sure thing, kiddo. I'll see y'all later. Brunch at eleven."

He steps into the house and I pull Callie closer to me. "Warm enough, Darlin'?"

She nods. "Yeah. You're always really warm, so I'm nice and toasty now. Did you sleep okay?"

"Yep. Same as always. I swear I love that mattress. I think it sleeps better than the one we have at home."

"Maybe. Speaking of which, are you gonna give up your lease when it comes due in a couple months?"

Callie and I haven't talked about my apartment in several weeks. And even though I'm practically living with her and Elliot, I still have a lot of stuff at my place. "Is that what you want?"

She smiles. "Well, you've not spent the night at your place since way before Thanksgiving. Don't you think it's a waste of money at this point?"

"Yeah, probably. But I didn't want to push you if it wasn't something you weren't ready for."

"I'm good if you are. Some people would probably think it's kind of soon, but most people don't know that we started our relationship by living together, so I think it's right on track for us."

I nod. "Probably. Okay. Yeah. I'll do it. What do you want me to do about my rent?"

Callie frowns. "What do you mean?"

"Well, right now I pay rent. You said your house is paid off. What do you want me to do with the money I normally put toward rent?"

She shrugs. "You don't have to do anything. We can talk with Elliot about how we want to split utilities and groceries and stuff. You can put whatever else in savings."

"Okay." I nuzzle her neck. "What do you want to do today?"

"We'll have the afternoon free. We could go on a walk through the woods. It's supposed to actually warm up a bit today, so it should be nice."

"Sounds perfect. Hey, I'm sorry about last night. I shouldn't be pushing you to talk to Maddie. I know you'll eventually work up to it. I only thought it would make this trip go a bit smoother if you went ahead and got everything out in the open with her."

Callie sighs. "I know. And I love you for wanting to help

me work through all my shit. I really do. I don't want to ruin Christmas. I feel like, if I go ahead and have it out with her, she and I will both be in a funk. At least this way, I can pretend to still be okay until we get through all the festivities. I know I can't avoid her forever. And I'll try to talk to her before we go home."

CHAPTER TWELVE

CALLIE

Jonas and I have a quiet day after brunch with the family and finally take a walk though the woods around three and when we get to the top of a hill, I point out where Clint's parents' house is.

"Oh, wow, I never noticed that during the summer. Is their place bigger than this one, damn."

I nod. "Yeah, you can't really see it until all the leaves are gone. Their place is nice. They have a pool and hot tub."

"So, how does Clint fit in with everything?"

"Well, his father is a judge, too, so Dad and Judge Branch ran in a lot of the same circles. Clint and I went to school together from middle school on. His parents bought one of our tracts of land when we were in high school and they spent summers up here like we did, so Clint and I spent a lot of time together."

He considers. "So, how old were you when you kissed him?"

I chuckle. "Fourteen. I asked him to kiss me so I would at least know what it was like before I started driving. He was still trying to figure out who he was and stuff, so I think it was still experimental for him. He was popular, played lacrosse, had a lot of girlfriends and guys on the low. But, he was nice to me."

"But nothing more?"

I shake my head. "No, kissing him was fine, but I wasn't ready to do more." I shrug. "What about you, who was your first kiss?"

He thinks for a moment. "Jen Waters. I was twelve. We were at our first boy-girl party."

I smile. "Did you play one of those games where you get in the closet and see how far you can get in seven minutes?"

He laughs. "Not hardly. I mean, there was a closet and I'm sure some kids got in it, but it was old fashioned Spin the Bottle."

"I see. And was your first kiss everything you thought it would be?"

He shrugs. "Probably about like first everything else. I don't know if your first *anything* lives up to expectation."

I nudge him playfully. "I don't know, our first time was pretty great."

He pulls me to his side. "Hell, yeah it was. But you know what I mean. For a guy, the first time you do anything, you're trying not to blow in, like, ten seconds. And for a girl, I would imagine it's painful."

I nod. "Yeah. Definitely. Probably good to go ahead and get the first time out of the way. Like the first pancake. It never turns out quite right." I chuckle. "And then, sometimes, your first pancake lasts four years and when you finally get your second, you can't understand how you didn't toss the first one after about a week."

He laughs. "Although I've never been compared to a pancake before, I guess I'll take it."

We walk on for a while longer in companionable silence

and make our way back to the house and I notice Jonas yawning. "You tired?"

He nods. "Yeah. It took me a while to fall asleep last night."

I quirk a brow. "We can always go up for a nap. We've still got a couple hours till supper."

He smiles. "That would be nice. Want to come cuddle with me?"

"Happily."

We walk up to our bedroom and I strip out of my jeans and sweater, leaving me in only a camisole and panties. "Darlin', I don't know how you expect me to nap when you're all half-naked."

I laugh. We'd had a very similar exchange to this one during the summer. "What, you no longer have superior self-control anymore?"

He smiles. "Not now that I've actually had you, I don't."

I shrug and give him a smug smile. "Whatever. I can't nap in jeans, so you'll just have to deal." I set my glasses on the nightstand and climb under the covers and a moment later, he joins me and I can tell he's also taken his pants and flannel shirt off, leaving him in only a tee shirt and boxer briefs.

He pulls me to him and I roll over to face him. "How come you had trouble falling asleep? It's not like you. You're normally out in about two minutes."

He huffs a soft laugh. "How would you know? You're out before I am most of the time."

"Probably, but still. Was there something bothering you?"

He considers for a moment and kisses my forehead. "I was mad at myself for what I said to you while we were getting ready for the party. I didn't think about the way Dominic had done you when I said what I said and I was so pissed I'd do anything like that."

"I'm fine. Promise. I'm pretty sure I can put you in your

place when I need to. You're the one who showed me I'm worth standing up for myself. So, I can fight back." I plant a kiss on his chest and snuggle closer to him.

"Oh, I know you can. I'm glad you do. I don't want you to ever feel you can't do it with me. Tell me when I'm being an ass. Sometimes, I need to hear it." He tilts my face up and gives me a soft kiss.

───────────

After our nap and supper, we all trek out to the fire pit and Jonas and I pile into a chair and cover up with a blanket. I've changed out of my jeans and sweater into a pair of comfy leggings and one of his hoodies.

Dad and uncle Lance are scoring the chestnuts no one will end up eating and placing them into a large cast iron dutch oven and setting it to the side of the fire pit. Mom, aunt Meredith, and Maddie all have full glasses of wine. I've opted to not drink tonight since I got a little too tipsy last night and I really want Jonas to take me to bed tonight.

Maddie and Dominic are sitting beside one another, which I find strange. When we were here during the week of the wedding, she constantly sat in his lap. *Trouble in paradise or simply the honeymoon lovey-dovey phase is over?*

"Callahan, was that Clint at the party last night you were talking to?" Maddie asks.

"Yeah. He's in from DC."

Maddie smirks. "Did you tell Jonas Clint was your first kiss?"

I feel like Maddie is only trying to stir up shit at this point because her remark was pointed and I can't figure out if it's because of what I said to her yesterday and she's trying to retaliate. "Actually, I did. Jonas and I don't have any secrets."

Jonas squeezes my knee and whispers in my ear. "Careful, Darlin'. Don't make it easy on her to rile you. Stay cool." He presses his lips to the side of my neck and my pulse jumps.

Maddie says, "I always thought Clint was probably gay, so I was surprised when I found y'all together back then."

Clint's secrets are not mine to tell, but I know he's not *out* here, so I don't respond and sip on the bottle of water I brought down to the pit with me.

Jonas whispers, "She doesn't know? Is he not open?" The shake of my head is so subtle, only he would be able to perceive it.

"I mean," Maddie continues, "he always dressed so well and was always hanging out with Emery Shaw. I figured they were together. Speaking of Emery, I saw him at the party, too, I wonder if they came together."

Emery was Clint's first boyfriend, but neither of them were out in high school, although I'm pretty sure Emery is now. "No, I didn't see Emery, just Clint. And simply because a man dresses really well doesn't mean anything, Maddie. This isn't the nineties. Some men just like to be fashionable."

She scoffs. "Oh, come on, Callahan, you know Emery's gay. There's no way Clint's not, too."

"I hung out with both of them, what's your point?"

"Maybe you should be careful who you associate with. In our circles, being gay or being associated with someone who is, is still frowned upon."

Rage swells within my chest. "Wow, Maddie, I didn't realize you were so homophobic. And what—"

"Girls, that's enough." My father cuts us off, using his judge tone which brooks no argument.

I'm still practically vibrating with anger and don't even realize my hands are clenched into fists until Jonas goes to uncurl my fingers. "Relax, Darlin'." I let him turn my hand face up on top of my thigh and he drags his fingers lightly back and forth across my palm. The action is instantly soothing and I start to calm down a little. "If you're good, I'm make sure you get a really great distraction later."

I take a deep breath and try not to blow up at Maddie in front of our entire family. I don't know how I never noticed how close minded she is or how snide she can be. Maybe seeing her confess to knowing exactly how Dominic treated me and still agreeing to marry him has opened my eyes to who she truly is.

CHAPTER THIRTEEN

JONAS

I can tell Callie is even more on edge than she was earlier while we sit at the fire pit. I know she would have loved to give Maddie a real piece of her mind and I'm pretty sure if Alex hadn't stopped their argument, it would have escalated to a point Callie would prefer to avoid at the moment. If for nothing else than to keep the peace until after tomorrow.

Callie slumps against me and I pull her closer. "Do we need to go up? Or can we sit here a while longer?" I ask. "I'm really enjoying this fire and you sitting in my lap. And you've got these leggings on, it'd be a shame to waste the opportunity to feel you up." I nuzzle under her ear and her breath catches.

She shifts in my lap and it's barely noticeable, but lord, help me, if she doesn't spread her legs. She takes my hand and places it high on her thigh. My pulse ratchets up and my dick instantly stands at attention. And I know Callie feels it, because a soft, smug smile plays at her lips.

We're far enough away from everyone that when my hand slides further up her thigh and her breath hitches, no one can see the way her chest swiftly rises or the blush that colors her cheeks. Callie pulls her hand out from under the blanket and wraps her arm around my neck, shifting further.

I trace lazy circles on her inner thigh. "Damn, Darlin'. You're dangerous. I like it. I know it's not a roller coaster, but it's still pretty hot."

She bites her lip and I know she's thinking about the fantasy she told me about over the summer. Her fingers play in the hair at the nape of my neck and she looks into the fire as if nothing is going on. Even as my fingers graze the fabric that covers her pussy, she doesn't react, except her nostrils flair the tiniest bit and in the firelight, I watch as her pupils dilate.

I hear Alex and Lance talking about the chestnuts being done and they take them into the house, Vicki and Meredith following. "Have a good evening, kids. We'll see you all in the morning."

"Goodnight," Callie calls and I don't miss how her voice is a bit breathy. She leans her head on my shoulder and brushes a kiss down my neck before whispering in my ear, "You gonna do something with those fingers besides tease me?"

My free hand is comfortably draped around her waist and I give her a squeeze and she squirms and squeals when I hit the spot I know is ticklish. I use the opportunity to cover the fact I've slipped my hand inside her leggings. Her eyes catch mine and she quirks a brow.

Callie turns her torso toward mine a bit as if we're simply having a private conversation. She nonchalantly tucks a hair behind my ear and leans in to give me a brief kiss and I slide my fingers down. My eyes widen a bit. "No panties? Damn. Did you plan this?" I ask, impressed.

She shrugs with one shoulder and smirks. "Maybe. Are you gonna take advantage of it?"

I grip the back of her neck with my free hand and cover her mouth with mine. She winds her arms around my neck and deepens the kiss as I search out her clit. She inhales sharply, but it's enveloped by our kiss. My fingers slip lower and I have to bite back a groan at how wet she is. *Damn, Callie.* She smiles against my lips. "You like? It's all for you."

I press my forehead to hers. "Shit, Darlin'. If we were out here alone, I'd show you exactly how much I love it."

She chuckles. "Do they show any signs of leaving anytime soon?" I covertly glance over Callie's shoulder and see both Maddie and Dominic on their phones.

How romantic.

I work Callie's clit in sure circles and she huffs a soft sigh. "They're both on their phones."

She rolls her eyes and I pull her mouth back to mine for a greedy kiss. She fists my shirt in an attempt to bring me closer and I'm ready to say screw Maddie and Dominic and the horses they rode in on and just get down to it out here. If they want to watch, more power to them. Maybe I could show Dom a thing or two.

But another part of me feels like Callie wants this, wants to be sneaky and not let on. She wants the danger, the thrill. And no doubt, it's fucking hot. Her hips writhe the slightest bit and I feel like I'm dying. I'm straining against the zipper of my jeans I'm pretty sure when I finally do get Callie in a place I can take off my pants, I'm gonna blow my load in about thirty seconds.

"Do you want to go to bed?" I ask. She raises a brow and shakes her head. I can't help but smile in surprise. "Okay, Darlin'."

I see Dominic rise from his chair and I think for a moment we're home free, but he simply puts another log on the fire before returning to his seat. I huff out a small, frustrated sigh and Callie takes my face in her hands. "Eyes on me. I don't care about them. Think about where your hand is. You've got a job to do."

I nod slowly and drag my eyes from hers to her lips and back up. "Yes, ma'am." She kisses me and I slip two fingers into her pussy and thumb her clit. Callie lets out a soft moan into my mouth as I work her with my hand. She doesn't give anything away, except that she's gripping my shoulders and her breathing has begun to grow a bit labored.

I drag my mouth to her ear. "You want me to make you come, Darlin'?"

Her answer is a soft and breathy, "Yes." My arm is beginning to grow tired from the angle I'm forcing it into so we can keep this discreet, but knowing how much closer Callie gets to her release spurs me on. "Don't stop, Jonas. Shit. I'm so close. Please." And I don't. I keep up the speed and stroke she likes and in a moment, she clenches and I claim her mouth to swallow up her soft groan as her climax overtakes her.

I withdraw my hand from her pants and we stay, not moving, for a full couple minutes as Callie comes down. I brush a soft kiss across her lips. She pulls back and looks into my eyes, a playful smile pulling at the corner of her mouth. She leans in to whisper in my ear, "Can you walk, you think?" I can't help but laugh and nod. "Then take me to bed and fuck me properly, please."

"You've got it, Darlin'." She rises from my lap and makes sure to leave me the blanket for me to carry draped over my arm. I give a salute to Maddie and Dominic. "Goodnight, y'all."

Callie and I book it up to the house and I barely have our bedroom door shut and locked before she's yanking her shirt over her head. "Fuck, that was hot. Do you think they knew?" She hurriedly finishes stripping and I do the same.

"I don't give a shit if they knew. Damn, Darlin'. I knew you had some freak in you." She laughs and I pull her to me and cover her mouth with mine. Our kiss is frantic as we shuffle toward the bed. When he get there, Callie climbs up and pulls me down to her. I settle myself between her thighs and slam into her. She exhales a sharp gasp. Our movements, typically easy and rhythmic, are desperate and it's as if we're both chasing a crazy high.

"Fuck, Callie. You feel too good."

She huffs a soft laugh. "That's because you got me all hot by the fire." She lets out a long moan. "Shit. You feel good, too."

My climax begins to build, my balls starting to draw up, my abs tensing, my breathing coming in rasps.

Callie reaches to down to work her clit and it takes every ounce of control I possess to hold off until she goes over. She clenches around me and her mouth falls open with a ragged exhale. My own release follows seconds later with a shuddering, guttural grunt.

I lie next to her, my face buried in her neck as we come back to ourselves. "Well," Callie says between breaths. "Merry Christmas to me."

I can't help but laugh. "Definitely a merry Christmas. Damn."

CHAPTER FOURTEEN

CALLIE

When I roll over on Christmas morning, still sleepy, I reach for Jonas and he pulls me into him. "Sorry, did I wake you up?" I ask.

He kisses the top of my head. "No. I woke up right before you did. Merry Christmas, Darlin'."

"Merry Christmas."

Jonas sighs. "What time do y'all usually get moving and open gifts and stuff?"

I snuggle closer to him. "We usually eat around eleven and then go down to open presents and watch movies."

"Good, so we don't have to get up yet?"

I shake my head. "Nope. I'm too comfy anyway."

Jonas smiles down at me. "Well, do you want your present from me now?"

I look up at him. "You mean last night wasn't gift enough?"

He laughs. "Well, yeah, it was exceptionally good, but do you want your gift now or later?"

I smile. "Sure. We can do them now." I hop out of bed and

run into the bathroom and quickly freshen up. Jonas does the same and I grab his gift from my suitcase and return to the bed.

When he climbs back into bed, he hands me a small box. "You first," he says.

I pull the ribbon from the package and rip the wrapping paper. It's a jeweler's box, but it's larger than a ring box. I open it and a teardrop shaped pendant inlaid with tiny diamonds on a white gold chain sits on a small tuft of velvet. "Jonas, it's beautiful."

He smiles as he takes the necklace out of the box. I turn to allow him to clasp it around my neck. "The diamonds came from Nana's engagement ring my granddad gave her. It was one of those cluster rings that were real popular in the sixties and seventies, but I knew it wasn't really your style, so I asked Nana if she minded if I repurposed it. I know you have a family ring you want to wear, but I figure this can also be good luck, since Nana and Granddad were married for over fifty years."

My chest tightens and tears burn my eyes as I look down at the necklace. "Jonas, I don't even know what to say. I love it. Thank you." I turn back to him and give him a kiss before handing his gift over. "Your turn."

He opens his gift and he's surprised. "You had my watch repaired?" The watch in question belonged to his grandfather and had stopped working around the time we got back together. It's an antique Omega Seamaster divers watch from the 1960's his grandfather received as a gift when he graduated from Annapolis.

I nod. "Yeah, I also had the band replaced to make it a bit more modern. But the jeweler said if you didn't like the band, they could exchange it. They also offered me a ton of money for it, because it's in such good condition, but I figured you were pretty attached to it."

His eyes soften and he chuckles. "Thank you, Callie. So

much. I love it." He takes the watch and fastens it to his wrist and takes my face in his hands and gives me a deep kiss. "I love you, Darlin'. Did you know that?"

I smile. "I did, actually. But it's still nice to hear. I love you, too."

***

The rest of Christmas Day passes pretty uneventfully and we enjoy brunch, gifts, and movies with my family. Thankfully, I'm able to successfully avoid a confrontation with Maddie. And as Jonas and I lie in bed later that night, we talk over our day. "I think your uncle Lance absolutely loved the first edition Frost we got him."

I chuckle. "Yeah, I didn't think he would ever put it down."

Jonas pats his stomach. "I'm gonna have to go for a run tomorrow. All this heavy food is gonna kill me when I get back to the gym."

I roll my eyes. "Have at it. I'll be here, sleeping while you're up at the crack of dawn pounding pavement."

"Sure. And then when I come back from my run all cold and clammy, I'll pull you into a hot shower with me."

I quirk a brow and lean into him. "Now that, I can get behind. Yes, please."

"What's the rest of the week look like? Any more parties or anything?"

"Not that I know of. I'd like to go to Dollywood and see the lights one evening. It's so pretty this time of year."

He nods. "Yeah, we can definitely do that. And didn't you want to have lunch or something with Clint?"

"I'd like to try to. He's leaving the day after New Years as far as I know, so I might have to play it by ear." Changing the subject, I huff an angry sigh. "Speaking of Clint, I could have punched Maddie in the face for the way she talked about him. Hearing her say those kinds of things makes me think I don't even really know her anymore.

"I used to think she was sweet and kind. But now, after what she did to me and knowing how she truly feels about things, I can't believe I ever was that close with her. I wonder if she's always been this way or if it's since she got with Dom?"

Jonas shrugs. "We can't choose our blood, but we can choose our family to an extent, thankfully." He pulls me to him and presses a kiss to my temple. "I choose you, Darlin'. You and Nana and Teagan."

I smile. "I choose you, too. I guess I should be thankful I'll only have to see her at Thanksgiving and Christmas. Hopefully not both in the same year."

"What about summers?" Jonas asks. "Will you not want to come up for summers? Especially once we have kids."

Hearing him talk about kids makes me both nervous and excited, because it means they'd be his kids, too, and seeing Jonas as a father is something I can't wait to see. I shrug. "Ideally, I think we'd spend a few weeks here. Especially if we both have jobs with summers off. And I could always try to coordinate those trips for when Maddie and Dom *won't* be here.

"But it probably wouldn't matter anyway, they both have jobs that require Monday to Friday schedules, at least until Maddie starts having kids. I'd bet money she quits working once she has a baby, if not before. Then we may have to reassess. Although, they may be *vacation* people who spend weeks at the beach or something."

He chuckles. "You say *vacation* like it's a bad thing. You don't like vacations?"

I shrug. "A vacation to me is simply not being at school or work, so home can be a vacation. I'm not opposed to vacations, but the way my family does vacations, it's more like a down payment on a house or the total of a luxury vehicle. Plus, we're less than an hour from the beach, so I don't necessarily feel the need to make a big trip, when we can come here for free. You know, aside from a plane ticket and rental car.

"Did you go on a lot of vacations growing up?"

He shakes his head. "No, we came to Gatlinburg and went to Savannah once. But, yeah, since we were so close to the beach, Nana and Granddad didn't see the need for vacations. Granddad would take me camping."

"Do you like camping?" I ask. I've never heard him talk about camping, so if he does, I'd be surprised.

"Not really. Granddad did, though, so I went with him. And I enjoy the memories I have with him doing that."

I nod. "Okay. Yeah, not much of a camper myself. The lake house is about as close to the outdoors as I want to get." We both laugh.

CHAPTER FIFTEEN

JONAS

When my alarm blares at six A.M., I almost regret setting it. But then I realize it's been over three days since I've had any sort of workout and if I don't get out and at least do a little something, I'll regret it more.

I check the weather and see it's a chilly thirty-seven degrees and I slip on some compression leggings and then my workout shorts, followed by a tee shirt and hoodie. I pull on a beanie and my socks and sneakers and tuck my phone in my pocket.

I head out the front door and stretch in the driveway. After a quick warmup, I push my earbuds in and turn on my running playlist, curated to keep my heart rate up.

The sun is still a good half-hour from rising, so I start a slow jog down the winding driveway. Once I get to the end, I take a left, heading further down the road. With the chill, my lungs take a bit to adjust, but soon, I'm able to averaging a ten-minute mile, which, given the hills I'm running, isn't bad for me.

I take the road until it dead ends a few miles up and turn around. The sun is just starting to make itself known and I curse myself for forgetting my sunglasses since I'm running into the sunlight as it rises above the trees. By the time I get back to Clint's house, I'm shading my eyes and then I stop in my tracks.

Dominic is coming out of Clint's house and even though the front door of the house is a few hundred yards off, I don't miss the intimate way Dom caresses Clint's cheek as he steps off his porch. *What the fuck?* Dominic cuts across the yard and into the woods and I hightail it back to the house.

By the time I make it in the front door, from my near sprint, I'm winded and drenched in sweat. I'm standing in the kitchen drinking a glass of water when Dominic attempts to sneak in the back door. He doesn't see me and when he's nearly to the stairs, I say, "Good morning for a walk through the woods, huh, Dom?" I keep my tone nonchalant.

He freezes and turns a few seconds later and sees me standing with my back to the sink. I don't miss the flush on his cheeks as he stalks toward me, fists clenched. He stops about five feet from me. I level him with a gaze. "I know I enjoyed my run. Especially up that way." I gesture toward Clint's house. "I didn't know you went for early morning hikes."

I continue sipping my water and Dominic finally finds words a few seconds later. "I don't know what you think you saw, but I don't think I like what you're insinuating."

I shrug. "I'm not insinuating anything, only making conversation." I set my glass down and sigh. "I don't know if you've noticed, but things have been a little tense between Callie and Maddie. Especially after what Maddie said about Clint on Christmas Eve. Really since before the wedding, but after the comments Maddie made, Callie's even more upset. Our roommate and good friend, Elliot, is gay, so Callie takes offense to homophobic behavior."

Something tics in Dominic's jaw and I continue, "I don't know if they'll be able to make up, but I know for our sake, it would probably be better if they at least hashed things out before we all go home. I don't look forward to all the future holidays with the family if there's gonna continue to be tension."

Dominic sticks his hands in his pockets and for the first time, I notice how rumpled his clothes are, as if they've been on the floor for several hours. "What makes you think you'll be around for a lot of future family holidays?"

I smile. "Oh, I'm not going anywhere. Callie and I are getting married, we've not decided when, but probably sooner rather than later."

"I don't know about that."

I shake my head. "You still think at some point, Callahan is gonna miraculously come back to you? If you truly think that, you're delusional. She knows what she's worth now and it's a hell of a lot more than you can offer her. And do you really think Maddie will keep you if she finds out what kind of *extracurricular activities* you might be a part of?"

Dominic spits out, "You don't know shit."

I shrug, keeping my voice even. "Maybe, but perception is key in most situations. And pictures typically tell a better story than words anyway." Totally a bluff, but he has no way of knowing that.

All the color drains from his face and I realize, for the first time since meeting him, he's nervous. "What do you want?"

I shake my head. "I don't want anything. I'm not the black-mailing type. I find it beneath me, to be honest."

He clenches his jaw. "Then why even bring it up?"

"So you know to be careful. You never know who sees what. Although, is that the life you want, to be sneaking around for the rest of your life?"

"I'm not sneaking around."

I smirk. "So, you normally come out of a man's house at

seven in the morning, clothes rumpled? And are you typically so intimate with a man you'll touch his face like that?"

Dominic closes the distance between us, his voice seething. "You don't know what the fuck you're talking about."

I shrug. "Maybe not. But seriously, Dominic, why would you be with someone who's bigoted? Someone you can't truly be yourself with? What kind of life is that? And believe me, I have a lot of issues with you for how you treated Callahan and how much you hurt her. Honestly, I could care less if you drop off the face of the earth, but still, do you not think people could accept you as anything other than the perfect Prescott heir?

"I mean, I know Maddie was more interested in a good match than anything, but was it like that for you, too?" *Fuck.* I didn't mean to say the last part, because that's Callie and Maddie's business. But Dominic doesn't notice, as he currently considering everything else I've said.

He slumps. "You have no clue what it's like to be me." *Shit, could he really be an actual human with feelings and emotions?*

I nod. "You're right, I don't know what it's like to come from lots of money and privilege and expectation. But I do know what it's like to go through life with a label and people thinking you are something because of who your parents are. My mom is a drug addict. I've not seen her in fifteen years. I honestly don't know if she's even still alive. So, I know what it's like to be judged based on who your family is, even if it's not the same way you've been viewed.

"But I know it's not worth living half a life. I did that before I met Callie. And until I met her, I didn't think I deserved to be happy because of something I'd done in the past. But, at least I'm honest with the people I love." I hold his gaze. "I had a really good run this morning, except the sun was in my eyes for the whole last quarter mile before I got to the driveway. I couldn't see shit, you know?"

He releases a breath and gives me a slight nod. I go to step past him and he grabs my bicep and he looks into my eyes. "Cal seems really happy."

I nod. "She is."

He doesn't release me. "I was terrible to her."

I nod again. "You were. But I think there's redemption available for almost everyone. Maybe even you."

"You're really gonna marry her?"

"Yeah, I am."

"You're a lucky man."

"I'm well aware. There's nothing like having Callie's love."

He nods and lets my arm go. "You're right about that."

I hear Callie's and my bedroom door open, so I step to the coffee maker and switch it on. I say, a little louder than is probably necessary, "I bet you feel like shit falling asleep in the media room, huh, Dom? What movie were you watching?"

He's quick on his feet. "*Forrest Gump*. And yeah, I totally have a crick in my neck."

When Callie reaches the bottom of the stairs, she looks from me to Dominic. I know she thinks this is weird, because Dominic and I don't talk. Ever. At least not since he and I had words over the summer. I put a pod in the Keurig and start a cup of coffee for Callie.

She comes over to me. "Everything okay?" Her eyes dart to Dom and I nod.

I brush a kiss across her lips. "Fine, Darlin'. I just ran into Dominic as I was coming in from my run. He was telling me he fell asleep in the media room last night."

Her expression is skeptical as I hand her mug of coffee over. She takes it and I start another. Callie leans against me and when Dominic says, "Cal," she immediately tenses.

I give her hand a reassuring squeeze and she looks at him. "Yeah?"

"Jonas said y'all were talking about getting married. That's great. I'm happy for you." She looks up at me, dumbfounded and for a solid five seconds, she's unable to form words.

When she finally speaks, her voice is soft. "Thank you."

He nods and then to my surprise, says, "I'm sorry, Cal. For the way I treated you. I was a dick and I'm glad you've found someone to treat you the way you deserve. I hope someday, you can forgive me for my past behavior. Jonas is a good guy and I told him how lucky he is to have you."

Callie's mouth falls open in shock and her eyes travel from Dom to me and back to him. "I'm lucky to have Jonas, too. Thank you, Dom. Your apology means a lot to me. I hope you and Maddie are happy, too."

I reach for my coffee mug and it blocks Callie from seeing Dominic's expression change and his jaw clench. I take her hand. "Come on, Darlin'. Let's go up to the porch."

CHAPTER SIXTEEN

CALLIE

I can only nod when Jonas tugs me toward the stairs. I follow him up and he grabs a couple blankets from a basket next to the sliding door leading to the porch. He sits in a chair and pulls me down into his lap and covers us with the blankets.

I can't hide the shock in my voice. "Did I hallucinate or have some sort of stroke? Or did that actually happen?"

Jonas sips his coffee and nods. "Yeah, it did. Maybe Dominic is actually a human person, capable of emotions like remorse and regret."

I shake my head. "I don't even know what to think."

He shrugs. "Maybe it's an olive branch. Maybe he knows y'all are gonna have to see each other for years and years since he's married to Maddie and he's tired of all the tension."

I quirk a brow at him. "Did he tell you all that?"

Jonas shakes his head. "No, but it's what I'd be thinking if I were him. You know, and that I'd lost the best thing I'd ever had and I can see that she's moved on and is really happy." He smirks.

I roll my eyes. "It's just weird. It came out of nowhere."

"Magic of Christmas, maybe? And maybe since you've made peace with Dominic, it seems, you can get things out in the open with Maddie."

I clench my jaw. "I don't even know where to start with her. Do I start with the betrayal or the bigotry?"

Jonas sighs and shrugs. "I don't know, Darlin'. I think it's all liable to come to the surface once you get going. Maybe take her to lunch. Have an actual conversation somewhere besides this house."

I consider. "Maybe. Oh, I got a text from Clint this morning. Why he was up so early, I don't know, but whatever. He invited us over on New Years Eve for a little get together. Watch the ball drop, drink ridiculously priced bottles of champaign, dress up a little. What do you think?"

He thinks for a moment and then quirks a brow and I know he's about to say something I'm probably gonna fuss about. "Okay, sure."

"Really? I thought for—."

"If—."

I roll my eyes. "There it is."

"If you talk to Maddie. I don't want to start a new year with y'all having all this animosity. It's bad luck."

I chuckle. "I wasn't aware you were superstitious."

"I'm not, really, I just feel like, why bring this year's drama into next year, you know?"

As much as I hate to admit it, he has a point. I slump and let out a groan. "Fine. I'll talk to her. Maybe I can get her to go shopping with me to buy a dress to wear to Clint's party. Do you want me to pick you up a new shirt to wear with your suit?"

He shrugs. "Sure. Whatever you want." He runs his nose along my jaw. "As long as I get to take the dress off of you after the party, wear whatever you want, Darlin'."

I turn my face to him. "You gonna unwrap me like a present again?"

He takes my coffee mug and his and sets them on the table and pulls me closer to him. I wind my arms around his neck. He gives me an amused grin. "I don't know if you could be that patient again. It almost killed you that night. I could see it all over you, how jumpy you were."

I give him a sheepish smile. "You're not wrong. I kept thinking, 'this is so strange, I don't know what to do with my hands, I feel stupid'. Lots of different thoughts going through my mind."

He runs his thumb along my bottom lip. "I only had one thought that night."

"Oh, yeah?"

He nods. "She's fucking beautiful and she's mine."

I blush and I bite my lip. "I am yours. Then and now."

He presses a kiss to my lips. "And I sure am thankful."

———

During brunch, I glance at Maddie across the table as she sips her bloody Mary. "Maddie?"

She looks at me, obviously surprised to find me speaking to her. "Yeah?"

I try to keep my features and tone even. "I need to buy a new dress for a New Years Eve party, would you be able to come help me pick one out? Jonas and I are probably gonna Dollywood tomorrow, but I was thinking if you're not doing anything, maybe the next day, you and I could grab lunch and go shopping? Catch up?"

She swallows the bite of food she's been chewing and dabs her mouth with her napkin. It feels like she's stalling, trying to formulate what she wants to say. She finally shrugs. "Sure. Okay."

Dominic says, "Hey, Jonas, since the girls will be gone, you want to go do something? Do you play golf?"

I want to laugh at the absurdity of what I'm witnessing. Dominic and Jonas willingly spending time together was definitely not a square on my bingo card for the week. Jonas smiles. "Unfortunately, the only type of golf I play is of the mini variety."

I pipe up. "Don't bet against him, either. You'll get hustled. He's really good."

Jonas and I laugh and then he says to Dominic, "You know what, I'm always up for a challenge, so sure. I'll have to rent some clubs, but let's do it."

Dom nods. "Okay. I'll set up a tee time. Alex, Lance, care to join?"

Dad shakes his head. "Sorry, I've got some motions I need to review for when the courts open up after New Years. I've put them off as long as I can."

Uncle Lance says, "I think I'll pass, too. My arthritis isn't a big fan of the cold these days. I'll probably stick around the house and read."

And because why not, Mom and aunt Meredith make a plan to go to *the club* for lunch. Jonas leans over to me and whispers in my ear. "Look at you, helping everyone connect. I'm proud of you for making baby steps." He kisses the sensitive area just below my ear and a pleasant flush creeps into my cheeks. His eyes travel down my face and he smirks at me.

CHAPTER SEVENTEEN

JONAS

After a great day and evening at Dollywood, where I am unsuccessful in my attempts in getting Callie to fool around on a roller coaster, like the fantasy she told me about over the summer, we curl up in bed.

"How many miles do you think we walked today?" I ask.

"According to my phone, about eight."

"Wow, I knew it was probably a lot. But I had a really good time, I wouldn't mind making it a tradition."

She nods. "Yeah, I love looking at the lights."

"Are you ready for your shopping and lunch date with Maddie tomorrow?"

Callie sighs. "Not in the least. But I need to get this over with. I'm tired of being so angry. She might be angry with me by the time I'm done with what I have to say to her, but at least I'll have it all off my chest. Are you ready for golf? I still can't believe you're gonna willingly hang out with Dominic. It's so strange."

I shrug. "Maybe it won't be too bad. He'll probably kick my

ass, since I don't play golf, but it still might be fun. I can drive the cart all over the course."

She chuckles. "Driving the cart was always my favorite part."

I have a thought. "Why don't you check in with me when you and Maddie are done shopping and stuff, maybe if y'all are in a decent place, we can all go out for supper or something."

Her mouth falls open. "Okay, who are you and what have you done with my man? What happened to 'I'd rather walk on glass barefoot than have dinner with them'?"

I sigh. "We're not gonna be able to avoid them for the rest of our lives. You and Dominic are cool now. Well, as cool as you're probably ever gonna get. The only beef I had with him was how he treated you and it seems like he knows what an asshole he was. I'm willing to try to at least be civil. And maybe Maddie will also recognize her errors and try to be better, too. And if nothing else, we won't be able to say we didn't try, right?"

Callie shakes her head. "You really are too good for me. I love you though, for wanting to try to see the good in others."

I take her face in my hands. "Well, you seemed to think there was some good in me, in spite of my wayward, woman-izing ways, so I figure the least I can do I prove you right." I press a kiss to her forehead.

Dominic and I are quiet on the way to the golf course. We eventually make small talk about football and fraternities and I end up not having to rent clubs, as Alex lends me his. When we're walking between holes, Dominic says in a low voice, "I appreciate keeping what you saw the other day to yourself."

I shrug. "I didn't see anything. The sun was in my eyes, remember?"

He nods. "Still, after what I did to Cal, I could understand if you wanted to ruin me."

"I don't make a habit of intentionally hurting people or blowing up their lives, regardless how I feel personally about their past actions. Because there were a lot of times over the week we were here during the wedding, I would have gladly punched you in the face. And if Callie had asked me to, I probably would have." I glance at him. "Can I ask you something, though?" He gives a halfhearted shrug, so I continue. "Are you happy? With your life? With Maddie?"

He considers my questions for a long time. "Those are really loaded questions. And the easy answer is yes. The harder answer is, it's complicated."

"Is Clint a one off? Or does that sort of thing happen a lot?" He blanches at my question and I press on. "Listen, I'm not here to judge or bust your balls. I didn't tell Callie about what I saw and I don't plan to, it's not my place. I could understand, in your position, your standing, if you don't have anyone to talk to. And who am I gonna tell, right? I don't know the people you know, other than Callie's family."

He's quiet for a minute. "I'm not gay. I love women. And I love Maddie. But, I am attracted to men, too."

"Okay, nothing wrong with that."

He sighs. "Yeah, except what Maddie said the other night, at the pit, about things being 'frowned upon'. She's right. Things are different for people like us, with the connections and families we have.

"And I can't tell Maddie the things I *need*, because of how ingrained all that kind of stuff is with her."

I shrug. "You might be surprised. Have you even talked with her about it?"

His face flushes and he looks down. "No. You saw how she was, the way she talked about Clint and Emery. Plus, she's super vanilla."

I chuckle. "Callie said the same thing about you. Sounds like she was mistaken."

His head snaps toward me. "Y'all talked about us and our sex life? That's fucked up."

I shrug. "Not really. Callie's not a prude. Surely you know that. And we really don't have secrets. Not about each other anyway. I know you were the first guy she was with and how long y'all hooked up and stuff."

He nods. "Yeah. And if I'd had any sense, I'd have married her instead of Maddie."

I should be angry by his words, but I honestly feel only pity for him. Because I know what it's like to give Callie up. Thankfully, I was fortunate enough to get her back. "Well, lucky for me, you didn't. And I am, that's for sure. Although, you know Callie doesn't want the kind of life you and Maddie or her parents have, so do you think y'all would have really been happy?"

He shrugs. "I don't know, but I know the grass isn't always greener. Maddie's not necessarily who I thought she was. Cal's got sass."

I smile. "Yeah, she does. Although, I don't know about you, but I don't like being on the bad end of it. She's got claws when she needs to."

He nods. "Yeah."

We reach the next hole, so I turn to him. "Listen, I'm not gonna tell you how to live your life. God knows, I've made some epic mistakes in my own life. But you have to decide what you're willing to live with. Are you willing to sneak around and have the possibility of Maddie finding out the truth, and the possible fallout of that?

"Because I know, from Callie, when Maddie gets drunk, she *talks*. If you really love her, can you tell her what you need? She might surprise you. Or, she might decide it's too much and she can't get past it. In which case, at least you know one way or the other."

His expression is concerned. "What did Maddie tell Cal?"

I shake my head. "That's between them. I'm not getting in the middle of it. But it's one of the reasons things have been so icy between them since the wedding."

He nods, considering everything I've said. "Okay. Well, can we get back to playing the game? I think I'm done with all the touchy-feely shit."

I shrug. "Sure."

CHAPTER EIGHTEEN

CALLIE

"So, what do you think about this one?" Maddie holds up a short red dress.

I consider. "I think I want something long. And red's not really my color."

She nods and continues to flip through the rack of dresses. After a moment, she sighs. "Are you ever gonna tell me what I did? Or are we gonna pretend like everything's back to normal?"

My hand freezes in mid-air and I turn to her. "You want to get into this now?"

She shrugs. "I know I did or said something and the only thing I can think of it was the night of the bachelorette party, because before that, we were fine. And after, you haven't even looked me in the eye very much."

I swallow and check my phone and see it's almost an acceptable hour to have a drink. "Want to go get a drink?"

Her face blanches. "Will I need one?"

I shrug. "I don't know, but I might."

She blows out a breath. "Okay."

We make our way to one of the bars at the mall and both order a glass of wine. Once it comes, I take a sip and steel myself to finally have this conversation with Maddie. She looks at me expectantly. "The night of the bachelorette party, you got really drunk."

She nods, a pained expression on her face. "Don't remind me. I can't look at a lemon drop the same way."

I swirl my wine in my glass and can't meet her eyes. "Well, while you were drunk, you told me you knew how long Dominic and I had been together. You said you knew the whole time." I glance up and all the color has drained from her face and I continue. "I asked you how you could be okay with the way he treated me and you told me you were ready to settle down and it was a good match."

I take a sip of my wine and try to fight the tightness in my chest. "And I was really hurt, Maddie, because I truly loved him and he had no problem casting me aside when you became available. And it turns out you knew everything and had no issues with what he'd done because as long as things worked out for you, it didn't matter who got hurt."

Maddie opens her mouth to say something and I cut her off. "And then, what you said the other night at the fire pit; the hateful things you said about Clint and Emery. I've never thought of you as a homophobic person. And one of my best friends is gay, so I take major offense to what you said. And it makes me look at you differently.

"I've always put you on this pedestal, because of how everyone treated you versus how they treated me. I always thought you had to be better than me. But I don't feel that way anymore. And I'm not saying I'm better than you, because I'm not. But I guess, the blinders are off for me as far as you're concerned."

Maddie drains her glass and signals for the bartender to

pour her another. Once he walks away, she visibly deflates. "Callahan, the stuff I said about Clint and Emery wasn't about them, not really. I was angry. I was lashing out. I don't have anything against them. I really don't. Emery and Clint are both good guys. At least, I always thought Emery was until I saw him kissing my husband."

My eyes go wide and my mouth falls open in shock. "What?"

She looks away and nods. "Yeah, at the Christmas party. They were out on the porch. *Your* porch. Dom told me he had a headache and was gonna go lie down. I was in the middle of a poker game with your dad and a few other people. And I went up to check on him a little while later and I felt the cold coming in and I thought for sure it was gonna be you and Jonas out there, because I know it's your favorite spot. But it wasn't. I don't think they even know I saw them, but I felt humiliated."

She looks back at me and tears are welling in her eyes. "And as far as what I said when I was drunk, I'm really sorry. I was always so jealous of you for having Dom first. And then when he finally pursued me, I thought I'd won big. Turns out, you're the only winner in all this. Because, damn, what I'd give to have Dominic look at me the way he still looks at you or the way Jonas looks at you."

"You, jealous of me? What are you talking about? And Dominic doesn't look at me." The second part might not necessarily be true, as Jonas told me the week of the wedding that Dominic would watch me. And not to mention him trying to hook up with me while Maddie was gone for the day a few days before the wedding.

"Callahan, you've never given a shit what our family thinks. You've always been content to do your own thing, be your own person. I've never been brave like you. I didn't even question what my path was, let alone make my own choices.

And Dominic still looks at you. The other night, when you and Jonas were making out at the fire pit, he couldn't take his eyes off you." She quirks a brow. "And, honestly, I couldn't either. I know y'all weren't *just* kissing over there." I blush and I look down into my glass. She continues. "You and Jonas seem to be on fire all the time. It's never been like that for Dom and me. And I know now it never will be. I'll never be enough for him."

"Are you gonna talk to him about what you saw? What if it was just a kiss? Maybe he was drunk and curious. Emery's a nice guy, people are drawn to him. Not that I'm saying what Dominic did was okay, in the least, but maybe there's a plausible reason.

"And you know, I spent a hell of a long time not thinking I was enough for Dominic. Four years, in fact. I finally had to learn to be enough on my own. Ironically, I didn't see that until I met Jonas and he showed me I didn't need someone else to make me *enough*. I was worth more than what someone was or wasn't willing to give me. I had to truly look at what I wanted and needed.

"And I know, if I had ended up with Dominic, I would have been miserable. We don't want the same things. We never have. So, honestly, you saved me and I should be thanking you. Because if you hadn't married Dominic, I never would have met Jonas."

She frowns. "What do you mean?"

I blow out a breath. "Can I tell you a secret?"

She laughs. "Sure, I mean I told you all my dirt today, so why not?"

"The 'blind date' Jonas and I went on?" When she nods, I continue. "It was the plane ride to come to the wedding. I'd never met him before that."

Her expression registers shock and her mouth falls open. "Okay, so I'm gonna need a lot more information, Hanny."

I smile. "Well, to be honest, I was still hung up on Dom when I got the invite to your wedding. And I didn't want to show up without a date and let him see that, so I asked Elliot to be my plus one. He was gonna pretend to be my boyfriend. But he decided pretending to be straight for a week was too much for him and the part about Jonas and him working together and him owing Elliot a favor, all true. I was a favor. And I was on the phone with Elliot when Jonas walked up, so the 'blind date' part wasn't totally fabricated, I only made up the where and when of things."

"Holy shit, Callahan. So, you and Jonas pretended to be together the whole week? How did you fake all that stuff, because damn, it was convincing."

I laugh. "Well, for a few days, it was pretend. We flirted and played things up in front of everyone. We never planned on sleeping together, it was all supposed to be for show."

"But y'all were practically all over each other the whole week. You're telling me y'all didn't have sex? Because, with the way he looks, how did you restrain yourself? That man is sex on a stick." I nod and huff out a small laugh. A thought hits her. "So, are y'all still faking this, because, I don't buy it. Y'all are too good."

I shake my head. "No, when we came up for the wedding, it was fake, until it wasn't. I fell for him. And he told me before we ever slept together he didn't do commitment, he didn't do relationships. And in spite of that, I still slept with him, knowing I'd have to give him up when we got home.

"And I did. When we got back from the wedding, we went our separate ways and I didn't see him until right before Halloween. I hadn't called him, he hadn't called me. But we ran into each other at a bar. And he told me he'd had feelings for me at the wedding, but because of some of his own issues, he couldn't admit it to himself. He knew how Dominic had treated me and he thought that until he could tell me what had happened to him, he didn't deserve me, because he didn't want to hurt me." I sigh. "But now, here we are."

She shakes her head. "See, that's what I'm talking about. You're brave, Callahan. I could never do anything like that."

I shrug. "I didn't feel very brave. It felt pretty pathetic, if I'm honest. I told Jonas if I'd really had balls, I would have showed up and owned my shit. But I couldn't. But he was definitely a good distraction that week." I quirk a brow.

"Jonas is a good man, Callahan. You're lucky."

I nod. "I am. I think Dom has the potential to be a good man, too, Maddie. He apologized to me the other day for how he'd treated me. And I never, in a million years, thought I'd see the day he'd admit he'd ever done anything wrong."

Maddie's face falls. "I don't know what to do. About Dominic."

I shrug. "I think you have to talk to him. Figure out what y'all want. Do you love him?"

She nods. "Yeah, I think I do, but what if," she lowers her voice to a whisper, "he's gay?"

I sigh. "I don't know. I don't think he is, not totally anyway. And that's not to say if you're gay, you can't be in straight-passing relationships for years and years, I know that happens, but I know he loves you. He told me.

"But this is something you're gonna have to talk with him about. This is *your* marriage. You have to decide what you are and aren't willing to live with."

Maddie sips her wine and lets out a deep sigh. "I've missed you, Hanny. Talking with you, having you in my corner. I'm sorry for all the shitty stuff I said and did. I understand if you can't forgive me, because a lot of it, if I were you, I don't know if I could."

I sip my own wine and look down into my glass. "Maddie,

I'll be real honest. I don't know if we'll ever be as close as we were. I'll always love you because you're like a sister to me, but I was so hurt by what you did. And honestly, what you did to me feels a lot worse than what Dominic did to me, because it's you. And I never expected for you to hurt me like that."

A tear rolls down her cheek. "I know. I understand. I'm glad we finally talked, though."

I nod. "Me, too. And I'll still be here to talk if you need me. Regardless of what's happened, we're still family and I want you to be happy."

"Okay. Now, do you want to go find you a smoking hot dress for your New Years party?"

I smile. "Yes, please."

CHAPTER NINETEEN

JONAS

After our golf game, where Dominic predictably wipes the floor with me, I call Callie to see if she and Maddie want to meet for supper.

"Let me ask Maddie," Callie says. I hear muffled voices and can't make out what she's saying, but she's away for a while. She finally comes back on the line and sighs. "Yeah, we can do that. Want to go to the steak place where Maddie and Dominic had their rehearsal dinner?"

I relay the information to Dom and he shrugs, "Okay."

I tell Callie, "Sure, Darlin' that'll work. Are y'all ready now? Dominic and I are done with our game, so we're chilling at the club bar having a beer."

"Yeah, we had a light lunch, so both of us are pretty hungry. We shopped until we dropped."

I'm glad she appears to be in better spirits and I hope it means she and Maddie got everything sorted. And once we finish our beers and pay our tabs, we head out to meet the girls.

When we get to the restaurant, Dominic puts our names

down on the list and we wait for Callie and Maddie to arrive. "You're not gonna tell Cal what I've said, are you?"

I shake my head. "I don't spill secrets that aren't mine. I think you need to talk to Maddie, but no, I'm not gonna tell Callie. It's not my place."

He looks relieved. "You're not so bad, Jonas. When Cal showed up with you for the wedding, I saw how happy she was and the way she looked at you, I was jealous. But she deserves to be happy after what I put her through. Don't take her for granted."

I nod. "Don't plan on it. Callie's the best thing in my life."

A few minutes later, Callie walks in and I never can get over how beautiful she is, even in simple jeans and a sweater and her hair in a ponytail with minimal makeup. The way she smiles at me when she sees me, the way her eyes light up, I hope it never stops. Maddie trails behind her and I notice she doesn't smile or really even look at Dominic when she comes in. *I wonder what that's about?*

Callie walks over and I pull her into my arms. "Hey, Darlin'."

She gives me a kiss and a sweet smile. "Hey, yourself. Did you have a good time?"

I nod. "Yeah, of course Dom beat the socks off me, but we knew it would happen."

He smiles. "If it's any consolation, I was on the golf team in high school and college."

I consider. "Actually, that does make me feel better."

After supper, on the way back to the house, I ask, "So, how did everything go with Maddie? Y'all seemed like you were on better terms."

She nods. "We are. I was honest with her about how I don't know if I'll ever be able to feel as close to her as I used to be, simply because she hurt me. And she understood. But I think we'll be okay." She lets out a sigh. "I also told her about us."

My eyes go wide. "What did you tell her?"

"The truth and that if she hadn't decided to marry Dom, then you and I never would have met, so I thanked her for it." She huffs a soft laugh.

I can't help but laugh with her. "Are you sure that was a good decision? What if she talks?"

Callie shrugs. "What's it matter now? We're together, we're happy, that's all that matters."

"You've got a point there. But if your parents found out, do you think they'd look down on me? I'd hate for them to think I took advantage of you."

"Are you kidding? They love you. I think, regardless, they'd still love you. That's not to say I want to shout our origins from the rooftops, but I honestly don't care anymore. Because I love you and I don't care how we started, it's how we finish, right? And I don't plan on being finished with you until we're old and shriveled and even then, you'll still be mine. You're stuck with me."

I smile. "You have such a way with words, Darlin'. But I love you, too."

The next few days pass pretty quietly. I get up in the mornings and go for runs and I don't see Dominic exiting Clint's house again. And for that, I'm thankful, because I don't like having to keep secrets from Callie, even if it's not really my secret.

Callie and I are getting ready to go to the New Years party

at Clint's and I'm putting the finishing touches on my hair, which is a bit longer than I like and my curls are a bit wild, but it's not terrible. Callie is swiping some mascara on and I'm still not used to seeing her without her glasses. She so rarely goes without them, part of me feels like it's a treat and another part of me doesn't feel like she's her without them.

Her hair is pulled into a simple, yet elegant, updo that showcases the graceful curve of her neck. She's still in her bathrobe and I have a hard time taking my eyes off her. "What?" she asks, catching me watching her in the mirror.

I shake my head. "I don't know if I'll ever get over looking at you. You're beautiful, Darlin'."

A slight blush creeps into her cheeks. "Thank you. But I'm not even dressed yet."

I nod. "I know. I don't know if I'll be able to withstand it. If you look this good right now, man, I'm liable to come apart once you put your dress on."

She rolls her eyes and chuckles. "How would you feel about telling my parents? About us getting engaged? We can pretend you proposed tonight." She winks. "It'd be our secret. But I'd like to do it before we go home. I mean, if that's okay with you."

I can't keep the wide grin off my face. "Really? Of course. I would have been happy to tell them at Thanksgiving, you know that."

She nods. "I know. And I appreciate you being patient with me."

She steps back from the mirror to assess her hair and makeup one last time before walking over to the closet to pull out her dress. It's a long, dark green velvet wrap dress. It's very nearly the same color as the dress she wore to Maddie and Dominic's wedding. And the color looks amazing on her. She lays it on the bed and sheds her robe and my mouth falls open. "Shit, Darlin', where you been hiding those?" She wears an extremely sexy black lace bra and panties set. "Are those new?"

She flushes and nods. "Just letting you know what you have to look forward to after the party."

"Damn, I might steal you away *at* the party."

She laughs and puts her arms into the sleeves of the dress and ties one side of the dress and then the other. The neckline barely gives a hint of cleavage and when she walks, she reveals quite a bit of leg. The necklace I gave her hits her perfectly and she wears simple diamond studs in her ears. She goes to swipe on some lipstick and I still her hand. "Not just yet." I pull her face to mine and kiss her deeply.

When I release her, her cheeks are flushed and her lashes flutter. "Well, okay." She applies her lipstick and gives herself one last look in the mirror.

"Callie, you already know you look amazing. What about me, am I up to snuff for a fancy party?"

She drags her eyes down my body and nods. "Definitely fuckable."

I can't help but laugh and she closes the distance between us and makes an adjustment to my tie and cufflinks. I'm wearing the same charcoal suit I wore to the Christmas party and changed out the black shirt for a burgundy one. "You look dashing, Jonas Merritt, and I can't wait to get you out of this suit later."

"Are we ready?"

"If you can carry my phone and lipstick, we are. I don't want to have to lug a clutch the whole night." I hold out my hand and she gives me her items. I stick them in the inside pocket of my jacket and we make our way down the stairs.

Alex and Vicki are sitting on the couch, which I find odd, because I'm not sure I've ever seen anyone sit in the living room anytime I've been here, but I guess they do. They both rise when we reach the main floor. Vicki smiles. "My, don't you two look beautiful. And yes, Jonas, you look beautiful, too."

Callie and I share a soft laugh. Alex asks, "Do y'all need a ride over to Clint's, so neither of you has to be DD?"

I shake my head. "Not necessary, but thank you for the offer."

Alex nods. "Sure, but if y'all need us, call. I know they're just right up the road, but it's no excuse to drink and drive."

I try not to let the innocent comment rankle me, since Alex doesn't know about my accident in college where I did exactly that. Callie gives my hand a reassuring squeeze. "Dad, we'll be fine. Promise."

He holds his hands up in a defensive posture. "Okay, sure. Only doing my duty. I see way too many DUI's in my court room after New Years. Force of habit, I guess."

Callie hugs her parents and we head out the door and I open the passenger door of the car for her and she climbs in. I wait until she makes sure her dress isn't hanging out of the vehicle to shut it and walk around and climb behind the wheel. I can't get Alex's comment out of my head. "Would your dad do a background check on me? Does he have those kinds of connections?"

Callie frowns and shakes her head. "I've never known him to do that before. And he says that to me every year. It didn't have anything to do with you. The year Maddie and Dom got together, I got so drunk he had to come get me from the party I was at. I had to listen to his lecture while nursing my hangover. Although, I don't know why he was lecturing me, since I didn't drive. I wonder if he did it simply to make my misery worse. I suspect if he'd known the reason for my inebriated state, he would have cut me some slack. But you're fine."

"Okay, not that I'm against your parents knowing about the

accident, but I'd prefer they not find out, if I'm honest. I guess I'm just paranoid."

"Jonas, it was so long ago and you're not the same person you were then. Everyone makes mistakes when they're young."

I nod. "I know."

CHAPTER TWENTY

CALLIE

We make the drive over to Clint's in less than five minutes and it almost feels silly to have driven such a short distance, but with the cold and dark, I'm not complaining about being in a warm car. "Shit, is that a valet?" Jonas asks.

I nod. "Yeah, Clint's a little extra."

"Good thing we dressed up, then, huh?"

I laugh. "Yep." When the car rolls to a stop in front of Clint's wide front porch steps, a young man in a red jacket opens my door and helps me exit the vehicle. Jonas comes around and gives the valet the car keys and takes a ticket from him. He reaches for my hand and we walk toward the front door.

"You look beautiful, Darlin'."

"You already told me that, but thank you." And I do feel really pretty. I love wearing this color and I feel elegant and sophisticated next to Jonas, who looks like he stepped out a magazine. "You're very handsome." I lean in closer to him. "And I hope later, you'll hand some of that dick over."

Jonas laughs and it's deep and genuine. He brushes a kiss across my cheek. "Gladly."

The crowd at the party consists of a lot of the same type of people who were at my parents' party, with several faces I don't recognize. "Where would you like to congregate tonight?" God, I love this man. He knows I don't like to be on display and knows I'd prefer to hang out around the periphery because of how introverted I am. And even though he's a total social butterfly, he's willing to let me make this call.

"I guess over by the fireplace is fine." I gesture across the room, where a fire is lit in the large stone fireplace.

"Okay, head that way, I'll get us a couple of drinks. You want wine?"

I nod. "Yes, please."

He kisses my cheek. "You've got it. Be back in a flash, you know, as soon as I locate the bar in this place." I chuckle and walk over to the fireplace.

Jonas is gone for a while, which is not a surprise, considering how large Clint's house is, and it doesn't bother me to be on my own, so I'm not worried. I glance up at the mantle and the photos of Clint and his parents taken over the years. "I especially like this one."

I turn to see a man in his late sixties looking at a photo of Clint in braces. I smile. "Yeah, Clint was fun at that age." The man looks familiar, but I can't place him. He's very handsome for his age and dressed impeccably in a suit I know has to cost more than my car. He's about six foot with graying curly, close cut hair and green eyes.

"How do you know Clint?" The man asks.

"Our families go way back. We've been friends for years. How do you know him?" *Boyfriend, maybe? Although, I don't ever recall Clint going for guys this old, even if this guy is really good looking.*

"He works for me."

My stomach drops. I've been speaking with a US senator for the last few minutes and I had no clue. I instantly flush with embarrassment. "You're Senator Bailey. Of course. I'm so sorry, I should have recognized you. Don't tell anyone, they might revoke my Florida residency."

He laughs and extends his hand and I shake it. "Your secret is safe with me. It'd be a shame for Florida to lose a resident as pretty as you."

He winks at me and I blush, suddenly feeling like I've done something wrong, although I haven't. I glance around trying to see Jonas but when I don't see him, I say, "So, Clint told me how he got his job. It was very generous of you to give him a chance like that."

He smiles. "He earned it. I like to find new talent and foster it. He's doing a great job. I'm up six points over my opponent already for the next election."

I nod, impressed. "Wow."

"So, how long have you lived in Florida?" Senator Bailey asks.

"Almost two years. I'm finishing up my PhD at Florida State."

"Well, I hope you plan on staying afterward. Florida needs all the well-educated people we can get."

I nod. "I will. My fiancé is from there. We'll be staying there when we marry. I'm originally from here, but I love Florida."

"And where is your fiancé tonight? And I don't think I caught your name."

I'm sincerely wishing Jonas would appear and my eyes dart around the room, hoping to see him before bringing my eyes back to the senator. I keep my tone polite. "It's Callahan. Callahan Benson. My fiancé must have gotten lost trying to find the bar. Clint's never been good at making things conspicuous."

"Well, maybe I can keep you company until he gets back. Shame for beautiful women to be left unattended at big parties like this."

I shrug and reply nonchalantly, "I'm pretty introverted, so unattended is typically no problem for me."

"So, Callahan. May I call you Callahan?" When I nod, he continues. "What are you studying at Florida State?"

"Library sciences. I hope to become a librarian at a university or school. Which will be perfect for my fiancé as well, since he's a teacher and we'd both have summers off."

He nods. "Teaching is a noble profession."

"I can't agree more."

Bailey is about to say something, when Jonas comes striding over with a wide smile, two drinks in hand. "Sorry, Darlin', I feel like I earned these drinks, so I hope you enjoy yours." I laugh and take my glass of wine.

Jonas glances at Senator Bailey and the smile disappears and his eyes harden. He pulls himself up to his full height and I'm suddenly very confused, but go to make the introductions. "Jonas, this is—."

"Senator Halston Bailey," he finishes flatly. I'm so caught off guard by Jonas's tone, I don't even know how to read him in this moment, because I've never seen him be rude to someone, and especially a senator. I know he said he wasn't fond of his professional record but Jonas is nothing if not polite to a fault.

Senator Bailey either doesn't notice Jonas's stony demeanor or chooses to overlook it; he is a politician, after all. He extends his hand. "Very nice to meet you. I hear you're from Florida."

Jonas looks down at Bailey's hand and reluctantly shakes it. His jaw clenches. "Jonas Merritt."

Bailey smiles, his attitude totally professional. "I take it by your tone, you didn't vote for me. I get it, I'm not everyone's cup of tea. I hope I can still serve you proudly in the senate."

"So, Senator, what brings you to Tennessee? I would think you'd spend time with your family in Florida during the holidays." I'm trying to keep the conversation light since it appears Jonas isn't gonna respond.

Bailey looks down at me. "Actually, I'm heading back to DC tomorrow. My wife and her sister are leaving on a cruise, all my kids and grandkids are doing their own things, Clint was nice enough to extend the invitation to the party so I wouldn't have to spend the holiday alone."

I nod and glance at Jonas who has stepped closer to me and settled a hand around my waist, but simply stares at the label on his bottle of beer. I recognize the look on his face as the same one he had after he saw Leah's sister at Maddie's wedding. *What secret is that about?*

Bailey examines Jonas a bit more closely. "You know, Jonas, you look familiar. Have we met before?"

Jonas squares his shoulders and meets the senator's eye. "No, sir. But I believe you knew my mother." My head snaps to Jonas as he continues. "Nancy Merritt."

I feel like I'm at a tennis match as my eyes dart from Jonas's face to the senator's, which at the moment appears to have lost all its color. *What the hell is going on here?*

Bailey falters for a moment. "Wow, I haven't heard that name in a long time."

Jonas interjects. "Probably about thirty years, I'd say."

"Yes, I'd say that's about right. How is Nancy?"

Jonas shrugs. "I wouldn't know. I haven't seen her in fifteen years." His tone is bitter and I'm at such a loss. He takes my hand. "If you'll excuse us, Senator." He doesn't elaborate or wait for a response, simply tugs me away.

I glance over my shoulder at Bailey, who looks down into

his glass of amber liquid. I realize Jonas is pulling me toward the front door. "Jonas, what's going on?"

"I'm sorry, Callie, I can't be here right now. Can we please go?" He almost sounds like he's pleading.

I'm thrown for a moment. "Oh, um. Yeah, sure. Of course." I set my glass down on a table right before we go out the door. When we make it outside, Jonas hands our valet ticket over and we wait for them to bring the car. I know he won't want to talk about whatever this is regarding until we're alone, so I don't even ask. I try to read his face and body language; his expression is tight and he looks as though he's grinding his teeth. His body radiates something that feels an awful lot like rage. I've never seen him like this and I don't know what to make of it. I know it has something to do with Bailey and possibly Jonas's mother, but I have no clue what.

A few minutes later, the car is brought around and the valet opens my door and I climb in. Jonas slides behind the wheel and starts the car and peels out. Once we're out on the road, he passes the driveway to the house. I try to keep my tone light. "Where we going, honey?"

"I don't know. I just need to drive for a bit, is that okay?"

I run my hand down his arm. "Of course. Whatever you need. If you want to go somewhere and park, I can show you where to go. Just let me know."

I see him nod in the dim light from the car's instrument panel and we don't talk for a while. Jonas finally breaks the silence after we've been driving about twenty minutes. "Where can we go?" His voice is low and I almost don't hear him.

I direct him to a back road that dead ends down a dirt drive. Once we get to the end and park, he asks, "Where is this?"

"We own this land. Maddie and I used to come here when we were in high school and hang out. No one comes out here."

He nods and cuts the engine. "Do you want me to ask?" This is our go-to when one of us is dealing with something, and it's our way of asking if the other wants to discuss what's bothering them.

He sighs. "Not really, but yeah."

"Okay, what's your deal with Bailey?"

Jonas is quiet for a while and I almost think he's not gonna talk about it, but I simply let him work at his own speed, and hope he eventually gets there. "My mother worked for Bailey when he was running for state congress. She was right out of high school and trying to get some experience before college, because she wanted to major in political science. I know that probably seems strange, considering she's an addict now and I haven't seen her since I was fifteen, but she used to be something. She had aspirations. She was so smart. And she was beautiful. Think a brunette Christina Hendricks. Do you know who she is?"

"Yeah, she was in *Mad Men*. Wow, I bet she was gorgeous. That explains why you are, too."

He continues, his eyes fixed on something out the windshield. But it's pitch dark, so I know he's not really looking at anything. "Well, she worked for him as an aide. She was instrumental in getting him elected, actually. She helped draft the stump speech he gave at his last rally. It was really powerful. All about changing things that didn't work in the state, specifically social programs and education. It was a great speech."

He thinks about what he wants to say for a long moment and I try to be patient. "There were a lot of late nights during the campaign and Bailey's wife and kids stayed at their home while he campaigned. His wife didn't like being a politician's wife. She didn't like the spot light, didn't want it for her kids. But he did it anyway, I guess. Anyway, my mom spent a lot of time with him. And there was a night where Mom drank too much and things went a little too far with Bailey."

I gasp. "Did he... I mean..." I don't know how to even ask it.

He shakes his head. "No, she wasn't assaulted. He was in a position of power though, so as far as it goes, I feel like he took advantage of her. And then, when she wouldn't continue to sleep with him, he fired her. She said to do it once was a drunken mistake, an error, to do it more than that, would have been an actual choice she kept making and he was married and had a family, so I guess she didn't want to be a home wrecker."

"How do you know all this?"

"Nana told me. You know her, she doesn't sugarcoat. I asked one day what might have driven my mom to the drugs, because it was after Bailey ran for US Senate when things got bad and she left."

"Jonas, I'm so sorry. That's awful."

He snorts, but it's bitter. "That's not even the worst part. He's my father, Callahan."

My stomach drops and my mouth falls open in shock. "I thought you didn't know who your father was."

"No, I said I'd never met him. There's a big difference. I hoped I never would."

"I don't even know what to say. Does he know?"

"Yeah, he knows. My mom went to him when she found out she was pregnant and he threw money at her and made her sign an NDA. He didn't care he was gonna have a bastard running around, as long as it didn't interfere with his political future. He paid her for a few years. And then stopped. And that's when we moved in with Nana and Granddad."

He slams his fist on the steering wheel and I jump. "I always thought if I met him, I'd have all this stuff I'd say. About what a sorry asshole he was. About how I turned out just fine without him. How it's his fault my mom left. How he's the worst sort of man; one who uses women and casts them aside. How I hope he's happy knowing he has a son who's nothing like him." He seems to consider something. "Although, maybe that's not true. I've chased a lot of skirt. So, maybe I am. But I couldn't say any of it; when I saw him with you, all I could see was red. And I know if I hadn't come along, he probably would have tried to get you into bed. Because he preys on young, beautiful women."

I think back and although he never touched me or said anything untoward, he was very good looking and exuded confidence and power and were I single, I can't say I wouldn't have found him charming. And knowing me, if he'd tried to seduce me, I would have gone willingly.

Jonas says, "He has three kids with his wife. I have a brother and two sisters I've never met. I have nieces and nephews. I have this whole other family and they have no clue.

"So, you asked me why I was so big on not flirting with a woman when she's had too much to drink. Part of it is about consent, like I said, but the other part is, I don't ever want to be *him*. I refuse to ever feel like I've taken advantage of a woman or have them feel that way.

"And I think part of me, after I met you, and found out what Dominic did to you, I saw it as just another way I could be *not him*. I could vicariously get revenge on my own father by helping you get over Dom. Like, maybe if my mom had had someone who showed her how wonderful and amazing and better off she was, she would've been okay. And she'd still be around." His voice breaks at the last and my chest tightens with emotion.

"I don't have any words at all for you, Jonas. Except to say, you told me we can't choose our blood, but we can choose our family. And I think in this case, especially, it's true."

CHAPTER TWENTY-ONE

JONAS

I think about what Callie is saying and I know she's right. I know he's not my family. I wouldn't choose him to be, even if I could, simply based on what I know about him and what he did.

I turn to Callie, who I can't really see because it's so dark. "I'm sorry we left the party. I know you were really looking forward to it. I was looking forward to it, too."

She reaches for me and nearly pokes me in the eye. When I yelp, she retreats. "I'm sorry. It's too dark in here."

I reach up and turn on the dome light and when it comes on, she reaches for me again. She takes my face in her hands. "Jonas, don't even worry about the stupid party. I knew when you saw him, something was majorly wrong. You're not a rude or stony person and I knew there had a to be a good reason and when you said you wanted to leave, I didn't even think twice.

"I wish I had the right words to tell you. You're so much better in a crisis and building someone back up than I am." A thought hits her. "When I ran away after the barbecue the week of the wedding, you asked me if wanted to hide or show Dominic I wasn't affected by him. Do you remember that?"

I nod. "Yeah, it's when I told you that your eyes change color depending on your mood."

She smiles. "Yeah, it was. Man, that was good speech. Anyway, I'm gonna ask you the same thing. He knows who you are. Do you want to hide out here, or do you want to show him how much better off you are without him? You can hold your head high and know that you are a good man, because you are, Jonas. You are the best man I know. We can still go back to the party and ring in the new year. We can drink really expensive champaign and have a good time. If it's what you want.

"If you'd rather go home and forget the whole thing, we can do that, too. Whatever you want."

I sigh. "I hate when you use my own logic against me, Darlin'. It's not fair."

She shrugs and gives me a sly smile. "All's fair in love and war, right?" Her expression grows serious and she takes my hand in hers. "But if it's too much, I get that, too. Just tell me what you want to do and we'll do it."

I think for a moment and check my watch. "It's ten-thirty, it's a little early to go home, don't you think?"

"So, that leaves staying out here, which, it's not a bad plan. We can always make out like high schoolers, but this car is a bit small for anything more than kissing. Or, we can go back to the party and make a good memory, in spite of your sperm donor."

I can't help but laugh. I pull her face to mine and press a kiss to her lips. "I'm glad you were with me tonight. There's no one else I'd rather have by my side when the shit hits the fan than you. You claim to not be good in a crisis, but you were pretty good tonight." I sigh. "Let's go back to the party. I may need you to distract me at some point, though. You think we could maybe find a closet or something to sneak off to?"

She laughs. "I'm sure we can think of something. You give me some sort of signal and I will whisk you away to a dark corner and untie my dress."

We drive back to the party and arrive at Clint's a little before eleven. The valet pretends we didn't leave an hour ago and come back and we walk into the house and Callie and I go find the bar together and get a drink.

We meander through the house and I pull Callie to my side. "How many bedrooms does this house have?"

"Ten, I think, and a full basement apartment."

"How do you even use ten bedrooms? I don't even know that many people I like enough to want to put them up."

She laughs. "Yeah, me neither. Our house only has six."

"It's still a lot of bedrooms."

She shrugs. "Not if you really think about it. You have a bedroom for Mom and Dad, Uncle Lance and Aunt Meredith, Maddie, me, a guest room, and the last bedroom will probably eventually be a bunk room for when Maddie and I have kids."

"How many of those you want, you think?" I ask.

"Honestly, I've never thought about how many, only that I want them. Although I grew up with Maddie, I was still an only child and sometimes, it's lonely, so I know I want more than one."

I nod. "I can get behind you on that."

She leans into me. "I hope you can get on top of me, too."

"Darlin', you're killing it tonight. That mouth is gonna get you in some trouble."

She raises a brow. "It'd be good trouble, I'm sure." We make our way back toward the living room and Callie spots Clint. "Let's go say hi to him, so we can duck out right after the ball drops. I don't plan on wearing this dress much past then."

The idea of getting her out of her dress is entirely too appealing to disagree with her plan. "Sounds good to me."

Callie and Clint embrace in a friendly hug and I take a pull from my beer. Clint turns to me once he releases her and we shake hands. "I'm glad y'all could make it tonight. You both look wonderful."

"Thank you for having us. This place is pretty incredible."

Clint looks around as if taking in the space anew. "Yeah, Mom and Dad did pretty well with it. Oh, did y'all see Senator Bailey was here? I was so surprised he actually came. I extended the invite to be polite since he was gonna be alone tonight. I honestly never expected him to actually show."

I try not to react and Callie says, "Yes, we met him. He had great things to say about you."

Clint smiles, obviously pleased. "Really? Well, that's nice. Okay, well, I'll let y'all go mingle. The champagne will be served a few minutes before the ball drops, so be on the look out. Happy New Year to you both."

"You, too, Clint," Callie says as we turn to walk away from him. She looks up at me and quirks a brow. "Want to find a dark corner somewhere and make out until it's time for champagne?"

"Really? You don't want to mingle some more?" Not that I'm opposed with sneaking off with Callie, it's one of my favorite things to do, but I don't want her to feel like she's sacrificing anything by missing the goings on here.

She rolls her eyes. "With very few exceptions, this is the exact same party as the one at our house at Christmas." She starts tugging me in the direction of a door. "And besides, I'd rather let you feel me up than make small talk."

I chuckle and nod. "Yeah, that's pretty nice. Where are you taking me?"

She doesn't answer and simply glances around before pulling me into a room and shutting the door. She turns on a light and I see it's a laundry room. When I look around at the large space, she says, "Don't have to worry about anyone coming in here. Not likely someone will need to do laundry tonight."

She clicks the lock on the door and closes the distance between us. I start to pull her to me and she walks past me to a counter and hops up to perch on the edge. I turn and follow her. "You know, Darlin', for someone who is opposed to fooling around in public, you sure aren't opposed to risk. I'm not complaining, believe me, I just find it hard to reconcile. You said you thought you'd be really vanilla, but first the fire pit and now sneaking away at a big party, I've got to admit, it's pretty hot."

She grabs the lapels of my jacket and pulls me between her knees, the skirt of her dress parting almost to the hip, making my dick promptly swell. "I don't think it's me. I think it's you that makes me want to be this way. The way I want you all the time, I don't know if I'll ever get used to it."

I run my hands up the outside of her thighs, feeling the velvet of her dress under my hands, to settle them on her hips and pull her closer to me. "I don't want you to get used to it. I don't plan on ever letting you get away, so it's in my best interest if you always want me. Because I know I sure as hell want you. I want you to always look at me like you do from across the room, like you're picturing me naked. I want to see your eyes light up when you see me, that beautiful smile you have only for me."

Callie takes my hand and guides it to her inner thigh and places it to the outside of her panties, her eyes never leaving mine. "This is only for you, too. Always." I cup her sex and rub her clit through the lace and she huffs out a soft breath.

I'll never get used to feeling her under my hands, how hot and pliable she is, the sounds she makes when I touch and taste her. I take her hand in my free one and place it over my heart. "And this is only for you, always."

Her eyes soften and she gives me a sweet smile. "I'll take it. Gladly."

CHAPTER TWENTY-TWO

CALLIE

Jonas's fingers are doing delicious things to me as I sit perched atop the counter in Clint's laundry room. I don't think I'll be waiting to get home to take this dress off. His lips crash against mine in an urgent kiss that makes my toes curl and sends a jolt of desire straight to my core.

He moves my panties to the side and slides two fingers into me and I moan into his mouth. Jonas breaks our kiss and I gulp in air. "Untie your dress, Callie. I want to see you."

My heart pounds as my fingers fumble with the strings keeping my dress closed as he continues to work me with his skillful hand, but after a few seconds, I have them undone. I pull the dress fully open and lean back on my hands. Jonas's eyes drag down my face and torso to my thighs, spread wide for him. "Damn, Darlin', I could look at you forever."

"You better do more than just look," I say between ragged breaths as my hips writhe against his hand, needing more friction.

He palms my breast and pulls the cup of my bra down right before his mouth descends and he flicks a tongue over the nipple sending sparks of electric heat to my center. I pull his mouth to mine for a greedy kiss as I loosen his tie and unbutton the first few buttons of his shirt. I lick and nip my way down his neck to his collarbone.

Jonas grips the back of my neck and captures my mouth with his own as he withdraws his fingers. I groan at the sudden absence but I hear him working to unbuckle his belt and drop his pants and a second later, he shoves my panties quickly to the side and he slams into me, nearly knocking the breath from my lungs.

He grabs my hips as he claims me, his movements deep and powerful, and I can only hang on to him as my pleasure swiftly builds. Jonas's breaths are shallow and hot on my ear as he whispers, his voice husky, "You feel so fucking good, Callie. I love you. Come for me, Darlin'."

I reach down to work my clit, already so sensitive and only a moment later, my release overtakes me and Jonas kisses me to muffle my cry as I clench around him, sending him into his own climax. After a few more sharp thrusts, he comes with a shudder and harsh sigh. He rests his forehead against mine as our breathing levels out.

"You think it will always be like this for us?" I ask. "When we're old and gray? You think we'll still be sneaking away during parties for a quickie?"

Jonas chuckles. "If I have any say in it, it will be." He brushes a soft kiss across my lips and steps back. He finds a roll of paper towels and we hastily clean up before righting our clothes.

"You go out first," I tell him. "I'll come out a minute later."

He smirks. "Oh, so now, you don't want people seeing us? Where's the fun in that? Do you really care if these people see us coming out of a room together?"

I roll my eyes. "No, I guess not. But I don't necessarily want to scream 'I just got fucked', you know."

He laughs. "Well, you can see it all over you, anyway. You're all flushed and your eyes are sleepy. It's sexy, Darlin'. I love the way you look after sex."

My blush deepens and I pick up his wrist. "Five minutes to midnight. We better head out and get some champagne before the countdown."

He takes my hand in his and pulls me out the door. Thankfully, no one notices us, as everyone is congregating in the living room as servers bring around glasses of champagne. Someone has switched on the large television over the fireplace and Time Square and the ball are on the screen with the countdown flashing in the corner.

Once we have our glasses, I take a sip and the bubbles tickle my nose. Jonas turns to me. "I'm glad we came back tonight. Marry me?"

I laugh. "I thought we already established I would."

He grins. "I know, but since we're gonna tell your parents I asked you tonight, I didn't want it to be a lie."

I grip his face in my free hand. "In that case, a million times, yes." My heart squeezes with love for this wonderful man. A man who's kind and caring and compassionate.

Jonas takes my hand in his and kisses my palm. He's about to say something, when someone starts a ten-second countdown. We join in on the countdown and when the new year hits, Jonas pulls my face to his for a tender kiss. "Happy New Year, Darlin'. I love you."

"I love you, too. Happy New Year." We finish our champagne and decide to head out. As we wait for the valet to bring the car around, Jonas pulls me into his side and I burrow against him for warmth. He stiffens and I follow his gaze and see why. Senator Bailey is coming out of the house with a young blonde in tow. By the looks of her, she can't be older than twenty-five and I'm suddenly filled with disgust. "Any chance she's one of his daughters?"

"No," Jonas spits out.

"Aside from the fact he's married, he's old enough to be her father and then some."

"Yeah. Who knows how many kids he actually has, though. I can't be the only bastard he's got out there."

I look up at him and grip his face. "Don't call yourself that."

He shrugs. "Why not, it's true. I'm illegitimate. That is, by definition, what a bastard is."

Our car is brought around and we climb in. I have a thought. "You know, your mom signed an NDA, not you. You could always go public, or threaten to."

He shakes his head as we pull out of Clint's driveway. "No, if I was gonna do that, I would have done it years ago. I don't give a shit about him. I don't want people know I share blood with a scumbag like him. I hope I never see him again, honestly. Once was enough for me."

I nod. "Me, too." When we get back to the house a few minutes later, I see the lights are still on. "Guess some people are still up. Want to go in and tell everyone the good news? Or do we need to go to bed and I can distract you from tonight's earlier events?"

Jonas takes my hand and presses his lips to a knuckle. "I'm good, Darlin'. I'm not that delicate. Let's go tell your parents, if they're up. I can't wait to make this thing official."

He starts to open his door and I place my hand on his arm. "Hey." When he turns back to me, I take his face in my hands. "I love you. I can't wait to be your wife. I can't wait to marry you and someday, in the pretty distant future, make lots of curly-headed babies with you."

Jonas smiles. "At least, more than one, right?"

"Right." I give him a quick kiss before we exit the car. As we open the front door, I see my parents, aunt Meredith, uncle Lance, Maddie, and Dominic sitting at the dining room table playing cards. They all greet us as we come inside.

We walk over to the table and I take Jonas's hand in mine. Even though I'm the most sure about this decision as I've ever been about anything, I still can't fight the nerves that settle in my stomach at the prospect of telling my family I'm getting married.

Mom looks up at me as she deals cards. "How was the party?"

I smile brightly and glance at Jonas, who is also smiling. "It was great. Really great, actually. I have an announcement." She stills her hands and everyone looks at me expectantly. "Jonas and I are getting married. He asked me tonight and I said yes."

Everyone erupts in a flurry of *congratulations, great news, wonderful*. Mom's grin widens and she rises from her chair to come and embrace me. "Oh, honey, this is such good news. I'm so happy for you."

Dad stands and shakes hands with Jonas. "Son, I'll forgive the fact you're a Florida fan on account of how happy you make my daughter." Jonas laughs and my father says, "Welcome to the family."

"Thank you, Alex. I hope I can continue to make her as happy as she makes me."

Maddie pipes up, "So, when are you thinking for a wedding?"

I shrug. "Not sure yet. Soon, but nothing set in stone. And small. Just the family and a couple of friends."

Dad nods, pleased. "Well, works for me."

I look around and notice my mom isn't in the room. "Where did Mom go?"

She comes back in a moment later. "I'm here. I just wanted

to go get this." She holds up a small velvet box. When she sees the question in my eyes, she smirks. "I had a hunch. I went to the bank yesterday and got it out of the safe deposit box. I also took it to be cleaned, so it's ready for you." She extends the box to Jonas. "Jonas, would you like to do the honors?"

Jonas looks surprised, but nods and takes the proffered box and opens it. I can't hold back my small chuckle of amusement when he sees the ring and his eyes go wide. As much as I eschew my family's money, I honestly adore this ring and have looked forward to wearing it since the day my mother showed it to me at the age of fourteen.

Just over two carats, it's a cushion cut flawless diamond set in platinum, surrounded by intricate filigree work around the setting, with smaller diamonds along the shoulders of the ring. Jonas takes the ring from its box and slides it on to my finger before bringing my hand up to his lips and kissing the back of it. "Beautiful, Darlin'."

CHAPTER TWENTY-THREE

JONAS

It's after one AM and Callie and I are still awake, cuddled in bed. I take her hand with the honking ring and hold it up. "You sure you're gonna be able to lift that thing every day? Jesus, what a rock."

She laughs. "You should've seen your face. It was like you'd been blinded or something."

I nod. "I think I nearly was. I mean, I figured it would be pretty, but damn, I didn't think it'd be that big."

"I could care less how big it is, although I love it. It's got history. And my great-grandparents were married for almost seventy years, so it's got good vibes, too."

"Well, between your ring and necklace, that's well over a century of good luck, so we should be good."

Callie rolls over and rests her chin on my chest. "I don't think we need luck. As long as we're always honest with one another and choose to be in this thing every single day, we'll be fine. There may be times we don't necessarily *like* each other. We'll fight, we'll have problems. But as long as we always remember we *love* each other, and choose *us*, we'll be okay."

I shake my head, impressed. "Man, Darlin', I think you just wrote our vows. That was pretty good." I lean down and plant a kiss on her forehead.

The next few days, before we go back to Florida, Callie and I spend a lot of time simply relaxing and enjoying each other's company. She and Maddie appear to be in a pretty good place and even things with Dominic appear to be decent as well. I don't know if we'll all ever be best of friends or anything, but knowing family gatherings and holidays won't be filled with so much animosity makes me feel better for Callie's sake.

Things with Maddie and Dominic, on the other hand seem volatile. They are hardly speaking to one another, at least, that's what it looks like as an outsider. Definitely not lovey-dovey like they were before the wedding. I haven't spoken with Dominic about things, because honestly, their relationship doesn't affect me, so I leave it. I think Callie is a bit worried about Maddie, just out of love for her. But she hasn't said anything to me about any conversations she's had with her and I don't ask. Again, it doesn't affect me, so I leave it.

When we get back home a couple days before I have to return to work, we FaceTime with Nana and tell her the news and show her Callie's necklace and ring. She is overjoyed for us and tells us she expects us to have a honeymoon baby, because "I'm not getting any younger, you know."

Callie and I both roll our eyes, but honestly, it wouldn't be the worst thing, because I do want Nana to at least have a memory of me with a child before she's gone. The thought of losing her grips my chest with such pain, but the rational side of me knows she won't be with me forever and I should simply enjoy whatever time I have left with her.

As rocky as Callie's relationship with her parents has been in the past, they're currently in a good place, at least until they try to discuss wedding plans. Vickie is trying to convince Callie she really does want the big wedding, but I'm proud of Callie for standing her ground for what *she* wants, which is anything but. And yet, we persevere.

Elliot, who's been dating Russ since shortly after Callie and I reconnected, have decided to move in together. Callie and I were shocked when Elliot told us after we got home at Christmas. I guess it's a good thing I'll be letting my apartment go, since we'll need the money from my rent to supplement Callie's income so she can continue to work at the library with Nana and not have to get another job making more money.

Callie will be entering the last year of her PhD program and I know this year is probably gonna be very stressful for her, so I plan on doing everything I can to alleviate any kind of pressure for her as far as wedding planning goes. As it stands, we're thinking a summer wedding, since we'll both be out of school and we can spend the break as newlyweds.

The Friday following Valentine's Day, Callie receives a call from Maddie and she takes it into the bedroom, so I figure it has something to do with Dominic and I return to cooking supper, knowing if she thinks I need to know, she'll tell me.

Twenty minutes later, as I'm draining pasta for spaghetti, Callie comes into the kitchen and wordlessly pours herself a glass of wine. I can tell she's been crying. "Do you want me to ask?"

She drains her glass and pours another. I continue dinner preparations and by the time we sit down to eat, Callie's finished her second glass of wine, but doesn't pour another. "Maddie's pregnant. And Dominic's been having an affair."

"Shit. Does she know who with?"

"Clint." When I don't act shocked, she levels me with a gaze. "Why are you not reacting, like, at all?"

I blow out a breath. "Because, I saw them together at Christmas. That morning when I went for a run and Dom and I were in the kitchen, I saw him coming out of Clint's house. We had a discussion and I told him I wouldn't tell, because it wasn't my place."

All the color drains from Callie's face. "And you didn't think to mention it? Not even to me?"

"It wasn't my secret to spill. Not my marriage. I told Dominic he needed to talk to Maddie about what he was going through."

Callie's expression registers disbelief. "Whoa, so you talked to *Dominic,* but not me? Jonas, what the hell?"

"Callie, it wasn't my place. I'm never gonna be his biggest fan, but I'm not gonna ruin someone's life just because they're a dick. And honestly, I thought the thing with Clint was a one-off."

She does pour herself another glass then and I don't say anything, because she's understandably pissed. After she takes a sip, she says, "Maddie saw him with Emery at the Christmas party. They were making out on my porch. That's why she said the stuff she did at the fire pit about Clint and Emery. She was doing it as a slight to Dominic, not truly because she's homophobic, or so she said."

I quirk a brow. "And you didn't tell me? You don't get to be indignant if you're keeping secrets, too, Darlin'."

She lets out a heavy sigh. "I know. I'm sorry. But my secret's not as big as him sleeping with someone else."

"How did Maddie find out about Clint?"

"She'd gone to the doctor and found out about the baby and wanted to surprise Dominic with the news at work. She walked in on them in his office. Clint's apparently been coming in every couple weeks since Christmas and they *have lunch* together. Behind a locked door. All afternoon. Dominic's assistant tried to put Maddie off, but she was so excited about the baby, she'd called Dom when she was standing outside his office and she heard his phone ringing and muffled voices and she made the assistant unlock the door."

"Shit."

Callie nods. "Yeah, she thought she was gonna find a woman in there, which would have been bad, too, but I think she would have taken that better, simply for appearance sake alone."

"So, what is she gonna do?"

"She's not sure. I told her when she saw Dom with Emery, she needed to confront him, but I don't think she ever did."

"I told Dominic he needed to talk to Maddie, too. Is she gonna divorce him?"

She shrugs. "You know she's so caught up with the way things look, she might stay with him and look the other way, so she's spared the embarrassment. I told her it's not a life she'd want. But, now, with the baby coming, I thinks she's even more conflicted."

I take Callie's wine glass and drain it. "Well, damn. Do Lance and Meredith know? Or your parents?"

She shakes her head. "No, I think the only reason she told me is because I already knew about the Emery situation. Otherwise, I think she would've kept all this to herself."

"And have they talked? What does Dominic say he wants to do?"

"She said he told her he still loves her, but she's not sure how she feels now, knowing he's a cheater."

I sigh. "Damn. I didn't see this coming. Not so soon anyway. I mean, I know I said before they got married, in ten years he'd be having an affair, I guess I missed the mark on that.

And I know I said they'd get some kind of karmic retribution, but man."

"Jonas, now is not the time for you to be reveling in other people's misery. I feel bad. I might not if Maddie and I hadn't reconciled, but we did. And there's a baby. This is bad."

I shake my head. "Who's reveling? I'm not. I was simply pointing out something I said before they got married. That's all. I know it's bad. I feel bad for Maddie. Not *so* much Dom, but still. It's a shitty situation, all the way around."

Callie picks up her wine glass and finds it empty and scoffs. "Really? That was the last of my favorite cab. You don't even like wine."

I shrug. "Sorry, Darlin'. It was at hand and I needed a drink after all this news. I'll pick you up a bottle on my way home tomorrow."

We eat in relative silence, both of us trying to absorb everything we've discussed. As we're clearing dishes away and I'm loading the dishwasher, Callie drops a bomb as she's leaving the kitchen to go take a shower. "By the way, Maddie's gonna come stay with us for a couple weeks while she decides what she wants to do. She'll be here tomorrow. Thanks. Love you."

CHAPTER TWENTY-FOUR

CALLIE

I'm starting the shower when Jonas bursts into the bathroom. "Excuse me? You didn't even talk to me before you got us in the middle of Maddie and Dominic's conflict? Who's keeping secrets now, Callahan?" His tone is angry and he so rarely calls me by my full name anymore, it catches me off guard when he does.

"What was I supposed to do? She asked if she could stay with us for a little while. She knew Elliot had moved out, because I told her about him and Russ moving in together. She's family, Jonas."

"It's not our place to get involved. You should've stayed out of it."

"You don't get to tell me who I can have come stay in *my* house," I reply, indignant.

Jonas stiffens and I can tell he is beyond pissed and more than a little hurt. He narrows his eyes and says in a low voice, "Just because this is *your* house, doesn't mean I don't have a say in who comes here. I live here, too. And if we're gonna be married, it's *our* house, remember? It's not yours or mine. It's ours. It's *us*. Isn't that what we said? That we choose *us?*"

I know he has a point and I hate that we're fighting. Especially over something that doesn't even concern us. I've never thrown the fact I own our house in his face before and now I feel like shit. I take my glasses off and put them on the sink and pinch the bridge of my nose. I close the distance between us and rest my forehead on his chest. "I'm sorry. I fucked up. I should've told her I would talk to you and get back to her. I should've consulted you. This is *our* home. I won't do that again."

Jonas wraps his arms around me and sighs. "It's not that I have a problem with Maddie staying with us. Honestly, it's not. I just want you to be careful. After everything that's happened between you two, I don't want you to get hurt again. I know y'all seem to be in a better place now than you were, but she still betrayed you and I don't want to see you go through something like that again. It broke my heart for you, Darlin'. I don't like to see you hurting."

I look up at him. "I know. And I love you for wanting to protect me. And I'm still a little gun shy as far as Maddie is concerned, even though we've worked through a lot of our shit, but I can understand her need to get away and gain some perspective. Hell, when everything ended with Dominic, I moved here. So, I get her wanting to run away for a little bit."

Jonas runs his knuckle along my jaw. "I'm forever gonna be thankful you ran here. Otherwise, we wouldn't have met. And I understand Maddie's need to escape so she can reflect and decide what she wants to do. I don't want us to fight because of them. They've caused you enough turmoil in the past. I don't want it to affect us."

I go up on my toes and press a kiss to his lips. "Um, does this constitute a fight?"

He quirks a brow. "I think it's pretty safe to say this was a fight. At the very least, a spirited argument."

I run my hands under his shirt. "So, does that mean we can have make up sex?"

He smirks. "I think it can be arranged."

I step back and pull my shirt over my head. "Care to discuss it in the shower? Maybe we can come to some sort of agreement." I continue stripping off my jeans, my bra, my panties and Jonas watches me undress. "Just think about it." I step into the tub and less than ten seconds later, Jonas comes in behind me. I can't help but chuckle. "I'll never understand how you get naked so quickly."

He takes my face in his hands and presses me against the shower wall. "Just another of my superpowers, I guess." He claims my mouth in a deep kiss and I wrap my arms around his neck.

He slides his hands down my arms and grips my wrists and pries them from behind his neck and puts them above my head and a thrill runs through me. He holds both my hands in one of his and runs his free hand along my side, lightly brushing my torso with the tips of his fingers. The teasing movements scatter goosebumps up my arms.

Jonas continues torturing me with his featherlight touches. He circles a finger around my nipples until they harden to sharp points. When I try to press my thighs together, he gives me a knowing smile and nudges my knees apart with his own. "No, Darlin', you're going wait for it."

My breath hitches. "You know you want me. You wouldn't have followed me in here if you didn't." I glance down at his dick. "Look at you, you're already so hard, you can barely stand it. Why don't you go ahead and put both of us out of our misery and fuck me already?"

Jonas laughs, but it's not playful or amused. It has an edge to it and it sends a shiver down my spine. "You know who has better self-control between the two of us. I can last hours without needing to give in. You, on the other hand, tend to get pretty needy." He leans in and kisses his way down my neck and chest, as if to emphasize his point and I can hardly bite back a moan as his mouth descends on my breast.

My thighs squeeze against his knee, unable to create any friction and Jonas chuckles as his tongue flicks over a taut nipple. I huff out a sharp, frustrated sigh. "See, Darlin', you're dying already and I haven't even gotten started."

"Jonas, please." My words come out in a near whine and I honestly don't even care.

"Please, what, Callie?"

"Please don't tease me. Make love to me."

He levels me with a gaze. "You don't want that. You want me to fuck you. And that's exactly what I intend to do. After I feel like you've earned it."

My heart races. We've not ever played like this before and I can't deny I find it both a bit unnerving and a big turn on. I know Jonas would never do anything to hurt me or make me truly uncomfortable, but hearing the edge in his voice and his behavior tonight sends a jolt to my core and honestly, I'm interested to see where this will go. I bite my lip. "Do I need a safe word? I feel like I might need a safe word. You know, just in case."

For the first time since we got in the shower, a small smile twitches at Jonas's mouth, seemingly causing him to break character, but it's gone just as quickly. "Sure, Darlin', say *Cabernet* and everything stops." He brushes a kiss across my cheek and it's tender, even as his fingers drag up and down my torso and thighs, still teasing me relentlessly.

"And what if we run out of hot water?" I ask, nearly breathless.

He gives me a wicked grin. "Well, then, I guess temperature play also gets added to the menu for tonight."

I hold Jonas's gaze. "I don't like to be cold."

"Then you better hurry up and earn this cock, Darlin'." His words send heat through me.

"And how do I do that?"

His pupils are blown wide and it makes his brown eyes look nearly black as his gaze slides down my face. "Well, I'm gonna let your hands go and you're not gonna touch me. And then, I'm gonna lick your pussy until I feel like you've had enough. And then, if you're very, very good, I'll fuck you." Need coils low in my belly. "Can you do that? Not touch me?"

I nod and he releases my hands. And although the only thing I want to do is run my hands down his muscled chest, I obediently put them to my side. "That's my girl," Jonas says. "Be good now, Darlin'." I close my eyes as I feel his mouth travel down my chest before his lips close over a hardened nipple.

His tongue flicks over the tight mound and I roll my hands into fists to keep from reaching for him. Being unable to touch him makes my pleasure, and therefore, my need for him more acute and I gulp in ragged breaths of air as he licks and suck and nips my breasts.

His fingers trail up my thigh and when his thumb presses into my clit, I gasp. He works it in easy circles and my hips rock against him. "No, Callie, don't move."

My eyes pop open. "Jonas, that's not fair. You already said I couldn't touch you. Now I can't move?"

He shakes his head. "If you move, that's touching. Be good."

I roll my shoulders in irritation. "Who knew you were such a sadistic fuck?"

He laughs, even as he drops to his knees. "Not gonna lie, I do get a little pleasure seeing you frustrated like this. But, I promise, Darlin', you'll get off. More than once. You just have to give up control. Let me do this." He plants a kiss next to my belly button before tugging the skin gently between his teeth, making me hiss.

His mouth descends lower and Jonas lifts my leg over his shoulder. He nips his way up my inner thigh and I can feel my nails digging into my palms to keep from running my fingers through his curly hair. The first swipe of his tongue up my sex makes a moan fall from my mouth. "Shit, Callie, I love the way you taste. Always so sweet."

I close my eyes and lean my head back and try not to move as his lips close over my clit. He suckles the sensitive bud and my hips buck reflexively. "Fuck". It comes out as a whimper and I can already feel my first orgasm building with the magic Jonas is working with his mouth. I told him last summer he did magic things with his tongue, and I was not exaggerating. When his fingers enter me, my hands move to touch him and I pull back at the last second, for fear he stops what he's doing and I really don't want him to do that.

My breathing grows shallow and labored and in the steam of the shower, I'm forced to drag in lungfuls of humid air. My climax builds and builds and when I can no longer hold back, it crashes into me suddenly and fiercely, nearly bringing tears to my eyes. I cry out with a harsh low groan and expect Jonas to rise and to feel his cock enter me, but he doesn't.

He continues to lick and suck and nibble my clit until a second, sharper orgasm rips through me and my moan sounds almost like a sob. "Jonas, please. Shit. Too much." I know he gave me a safe word and I sincerely debate saying, but I never thought I'd need it. I'd really only asked for it as a joke, but I'm seriously weighing my options at this point.

Trying not to move has made my limbs shaky and my hands are cramping from clenching them into fists. When I feel like

I'm about to die with Jonas's mouth still relentlessly working my pussy, he finally pulls back and I gasp in relief. "Darlin', you were so good for me." My heart is pounding against my ribs and I'm trying to simply breathe as he stands. He runs his hands lightly down my arms and uncurls my fingers and massages my palms.

I don't trust he'll let me touch him, so I don't move since I don't know what else he has planned. Jonas brushes a kiss down my neck. "Damn, your pulse is racing. Tell me, Darlin', do you want my cock?" I nod. "Tell me, Callie. Use your words. You've got such a big vocabulary, with all those books you read, surely they've not all escaped you."

My head is swimming and it is honestly difficult to form coherent speech in this moment, but I finally manage to string a few words together.

"Jonas, I want your cock. Please?"

He lets out a soft laugh against my neck. "Even said please. Such a good girl." He hooks my leg around his hip and I feel his hard length pressed against my entrance. "I'm gonna fuck you now, Callie. Are you ready?"

"God, yes."

He slams into me and I exhale sharply. His thrusts are claiming and powerful. He presses my knee higher to drive himself deeper and a long moan falls from my mouth as Jonas continues to batter me with his relentless movements. He tangles his hands in my hair and he pulls just enough to get my attention. "I'm not your roommate. I'm not your friend. I'm gonna be your husband. You are fucking *mine*. You don't get to keep secrets from me. You don't get to pretend I don't have a say. You hear me?" His words come out in a near growl, his breath hot against my ear. I try to respond, but I'm so near a climax, I can't get the words out. Jonas bucks his hips harder and I gasp. "Say, it Callie. Tell me you're mine. Tell me you won't keep secrets."

"Fuck. Yes. I'm yours. No secrets," I barely manage to croak out as I'm wrecked with my final orgasm. A deep sob wells in my chest as I let go. I clench down and with a final, powerful thrust, Jonas joins me in his own release. He crashes his mouth against mine for a searing, possessive kiss as he gently sets my leg down.

My knees are watery and he supports me, even as he turns off the shower that went cold some time ago. He wordlessly wraps me in a towel and then himself, before helping me out of the tub.

CHAPTER TWENTY-FIVE

JONAS

I watch Callie's face as I help her get dried off. Her eyes appear to be glazed, possibly from endorphins and the come down. She's nearly catatonic as I guide her to the bedroom and pull one of my teeshirts over her head. I don't know whether to be proud of myself for fucking her into such a stupor or concerned for her and her inability to speak at the moment.

I pull on a pair of underwear and towel dry Callie's hair before running a wide-toothed comb through the long strands and working them into a quick braid like she likes. She lets me fuss over her without commenting and after I turn down the covers on the bed, she climbs in.

I go into the kitchen and grab a bottle of water and bring it back. I twist the lid off and hand it to her. "Here, Darlin', drink this." She sits up and sips the bottle of water and I climb into bed beside her and pull her against my side. I can't resist asking, "Do you wish you'd used the safe word?"

After a moment, she shakes her head. "No, I'm just still a bit dazed. That was... intense."

"Too much?"

She huffs a soft laugh. "Fuck, no. Shit." She looks at me and her eyes appear to be a bit clearer. "Maybe I'm not as vanilla as I thought I was. Where did that come from, though? We've never done anything like that before. Is that the way you want it all the time? To control it so much?"

I plant a kiss on the top of her head. "I wouldn't say we've *never* done that before. Our first time, do you remember when I made you stand there and let me undress you? That was me controlling things, wouldn't you say? But no, I don't need it like that. Not gonna lie, I like it sometimes."

She nods and a slight blush colors her cheeks. "I think I like it sometimes, too." After a beat, she says, "That stuff you said, you were right. I didn't treat you like my soon-to-be husband. I'm sorry, I won't do that again. It was disrespectful."

I take her face in my hands. "No, I'm sorry. I shouldn't have said any of that; not during sex. I won't do it again. I was pissed when you said this was your house and I should've never taken it with me when I climbed into the shower. I'm sorry, Callie." I am sorry. I could kick myself for bringing my personal shit into sex.

She squeeze my wrists in reassurance. "I'm okay. I knew you were pissed. I knew what I'd said hurt you. But I'm fine. I know sometimes we'll be frustrated with one another and if it comes out during sex, so what? I'm not scared of you. You're never gonna hurt me, I know that. Honestly, it was pretty hot, seeing you get all alpha like that.

"And it would be one thing if you did all that stuff and were super dominating and just left me in the shower or didn't take care of me after, but you did. You were gentle with me and helped me come down and even got me a bottle of water and braided my hair and checked in with me. All very textbook aftercare behavior."

I roll my eyes. "Aftercare? You make it sound like it was

some kind of dom/sub scene. Like out of one of your smutty books."

She shrugs. "I mean, kinda. But I liked it, so don't think I'm not okay with it. I think you know me well enough to know if I wasn't, I would let it be known. It was hot." She presses a kiss to my lips and sets the bottle of water on her nightstand before snuggling down in the covers. I turn off the light and lie down and pull Callie to my chest and drape my arm around her. She's out in a matter of minutes and for a while, I simply listen to her sleep before I fall into my own exhausted slumber.

When I wake up, Callie is still asleep and has rolled over to face me sometime in the night. I lie and watch her sleep for a bit. She's so beautiful and most of the time, she has no clue. She has no clue how men's eyes follow her when she walks down the street or how sexy she is without even trying. Most of the time, she's barefaced, or only wears a swipe of mascara on her blonde lashes.

And when she tries, when she dresses up or has an event, she is show-stoppingly stunning. But because she's so humble, she never sees it. Although, I think I love her the most exactly like this; when her hair is coming loose from her braid and her face is relaxed and her lips are pursed in sleep. She's normally up before me, so it's rare I actually get to see her sleeping and I take advantage when I can.

As if she can sense she's being watched, her eyes flutter open and she gives me a sleepy smile. "Good morning."

"Good morning, Darlin'." I pull her to me and press a kiss to her forehead. She throws her leg over my hip and rests her hand on my waist as she snuggles closer to me. "What time does Maddie's flight get in today?"

Callie sighs. "Around four-thirty, I think."

"Will we need to go pick her up?"

"No, she's renting a car. I told her we could, but I don't think she wants to be trapped while she's here. You know, in case she wants to get out while we're both gone."

I nod. "Sure. Sorry about last night."

She waves my apology away. "Totally forgiven and forgotten. Same?"

I chuckle. "Yes, Darlin'. Want some coffee? I'll go make some and bring it back if you're wanting to be a little lazy this morning. I'm happy to come back and cuddle you some more, as much of a hardship as it would be for me."

She snorts against my chest. "I'm so sure. No, I need to get up. I've got to get the guest room made up for Maddie and do some laundry and go get groceries. Ugh. Sometimes being a grown up sucks."

"Yeah, but some parts are nice, don't you think? The part where you can live with your spouse-to-be and have crazy shower sex and stay up late watching R-rated movies."

"True, those parts are nice. The other parts, though, bills, jobs, aches and pains as you get older, not so much."

I laugh. "Like you're old? Miss twenty-five. When you're thirty, you can complain."

"Well, I sure feel old today. I'm pretty sure you drained some of my life force away when we had our crazy shower sex last night."

"Could be why I feel so good this morning." I roll out of bed and Callie groans and reaches for me.

"You're stealing all my warmth. Come back."

I lean down and kiss the side of her head. "I'll be back when I make coffee." I leave her in the bed and pad into the kitchen to brew a pot of coffee. By the time I'm pour her a mug, she comes walking in.

"It's not the same in bed without you," she says with a pout that makes me smile.

I hand over her mug and pull her to my side. "I'm sorry, Darlin'. I'll try to make sure you get up first from now on, alright?"

"Yes, please."

CHAPTER TWENTY-SIX

CALLIE

After we've had our coffee, Jonas and I settle into our normal Saturday routine if I'm not working. We fix breakfast and watch our weekend morning shows. I toss in a load of laundry and make the grocery list. "You want to come with me to the store?" I ask Jonas as he's folding a load of towels.

"I can, but if you want, I can stay here and get the guest room made up so you won't have to do it when you get back."

I nod. "Okay, I like that idea better. Thank you."

"Sure, Darlin'. Want to order pizza tonight, since Maddie will be coming in? That way we don't have to cook?" I can tell he's trying to be more supportive of Maddie coming to visit and it makes me feel even more guilty than I did last night about everything I said. "Callie, I'm fine. Stop dwelling. She's coming, I'm good. We're good."

I sigh and roll my eyes. "Just because you can read me all the time doesn't mean I don't want to pretend I can keep my thoughts hidden every once in a while, you know."

He chuckles and gives me a halfhearted shrug. "Sorry,

Darlin'. What can I say, you're my favorite book. I love to read you over and over again. So, pizza, or no?"

I nod. "Pizza would be good. Want me to pick up some Stella for you? Or you want something different?"

"Stella's fine. Since Maddie's pregnant, you won't have to worry about her drinking all your wine."

I scoff. "No, I just have to worry about you drinking it. For someone who doesn't like wine, for some reason, whenever I have a bottle of that cab, you manage to drink about a third of it."

Jonas laughs. "It's actually a pretty good wine. Might want to get two bottles."

I consider. "Not a bad idea. I'm hoping while Maddie's here, she can help me with some wedding planning. Maybe she and I can go look at dresses while she's in town. June's gonna be here before we know it and we have basically nothing planned."

"You sound like you actually want to plan a wedding. Big change from 'I'll go to Vegas and show up at Thanksgiving with a husband'."

I sigh. "Yeah, I know. Guess that's what healing will get you. I said all that back when I was bitter and broken. You can't hold it against me. You know I still don't want a big to-do. I only want you and me and our families. That's it. I want to wear a pretty dress and see you wear a gorgeous suit and then have fabulous married sex with you. Preferably at the wedding."

He laughs. "Damn, I like the idea of that. Well, whatever you need from me, let me know. I want to do the whole cake tasting thing. You know I love wedding cake."

I roll my eyes. "I think the cake is the only thing about the wedding you *do* care about."

He sets the last folded towel down on the stack of others already folded and comes over to me. "Not true. I can't wait to be your husband. I can't wait for you to be Callahan Merritt. I mean, unless you want to keep your maiden name or hyphenate. We haven't really talked about it."

"Nope, I'm totally stealing your last name, mister. It's the least you owe me for stealing my heart." A goofy grin crosses my face and we both laugh.

"Cheesy, Darlin'. But I like it." He gives me a quick kiss before taking the towels and putting them in the linen closet.

I make it back from the grocery store by four and get everything put away just as Maddie texts me to say her plane has landed and she should be arriving by about five. Sure enough, she pulls in the driveway at five after five and Jonas heads out to help her with her bags. And to my shock, she has two large suitcases, as if she's brought nearly her entire wardrobe. Jonas and I exchange nervous glances when we both see how much luggage she's carted here for *only a couple weeks.*

Maddie comes in the door and immediately rushes over to me and throws her arms around me. I can see on her face she's been crying and I don't know how to help her, so I simply rub her back and mouth *help me* to Jonas over Maddie's shoulder.

He shakes his head and mouths back *you're on your own.* His smile is a bit more smug than I'd like, but I can't blame him. He would prefer we were not involved in this at all. And although I know he's not gonna do or say anything to Maddie to make her feel unwelcome, he's probably not gonna go out of his way to be a big help to her other than to extend hospitality, either.

When Maddie pulls back, I rub my hands down her arms. "How was your flight?"

She shrugs. "Fine. Some turbulence, but I'm so nauseated already, I never noticed."

I nod. "Well, can I get you anything? Crackers, a cup of tea?"

She shakes her head. "I think I'm gonna lie down for a while. I've not been sleeping very well."

"Sure. We're gonna order pizza later. You still like sausage and bacon?"

All the color drains from her face and she blows out a breath. "No, thanks. I'll probably have some toast if I get hungry later. Pizza hasn't really been my friend lately."

I put my arm around her shoulder and guide her to the guest room. "Your place is really nice, Hanny. It's very you. Thank you for letting me crash with you and Jonas. I'll try to stay out of your way while I'm here. I really just need time to think." She draws in a shaky breath and tears well in her eyes.

"Sure, Maddie. Get some rest. The bed has clean sheets. Bathroom is right down the hall. Help yourself to whatever you'd like in the kitchen. Let me know if you need anything, okay?"

She nods. "Okay." She walks into the bedroom and shuts the door.

Over the next few days, I don't see Maddie much. She stays in her room and sleeps a lot. I don't know if it's because she's pregnant, or because of depression or what, but she doesn't eat with us or really interact and it's almost like she's not even here, so Jonas and I go about our regular routine. I check on Maddie a couple times a day and can see she usually has on clean clothes and looks like she's showered, so she must at least be doing that while we're gone during the day.

I'm still worried about her, simply because she's family, even if we'll never be as close as we once were. I sincerely hope she finds peace with whatever decision she makes regarding

Dominic and their relationship. I hope for the sake of her child she doesn't go back to Dom because it's the easy thing. I know in the long run, she'll be miserable and so will he and their child. But with as worried as she is about appearances, I wouldn't put it past her to simply stick it out.

As I'm leaving class the Tuesday after she arrives, I'm still thinking and worrying about Maddie, looking down at my phone to text Jonas to remind him I have study group tonight, when a figure steps in front of me. And because I'm not paying attention, I nearly run right into them. It's not until I look up into the face of the person I nearly collide with, I see who it is. I'm both shocked and disgusted to see Senator Halston Bailey standing in front of me. I try to keep my features neutral. "Senator. Excuse me." I attempt to walk past him, because I sure as hell don't want to see him and don't have a clue as to why he'd be here in the first place.

He steps into my path. "Callahan. Lovely to see you again. Do you have a moment?"

I'm so far beyond confused and he takes my inability to comprehend that he's actually sought me out and thus, my inability to form words, as his cue to speak freely. "Good. I'll try not to take up much of your time. I don't know what you might have heard about me, and I can see by the look on your face you've heard *something*, but I only want to talk."

I'm suddenly filled with rage on behalf of Jonas. And in spite of Bailey's calm demeanor and polished exterior, he's *nervous*. He's fidgety and keeps raking his hands through his hair. I've seen Jonas do it a hundred times whenever he's anxious or upset. *I guess some behaviors really are ingrained.* I finally find words and can barely contain my anger, even as I manage to keep my tone even.

"I'm sorry, Senator, what would you be referring to? I've heard a lot of things. None of them good where you're concerned. And beyond that, why would you care what I think? Why are you here?" After a beat, I say, "You know what, I don't even care. Good day."

I turn to go the way I came, simply so I can get away from him, and Bailey says, "I know where Jonas's mother is."

I freeze in my steps and turn to face him and narrow my eyes. "Excuse me?"

"Nancy, Jonas's mother. I know where she is."

"Why do you know that?"

He sticks his hands in his pockets. "I knew who Jonas was when he said who is mother was. I'm not stupid enough to think he's not aware of who I am to him. When he—."

"You're *nothing* to him." I cut him off and can't keep the bite out of my tone.

He nods. "Yes, well. I do have the information as to Nancy's whereabouts if you think Jonas would be interested."

"Why come to me? Obviously, if you found me, you could've found him."

He shrugs and almost manages to appear humble. "I get the feeling he'd rather not see me, based on his reaction at Clint's party. I thought you'd be the better in. But I'll be honest, you're pretty intimidating, young lady."

I scoff and roll my eyes and shift my bag from one shoulder to the other. "What do you want? Why would you do this?"

He looks down at his feet for a moment. "I'm not a good man. I've never claimed to be. I've made a lot of mistakes over the years. And when Jonas's mother came to see me to tell me she was pregnant... Well, I'm not proud of what I did back then. I wasn't a young man, but I was an immature man. I made a hasty decision based on what I thought was best for me.

"Honestly, when I never heard from Nancy after I stopped sending her money, I assumed she'd had an abortion or put the baby up for adoption. She was very young, after all. So, I rarely gave it another thought. But when I met Jonas at Clint's party, I realized, that wasn't the case. He looks exactly like my son, Ashton, except for the eyes. Those are his mother's. I looked into Jonas. He's a good man."

"He's the best man I know. And it has nothing to do with you."

He nods. "Yes. That's obvious. And I can, in no way, make up for the past or the mistakes I've made, but I thought if I could find his mother and help them reconnect, then I could at least do one good thing."

"And what do you want for this good deed of yours? I'm not naive. You're a politician. There's no way you wouldn't have some sort of reason."

"I'm planning on running for governor after my next term in senate."

I snort bitterly. "So, you're just wanting to ensure your skeletons stay buried, is that it? You know, I tried to get Jonas to go public. You know what he said?" Bailey's jaw clenches and I continue. "He said if he wanted to do it, he would have done it already. He has no desire to be connected with you in any way. He's made peace with who he is in spite of who *you* are."

The senator runs his fingers through his hair again and I'm struck by how similar the mannerism is to what Jonas does. He says, "Well, I only wanted to offer. I'd be happy to send the information to you or him, but I'd prefer to give it to him in person if you think he'll meet with me."

I huff out a small, hollow laugh. "I can almost guarantee you he will not want to see you. Once was enough for him."

He extends a business card to me. "Be that as it may, I would like to meet with him, if he's willing. My personal cell is on the back. Even if he won't meet with me, but still wants the information, I can send it via email or currier. I'll be in Florida for the next week, and won't be back until later in the year, when we adjourn."

I look down at the card in his hand and seriously consider not taking it, but this is Jonas's mother. Dorothy's daughter. If there's any way they can be reunited, I have to give Jonas the option. I sigh and take the card. "Even if you do this, you know it will never mean anything other than what it is, right? You'll never be more than what you are currently. Which is nothing."

He nods. "Yes. I'm not expecting that. Like I said, I simply want to do at least one good thing for him." He steps back. "I won't take any more of your time. Thank you for hearing me out. Have a good evening, Callahan." He turns to walk off.

I pull my phone out and text my study group to tell them I won't make it and climb in my car to go home to try to figure out how to blow up Jonas's life.

CHAPTER TWENTY-SEVEN

JONAS

I know Callie is supposed to be at study group tonight, so I'm surprised to see her come in the door. I picked up burgers for Maddie and me, even though she has only nibbled hers. So I don't know if Callie's eaten.

I rise from the couch after she sets her stuff down in a chair and follow her to the kitchen. She doesn't even acknowledge me and immediately pulls out a bottle of wine and a glass. She pours it almost completely full and I know without having to even ask, something's happened. "Hey, Darlin'. Study group get cancelled? I wasn't expecting you for at least a couple more hours. Have you eaten? I can make you something real quick."

She's practically guzzling her wine and I try to wait for her to lower the glass so she'll speak, but I'm beginning to get anxious. She doesn't put the glass down until it's empty and then she goes to pour another and I reach and stop her from tipping the bottle and lift her chin. Her eyes are the grayish blue of when she's upset. "What happened, Callahan? What's wrong?" I try to keep my voice low so Maddie won't overhear. She's curled up on the couch watching a movie, which is actually an improvement for her, because at least she's out of her room.

Callie takes a deep breath. "We need to talk."

My stomach drops and I rake my fingers through my hair, suddenly nervous. She sees the gesture and all the color drains from her face. "Callie, what's wrong?"

Her eyes flick to the couch where Maddie is stretched out before coming back to mine. "Take me for a drive?" She sounds nearly panicked.

I nod. "Of course. Let me get my keys." I walk into our bedroom and grab my keys and phone from my nightstand and walk back toward the front door. I see Callie has a to-go cup I'm sure doesn't contain coffee, but I don't say anything. She obviously needs a little liquid courage for whatever reason, so I let it pass. "Maddie, we'll be back."

She simply waves to us as we walk out the door. I open the passenger door for Callie when we reach my care. After she's in, I go around to the driver's door and climb behind the wheel and start the car. "Where to, Darlin'?"

She shrugs. "I don't care, really, I didn't want Maddie to overhear. It's a small house, so even if we went in the bedroom, she might have heard us talking."

I nod and back out the driveway. I drive a couple of miles down the road and pull in at a park where I sometimes go to run. I park the car, and crack the windows so it doesn't get stuffy when I cut the engine. I turn to Callie and take her hand in mine. "Are we okay, Darlin'? Hearing 'we need to talk' is one of those things that strikes fear in the heart of every man in a relationship, you know."

She huffs a small laugh and kisses my palm. She looks into my eyes. "You and I are fine. I'm still trying to process. It might take me a minute. But, I swear, we're fine. I love you."

I sigh in relief. "Okay. Well, now that I know that, I can breathe. Take your time."

She sips her wine for a moment and then seems to come to some sort of conclusion in her mind. "Have you ever tried to find your mom? You know, since she left?"

I'm caught off guard by her question, because it's so far out of left field. We've never really talked about my mom, so to hear Callie bring her up after something's obviously happened, it's strange. But because I feel like she's got a certain place she's trying to get to in this conversation, I answer the questions simply. "Nana and Grandad hired a private detective a few months after she left. And for several months, they paid this guy to track down leads. But, either, she left the state, or something, because he never could find her. And my grandparents couldn't afford to keep looking. And when she never tried to contact me at all, I assumed she didn't want to be found or didn't want to see me anymore, so I didn't look."

Callie looks at her lap, absorbing my words. After a moment, she asks. "If you knew where she was, what would you do? Would you want to see her?"

"Callie, what's going on? What's my mother have to do with anything?"

"Answer the question, Jonas. Would you want to see her if you knew where she was?"

I try to picture my mother before she got on drugs. I try to think about the good times we had. How she'd make me pancakes with sprinkles on my birthday. How she'd ruffle my hair and call me squirt. How she'd sit in bed with me and read comic books, even though she didn't really like them, simply to take an active interest in something I liked. How she'd cheer me on in peewee basketball. How when I won the state spelling bee when I was eleven, she put the newspaper article up the fridge and told everyone who came over how proud she was of me.

Then I remember what she was like after. How skinny she got. How she stole money from Nana and Granddad. How she'd hit me sometimes. How I was embarrassed to bring people over for fear she'd be high. How, when she left, I wasn't even really mad or sad, I was relieved. Because at least, I was safe with my grandparents.

My chest suddenly feels tight and tears burn my eyes. "I don't know. It's a really loaded question. I think it would depend on which Nancy would be there. Sober or strung out? They're two totally different women. Why?"

"Halston Bailey came to see me at school today. He was waiting for me when I got out of class. He says he knows where your mother is."

My breath hitches hearing his name. And learning he has information about where my mother is so absurd I nearly start laughing. But all that comes out is a gruff rasp. And then I think about how he is with women and I immediately worry about Callie. "Did he hurt you? Did he do anything to you?"

Callie's eyes soften and she takes my face in her hands. "No, he was very respectful, contrite, even, which was totally strange."

"What did he say? How does he know where she is? What does he want?"

She drops her hands and takes mine in hers again. "He said when your mother came to see him all those years ago and told him she was pregnant, he *made a hasty decision*. That's what he said. It nearly sounded like he has regret over things, but he never came out and said it.

"He said when Nancy never came back or tried to get more money or anything, he assumed she'd had an abortion or put you up for adoption because she was so young. But he said when he saw you at Clint's party and you told him who your mom was, he realized she'd had you.

"And when you said you hadn't seen her in fifteen years, he did some looking. I guess, with his connections, she was pretty easy to find, because he says he knows where she is. And if you want the information, he wants you to have it. He said he's never claimed to be a good man, but he could at least do this."

My stomach knots up at the thought of seeing my mother again after all this time. "What does he want for the information?"

"He's running for governor and wants to make sure things stay quiet." She huffs angrily. "You better believe I tore into him about how if you wanted to go public you would have done it long before now and how you don't ever want to be connected to him. But he also would like to give you the information in person. I told him you'd probably refuse, and he said he'd still send the info if that was the case.

"But I know you've always had things you wanted to say to him, so this might be a good time to get all that stuff off your chest."

"How come he went to you?" I can't help but wonder if he wants to see me so bad, why he didn't track me down instead of Callie.

"He said he thought I'd be the easier one of us to deal with."

I chuckle. "That's because he doesn't know how ruthless you can be."

She smiles. "He does now." Her expression grows serious. "You know whatever you decide to do, I'll support you. If you want to see him and tell him all those things you always wanted to say, you should. And I think you owe it to yourself to find your mom and if you guys can reconcile, you should. I think Nana deserves it too."

"Does he think if I see him we'll have this magical Hallmark moment?" I can't keep the bitterness out of my voice.

"No, I don't think that's what he's after. I honestly don't know what he's after, other than to meet with you and give you the info about your mom. He'll be in town for a week, then he returns to DC. And if you want to go, I'll be right there by your side if you want."

I look at Callie and her expression is compassionate and loving. "What would you do, Callie? If you were me?"

"I can't tell you what to do, our life experiences are totally different. I know if I'd had the opportunity to tell Dominic off last summer and I hadn't done it, I'd regret it. It was cathartic for me to get all the stuff I needed to tell him off my chest. I think I don't want you to have any regrets. Whatever that looks like for you."

We sit in the quiet for a while and I start the car. "Are there any other bombs you want to drop on me tonight?"

She chuckles. "No. I think that'll do us for today. Want to take me home and I can distract you for a while?" Her tone is suggestive.

I examine her face. Although she doesn't look like she's anywhere near drunk, I know she hasn't had supper and all this wine will hit her at once. "How tipsy are you?"

"Just barely." She holds her thumb and index finger about a quarter-inch apart as if to emphasize her point.

"Eat something and then we'll talk."

"Okay. Well, take me home and make me something to eat and then I'll distract you for the rest of the night, how about that?"

"Sure, Darlin'." I start to put the car in gear and then I stop. "Callie, thank you for being my person. I'm glad I have you to help me work through all this shit." I take her face in my hands and press a kiss to her lips.

She wraps her arms around my neck and deepens the kiss. She tastes like her favorite wine and there's nothing more I would love to do than keep kissing her. Her mouth moves down to my neck and she says, "You know, I'd be happy to give you a distraction right here, too." Her hand slides up my thigh and inside the athletic shorts I'm currently wearing. My dick hardens instantly at the nearness of her hand and I reach down to stop her.

"What's wrong?" Callie asks, confused.

"I told you, you need to eat something."

She huffs a frustrated sigh. "I'm not drunk, Jonas. I'm fine."

"You know the rules, Callie."

CHAPTER TWENTY-EIGHT

CALLIE

"You know the rules, Callie," Jonas says, his tone even.

Anger wells up in my chest. "Dammit. I'm not drunk. And I'm getting real tired of this *rule*. Simply because I'm slightly tipsy, you won't even fool around with me? It's not like I couldn't still tell you no if I wasn't into something. But I also know you love me enough to never hurt me; not like that. I know you like to be in control all the time, but fuck, sometimes, tipsy sex is fun." I fold my arms and turn to stare out the windshield.

"Just because that was the only way you could have *fun* with Dominic doesn't mean that's how I want to do things." His voice has an edge to it.

"And just because I can't throw in your face every hookup you've ever had doesn't mean you can do it to me. Don't bring him up again, it's not fair to me."

"Well, what's fair about you pushing my boundaries, Callie?"

"You said drunk, Jonas. I'm not drunk. I'm tipsy. There's a huge difference. You've never seen me drunk. I promise it's a very different experience. I don't get drunk." I turn to him and see that he's gripping the steering wheel so tightly that his knuckles have gone white. His jaw is clenched and his brows are furrowed. I know the stuff with Bailey has caught us both off guard tonight and we're taking it out on each other.

I blow out a deep breath and put my hand on his jaw to force him to look at me. "You're not *him*, Jonas. You're not your father. You're never gonna be him. The same way you told me I'm not Maddie and I'm never gonna be her. I feel like, you've spent all these years trying to prove to yourself you're better than he is, when you can't even see that you always have been.

"You've never taken advantage of a woman in your life, I know that. And even when you very easily could have taken advantage of me when we met, you didn't. I was so vulnerable and desperate for attention, you probably could have seduced me on the first night if you wanted. It really wouldn't have taken much." I huff out a small laugh and I see his lips twitch as if he's trying not to smile.

"But you didn't. You made sure it was my choice. Everything we did. You made sure I felt good about myself before you slept with me. It was the first time in my life I felt truly sexy and desired. *You* helped me feel that. You are not your father. And I'm not your mother. You don't need to protect me, not from you."

Jonas slumps and leans his face into my hand. "I'm sorry, Callie. I don't want us to fight. I never thought he had such an impact on me, but I guess he did."

"Hey, I'm just glad to know I'm not the only one in this relationship who might have a little bit of damage. That part of things has always been a little one-sided and it was kind of lonely."

Jonas snorts. "Yeah, I guess I have some daddy issues I need to work though, huh?" After a beat, he turns his face and kisses my palm. "I'll meet with Bailey."

"I don't want you to do it only because I think you should."

He shakes his head. "No, I need to look him in the face and tell him all the things I've always wanted him to know. I think you're right about getting it all off my chest. And if I can learn where my mother is, I should. I don't think Nana's ever given up hope that she'd come back and if I can help her see her again, I want to do that."

I nod. "Okay. Do you want me to set up the meeting, or do you want to do it?"

He sighs. "I need to do it. I'll do it. You'll come with me, though, right?"

"Of course. I'll be right by your side." I lean over and kiss his cheek. "Now, can you take me home and feed me and take me to bed?"

"Sure, Darlin'." He puts the car in gear and a few minutes later, we're back home and I see a car I don't recognize in the driveway.

"Do you recognize that car?" I ask.

Jonas shakes his head. As we walk up onto the porch, we hear shouting. "What the hell?" I rush to open the door and see Maddie standing in the living room. With Dominic. Jonas and I both freeze when we see him and they both immediately clam up.

Jonas is the first one to speak. "Do you need us to leave so y'all can talk?"

Maddie glares at Dominic. "No, he was just leaving."

Dominic stands up straighter. "We're not done, Maddie."

"Well, I am." Maddie turns to go and Dom reaches for her. She jerks away from him. "Don't touch me." She pushes past him and goes into her room and slams the door.

He goes to follow her and I get in his path. "Dominic, don't.

Give her time. You know her. If you push her, you're not gonna get anywhere. How did you even know she was here?"

His jaw clenches and his eyes are fixed on Maddie's door. "It wasn't too hard to figure out. You're the only person she'd trust in this. She'd never tell anyone we knew about what was going on, she'd be too embarrassed. But I'm guessing she told you everything. Or, Jonas did."

I shake my head. "Jonas didn't tell me anything. Not until after Maddie did. He kept your secret, as pissed as I was at him for it."

Dominic glances over his shoulder at Jonas, who's making me a grilled cheese. "Really, he didn't tell you?"

"No. Jonas doesn't betray people." I can't keep the bitterness out of my voice. "Why are you here, Dom?"

"I want my wife back."

"Well, maybe you should have thought about her *before* you cheated."

"I know I fucked up. I'll never forgive myself for it. But I'm not leaving here without Maddie."

"You know she might not forgive you, right? She might not get past this. And you know your prenup has an infidelity clause. So if she divorces you, you get nothing, right? Is that the only thing you're worried about? Her money?"

His face contorts in anger. "I don't give a fuck about her money. I love Maddie."

I snort. "Then why did you cheat?"

His face falls. "I don't have a good answer. There's never a good answer. All the reasons I could give are shitty."

"Are you still with Clint?"

He shakes his head. "No. When Maddie caught us and I saw the look on her face, I realized what a stupid fucking mistake I'd made and I was so sick over it."

"So, it's only because you got caught? Wow. That's great.

So, what you're saying is, if you *hadn't* got caught, you'd still be fucking him? You're right, it is a shitty reason, Dom."

His jaw clenches. "I don't have to rationalize shit to you, Cal. You're not my wife."

I bark out a laugh. "Thank God. Because if it was me, you know I have no issues blowing shit up and you'd never even be able to show your face in front of your family and friends again by the time I was done with you. You're lucky Maddie cares about appearances. I would've blasted this shit all over."

"Callie, come eat, Darlin'." Jonas has my plate and and a glass of ice water sitting on the table. When I don't move from my spot, he comes over and kisses the side of my head. "Go on, it's fine. I won't let him go in there."

I glance up at him and he gives me a nod and a small smile, so I go eat my sandwich. Jonas is saying something to Dominic, but his voice is low and I can't hear what's being said.

Dominic's not so quiet. "You think I don't know that?! I already told y'all, I'm not leaving without Maddie."

Jonas folds his arms. "Well, she's obviously done talking to you for tonight. And Callie and I both have work tomorrow. It's getting late. Go get a hotel room and try again tomorrow. But not until one of us is home. I'll be home by four. Come back then. Maybe Maddie will be more open to talking then."

Dominic deflates. "Fine. I'll be here. I'm not going home without her. And I'm only in town for a few days." He hollers past Jonas. "You hear me, Maddie, I'm not going home without you. So you can be mad, you can scream at me, you can give me the silent treatment, but you'll do it at home." He turns and walks out of the house.

Jonas comes over to sit next to me at the table. "What did you say to him?" I ask.

"I told him he should have talked with Maddie after Christmas and this all could've been avoided."

I nod. "Yeah, he should have. But she should have talked to him, too, after she saw him with Emery. They're both at fault here. I mean, him more than her, obviously. But I'd have never watched you or anyone else I was in a relationship with kiss someone else and turned a blind eye."

Jonas snorts. "No, you'd kick my ass."

"Damn right I would. You only have yourself to blame for that. You're the one who showed me what I was worth, so I don't let anyone treat me bad anymore."

Jonas smiles. "I'm glad, Darlin'."

I hear Maddie's bedroom door open and she pads into the kitchen. "He's gone?" she asks.

We nod. Jonas folds his arms. "You haven't told him about the baby, have you?"

My head snaps to him and then to Maddie. "What?"

Maddie shakes her head. "No."

I frown at Jonas. "How'd you know?"

"Because he never once mentioned he wanted her to come home because of the baby or anything remotely close to that."

I realize he's right. "Maddie, you haven't told him?"

She sits down at the table and sighs. "No. When I saw him and Clint together, the only thing I could think was I needed to get out, get away. So I did."

"What are you gonna do? He's coming back tomorrow."

"I heard. I don't know. I know even if I leave him for good, we'll still be connected because of the baby, so I honestly don't know. But it's such a mess. I've been married less than a year and my husband cheated on me and I'm pregnant. So much for me thinking this was a good match. I thought he was so boring I'd eventually be the one who strayed simply for excitement. Jesus, I'm an idiot."

Jonas and I exchange surprised glances. I say, "Maddie, there are worse things than divorce, you know. There's staying in a bad marriage for years and years and both parties being completely miserable. There's raising a child in an unhappy marriage. I know you worry about what people are gonna think, but isn't it worse for you to be miserable for the rest of your life as opposed to maybe being a bit uncomfortable socially for a short time."

Maddie holds my gaze. "All that's real easy for you to say, Callahan, you're not even part of the social scene. You've always shunned it. You don't care. You've never cared. I do."

I shrug. "Well, then, you have do what's best for you."

Jonas says, "Just make sure it's something you can live with. Whatever it is."

"Do you love him, Maddie?" I ask.

She looks down at her hands. "I don't know. Not anymore."

"Then you never did."

Her head snaps to me. "You don't know that."

I scoff. "Yes I do. If you truly loved him, you'd be more upset about what he did than the way it looks. You'd be heartbroken. Inconsolable. Believe me." I glance at Jonas and he gives me a small nod as if he already knows what I'm gonna say. "Do you know what I did after I found out you and Dominic had started dating?"

Her eyes dart from me to Jonas as if she's surprised to hear me talk about this in front of him. "He already knows everything I'm gonna say, so it does't matter. Maddie, I moved five hundred miles away. I stayed drunk for two months. I got a fucking tattoo. I was still hung up on him when I came home for your wedding. It ate me alive. I loved Dominic. And he broke my heart. He chose you. He loves you. He came here without even knowing about the baby because he wants you back. If you don't love him, whatever. Let him go if it's what you need to do. But don't stay with him only because you're worried about what people will think. You're not the first woman whose husband cheated. You're not that special, Maddie."

Her mouth falls open as if she's shocked to hear me speak to her this way but then she closes it and nods. "You got a tattoo? Another one?"

I chuckle. "I have three, actually."

"Three? I thought you only had the one with the books?"

I shake my head. "No."

CHAPTER TWENTY-NINE

JONAS

Maddie doesn't say anything for a few minutes following Callie's speech and honestly, I'm so proud of her. A year ago, she'd have never told Maddie off like this. Hell, even before the wedding, she'd have never had the nerve. My girl has grown and I'm proud.

"I'm going to bed," Maddie says suddenly. "Jonas, you'll be here tomorrow when he comes back, right?"

I nod. "Yeah. I told him he couldn't come back unless one of us was here."

"Okay. Goodnight." She stands and walks into her bedroom.

Callie pushes her plate back and lays her head down on the table. "What a fucking day."

I can't help but laugh. "Yeah. I'm done. I can't handle anything else. Want to go to bed?"

"Yes, please."

I take Callie's plate and glass and put them in the dishwasher and pull her up from her chair. We walk to our bedroom and close the door. I turn the lamp on and Callie puts her glasses on the nightstand. I pull her to me and she wraps her arms around my waist. "I'm sorry about our fight."

"Me, too." I look into her eyes and see nothing but love in them. "I love you, Callie."

She smiles. "I love you, too. Can we promise we'll never go to bed angry or with unresolved stuff? I can't stomach the thought of sleeping next to you and us having something hanging over us."

I nod. "I think we can do that. I think we're both stubborn as hell, but we both don't like to let things fester for the most part. I know you've gotten really good at speaking your mind."

She rolls her eyes. "Again, all your fault. I told you you'd have no one to blame but yourself if I got to be too much to handle."

I lean in and brush a kiss down her neck and she lets out a soft breath. "You'll never be too much for me to handle, Darlin'. I love how fierce you are. I was thinking a few minutes ago how much you've grown.

"You'd have never talked to Maddie the way you did before the wedding. I'm so proud of you." I pull back to look at her face and she has a slight blush on her cheeks. "But you can still blush. I like it."

She chuckles. "I like that you can still make me blush."

"Let's see if I can make it spread," I say and wiggle my eyebrows. She laughs and I pull her face to mine for a kiss. It's tender and melts every bit of tension from the day for both of us. Callie leans into me and deepens our kiss. Her hands travel down my ribs and tugs my shirt up. She breaks our kiss to pull it over my head.

I start to move my hands under her sweater and she covers my hands with her own, stopping my movements. "Not yet.

Only for tonight, let go of your control." I drop my hands, even as my brain screams at me to take Callie in my arms and make her forget about what she's just said. But another part of me says letting her control things is in and of itself an act of control, so I let her continue.

She slides my shorts down, followed by my underwear. It's totally strange for me to be naked and her fully clothed, but I try not to think about it. I watch as her eyes drag down my body and I almost blush. *Is this what it's like, when I look at her? I feel totally exposed.* "Like what you see, Darlin'?"

"Always." After a beat, she says, "Get on the bed." I climb onto the bed and lie down with my head resting on my interlocked fingers and look at her. She pulls her sweater over her head and static crackles, making fine baby hairs in her long hair stand up. She pulls her hair over one shoulder and it falls past her breast. Her eyes don't leave mine as she unbuttons her jeans and pulls them slowly down her hips. Her movements are perfunctory, but with her eyes on me, it's undeniably sexy and my cock jerks. She notices and gives me a smug smile.

She reaches behind her back and unclasps her bra and lets it fall to the floor before climbing onto the bed, clad only in her panties. I go to reach for her and she stops. "You can't touch me yet. Put your hands back where they were." I reluctantly obey and once she's seemingly satisfied, she comes closer to me and straddles my waist. I blow out a breath and try to not think about how her ass is nestled right up against my dick and how all I want to do is grab her and roll her over.

"Is this hard for you, Jonas? To lie here and let me take care of you?"

I shift my hips, grinding myself against her. "I think you know how hard this is."

"Don't move. That's touching, remember?" Her tone is chiding.

"You're enjoying this too much, Darlin'."

She chuckles. "I am, but it's also to prove a point."

My hands clench behind my head, itching to reach for her. "And what's that?"

"That relationships are give *and* take. You can't be in control all the time. And as much as I love it when you do take control, cause damn, it's sexy, there are gonna be times when you'll have to be okay with *not* being in control. And I'm not only referring to sex. But for tonight, it is about sex."

I nod. "Okay."

Her hands trail down my chest and even though I'm not ticklish by nature, her touch is so light, I can't help but squirm at least a little. "Do you know how much I love your body, Jonas? It's my second favorite thing about you."

I smile. "What's the first?"

Her eyes soften. "Your heart." She places her hand over said organ and quirks a brow. "Which, at this moment, is beating rather quickly. I thought you were an athlete. Shouldn't your resting heart rate be lower?"

"Well, when you have tits this perfect right in your direct line of sight and you've been ordered to not touch them, it does tend to make one's pulse race a bit."

She blushes and straightens and pulls her hair up into a messy bun before planting her hands on either side of my head, in the space left by my folded arms. She rises up on to her knees until her breasts are directly above me. "Oh, you mean these tits?" I start to raise my head to take her nipple into my mouth and she pulls back. "No, that's not what we're doing. Don't move."

"Then, don't tease."

She gives me a wicked grin. "What, mister I-love-a-challenge can't deal with a little temptation? I thought you were a big strong man. Are you strong enough to just lie there?"

I huff out a breath. "Callie, you have no clue how strong I'm having to be in this moment to not roll you over and fuck you right this minute."

"Then I have you exactly where I want you." She lowers her mouth to mine and kisses me deeply and it's so strange to be kissing her, yet not be touching her in some way, but damn, it's hot.

Her mouth travels down my neck and her teeth graze my collarbone, sending goosebumps down, or rather, up my folded arms. She kisses her way down my chest and abs, keeping her eyes glued to mine.

When she reaches my cock, she plants a kiss on the head before taking it in her hand and stroking the shaft and I have to blow out a breath. "Jonas, I'm gonna suck your cock. You're not allowed to come."

I huff a soft laugh. "Well, you're not gonna be able to do it for long, because your head game has always been on point, Darlin'."

She shakes her head, even as she lowers her mouth. "Do. Not. Come." She takes me between her lips and her tongue flicks over the head and my hips reflexively buck in response. I almost expect her to reprimand me, but she doesn't. What she does do, though, is magic. Sheer witchcraft with her mouth and tongue and hands I've never understood how she's been able to do.

"Shit, Callie." I huff out a ragged breath and she chuckles and I have to roll my hands into fists to keep from putting my fingers in her hair. My breathing begins to grow labored as my pleasure starts to build and I'm biting down on my lower lip to keep my mind off of how close I am to letting go. My dick twitches and I know I have about thirty seconds until I'm past the point of no return. Twenty seconds. "Callie." My tone has a warning edge to it. Ten. Five. "Callie. Fuck." It's a near whine I don't even believe comes from my mouth. And just before I actually come, she pulls off of me and I gasp.

Callie rises to her knees and I watch as she works her panties down her hips and I focus on simply breathing. "I'm impressed Jonas. You were so good for me."

I say between shallow breaths, "Not as impressed as I am, Darlin'. Shit. That was torture."

She laughs softly. "I'm not done yet."

I groan almost painfully. "Can I touch you?"

She shakes her head. "Nope." She straddles me and plants her hands beside my head again. She kisses me deeply and I truly am in pain now, with how on edge I am. My body aches with need for release and my muscles are as tense as taut piano wire from trying to do what Callie's asked, which is nothing. When she breaks our kiss, I want to chase her face with mine. "Jonas, I'm gonna fuck you now. But you can't get off until I do. You think you can do that?"

"Callie, I'm about three seconds from blowing, so unless you can finish in that period of time, I sincerely doubt it."

"What, no more of that *superior self-control* you've always been so proud of?" Her tone is teasing and I can't help but laugh.

"Darlin', I told you, it went out the window the moment I had you. You stripped all of it away. With your mind and your heart and your sass and this fucking incredible body. And now, it's nearly non-existent."

She blushes and her eyes soften. Her hands trail up my chest and my folded arms. She pulls my hands from behind my head and uncurls my fists. She brushes kisses along my palms, where my nails have dug into the flesh, leaving half-moon indentations. She holds my gaze as she places my hands on her hips. I have to take a breath to try to control myself. The not being able to touch her all this time and now, with my hands on her soft skin, it's nearly too much. "Jonas?" Callie's voice is soft, all traces of her earlier teasing and playful command gone.

"Yeah, Darlin'?"

"Make love to me?"

"Is that what you want?" I squeeze her hip. "I'm alright. This whole 'Callie in control' thing is pretty hot." Even though, I'm pretty sure I'm dying, I want to let her to still call the shots in this moment.

She nods. "I miss your hands and mouth on my body. And while torturing you is fun for a little while, I want *you*. The real you. My in charge husband-to-be. Although, I'm really proud of you for letting me run the show for a bit. I know it was really difficult for you. So, yes, make love to me. Right the fuck now, if you please."

I sit up quickly and her breath hitches at the speed in which I'm upright. I grip the back of her neck to bring her face to mine for a deep, possessive kiss. Because in spite of her being in control tonight, she is *mine*.

I roll us over swiftly and Callie lets out this adorable little squeal. I look down at her beautiful face and she gives me a sweet smile. And as much as I'm ready to sink deep into her, I can't take my eyes off her in this moment. "Do you know how much I love you, Darlin'?" She bites her lip and reaches up to brush my curls out of my eyes and I continue. "I love you so much I can't breathe sometimes. When you walk into a room, it's like all the air leaves until you're next to me. When I look at you, I don't only see the next ten or twenty or fifty years; I see eternity. I see kids and a picket fence and a big goofy dog who's dumb but we still love him. I see lazy Sunday mornings making pancakes and Friday nights eating pizza and quickies when the babies are napping. I can't wait to teach our kids how to flip themselves off the rope swing at the lake house. I can't wait

until you take my last name. I love you so fucking much it physically hurts."

Tears well in Callie's eyes and I kiss them away. "I know
you think I control this thing, but honestly, I loose every bit of
control when it comes to you. You *own* me, Callahan. Every
part of me. Every corner of my soul, it's yours."

She lets out a soft laugh. "I think I just came. God, you're
sexy when you wax poetic. Please never stop."

I shake my head. "Never. You keep looking at me the way
you do, like you think I'm worth something, and I'll never stop
hoping to make it true."

"You're worth everything and more." She pulls my face to
hers and the kiss is tender and sweet and full of the love we
share. When I enter Callie, it's slow and easy and also full of
the love we share. A physical manifestation of the invisible cord
that binds us together. More the joining of souls than the
joining of bodies.

And when she comes, it's like she's surprised and expectant
at the same time and rapture is really the only word I have to
describe her expression. After a moment, when I, too, find my
own release, it's with a tear in my eye and my heart crashing
into my ribs.

Later, when we're curled together, sated and sleepy, Callie
says, "I know where I want to get married."

"Oh? Where's that?"

"The lake house. But not anything like what Maddie did. I
want to do it barefoot on the dock, just us and an officiant. No
bridal party, no big tent, only the family, Elliot and Teagan. I
want to have pizza and beer and ten different kinds of
cupcakes." After a beat, she chuckles. "Do you think all that
would sufficiently mortify my family?"

I laugh. "I can picture your aunt Meredith scowling when

we walk out onto the dock with no shoes. Can I forgo a tie, too? Just do shorts and a polo?"

"But I like you in a tie. You in a suit is one of my favorite things. And you might look kind of silly if I'm in a pretty wedding dress and you're that casual, don't you think? Granted, I don't have a wedding dress yet, but you know what I mean."

I plant a kiss on the top of her head. "It all sounds exactly perfect, Darlin'. I'm in."

CHAPTER THIRTY

CALLIE

When I pull into the driveway after class, Dominic's rental car is at the house and I try to mentally prepare myself for what I'll find when I go inside. As I walk in the front door, I'm greeted by the sight of Maddie and Dominic sitting at the kitchen table, not speaking to one another and Jonas sitting on the couch, reading a book and drinking a beer. I make a beeline to him and drop my bag on the opposite end of the sofa before slipping off my shoes and curling up next to him. "What's been happening?" I ask in a whisper.

He offers me his beer and I take a pull. "Nothing. He got here about an hour ago and they've not said anything. Like, at all. It's unnerving. I've been sitting here, trying not to eavesdrop, but turns out, there's nothing to eavesdrop on. They've barely even looked at one another."

I roll my eyes. "This is stupid."

He nods. "Tell me about it."

"I can't believe you've not said anything to them, to try to get them going."

"Are you kidding? I'm staying out of that mess."

"Chicken."

He nods. "Damn right. Have at it."

I take his beer and drain the rest and Jonas scoffs. "That was my last beer. No fair."

"Sorry, honey. You drink my wine, I drink your beer." I give him a sweet smile and a quick kiss before I rise from the couch. I drop the empty bottle into the recycle bin and stand at the dining table. I look at Dominic whose expression is both angry and hurt and then to Maddie, who looks like she'd rather be anywhere but here.

"Okay, y'all. Here's the deal. You each have sixty seconds to tell the other what, in this exact moment, you want to do. That's not to say in a month, you'll want something different, but in this moment only, what you want from the other person. Maddie?"

Her arms are folded stubbornly. "I'm not going first. I'm the injured party, I should have the last word."

I roll my eyes and let out a heavy sigh. "For fuck's sake. Fine. Dominic, go."

He looks caught off guard, but after I say, "Fifty seconds," he opens his mouth to speak.

"Maddie, I fucked up. I know that. I'm an idiot and I thought if you knew me, that part of me, anyway, you'd never have married me. And I love you and thought, well, I don't know what I thought, but it was a colossal mistake and I know now I'd rather have you and shut that part of me away forever than lose you. I don't need it. I need you. And I didn't realize exactly how much until I saw your face that day. And if you give me another chance, I promise, you'll never have to wonder or worry. I love you, Maddie. More than anything. I miss you and want you to come home. To our home."

I'm honestly shocked by the sincerity in his voice as well as what he's said, because for as long as I've known Dominic, he's never been one to gush or spill his feelings, but I guess, for Maddie, he will. "Maddie? Your turn."

Maddie's jaw clenches and she still doesn't look at Dominic when she starts speaking. "I could've gotten past the part about you being attracted to men. There are a lot of bisexual people who are married to one or the other and are perfectly happy. But you cheated, Dom. You broke our vows. And I don't know what I'm supposed to do about that. I have bigger things I need to think about now. Bigger than only you and me. And I know I'm not perfect. This situation has made me question if we got married for the right reasons, or if I thought you'd be safe and reliable." She looks at me and I feel like she's thinking about the confession she made to me at her bachelorette party. "And I don't know what I need to do right now."

"Maddie, what could be bigger than you and me? We're married. That's pretty big. I want to make this work. We've not even been married a year. Can't we just, I don't know, have a mulligan?" Leave it to Dom to throw in a golf metaphor. I nearly roll my eyes, but I'm looking at Maddie, who I can see is having some kind of internal debate with herself and I can't help but wonder if she's gonna tell him about the baby.

But she simply shrugs. "I don't know. I need more time. I need to figure things out for myself and figure out what I really want. And I can't do it with you in front of me."

I'm struck with a thought. "Guys, I'll be right back." I motion for Jonas to follow me and we step into the bedroom.

"Darlin', now's not really the time to take me to bed, there's a bit of a situation going on out there."

I roll my eyes and jab him playfully. "Very funny. Listen, I didn't want to offer this without speaking with you first, you know, since this is your home, too. But, we'll be going back to the lake house in three months for the wedding. What if Maddie stayed with us until we go to Tennessee? Three months was enough time for us to figure out we were miserable without each other. Maybe they'll figure out one way or the other if they want to work it out. I mean, it sounds like he does, but I think she's not even sure she really loves him. Maybe the distance will give her some clarity."

Jonas's cheeks puff with a held breath. He slowly lets it out and shrugs. "If you want to offer, I'm not gonna stop you. I can understand Maddie's current predicament. It's hard to know what you really think when the person you're trying to figure shit out about is in your face. It's three months. Sure. But, as soon as we say our vows, you're the only person I'm living with. At least until you give me little Merritts."

I laugh and throw my arms around his shoulders. "I love you. Thank you for agreeing to this. I know you think I'm a big softy when it comes to Maddie, but I don't want her to have regrets, you know?"

He nods and presses his lips to my temple. "I do. I guess, get back out there and offer to make Maddie a temporary roommate."

We exit the bedroom and Jonas retakes his seat on the sofa. I go to stand at the table and plant my hands on the tabletop and level both of them with a gaze. "Maddie, is it possible for you to work remotely? Will they let you do that?"

She thinks for a moment and I can tell she's confused by my question, but finally nods. "Yeah, I think so."

I blow out a breath. "Okay, here's what's gonna happen. And you'll let me finish speaking before either of you opens your mouths. Maddie, you're gonna stay here and work remotely. Dominic, you're gonna go back home. In three months, at Jonas's and my wedding, you'll see one another and decide once and for all, what you want to do. Until then, you'll not talk to each other or try to see each other, or have any kind of communication. Maddie, if you haven't decided by then you can live with Dominic and make things work, then I think you'll already have your answer. Dom, you need to do some definite soul searching and decide if you're really gonna be able to live whatever life you'd have with *just* Maddie. If that's not enough for you, then I think you also have your answer.

"Honestly, what y'all do doesn't affect me. I could care less, to be frank. Both of you have hurt me immensely and I've made peace with it and forgiven both of you. And maybe y'all need to figure out if you can forgive each other, too."

I look between the two of them and Dominic looks like he want to object, but finally nods. "Okay, I can do that."

Maddie looks surprised. "What am I gonna tell people, why I'm down here for three months? I already told folks I was just visiting."

I shrug. "Tell them you're helping me plan the wedding. I still need to find a dress and pick out flowers and stuff. So yeah, tell them whatever you need to. I don't give a shit. You can take or leave it."

Maddie looks taken aback by my bluntness, but she, too, finally gives a small nod. "Okay. Dominic, if I text you a list, can you ship some of my things? They'll need to be overnighted."

"Yeah." He gets up from his chair. "I guess that's it for now, right?" He looks at me and then at Maddie, who doesn't meet his eye. "I really do love you, Mads. That's not gonna change for me. I'll see you in three months. Cal, Jonas, take care of her for me?"

She doesn't respond, but with his last sentence, I see something soften in her face. I look at Dominic. "Of course. She'll be safe here."

Jonas stands. "Come on, Dom. I'll walk you out." The two men walk out the front door and I take the seat the Dominic vacated.

"You didn't tell him about the baby."

She shakes her head. "No. I need to know he wants me aside from that fact. If he finds out about the baby, he's gonna insist we make it work. And I don't know if that's what I want. And I need to figure out if I want him aside from the baby, too. I need to think like there's not one. Like, what would I do if there was no baby. I mean, I know regardless what happens, I'll always be connected to him *because* of the baby, but I need to know if I want him outside of that factor."

"I understand. For what it's worth, I think he really does love you. I've never heard him speak so emotionally about anything. So there's that."

As Jonas and I lie in bed, I'm struggling to keep my eyes open as he's telling me about one of his students turning the corner in her reading journey. I love hearing him talking passionately about his job as a kindergarten teacher. It was one of the first things I noticed about him; his love for the job and his love for the kids. Especially those who come from less than stellar home lives. "Oh, I also got in touch with Bailey."

I'm suddenly re-energized and sit up and look at him. "Really? And are you still gonna meet with him?"

"*We're* gonna meet with him, Darlin'. Sunday morning at ten. At the breakfast place on the highway."

"Ooh, the one with the really great eggs benedict?"

He chuckles. "Yes. I know how much you love that place, so even if the meeting is brief, you'll still get brunch."

"I love how you know me so well." I run my finger along his jaw. "Are you gonna be okay?"

He nods. "Yeah. I keep trying to remind myself if she's healthy, then it means maybe Nana can have her back. She deserves that. I don't know what kind of relationship I'm hoping to have with her, but just knowing she's alive makes me feel some sort of way, even if I'm not sure how I feel yet."

I kiss his cheek. "I don't think there's anything wrong with being uncertain. You've not seen her in fifteen years. Neither of you are the same people you were back then."

"I know. I'm glad you'll be with me, though, not gonna lie. I know I like a challenge, but this is one I don't know I could've faced down on my own."

"I'm happy to be there for you. I always want to be there for you. Forever."

CHAPTER THIRTY-ONE

JONAS

As much as I've been dreading this meeting with Bailey, simply because I have absolutely no desire to ever see him again, I can't deny I'm a bit excited about the prospect of reconnecting with my mother. But I'm trying not to get my hopes up, because if she's been on drugs this entire time, how much of the her I knew can still be there?

Callie and I arrive about ten minutes prior to when we've planned on meeting him, but when we enter the restaurant, Bailey's already waiting in a booth. I rake my fingers through my hair nervously and Callie squeezes my hand. "It's gonna be fine. We're here to find out about your mother and after that, we can leave. You're under no obligation to say or do anything else. If it gets too hard, you can go and I'll deal with him, okay?"

I look down at her and her expression is supportive and maybe a little hopeful. I nod and let out a long, slow breath. "Thank you for being here with me."

She gives me a soft smile and touches my cheek. "Of course. Ready?"

I huff out a small laugh. "Not in the least, but let's do it anyway."

Bailey stands when he sees us approaching. He's dressed fairly casually — for a senator— in a pair of navy slacks and light blue button down, sleeves rolled to the elbows. "Thank you for agreeing to meet me." He looks as though he's getting ready to extend his hand and maybe thinks better of it. He instead gestures to the seat across from his, inviting us to sit.

Callie slides in and lets me have the outside seat and she says, "Good morning, Senator."

As chatty as I typically am, I find myself at a sudden loss for words. I'm focused on Bailey's face, trying to see a possible resemblance. Callie told me Bailey said I looked like his son, so he must mean I also look like him. I see the curly hair, same as mine and I know his used to be a dark brown before it went gray. I have my mother's eyes, but perhaps, my jawline and nose are his?

Bailey runs his fingers through his hair and it catches me off guard, because I know I do the same thing and I'm instantly angry because I want *nothing* of him. It's bad enough half of my DNA and some of my physical features are from him, but mannerisms? It's not fair.

My thoughts are interrupted by a server bringing a pot of coffee to the table and pouring a cup for both Callie and myself. She goes over the specials, but I don't hear them. Bailey tells her he's not sure we'll need menus, but to check back later. She simply nods and walks away.

He sips his own coffee and after he sets his mug down, he says, "I'm sure you have a lot of questions."

"Only as far as my mother is concerned," I respond flatly.

He nods. "Yes." He reaches beside him on the booth and brings out a large manilla envelope. "All of the information is here." He sets it on the table and my fingers instantly itch to reach for it, but I don't want him to know how affected I am by this thing he's offering me.

Callie speaks then. "How did you find her?"

Bailey considers the question for a while, as if he's not sure how he wants to answer. He takes a sip of his coffee and I want to reach across the table and slug him for stalling. He looks at me, as if I'm the one who posed the question. "After I met you at New Years and you said you hadn't seen your mother in fifteen years, I surmised she had to still be living, otherwise, you'd have said she'd died. I took that to mean she'd left or gone missing or something, so I hired a private investigator."

"Why?" I ask.

A muscle in his jaw tics. "I'm sure Callahan told you about what I said when I tracked her down last week. And I can't make up for the pain I caused your mother or my lack of forethought or even common decency. But, as you're probably aware, I have extensive connections. And I could do this one thing for you. Not to make myself look good or make you see me as anything other than what I am, but to maybe do one good thing for a good man.

"I also looked into you, Jonas." I tense when he uses my name. I don't want to hear it on his lips. Callie squeezes my knee under the table as he continues. "You're very intelligent. Summa cum laude with a double major; even after what happened with your car accident. And Florida teacher of the year twice." Callie's head snaps to me, surprised. Bailey says, "You also take care of your grandmother and provide clothing and school supplies for a lot of your students when they don't have them. You're a good man. A much better man than I could ever hope to be; in spite of the hand life dealt you; which I know I had a part in. A man a father could be proud to call his son, if he was not such a coward and an ass. So, I wanted to do this one thing.

"And I know you want nothing from me. Callahan made that very clear. She's quite something, too, from what I've seen. I thought she was the safer option to reach out to you, but she's a little scary, if I'm honest."

In spite of myself, I chuckle. "Yeah, you don't want to be on the ass end of her attitude, that's for sure."

Callie elbows me good-naturedly and for the first time since we arrived, I relax a bit. A smile tugs at Bailey's lips and he clears his throat. "As I was saying, I know you don't want anything from me. But, your mother is in a rehab facility. She's been there for the past month." My stomach knots up, knowing my mother probably hasn't been clean the entire time she's been gone if she's now in a rehab.

"She's doing very well, from what the facility staff say. She's due to be released in two weeks. But she is allowed visitors. And I can't make up for all the years, but I can help her. I know you don't want anything from me, but if you'll allow me, I would like to help make sure she gets back on her feet. There is a halfway house dedicated to helping recovering addicts. She'd spend a year there and then hopefully, be well on her way to a good, clean life. I know part of the reason she got in the state she did has to do with me and the choices I made, so I feel responsible in making sure she gets the help she needs."

He takes another sip of his coffee and I don't yet trust myself to speak, so I simply sit and wait for him to go on. "I'm not sure if you know this, but without her, I wouldn't have been elected in the first place. She was a talented speech writer and hard worker, even as young as she was. And beautiful and captivating. But I'll not pretend as though I would have left my wife and children for her, in spite of how I may have felt about her. I was not a good man, I'm still not. But that's beside the point.

"I can help her, if you'll let me. I'm leaving this up to you.

Her rehab has been paid for, and if you'll allow me, I'd like to cover the cost of her housing at the halfway house. I know you're probably a very proud man and would prefer to do this yourself, but I know you can't afford it." He glances at Callie. "And I know your family is wealthy, but I know you don't accept their money, preferring to make your own way."

Callie stiffens next to me, as if she's surprised he knows things about her as well. Bailey says, "I can do this. I don't expect anything in return. I know it might sound strange, considering I'm a politician and my primary currency consists of quid pro quo." He holds my gaze. "I only want to do this one good thing. I'll never capitalize on it, I'll never speak about it in any paper or make it look like I'm some kind of hero. You have my word on this, as little faith as you might put in it. But honestly, it would be in my best interest if all of this stays quiet. I'm sure Callahan mentioned I plan to run for governor after my next term in the Senate."

When I nod, he says, "I've had my lawyers draw up a trust which will cover the expenses of the halfway house and a little bit extra for her to use how she will after she's fully back on her feet. I've put your name on the trust as well, so you can help her manage it."

"Like hush money?" I can't keep the bitterness out of my tone.

Ever the smooth politician, he's unfazed by my accusation. "Consider it back child support."

"Even if you do this, it doesn't mean I won't still look at you with anything other than disdain or contempt. I don't think forgiveness is in my vocabulary as far as you're concerned."

He nods. "That's fair. I've never expected to be forgiven for my many, many sins. But if, in some small way, I can make amends to someone I've wronged, I might be able to someday forgive myself."

I look at Callie but I know she can't make this decision for me. She won't, even if I ask her to. And he's right, I can't afford a year in a halfway house for my mother and I would be stupid to take this away from her if it can help her. Especially if it helps her stay clean and Nana can get her back. And after everything Nana's done for me, if I can do something for her, I should.

I examine Bailey's face and don't see a senator or the monster under my bed I've always pictured him to be. I certainly don't see a father, but if I look hard enough, maybe I can see a man. Just a man who's made innumerable mistakes, but so have I.

I blow out a deep breath and finally nod. "Okay. I'll let you help her. But like I said, don't expect that I'm suddenly gonna feel a certain way about you. You'll never be anything to me other than what you are."

"I know. I'm nothing to you. I expect it will stay that way. But, I will say this. If I could go back, if I could do things different, I would have made very different choices. I know you have no reason to believe me, but I would. When you get old, you look back at the decisions you've made in your life and you see several where you know you made colossal errors. And regarding your mother, and by extension, you, I know those will always be the decisions I regret most." He drains the last of his coffee and stands. "I won't take up any more of your time. I have a plane to catch. But thank you for meeting me and I hope everything works out for your mother. I'll have my lawyer reach out to you with the information about the trust and halfway house for Nancy. Best of luck to you both."

As he walks away, I feel a sudden tightness in my chest and tears I don't understand burn my eyes and I look down at my hands, clenched into fists in my lap. Callie presses her forehead against my temple. "Do you want to go home? I know you have

a lot to process here. We can go." Her hand slides down my arm
to uncurl my fists and intertwines our fingers.

I shake my head. "No, I'm hungry. And I promised you
eggs benedict."

She takes my face in her free hand and forces me to look at
her. "Jonas, be serious. This was a lot. I know you're not okay.
Hell, this didn't even concern me and I don't know if I'm okay.
So, if you want to go, we can. We don't have to go home, since
Maddie's there, we can go for a drive if you want."

I take her hand from my face and kiss her palm. "I'm
alright, Darlin'. Promise. It was a lot. And I don't understand
the way I'm feeling right now, but staying here and eating
breakfast isn't gonna change that. And I really am hungry. I
didn't eat very much at supper last night because I was nervous
about this meeting. And now that it's over, I'm starving."

She searches my eyes, checking to make sure I'm being
truthful. "If you're sure."

I press a kiss to her lips. "I love you for worrying about me,
but yes."

"Can we also talk about how you've been teacher of the
year twice. Like, best teacher in the whole state, *twice*?"

I shrug. "It's not a big deal."

Her eyebrows raise in surprise. "Not a big deal? It's a huge
deal. How did I not ever know this? I always knew you were a
good teacher, but Jonas, that's amazing." She gives me a soft
smile. "I'm proud of you. I know it's way after the fact and I
didn't know you when you got those awards, but still, I'm so
proud of you."

"Thanks, Darlin'. It was a big honor. And Nana came with
me to the ceremonies. She was proud, too. But I don't like to
toot my own horn." When Callie quirks a brow and her expression definitely says, *oh, yes you do,* I chuckle. "Well, not about
work. Not about my kids. I don't do my job for any kind of

recognition or accolades. I simply want to make a difference to them. I know it's only kindergarten, but I want to start their school careers off right. And you always remember the really good teachers and the really bad teachers and I want to be one of the really good ones."

She kisses my cheek. "You are one of the really good ones. You're one of the amazing ones."

CHAPTER THIRTY-TWO

JONAS

The evening after meeting with Bailey, Callie and I take Nana out for supper, as is our normal Sunday night routine but we've decided to keep the information about my mother quiet for now. I want to go see her first and get a feel for how she's doing before exposing Nana to her.

Callie offered to go with me to see my mother at the rehab, but I feel like I need to go on my own. And so, here I am, waiting in a sunroom at a spacious and obviously expensive rehabilitation facility that looks more like some sort of spa. A member of staff has brought a tray of iced tea and cookies and placed it on a small table next to where I sit.

My knee is bouncing nervously and I'm probably pulling my hair out, as many times as I've raked my fingers through it. But finally, a woman in khakis and a button-down top with the rehab's logo enters the room, followed by a woman who can only be my mother, in spite of how much she's changed in fifteen years.

I jump to my feet as she comes closer and feel like my heart is in my throat. I don't know what I was expecting, but she's a lot different than I remember. She used to have this long, thick, shiny, chestnut brown hair. Now, it's thin and short and shot through with more gray than brown, in spite of the fact she's not even fifty. Her eyes used to be so bright, and now, they just look sad, if free of the haze of drugs. Her skin used to be bright and rosy and now looks dull and the drugs have definitely aged her. She looks nearly as old as Nana. She's so thin, her cheekbones are sharp and her wrist bones are visible knobs above her hands. She's dressed casually in jeans and a thin blouse.

The staff member gestures for my mother to sit and looks at me. "Do you need me to stay?"

I shake my head and retake my seat. "No, I think we'll be okay. Thank you." She nods and walks back into the other room.

My mother glances at me nervously. "Hi," she says softly.

"Hello." She reaches for a glass of tea and her hands tremble. I immediately wonder if it's from all the drugs or simply nerves. "How are you?" I ask.

She takes a sip of her glass and finally appears to settle a bit. "Clean. Twenty-nine days."

I nod. "That's good to hear. Are they treating you well?"

"Yes. This is a great facility. I've been to others, but this is one of the good ones. I don't know how I got in, but I'll take it."

She doesn't know Bailey did this? "So, you've been to rehab before?"

She nods. "Yes, about ten years ago, and then again about six years ago. Homeless shelters tend to be connected to rehabs and sometimes they have room. So, I tried, but it didn't stick, obviously." She says the last sentence with a bit of bitterness. "How did you find out where I was?"

If she doesn't know Bailey is the one who got her in here, I'm not about to tell her. So I lie, sort of. "Private investigator."

She nods. "I'm sorry you have to see me like this."

I shrug. "I'm just glad to know you're alive. Nana and Granddad hired someone right after you left, but then they couldn't afford to keep looking."

"How is Momma?"

I smile. "She's good. Feisty and hounding me for great-grandkids."

"And Daddy?"

I look down. "Passed about five years ago. Heart attack."

She looks pained and bites her lip. "And do you have children? You said Momma's hounding you. Do you have them yet? Are you married?"

I shake my head. "No kids yet. I'm getting married in June. We'll probably wait a few years. My fiancée is still in school until the end of this year, so I know she wants to work for a little while before we have children."

She nods. "Well, congratulations. I can't get over how grown you are. You look exactly like..." She trails off and looks down into her glass of tea.

"My father. I'm aware."

Her head snaps up to me. "You know about him?"

I nod. "Yeah. Nana told me. When I asked her why you might have left. She told me about him."

Her eyes fill with tears. "I'm sorry, Jonas. I'm sorry I was weak and I couldn't be there for you. I was in a really bad place. Hell, I'm still in a bad place. I shouldn't have left you, but I thought Momma and Daddy were better for you. I knew I wasn't okay and when I hit you that last time, I couldn't live with what I'd done and I left."

My chest tightens. I'd almost forgot the night she left, she'd backhanded me and busted my nose. Until she mentioned it, I had forgotten. I simply nod.

She recomposes herself and wipes her eyes. "So, what do

you do with yourself these days? Did you go to college? Tell me about your fiancée."

"I'm a kindergarten teacher. Callahan, my fiancée, is getting her PhD. She's gonna be a librarian, hopefully at a school or university. Right now, she and Nana work at the same library in town."

"Is that how you met her, through Momma?"

I shake my head. "No, it was a blind date. Her former roommate works with me. He set us up. Her working with Nana was simply a happy coincidence, even though Nana had been trying to set us up, too. I just didn't know it was her."

She nods. "Well, that's good. And you're happy?"

"Yes, very. I had a few rough years, but since I met Callie, I've been very happy."

"I'm glad." She takes a sip of her drink and wipes the condensation from the side of the glass with her finger.

"What about you?" I ask. "What have you done in the past fifteen years?"

She blows out a breath. "Well, drugs mostly, if I'm honest. That's not to say I haven't had moments where I was clean. There were weeks and even months, here and there. But not a lot. I've been in and out of shelters and rehabs, as I said."

And because I can't stop myself, I ask, "How come you never came home? We would have made sure you got help."

"I didn't want you to see me like that. I know what I looked like when I left and what I look like now, but trust me when I say, I look good right now. And some of the things I've done over the years to pay for my habit, I'd rather you thought I was dead than face you knowing who I've been."

I don't want to think about what she may have done. What she may have had to reduce herself to because of her addiction. "Do you think you'll be okay this time?" is all I can think to ask.

She shrugs. "I have to say yes, because the alternative is I go back and I don't want to do that. There was a man who came around where I was staying and offered me a place here. Again, I don't know how I got in, but I've learned not to question things. I was at the point I honestly wanted to die, Jonas. I was in a bad, bad way. If I'd had any money, I probably would be dead. I would have intentionally OD'd. I was done." Her voice breaks and it makes something crack in my chest and I want to cry, but I don't.

"I'm glad you're not dead, Mom." She nods, but I'm not sure if it's because she's agreeing with me, or it simply gives her something to do. I clear my throat, trying to dislodge the lump that's formed. "There's a halfway house you can go to after you're released from rehab in a couple weeks. You can stay there for a year while you get back on your feet. I've looked into it. It seems like a great place. They'll support you and help you get a job. You can take classes and hopefully start to build a new life."

"I can't afford anything like that."

And because I don't want her to know Bailey has a hand in this, I lie to her again. "There's a grant. It's paid for. Will you go?" I don't feel bad about lying to her. I probably should, but I don't. I don't care how she gets there as long as she does. Because now that she's in front of me, I feel like I'm fifteen again and she's my mom and she'll ruffle my hair and make me pancakes and I don't want her to go away again.

"Will you come and visit me? And can I see Momma?"

"I'd like that. I haven't told Nana I found you yet. I wanted to see you first. But once you get into the halfway house, I can bring her or we can all go out to eat. We'll have to see what their rules are. Callie and I take Nana out to eat every Sunday evening, so maybe you can join us."

She nods. "Okay. I'll go."

"Thank you." And I am thankful. I'm thankful to have found her, even if it was because of Bailey. I'm thankful she's alive. I'm thankful she's here. I can only hope she's able to stay sober.

We sit and make small talk for a little while longer, until the same staff member who escorted her out to see me comes to stand beside my mother's chair. "I'm sorry to interrupt. Nancy, it's time for group."

Mom nods and sets her glass down. "Okay, I'll be there in a few minutes."

The woman nods and steps toward the doorway, attempting to give us a bit of privacy, but probably needing to make sure my mother follows through. We both stand and she looks at me. "I'm glad you came today. It's so good to see you." Her eyes are warm and she wears a soft smile.

"Me, too, Mom." I can't say much more since I'm trying not to get emotional.

She bites her lip, nervous, and extends her hand. I look down at it and pull her into my arms instead. I don't know if I planned it, but seeing her only expecting I would want to shake her hand breaks something in me. She's obviously surprised by my hug, but after a moment, she wraps her arms around my waist and I feel, more than hear her crying. She's trembling against me and I can't stop my own tears as they roll down my cheeks.

"Oh, my sweet boy, I'm so sorry." Her words come between sobs and all I can do is whisper words of encouragement to her.

After a moment, she pulls back from me and we both wipe our eyes. "I can come back and see you again. We can talk more about the halfway house. Maybe Callie can come with me. You'll love her."

She smiles and nods. "I can't wait to meet her." The staffer softly clears her throat to signal it's time to go and Mom says, "I guess that's my cue. Thank you, Jonas. For coming here, for finding me."

I nod. "Get better, Mom. Please."

"I promise. I'll try really hard." She turns to go and I just stand and watch her walk away.

CHAPTER THIRTY-THREE

CALLIE

I watch the clock and wait for Jonas to come home. I've been on pins and needles while he's been gone to see his mother. I offered to go, but wasn't surprised when he said he wanted to go it alone.

To distract me, Maddie made an appointment for us to go look at dresses and shockingly, I found *the one* today. It's perfect and it's me. Even Maddie, whose taste in wedding dresses is vastly different than my own, said my dress was exactly what she would have picked out for me.

She's been exceedingly contemplative since Dominic returned home without her. I'm trying to not pry, but would really like to know what she's thinking. She's working and takes video calls and conference calls in her room and although I should be used to seeing Maddie be in charge and on top of things, seeing her be the boss is strange to me.

I'm pulling some rolls out of the oven when Jonas gets home. I immediately set them down and go to him. I can tell he's been crying and I wrap my arms around his waist. He looks around. "Where's Maddie?"

"She went on a walk. She'll be back in a few minutes for supper. How was it?"

He sighs. "Surreal. She looked so different, but, *not*. Does that make sense?" When I nod, he continues. "She's really skinny, but I kind of expected that. She's agreed to go to the halfway house. I didn't tell her anything about Bailey. I told her there was a grant. I should feel bad about lying to her, but I don't. I just want her to get better."

"Of course you do. But it was good?"

He smiles. "Yeah. It really was." He gives me a quick rundown of how their visit went and although I know he's nervous about how all this will play out, he seems hopeful, so I want to support him.

Maddie comes in a few minutes later and we all sit down to eat. "Oh, Jonas," Maddie says. "Callahan found her wedding dress today. It's beautiful."

He looks at me, surprised. "Really, you found one? Wasn't this the first time you went looking? Is that weird to find one on the first time out?"

I shrug. "When you know, you know, I guess. But I love it. And I promise, it's not one of those over-the-top, satin monstrosities. It's very me. And I don't think you'll need a full suit, maybe nice slacks, a button-down and a vest. I think it will work better with my dress."

He smiles. "Whatever you say, Darlin'. Can I still go barefoot?"

Maddie scoffs. "You cannot go barefoot to your wedding. You're not getting married on the beach. It's tacky."

I shrug. "I found some sandals today, along with my dress, so you'll be the only one barefoot if you do. But have at it, you know I don't mind." I wink at him.

He sighs in mock-exasperation. "And here, I thought the

whole goal was to rile the family. How are we gonna do that if we're both wearing shoes?"

I laugh. "I'm pretty sure the pizza and beer will be sufficient."

Maddie's mouth falls open. "I'm sorry, pizza and beer? *That's* what you're planning?"

I nod. "Yep."

"Come on, that's not a wedding, that's a tailgate party. Will you at least have cake and dancing."

"Cupcakes and cornhole."

Maddie shakes her head. "I swear, Hanny, I'll never understand you. This is your wedding."

"Exactly. *My* wedding. Mine and Jonas's. We don't want all the crazy traditional stuff. We're not even having a bridal party." I consider. "Although, if we did, that wouldn't even be traditional. Elliot would be by my side and Teagan would be by Jonas's. So, yeah, it won't be traditional, but it will be fun. And that's all I care about."

"Who's Teagan?" Maddie asks, looking at Jonas.

He gives thought to how he wants to answer, because long-term friend with benefits is probably not the best explanation, even if it's true. He looks to me and I smirk and he sighs. "Teagan and I have been friends since college."

"How good of friends are we talking? Callahan, you're okay that he has a friend who's a girl? You're not jealous?"

I laugh. "No, I'm not jealous. I've met her. They have history. It's okay. Teagan's cool. I'd never get any sleep if I was jealous of all the girls Jonas slept with. What happened before me doesn't matter. And he chose me, so that's what matters."

Maddie nods and considers my words with what seems like a bit more than simply passing interest. She's quiet for the rest of supper as Jonas and I discuss our plans for the week and after we're done eating, she helps clean up, but quickly goes to her room and shuts the door.

While Jonas and I are climbing into bed a bit later, he asks, "Why do you think Maddie got so quiet after we talked about Teagan? And then she went straight to her room. She normally watches a little TV after supper."

I shrug. "Maybe she's thinking about what I said in terms of Dominic? That's the only thing I can think of."

He pulls me into his arms. "What do you think she's gonna do?"

I huff a laugh. "I have no idea. Hearing what Dominic said when he was here makes me think he really loves her, but it's Dominic, so, who knows? And I think this is the first time in Maddie's whole life where she's been betrayed or embarrassed like this and I feel like her ego has been more bruised than anything. Not that him cheating isn't bad, because it is, but she knows he picked her over me and I think it made her feel superior somehow. And knowing there might be someone out there who he might, at some point, choose over her, I think it's made her feel the way I've always felt over the years."

He nods. "And how does that make you feel?"

I shrug. "You'd think after they way the both did me, I'd be ecstatic they're both hurting, but I'm not. I don't want their marriage to fall apart, and honestly, I hope they work it out. And not only for the sake of the baby, because people shouldn't stay together simply for the sake of kids. I want them to choose each other. And maybe part of it is *because* they hurt me and if they let this break them up, then me being so hurt will have been for nothing." I look up at Jonas. "Well, not for nothing, obviously, because I wouldn't have you if they hadn't hurt me, but you know what I mean."

He nods and kisses my forehead. "Yeah, I know what you mean, Darlin'."

"And I feel like if they can make it through all this, they'll be a lot stronger in the long run."

"Yeah, you're probably right."

Changing the subject, I ask, "You want me to include your mother in the wedding plans?"

Jonas blows out a heavy sigh. "I don't know. Not yet. Let's see how things go. Not that I might not want her there, but I don't want to get my hopes up, as bad I already am."

"Sure. I get that. So, after seeing your mother again, how are you feeling?"

He shrugs. "I don't know. Like I said, I'm trying not to get my hopes up, but she's my mom, so it's hard to be objective. And then there's..." He trails off and rakes his fingers through his hair.

"There's what?"

After a moment, he shakes his head. "Bailey. I want to hate him and still think of him as the worst human in existence. Which, I know is entirely irrational, because that list includes people like Hitler and Stalin and Osama Bin Laden, but for years and years, I saw him as this major villain. He's been the reason I've done or not done so much in my life. And now, he's done this amazing thing for my mom and she might be okay only because of something he's done. And I don't know how to reconcile it with myself."

"He's human. Not necessarily good or bad, just... human. Humans are flawed by nature. Even the good ones."

He nods. "Yeah, and the same way you put Maddie up on this pedestal of goodness or greatness or whatever for all those years, I think I did the same thing to him with his badness. And it was easy to hate him after what he did to my mom and stuff. It's not so easy to hate him when he's in front of me and saying if he could go back, he'd make different choices. It's not as easy to hate him when I can kind of get why he did what he did. It's not as easy to hate him when he's doing this thing for my mom when I can't."

"It's easier to hate someone when you can't empathize with them."

He lets out a frustrated sigh. "Exactly. And I don't like that I might not hate him anymore. I've spent the last fifteen years hating him. What am I supposed to do if I don't hate him? What's it mean?"

"I think it means you're free. I think it means you have room in your heart and mind for better things. I'm not saying we'll send him Christmas cards or invite him to our kids' birthday parties, but it's okay if you don't hate him. It might even be okay if someday, you did want to do those things. Not that you will, but if you wanted to, it would be okay."

"I don't know about all that," he says with a quirked brow.

"Listen, no one knows as much as I do how badly family can hurt you. And you've got a lot of reasons to be hurt. But it's okay to also move past it. It's okay to let it go."

CHAPTER THIRTY-FOUR

CALLIE

The next three months leading up to the wedding absolutely fly. Between my classes, working at the library, study group, not to mention, spending time with Jonas, Nana, and Nancy, wedding planning kind of took a backseat. Thankfully, Maddie has really stepped up — with massive amounts of supervision by Jonas and me.

If it were up to her, we'd have a miniature version of her own wedding. But she finally got on board after we got into an argument about flowers and I threatened to take her home that night. But she hadn't made up her mind about Dominic at that point, so she got in line.

We told Nana about Nancy after she got settled in the halfway house. So far, she's over ninety days sober and Jonas is extremely proud of her, we all are. Nana was overjoyed to be reunited with her daughter and they'll both be coming to the wedding later this week.

It's hard to believe that less than a year ago, I was dreading going to Maddie and Dominic's wedding and now I'm getting ready for my own. Jonas and I have had almost no alone time since Maddie moved in and we're both on edge. I've been crabby because I've been so stressed and he's been antsy because the end of the school year is always a little crazy. There are so many last minute things in kindergarten; field trips, award days, parties. He's entirely wore out. We both are. Luckily, today is the last day of classes for both of us and we go to Tennessee tomorrow.

We'll have four whole days to decompress before the wedding and it will only be the two of us at the lake house. We are beyond ready. Maddie will be coming with Nana and Nancy later in the week before the rehearsal dinner. Teagan, Elliot, & Russ will be coming for the ceremony.

Today, though, I'm going with Maddie to an OB appointment. She's supposed to have an ultrasound and hopefully find out the sex of the baby. She's twenty weeks and barely starting to show. She knows, regardless of what she decides about Dominic, she'll have to tell him about the baby this weekend.

She's lying on the exam table with her shirt pulled up, waiting for the ultrasound tech to put the wand on her belly. "Okay, Madison, this gel might be a little cold," the tech warns, before squeezing the clear jelly onto her belly.

Then, after he puts the wand on her belly, there's the clear profile of a baby on the monitor. Maddie hasn't had an ultrasound since she first found out she was pregnant a few months ago. "Everything looks perfect. I'm gonna get a few measurements. Would you like to know the sex?"

Maddie doesn't answer right away, even though she's been so excited to find out if it's a boy or girl and I tear my eyes away from the screen to look at her and she's crying. "Maddie, what's wrong?"

"I don't want to know. Not without Dominic."

Realization washes over me and the tech seems unsure what to do. I look at him. "Can you turn the screen away and type the sex on the screen and print the images out and put them in an envelope?"

He smiles and nods. "Of course, I'd be happy to." After he hands the sealed envelope to Maddie, he waves goodbye and tells us to take our time.

I pull a tissue from the box on the wall and hand it to Maddie, who's still crying. "What's going on, Maddie? Have you made up your mind?"

She nods. "I didn't think I would care. I thought I could do this on my own. But when I saw the baby, I realized I want him here with me. I miss him, Callahan. Not talking with him or seeing him has been harder than I thought it would. I know we're gonna have to work through a lot of stuff, but I love him. I wasn't sure I did when he left, but I tried to picture my life without him and I can't. I don't want to raise this baby without him. I don't want to live without him anymore." She bites her lip. "What if he's changed his mind? What if he doesn't want me anymore?"

I roll my eyes. "Maddie, he's wanted you for years. I don't think three months will have made a difference. Plus, I know he's been texting with Jonas to check on you. But you can't tell him I told you. You're not supposed to know."

Her eyes go wide. "He has?"

I nod. "Yeah. So I think you're safe. How do you feel about seeing him this weekend?"

She wipes the gel off her belly and sits up, pulling her top over her tiny bump. "Nervous. Excited. Terrified." She laughs and I can't help but join her. She sobers. "Thank you, Callahan. For everything. You and Jonas have been wonderful to me. Way better than I deserve after what I did. But you'll never know how much these last few months have meant to me."

I wrap my arms around her for a tight hug. "We were

happy to have you. That's not to say Jonas and I aren't counting down the days until we have our house to ourselves again."

Maddie laughs. "I'd hope so. Newlyweds shouldn't live with anyone. Not that y'all still haven't been acting like newlyweds." She smirks. "I swear, y'all make me so jealous. All these pregnancy hormones have me so crazy horny and I haven't been able to do much about it. You and Jonas are all over each other all the time."

I snort. "And to think, we've actually toned it down a bit since you moved in."

Her eyes widen. "Well, shit. Good for you, Hanny. Damn."

I nod. "Yeah, I'm pretty lucky. We're looking forward to having a few days just us at the lake house before everyone gets there."

"I bet you are," she says knowingly.

CHAPTER THIRTY-FIVE

CALLIE

Jonas and I have shipped a lot of the stuff for the wedding up to the lake house, but still have a small suitcase apiece when we get ready to leave for the airport. "Okay, Maddie, you're gonna pick up Nana and Nancy for your flight on Friday, right?"

Maddie rolls her eyes. "Yes, Callahan, for the third time today. I know you're a nervous flyer, but we'll be fine. Our plane gets in a little after noon. Dad's picking us up and bring us to the lake house for the rehearsal dinner. We'll be fine. Go, enjoy your time with Jonas."

Jonas comes up behind me and wraps his arms around me. "Don't worry, we will. And I've gotten really good at distracting Callie during flights, haven't I, Darlin'?"

I can't keep the slight blush from my cheeks. His distractions on planes are quite nice. He plants a kiss on the side of my neck before going back into the bedroom to grab our bags. "Maddie, if you don't mind, just leave my car in long-term parking. I'll give you the spare and you can give it to me at the wedding."

"Sounds good. Are y'all ready to go?"

"Ready as we'll ever be," I say.

We all troop out to Jonas's car and pile in. After Maddie drops us off at the airport, we make it through security in what feels like record time and have a half-hour to kill prior to boarding. We sit curled together on a bench while we wait. He pulls me to his side and whispers in my ear, "Have I told you how much I'm looking forward to the next few days with you and only you."

I lean into him. "Maybe a few times. But feel free to tell me again."

"Well, I'm planning on making love to you in so many, many places while we're there. In our room, on the porch, in the media room, by the fire pit, maybe in the woods."

"Oh, really? You're not worried about poison ivy?"

He laughs. "Okay, maybe not the woods. But everywhere else is fair game."

"Sounds perfect to me. What do you want to do for supper tonight? Since it'll be about then when we get to the house."

He shrugs. "I'm sure we'll think of something."

Our flight is pretty smooth and I actually nap, which is probably more telling about how tired I am than how good the flight is. I wake up just as we're landing and Jonas is grinning at me. "Wow, Darlin'. I've never seen you sleep on a flight, but you were passed out."

I yawn and stretch. "Yeah. I can't believe it, either."

We get to the lake house about an hour before sunset and I unlock the house and Jonas takes our bags upstairs to our room. It's strange it being just us here, but I have to admit, it's exceptionally nice to have time for only Jonas and me for a few days.

I look around the kitchen and see a note on the counter.

· · ·

Thanks for taking care of Maddie for me.
I can't repay everything y'all have done,
But I hope the steaks and beer are a start.
Check the fridge. See y'all soon.
-Dom

Jonas comes down the stairs as I'm opening the fridge. Sure enough, there are two very nice ribeye steaks on the shelf, along with a six pack of beer. "What's this?" Jonas asks as I pull the steaks out of the fridge so they can come to room temperature before we grill them.

I gesture to the note. "Dominic, apparently. To thank us for taking care of Maddie. Did you tell him she's decided she'll take him back?"

He shakes his head. "No, I thought I'd let it be a surprise. But it was nice of him. I'm never gonna turn down steaks. I'll go start the grill. Want to season those and see if there are some potatoes or something we can have to go with them?"

I nod and look in the pantry and find some baby fingerling potatoes and wash and dry them before quartering and seasoning them and spreading them on a grill pan. I also see some salad supplies in the fridge and throw together a quick salad of butter and romaine lettuce, grape tomatoes, carrots, and cucumbers.

By the time the potatoes are almost done, Jonas has the steaks started on the grill and we're sitting on the patio having a beer. "This is really nice," Jonas says.

"Yeah, if you listen real quiet, you can hear it."

He frowns. "Hear what?"

I nod and take a pull on my beer. "Exactly. Nothing."

He laughs. "Yeah. It's really nice. Although, I fully expect to hear you later, Darlin'."

I smirk. "Oh, really, in what context?"

"You know what context. Since Maddie moved in, you've held back. Don't think I haven't noticed. I expect for you to make it up to me while we're here and when we get home."

I chuckle. "Apparently not enough she didn't notice. She kept talking about how jealous she was because I guess the pregnancy has made her really horny and she hasn't been able to do anything about it."

Jonas laughs. "Did you tell her we had actually cut back, especially when she was in the house."

I nod. "Yeah and you should have seen how fast her chin hit her chest. I told her how excited we were to have the house back to ourselves, but I'm still gonna miss her. We had a lot of fun, even though we butted heads a lot."

"Yeah, I know you will. But that's good. It means you guys are in a good place. If you didn't miss her, it would mean you weren't, so you'll be looking forward to seeing her again. Remember how you talked last year about not wanting to come here when she and Dominic would be here and holidays and stuff? Do you still feel that way?"

I shake my head. "No, I'll be happy to see her."

"So, see, it's all good." He jumps up to flip the steaks and check the potatoes. "About five more minutes."

I stand. "I'll go set the table. Do you care to bring everything in when it's done?"

"Sure. Be inside in a few."

Our steaks are fantastic and we both relax even more with our second beers and the good food. After we clean up the kitchen, Jonas shoots Dominic a quick text to thank him and sticks his phone back in his pocket. A few minutes later, his phone dings and he pulls it out.

Jonas frowns. "Dominic says to check on the fireplace mantle."

"Weird. Okay." I walk over to the fireplace and there's some kind of remote on the mantle and I hold it up. Jonas types something on his phone and a moment later, he looks up at me.

"He says to go upstairs and push the white circle on the remote."

"Why is he being so strange?"

Jonas shrugs. "Maybe another surprise?"

I sigh. "Well, I guess we have to go upstairs. Where, upstairs?"

"It says when we get to the top of the stairs, press the white circle."

We both walk up the stairs and when we get to the landing, I press the button on the remote. I look around, but don't see anything at first until Jonas nudges me and points out onto the porch. "What the hell?"

We walk toward the porch and open the sliding door. The furniture has been stacked in one corner and the perimeter of the porch is lined with flickering LED candles. Explains the remote. There's a made bed and a cooler next to it. "Am I hallucinating? Or is there a bed on my porch?"

Jonas shakes his head. "If you are, I am, too. Apparently, Dom is also a big romantic? Who knew?"

I walk over to the cooler and there's a note on top.

Don't worry, it's only inflatable.
Champagne and glasses are in the cooler.
It's the good stuff you like, Cal.

I can never take back the hurt I caused you,
But I hope you know how happy I am for
you and Jonas.
  Make some good memories in your favorite
place.
    — Dom

I show the note to Jonas. "Too bad he doesn't know we already made a memory out here, but this is really nice. Weird, but nice. Do you want some champagne, or do you think it's too much? I know you've already had two beers and don't like to do more than that."

He opens the cooler and pulls out the glasses and hands them to me and pops the cork on the bottle and pours us both a glass. I look at Jonas as I hand his glass over. "Did you know he was gonna do any of this?"

He sips his champagne and shakes his head. "He asked me what time our flight got in, but I didn't think anything of it."

I nod. "I don't know what to think about this."

He shrugs. "Maybe, he's trying to be a better person. He knows he hurt you and he's trying to make up for it. A little weird he'd do it by helping me get laid, but I'm not complaining."

I laugh. "You mean, get me laid."

"Whatever works, Darlin'. All I know is, I'm not leaving this porch until one or both of us can't walk."

I down my champagne and set my glass down. "I'm not planning on leaving this porch at all. No one will be here for three more days. I'm sleeping out here tonight. Naked, next to the man I love."

He raises his eyebrows, impressed. "Daring, Darlin'. I like it."

I level him with my gaze. "Finish your drink and get me naked. Or do you want me to do it myself?"

"Don't you dare." He drinks his champagne in one long gulp and then makes a face when the carbonation hits his nose and I laugh. "That was not very sexy. Sorry."

"I thought it was entirely sexy. Now, are you ready to get me naked?"

He laughs. "Damn, keep it in your pants, lady. We've got time."

"Sorry, it's the first time we've been alone in months. I'm a little eager, so sue me."

He closes the distance between us and takes my face in his hands. "I'm glad I'm not the only one. I've missed you. I know it might sound strange since we've seen each other every day since before Halloween, but I feel like I haven't seen you or really spent any time with you."

I nod and turn my face to kiss his palm. "Yeah, we've been so busy with school and work and wedding plans, it really does feel like we haven't seen one another. But we're here now. And once we get through the wedding, we're back home and it's only us and we have all summer before we have to go back to school."

He sighs. "I can't wait."

I put my hands on his hips and pull him closer. He claims my mouth and the kiss is deep and hungry and scorching and cliché as it sounds, in spite of how many times I've kissed this man, my knees go weak. I tug his shirt up until we're forced to break our kiss to pull it over his head.

I plant kisses on his chest and abs and work to get his belt and shorts undone and down his hips. Jonas lets them fall to the floor before pulling my face back up and covering my mouth with his as he unzips my dress and tugs it down my shoulders, trailing kisses down my cheek to my shoulders and chest.

I let out a contented sigh as my dress hits the floor. Jonas unhooks my bra and lets it drop. He trails his fingers lightly down my arms then back up my waist and ribs before cupping my breasts and brushing his thumbs over my nipples. I feel them tighten under his touch. "Have I ever told you how much I love your tits, Darlin'?"

I let out a soft laugh. "Maybe a few times, but I don't mind hearing it again."

His hand slides around and down my back to settle on my butt. "And what about your ass? Have I told you how much I love that?"

I nod. "Yeah, I'm pretty sure you have."

His finger skims under the waistband of my panties and he slowly guides them past my hips. They join the puddle of clothes at my feet. Jonas drags his hand up the inside of my leg until his fingers brush lazily against my sex, causing me to exhale slowly. "And what about your pussy? Have I told you how much I love that?"

He thumbs my clit and I inhale sharply. "You know, I'm not sure. You might have to show me."

He smirks. "Oh, I can do that. Might take me a little while to show you exactly how much. I'm pretty fond of it."

I hook my fingers in the waistband of his boxer briefs and tug them down, his cock popping free. I wrap my hand around it and stroke the shaft. "And have I told you how much I love your dick?"

Jonas closes his eyes and presses his forehead to mine. "Jesus, Callie. I love you."

"I think it's because my hand is on your cock," I say with humor in my voice.

He takes my chin in his hand and forces me to look at him

and pulls my hand away from his body. "Don't get me wrong, Darlin', that's really nice, but I don't love you because of that."

I meet his gaze, a small smile on my lips. "I know. I'm sure my wit and charm had something to do with it, too."

"I think you might be right. I'm pretty sure it was the *Brady Bunch* reference that did it for me."

I snort. "Oh, God. Let's not bring that up. I was mortified."

He brushes a kiss across my lips. "Well, mortification was pretty damn sexy on you. I found it quite endearing."

I roll my eyes. "And this is what you've chosen to shackle yourself to me for the rest of your life? Bad TV references and unending sarcasm?"

"Yes, and gladly. Now, tell me, these *shackles* you mentioned, can those be an actual thing? Like, can we get some and bring them into the bedroom?"

I roll my eyes. "Why don't you save something for later? Forever is a long, long time. Plenty of time to explore all your sadistic fantasies."

He gives me a wicked grin. "All of them? Darlin', you might regret it."

I shake my head. "Nah, I've never regretted anything with you." I sit on the bed and pull Jonas down with me. "Now, will you please make love to me?"

He smiles. "Happily, Darlin'." And then he does. Slowly and sweetly and perfectly.

CHAPTER THIRTY-SIX

JONAS

Callie and I end up spending the three nights before everyone arrives out on the porch. The air mattress is not especially conducive to amorous activities, but we make it work. And simply waking up on the porch is extremely nice. Having all these great memories to take back home with us isn't too bad, either.

Knowing folks will start arriving around noon, Callie and I take an hour to breakdown the setup Dominic put together for us and box up the air mattress and throw the sheets in the washer. We put away all the candles and fix the furniture. As we have our coffee out on the porch when it's back to the way it was, Callie says, "You know, I think back in the day, they had these things called 'sleeping porches'. I totally get the appeal. If we ever buy another house or build one, I definitely want one of those."

I laugh. "Deal. I could see us having one of those. Although, we'd probably only be able to use it like one month out of the year because it gets too hot and humid."

She nods. "Yeah, but it would be a fun month."

"Very true." I take a sip of my coffee. "So, you ready for the chaos that's about to ensue?"

Callie sighs. "No. But you know me. I don't like to be the center of attention and that's exactly what's about to happen. Remind me again why I agreed to do this and not go to Vegas?"

"Because you secretly want all the traditions. You want your dad to walk you down the aisle. You want your family and friends to see us vow to love and honor one another. And, you know how much I love wedding cake, so you wanted to make me happy."

She laughs. "Yes, I know how much you love cake. And yeah, I do want my dad to walk me down the aisle." Her expression grows serious. "But, is everything we're doing stuff you're happy with? I know I said I didn't want all the pomp and circumstance, but I didn't really ask you what you wanted. And now I feel bad because tomorrow's the wedding and it's all planned out."

I shake my head and give her a reassuring smile. "Darlin', all I ever cared about was getting to have you. I told you we didn't even have to get married if it's not what you wanted. I was happy to do whatever, wherever, as long as it was with you." After a beat, I add with a smirk, "The cake is a really nice bonus, though."

She nods, but I can see it in her face she's unconvinced. I level her with a gaze. "Callie, I swear. I'm good. You know how much I love cornhole and pizza. I love that this is gonna be a big party with our favorite people. I love that at the end of the day, you'll be my wife. And I especially love that when we go home, no one else will be there."

"Yeah, I'm pretty excited about that part, too."

For about another half hour, we finish our coffee and then I stand and hold out my hand to Callie. "Come for a walk with me?"

She smiles and takes my outstretched hand in her own and we walk back into the house and down the stairs. When we get to the kitchen, we see Alex and Vicki. Callie greets her parents with a hug. "When did y'all get here?"

Alex shakes my hand. "About fifteen minutes ago. I've got to admit, this pizza and beer wedding idea might take some getting used to, but I'm not gonna complain about not having to wear a tux and go through the whole rigmarole. You've made this so easy on us, compared to how Lance and Meredith had it with Maddie's wedding."

Callie laughs. "Glad I could help, Dad. Jonas and I are gonna go for a walk, we'll be back in a little while. Maddie and Dorothy and Nancy should be arriving after while, but we'll make sure to be back before they get here."

"Sure. Have fun. Supper will be done by seven. Jonas, thank you for letting me grill out. Y'all know I don't get to do it much. I got chicken and shrimp, so I thought we'd do kabobs."

"Actually, I'm allergic to shrimp."

Alex looks apologetic. "Oh, I'm sorry. I didn't know. I can fix the chicken and then do the shrimp after, would that be okay?"

I nod. "That should be fine. No problem, probably."

He looks relieved. "I'll try to keep it in mind for the future. I'm glad I found out. We don't need the groom getting taken out before the big day."

We all laugh and Callie says, "I'd very much appreciate it, Dad. I'd like to keep him around for a while, if you don't mind. He's pretty handsy — I mean handy." She blushes at her own flub and Alex chokes on his bottle of water.

I tug her out the door and pull her toward the walking trail. I can't hide my amusement at what Callie said. "I thought your dad was gonna have a stroke. He's not as young as he used to be,

Darlin'. You're gonna have to be more careful with your words, you know."

She elbows me playfully. "It's all that great porch sex. It's addled my brain. I blame you. Although, I wasn't lying. You can be pretty handsy."

"You're one to talk. I'm pretty sure you were the one begging me to get you naked when we got here."

She gives me a sly smile. "And I regret nothing."

I can't help but laugh. I put my arm around Callie's shoulder and pull her into my side. "One more day, Darlin'. That's all the time you've got left to bail."

"No bailing happening here. What about you? Are your feet feeling frosty?"

"Nope. Just right, as Goldilocks would say."

We walk along the trail in companionable silence for a few minutes before Callie asks, "What do you think's gonna happen with Maddie and Dominic?"

I shrug. "Honestly, I have no clue. I know from his texts, he still wants her back, but who knows if they'll be able to make it work for the long term. Maddie's sure she wants to take him back?"

Callie sighs. "That's what she said. And I'm inclined to believe her. I'm with you, though. I don't know if they'll be able to make it. Neither of them seems very good at communicating what they need to the other person. But we'll see, I guess." After a moment, she asks, "Do you think because of the way we started out, we'll have better luck?"

I frown in confusion. "What do you mean?"

She shrugs. "Well, when we first met, we talked about a lot of stuff we might not have if we were truly dating. Like all my shit with Dom, I don't know if you would've been privy to that. And the way you talked about picking up women and all that,

do you think you would have been so open about your...
antics?"

I consider for a moment. "Probably not. I mean, I like to
think if I was serious about a woman, I would have been open,
but with you, since we didn't have any intention of sleeping
together in the beginning, it was easy to tell you that stuff."

She nods. "Yeah, same. So, do you think it helps us or
hurts us?"

"I think it means there's nothing we can't talk about and
work through. We've probably been more real with each other
than with anyone else, wouldn't you say?"

"I know you've seen me at my most real. All terrible
sobbing and everything."

I plant a kiss on the top of her head. "I like it when you're
real, Callie. Although, since you're so easy to read, I don't know
if you could be fake with me, anyway."

She chuckles. "Probably not. Are you excited your mom is
coming?"

I blow out a breath. "Yes and no. Don't get me wrong, I'm
glad she gets to see us get married and meet your family and
stuff, but I'm worried I'll have to keep an eye on her, since this
is probably gonna be her first test as far as temptation goes. I
mean, her drug of choice isn't alcohol, as far as I know, but still,
it might be difficult for her."

"She's been doing really well. We can both watch her."
Callie looks up at me and touches my cheek. "You're not alone
in this."

I brush a kiss across her lips. "I'm thankful to have you
with me."

CHAPTER THIRTY-SEVEN

CALLIE

Just as Jonas and I are coming in the back door, Maddie, Nancy, and Nana are coming in the front. Maddie is dressed in a flowy dress that conceals her growing bump and if you didn't know she was pregnant, you wouldn't be able to tell.

She walks over to me. "Is Dominic here yet?" She keeps her voice low, but Jonas hears her and he leans over.

"He said he wasn't coming until the wedding. So he won't be here until tomorrow. He wasn't sure if you'd want to stay with him tonight, since y'all haven't talked or anything, so he thought it'd be best to wait."

Her face falls in disappointment. "Oh, okay. Well, I guess I'll see him tomorrow." Trying to keep her on more positive ground, I ask about their flight. "It was fine. Smooth. Dorothy kept trying to get the attention of this handsome older man across the aisle."

Jonas's expression registers shock. "She did what?"

Maddie chuckles. "I'm pretty sure she had him in mind for your mom, not herself."

He rolls his eyes. "I swear, Nana can't help herself. Always trying to play matchmaker." He steps away to greet his mother and grandmother and show them to their rooms.

I turn back to Maddie. "So, still feeling good about everything?"

She sighs and shrugs. "I don't know. I've got butterflies just thinking about seeing him and I'm excited to tell him about the baby, but I don't know how's he's gonna take the news. And I still haven't told my parents, so I feel like I have this huge secret."

I have a momentary thought that Maddie will hijack my wedding to announce her pregnancy and immediately tense. She touches my arm. "Don't worry, Hanny, I'm not gonna tell them until after the wedding. This is your big day. I'm not gonna take your spotlight, even though I know you don't like to be the center of attention."

Relieved, I smile. "Thanks."

"Of course. I really hoped Dominic would be here tonight so we could talk. We won't have much time tomorrow. And I'm so anxious, I want to get everything out in the open."

"Do you want me to have Jonas to tell him to come tonight? I'm sure your parents will probably think it's weird he's not here anyway."

She bites her lip and considers, clearly apprehensive. "Can he? Would it make me look too eager?"

I shrug. "I think he might think it's a good sign. What do you want to do?"

Her expression is hopeful, but her voice is soft. "Can you have Jonas call him? Please?"

I nod. "Sure. Supper's not for a couple hours. Should give him plenty of time to get here."

"Okay, well, I'm gonna go unpack." She looks around and leans closer to me. "Can you tell I'm pregnant in this dress?"

I shake my head. "Not really. If I didn't already know, I'd

never guess you were. A couple more weeks, though, and there'd be no way to hide it."

"That's what I thought. Let me know what Jonas finds out?"

"I will."

I find Jonas showing his mother around the house and greet Nancy when I see them. She gives me a quick hug. "Callahan, this place is amazing. It's like something out of a magazine."

I smile. "We really love it here. It's my favorite place. Make yourself at home. I'll introduce you to my parents in a few minutes. Would you mind if I steal Jonas for a moment, Nancy?"

She shakes her head. "Of course not. I'm gonna go unpack and make sure Momma is settled." After a beat, she looks at Jonas, her eyes a bit misty. "Thank you for trusting me to come this weekend. I know you're taking a big chance after everything. I promise, I'll be good."

Jonas gives his mother a soft smile. "I'm glad you're here, Mom. Really." Nancy heads in the direction of her bedroom and he turns to me. "What's up?"

I sigh. "Can you call Dom and see if he'll go ahead and come up tonight? Maddie was really disappointed when she found out he wasn't coming until tomorrow."

"Why can't she call him herself?"

"I think she's nervous about everything. Can you?"

He shrugs. "Okay. Sure. But I'm not playing chaperone to them tonight."

I chuckle. "Yeah, me neither. I think she's worried they won't have time to talk if he doesn't get here until tomorrow."

He nods. "Makes sense." He pulls out his phone and calls Dominic and I hear Jonas's side of the conversation, but don't really pay attention until his tone changes. "Oh, well, I'm just relaying a message, man. I thought you'd be excited considering... Yeah, but she wants you here, doesn't that mean anything... Don't do that. Don't play games. I honestly don't care one way or another, but you want her back, she seems to want the same thing. Get your ass here, Dom... Sack up and face the music... Good. Supper starts at seven. Be here."

He disconnects the call and the look on my face must be enough to prompt him to explain. He sighs. "Idiot thought he'd 'wait until tomorrow so he could make Maddie want him more'."

I quirk a brow. "Are you shitting me? He's the one who fucked up and she finally decides she wants him back and he wants to torture *her*? Good lord. Can we wash our hands of this yet?"

Jonas pulls my face to his for a quick kiss. "This was all your idea, Darlin'. You have no one to blame but yourself."

I roll my eyes and let out a deep sigh. "Yeah, yeah. You're not allowed to throw my bad ideas back in my face."

He smirks. "Oh, now what's the fun in that? You call me on my shit, I call you on yours. Isn't that what we do?"

I wrap my arms around his waist. "Yeah, I guess so. Fine. Yeah, this is all on me. Hopefully, after tonight, we'll be rid of this mess."

By the time supper rolls around, Dominic still hasn't shown up and Maddie is so antsy and fidgety, I can't stand it. I lean over to her, my whisper harsh. "Maddie, if you don't calm down, "I'm gonna scream. Eat your food. He'll be here."

She looks at me, her expression fearful. "But what if he doesn't—. I mean, what if he's changed his mind? What am I gonna do?"

I'm about ready to shake her and hopefully knock some

sense into her when Jonas nudges me. "Look." He gestures toward the house and Maddie and I both turn to see what he's pointing at.

Dominic is coming out the back door, his hands in his pockets, his expression unsure. I hear Maddie let out a breath. I expect her to jump out of her chair, but she stays glued to her seat. I look at her incredulously. "What are you waiting for? Go talk to him."

"I don't know if I can move. I forgot how good he looks. Doesn't he look good?"

I roll my eyes. "Maddie, if you don't get your ass over there and get this over with, I'm gonna throttle you."

She swallows nervously. "You think it's gonna be okay?"

I shrug. "I think unless you get over there and talk to him, you'll never know."

She nods and slowly rises from her chair and Jonas and I watch her walk over to where Dominic stands. We can't hear what is being said but when Maddie finally gets to him, she reaches for him and his face softens and he pulls her into his arms. They stay like that for a long time, before Dominic turns and pulls Maddie into the house with him.

I look at Jonas and we both breathe a sigh of relief. I lean into him. "You know, I never in a million years thought I would care whether they were happy, after everything, but, I actually hope they are. What do you think it means?"

Jonas presses a kiss to my forehead. "I think it means you're free. Isn't that what you told me, when I said I didn't hate Bailey anymore? That I was free? Maybe you are, too."

I nod. "Looks like it."

CHAPTER THIRTY-EIGHT

JONAS

As someone who is not a big fan of weddings, I have to say, Callie's and mine was pretty perfect. It was laid back and casual and as she came down the aisle on Alex's arm, my breath caught. She was so perfect in her dress; a simple cream lace number that flowed over her curves and when she'd said it was *her*, she was right. I couldn't imagine her in anything else. Her hair looked like gold in the waning sunlight, swept into a loose braid over one shoulder. She'd chosen to wear her contacts for today and she had a large bouquet of hydrangeas and roses and wore the necklace I'd given her for Christmas.

We both had tears in our eyes as we said our vows and promised to always choose *us*. To never go to bed angry. To laugh at each other's bad jokes. To love each other, even when we don't like each other. And when I kissed my wife for the first time, I knew I never wanted to stop kissing her for the rest of my life.

We played cornhole and ate pizza and drank beer and laughed with our family and friends until the wee hours. And when Maddie and Dominic snuck away after the ceremony to come back an hour later, both looking a bit flushed and disheveled, Callie and I exchanged knowing looks.

And when we went up to our room, I surprised Callie by having all the candles from the porch put in our room for some romantic lighting. She looked around, surprised. "This is beautiful, Jonas. When did you have time to do this?"

I give her a sly smile and wink. "I worked a little magic while you were taking pictures before the ceremony."

"Well, you did good." She wraps her arms around my waist and pulls me to her. "Are you happy?"

I brush a stray hair off her forehead and look into her dark blue eyes. "So, so, happy, Darlin'. Thank you for marrying me."

She smirks. "It was the least I could do, really, for all those great orgasms you give me."

I can't help but laugh. "We should've put *that* in the vows."

"Well, we could always have vows just for us. Like, Jonas promises to give Callie untold numbers of orgasms for the rest of their lives and make her grilled cheeses. And Callie promises to not get mad when Jonas can read her every thought."

I laugh and nod. "Okay. And Callie promises to never to stop letting Jonas give her untold numbers of orgasms. And Jonas promises to someday give Callie at least two curly-headed Merritt babies. And Jonas and Callie both promise to continue to put each other first for the rest of their lives. And Callie promises to let Jonas have a puppy for Christmas."

Callie laughs. "Wow, a puppy? That's a pretty specific vow. We'll see what we can do. For now, though, can you make love to your wife?"

I release a contented sigh. "Man, I like the way that sounds. *Wife.* It sounds so... permanent."

She rolls her eyes. "Well, that is the idea."

I take her face in my hands and brush a soft kiss across her lips before letting my eyes scan her face. Her blue eyes, growing dark with desire. Her lips, slightly parted from where I'd kissed her. The slight blush coming into her cheeks like it always does when I look at her, even after all these months. I lean in to trail kisses down her neck.

I reach around behind her and start unzipping her dress when there's a knock at the door. I freeze and Callie lays her head on my shoulder and sighs in frustration. Her words are muffled, but I hear her say, "I swear, if that's Maddie, I'm gonna scream."

I can't help but chuckle. "She must have some kind of radar for when we're about to get freaky and needs us to build a little more anticipation."

She rolls her eyes, but walks over to the bedroom door. I follow close behind her and she takes a deep breath before turning the nob. When she opens it, Maddie and Dominic are standing on the other side.

Maddie lets out a relieved sigh. "Oh, good. You're not naked yet. Do y'all have a minute?"

I can't help but huff a soft laugh, but Callie pinches the bridge of her nose. "You've got two minutes." She gestures for them to enter and then closes the door behind them. "Go."

Maddie and Dominic exchange glances for a quick second. "Well, we wanted to thank you both for everything. Y'all really helped us work through a lot of things and even though we're nowhere near back to where we were, we'll get there. We're gonna go to counseling and hopefully learn to be better for each other."

She looks at Callie, her eyes welling with tears. "Callahan, after everything I've done, I'll never be able to tell you how sorry I am for my actions and the way I treated you. You are such a good cousin and friend to me and so much better to me than I deserve."

Dominic interjects. "Maddie and I spent a lot of time

talking last night and we both owe you such a huge apology for the way we both took you for granted and treated you so poorly. I know you said you forgive us, but we both understand if you never get over what we did." Callie lets out a shaky breath and I squeeze her hand in reassurance.

Maddie takes a deep breath. "But we wanted also thank you, Jonas."

I'm taken aback. "For what?"

She smiles. "For loving Callahan. For helping her become the person she was meant to be. You've helped her grow and become more confident and the fact she was able to tell both Dominic and me off the way she did, that's major. And you're so good for each other. You know, I told Callahan the week of our wedding I had a good feeling about you two. And that was before I knew the truth about everything with y'all. But I stand by it. Y'all are the real deal and I'm really happy for you."

I nod. "Thanks, Maddie."

She gives me a soft smile and looks at Dominic, who gives her a small nod. "We also had a question we wanted to ask you both. And if you say no, we completely understand, but we can't think of anyone we'd trust more for this." She looks at Callie and appears nervous, but continues. "We wanted to know if you and Jonas would consider being godparents to our son."

Callie's expression softens. "A boy? It's a boy?"

Maddie nods and tears stream down her face. "Yeah, and there's no two people we'd rather have raise him if something happens to us than the two of you. You're the best people we know."

Callie looks at me and I shrug, as if to say, *up to you*. She swallows and turns her face back to Maddie. "Wow, Maddie, I don't even know what to say."

She nods slowly. "I know this is asking a lot, so if you need to take some time to think about it, we understand."

I squeeze Callie's other hand and she glances at me. I give her a wink and a tiny nod and she smiles, instantly understanding that I'm good with whatever she decides. She looks at Maddie and then Dominic and nods. "We'd be honored. Of course. We'd be more than happy to be godparents."

Maddie throws her arms around Callie and they embrace. After a moment, Callie pulls back. "Not that I don't appreciate both of you coming here for this lovely heart-to-heart, but Maddie, you have impeccable timing when it comes to interrupting Jonas getting me naked and now I need you to go. It's my wedding night, for crying out loud. I say this with love, but go away and don't come back. For the next several hours at least."

Maddie blushes and giggles. "Yeah. Sorry about that. We'll go. Right now. Congratulations, Hanny. I'm so happy for you."

Callie smiles. "Thanks, Maddie."

Maddie and Dominic leave and Callie locks the door.

CHAPTER THIRTY-NINE

CALLIE

As I lock the door, Jonas comes up behind me. "So," he says, his voice low and husky. "Where were we?"

I can't help but smile. "I'm pretty sure you were getting ready to take this dress off of me. Would you like to do that now?"

He places a soft kiss at the nape of my neck. "Depends, will I like what's underneath it?"

I huff a small laugh. "Do you like *nothing*?"

Jonas nuzzles the sensitive spot under my ear that always gives me goosebumps. "Are you telling me you went commando to our wedding, Callie?"

I turn my face toward him and smirk. "Isn't that what *nothing* usually means?"

"Well, well. I know I've said it before, but I truly think you've got some freak in you, Darlin'." His fingers slowly unzip my dress and his mouth follows the descent of the zipper, planting soft kisses down my spine. "Did it make you feel sexy to know you didn't wear anything under this thin dress? To know that if I'd known, I would have had to steal you away before we'd even had supper."

My skin tingles as his lips brush against my body. "Yes, actually. It felt like this dirty secret only I knew."

"And can I tell you a secret?" he asks, his breath warm as he comes back up to whisper in my ear.

"I think if we got married and you can't tell me a secret, we'd be in trouble, don't you?" I inquire, my tone playful.

"I, too, wore nothing."

I turn to face him so quickly, he nearly stumbles back. "You aren't wearing underwear?"

He smirks. "Nope. Thought it'd be a nice surprise for you."

We both laugh, even as he tugs me toward the bed. I look him up and down. "Show me."

"Nah, I was getting you undressed first."

"Well," I say, reaching to unbutton his vest and slide it down his shoulders. "No one is stopping you, but I'm still getting you naked right now, so do with that what you will."

Jonas grabs my face and kisses me deeply. So deeply, in fact, my hands stop their movements and the only thing I can do is hang on to him to keep my knees from buckling. When I come up for air, I ask, my chest heaving, "Where you been hiding that kiss? Damn."

Jonas laughs and it's not until he's kissing his way down my chest that I realize he's gotten my dress off of me and it's now a puddle at my feet. My mouth falls open in surprise. "How the hell did you do that?"

He wiggles his eyebrows and turns me to sit on the bed. "Just that good, I guess."

I reach for him and he steps between my knees. He shucks his vest and my fingers make quick work of unbuttoning his shirt before moving on to his belt and pants.

When they finally fall past his hips, I see he was telling the truth about not wearing underwear. I hold him at arm's length as my eyes travel from his face down his torso and hips. "I can't believe all of this is mine for the rest of my life."

Jonas plants his hand on either side of my hips on the mattress and lowers his face to mine until our lips are almost touching. "All yours, Darlin'. Forever."

I scoot back onto the bed and pull him down with me. I hook my legs around his hips and pull him closer. I trail my hands down his chest and abs and wrap my fingers around his cock and stroke him leisurely. Jonas's eyes don't leave mine and after a moment, his breathing grows labored and he pulls my hand away from his body and braces it against the bed with his own.

He lowers his mouth to mine for a tender kiss. I attempt to extricate my hands from his to pull him closer, but he doesn't let me go. "But guess what?" I quirk a brow and he continues. "You're mine, too. Especially right now. I've got you right where I want you."

I nod. "You don't see me trying to get away. What do you plan on doing with me?"

His expression grows considerate. He plants soft kisses on my cheeks and forehead before moving down to my neck. "Well, for starters, I'm gonna kiss nearly every inch of your body and you'll lie there and let me do it."

"Oh, you think so?"

He raises up to slowly nod at me, a wicked grin on his face. "Yeah, I do. And then, I'm gonna make you come with my tongue. Not entirely sure how many time yet." His words make my heart rate tic up.

I bite my lip. "And then what?"

"And then, Darlin', when you're not sure you can take it

anymore, then and only then, will I finally fuck you good and proper until we're both beyond exhausted and happy and neither of us wants to ever get out of this bed again."

I feign nonchalance, even as heat curls through my middle and my breath comes in near sighs of anticipation. I relax my hands and give him a soft smile. "I don't know if I'll ever get used to you taking control like this. I don't know why it makes me so hot, but hearing you tell me exactly what you want to do to me, and knowing what it's gonna be like, I don't know if I can stand it."

"So, are you gonna lie there and let me do what I've been thinking about all day?"

I nod. "Happily. Although, can I touch you?" I ask, my tone hopeful. Because as much as I want him to do all the things to me he's described, I want to feel him under my hands while he does them.

Jonas brings one of my hands to his mouth and kisses my palm. "Will that make this more enjoyable for you?"

I nod. "Immensely. Even though, sometimes it's hot to not be able to, tonight, I want to touch you. To feel you. To connect with you."

"Sure, Darlin', you can touch. But, no helping."

I frown in confusion. "What do you mean, no helping?"

He trails kisses up my arm, but keeps his brown eyes glued to mine. "What I mean is, you can't touch yourself. At all. I know it might be difficult for you, but can you do that?"

"If it means I can touch you, I can definitely keep my hands *not* to myself."

Jonas lets out a low laugh. "Good." He takes my hand and places it on the back of his neck as his lips graze my collarbone, moving southward.

As is his custom, he likes to drag out the torture that is my pleasure and true to his word, he proceeds to brush his lips over nearly every square inch of my body. Well, every square inch except the areas that would push me over the edge. He doesn't kiss the sensitive places he knows set me alight with need. And this, in and of itself, begins to drive me crazy.

"Jonas," I breathe. "What are you doing to me?" I'm practically tingling with my building desire.

His mouth is moving up my skin, lightly dropping soft kisses up my shin. "I'm worshiping you, Callie. I want to be able to say I know every place on your body better than my own and which places are the ones that bring you pleasure. I'm sure there are some I haven't found yet. And I don't plan on stopping until I find them. He nips at a place right above the inside of my knee and I inhale a sharp breath with the jolt that shoots to my core. "See, just like that. All these months, I've made love to you and never knew that one spot was one that did something for you. It's something a husband should know about his wife, don't you think?"

My breathing grows more ragged as his lips travel higher on my thigh. "I think I'm about to die. I swear, it's your life's goal or something to make me beg, isn't it?"

He winks at me. "I'm not above making you beg. I enjoy it quite a lot actually." He tugs the sensitive skin of my inner thigh between his teeth and I gasp. "But tonight, I'm not gonna make you beg, Darlin'."

His mouth descends on my pussy and I'm caught totally off guard and can't bite back the moan that leaves my throat as his lips close over my clit. "Fuck, Jonas." I hear him chuckle softly and the vibrations from the sound makes my hips buck with the acute sensation. My hands tangle in his hair and all I can do is ride it out as my release starts to build with every perfect flick, every gentle nibble, every exquisite suckle.

When my climax rips through me, Jonas doesn't stop working his mouth, he simply slides two fingers into me and crooks the digits, hitting exactly the right spot to trigger another, more intense orgasm moments later.

And even then, he doesn't stop. Not when two turns into three and my legs start to shake. Not when three turns in to four and I struggle to breathe or form words. It's only when I lose the ability to make sound at all, Jonas takes it as his cue that he's reached some sort of finish line that his mouth leaves my swollen, oversensitive clit. "Had enough?"

It's all I can do to nod as he tugs my hips down the bed before slamming into me. And although I'm utterly exhausted already, once Jonas starts to move within me, I begin to come back to myself, even as the endorphins and hormones rage in my brain. He grips my face, forcing me to look at him. "Fuck, I love the way you feel." He brushes a soft kiss across my lips and I grip his waist as I rock my hips to drive him deeper. His thrusts grow more urgent as he begins to chase his own release.

Jonas presses my knees back and raises up onto his toes, causing the angle of his impact to change suddenly and I'm shocked to find myself growing closer to one final climax. When I finally let go with a sharp rasp, he finally gives himself permission join me. And I watch his face as his eyes squeeze shut and his mouth falls open and a deep grunt leaves his throat with the last brutal pumps of his hips.

He nearly collapses into me and I wrap my arms around him as his breaths come hot and labored against my neck. I feel the sweat on his chest and back and know that I, too, am covered in perspiration by the way my hair is plastered to my neck and forehead.

We don't move for what seems like hours, but in reality is probably mere minutes. And after a while, I start to notice how heavy Jonas is and I nudge him, still unsure if I can form words.

He rolls over and I inhale a deep breath. He pulls me into his arms and I rest my head on his chest. I struggle to stay awake, especially as he begins to trace lazy circles on my back with the tip of a finger. "Well, you were right," I say.

"About what, Darlin'?"

"I never want to get out of this bed again."

EPILOGUE
JONAS — NINE MONTHS LATER

As is our tradition, Callie and I traveled to the lake house for Christmas. During our visit, we got to spend a lot of time with our godson, Chance. He has Maddie's curly red hair and the Benson nose, but he has Dominic's eyes and coloring. He'd just started laughing and Callie and I took turns simply making him giggle.

Dominic and Maddie appear to be in a better place and say the couples counseling they've been going to has been very helpful. They laugh and smile at each other and seem to genuinely be in love. Although it's hard to believe, Callie and I are thrilled for them. It's truly a change from the way things were nearly two years ago.

Callie successfully completed her PhD and secured a position at the local high school when there was an opening. It's great we'll have the same schedule and always have summers off to spend time together.

We did end up getting a dog for Christmas, if not a puppy. We decided to go the rescue route, and brought Homer, a great dane mix, home the week following our return from the lake.

He's ginormous and thinks he's a lapdog. He's also goofy and adorable and we love him.

Last week, my mother celebrated one year sober and will leave the halfway house in another month, so we've been looking at houses and apartments. She's taken Callie's old job at the library with Nana and by all accounts, is thriving. Thanks to the money Bailey left in trust for her, she can put a down payment on a small house.

And in spite of the animosity I have toward him, I can't disregard this wonderful thing he did for my mother. He was able to bring her back to me and I now have a good relationship with her. Which is why, at Callie's urging, I'm sitting in the same restaurant as a year ago, waiting on him to arrive.

He was shocked to get my call, but I feel like I owe him thanks for what he did, so I invited him to have coffee the next time he was in town. I catch myself nervously raking my fingers through my hair and immediately stop, since I still don't necessarily like that I share my father's mannerisms.

He enters the restaurant and walks back to the booth where I sit. And to his shock and maybe even my own, I stand and shake his hand. "Jonas, good to see you." I nod and he sits opposite me. A server brings over a pot of coffee and pours us both a cup. When she walks away, Bailey says, "I was surprised, to say the least, to get your call. Not that I'm not pleased, obviously."

I'm beginning to wish I'd dragged Callie here with me, but I wanted to try to do this on my own, so I didn't. I nervously twist my wedding band on my finger. "Yes, well, thank you for agreeing to meet me."

"I was happy to do it." He notices me fidgeting with my ring. "How's married life treating you? How is Callahan?"

"Good. She's happy to be done with school."

He nods as he sips his coffee. "Any plans for kids?"

RACHAEL OGLE

"Not for a while. We just got a dog, so he takes a lot of our attention right now. Maybe in a few years."

"Children are a blessing. All of them." He holds my gaze and I'm not sure how to feel about what he's said.

I blow out a breath and decide to cut to the chase. "So, the reason I wanted to see you is because I wanted to thank you. My mother is doing exceptionally well and she'll be leaving the halfway house in a few weeks. And I know without you, it wouldn't be possible for her to be doing as well as she is. So, I wanted to say thank you, in person. And with the trust, she'll be able to put a down payment on a house, so thank you for that as well. It was very generous."

His throat bobs with a swallow and he runs his fingers through his hair. "It was the least I could do, really. I wish I had learned about... things sooner, and maybe she could have come back to you sooner."

"I'm just happy to have her back."

We sit in silence for a few moments and I don't know what else to say, since I've already said everything I came to say. Bailey drains his mug. "Well, I'll be on my way. I'm sure you have a busy life to get back to."

He starts to stand and because I can't help myself and it's bothered me since the last time I saw him, I ask, "What would you have done differently?"

He retakes his seat and signals for the server to refill his coffee. When she leaves, he blows out a breath. "It's hard to say exactly. I would have done a lot of things. I can't say I wouldn't still have pursued your mother, as bad as it sounds, since I was married. Because if I said that, then you wouldn't be here now. And I'm sure Callahan would prefer you were." After a beat, he continues. "I would've been a part of your life, somehow. Regardless of the impact to my career. I would have provided for you."

He takes a sip of his coffee. "But then, to say that, makes me wonder how differently you would have turned out. And this may sound like some kind of copout, but without my influence, the man you are is probably vastly greater than the man you would have been if I had been involved. I look at you and my daughters and other son and with my provisions and influence on their lives, they've all turned out fine, but you definitely are something else, Jonas."

I look down into my own mug, unsure how to take what he's said. He takes my silence as an invitation to continue. "And I wonder how much of who you are is because of who your mother was or if you got any good from me, or if it's only because it was who you were meant to be and everything that's happened to you. It's infinitely easy to play *what if*. It's harder to accept the mistakes you've made and learn from them. And so, part of me is glad you didn't have me, because I probably would have ruined your life. You have a good life."

I nod. "I do. I wouldn't trade my life for anything. It's still nice to know you're not above admitting your mistakes. I wasn't aware politicians could do that," I say with a smirk.

Bailey is surprised by my comment and laughs. "Yes, well, we sometimes have human tendencies, even if we're more reptilian in nature most of the time."

And in spite of myself, I laugh, too.

I spend another hour with Bailey and I have to admit, it's not terrible. He's a good conversationalist and if I didn't have this history of hating him, I might find him pretty likable. And by the time I climb in my car and head toward the house, I find that maybe I don't hate him anymore. Maybe Callie was right and he's human. Not good or bad. Simply *human*. Flawed and imperfect and real like the rest of us. And maybe even he is capable of redemption. Maybe we'll never be family, but I might not have to live and die by the things he did or didn't do anymore. Maybe Callie's right and I'm free.

When I walk in the front door, Callie is folding a load of laundry. She drops the towel she's just picked up and comes over to me. I give her a quick kiss as I shuck my windbreaker and hang it on the hook by the door after bending down to give Homer a scratch behind the ear.

"So, how was it?" she asks. "I assume it wasn't horrible, since you were gone almost two hours. I mean, unless we need to hide a body. You didn't pull a Dexter, did you?"

I can't help but laugh. "No, he's still among the living. It was fine. He's actually pretty funny, as much as I hate to admit it."

She nods. "So, what does this mean?"

I shrug. "Maybe it means we send him a Christmas card."

ABOUT THE AUTHOR

For as long as she can remember, Rachael has been a voracious reader. At the age of eleven, she discovered her grandmother's stash of clench-cover romance novels and she was forever changed. A lover of many, many fictional men and one very non-fictional one, she strives to write real and emotional characters who always get their happily ever after. Rachael lives in East Tennessee with her husband and two sons on their family farm. When she's not tackling her endless TBR, she can be found drinking all the coffee in existence.

ALSO BY RACHAEL OGLE

www.ingramcontent.com/pod-product-compliance
Lightning Source LLC
Chambersburg PA
CBHW060810120726
47909CB00006B/1851